## The critics on Cristina Odone

'A delightful novel that leaves the reader pondering its many subtle themes' *The Times*

'The novel is subtle and scary, a study of our weaknesses, desires and deceptions and of the pitfalls of pursuing single-minded solutions to our troubles' *Independent*

'Grippingly interwoven plots ... [a] passionate and wholesome narrative style, enviably neat, snappy and lyrical' *Spectator*

'A pulse of real humanity runs through the story, making it a delightful read' *Daily Telegraph*

'A moral puzzle written in clear, elegant prose ... [an] elegant and enjoyable portrait of a febrile, self-questioning, pre-millennial country' *Literary Review*

'An exceptionally sophisticated read from a born writer. Odone is exceptionally astute about the cut-throat world of both the media and political arena without stooping to cynicism. She is equally perceptive in her observations of a marriage in crisis' *Stirling Observer*

'Odone displays an impressive deftness in creating a lingering sense of place and time that marks her out as a novelist of great promise' *New Statesman & Society*

'A compelling portrait of the clash between religious and secular agendas ... [Odone's] writing has a lyrical, lingering quality that is well-suited to conveying ambiguity' *Independent on Sunday*

Cristina Odone is Italian and was brought up in Italy and America before attending Oxford University. She is the Deputy Editor of the *New Statesman* and was formerly Editor of the *Catholic Herald*. Cristina Odone broadcasts regularly for both television and radio.

*By the same author*

The Shrine

# A Perfect Wife

CRISTINA ODONE

PHŒNIX

A PHOENIX PAPERBACK
First published in Great Britain by Orion in 1997
This paperback edition published in 1998 by Phoenix,
a division of Orion Books Ltd,
Orion House, 5 Upper St Martin's Lane,
London WC2H 9EA

A CIP catalogue record for this book
is available from the British Library.

ISBN: 0 75380 472 7

Printed and bound in Great Britain by
The Guernsey Press Company Ltd.,
Guernsey, Channel Islands

For Francesco

# Chapter One

'I suppose I've loved you since the first time I saw you, walking down the aisle beside my best friend.' Victor sighed among the cream and gold stripes of the sofa.

'Darling Victor . . .' Nina stood at her desk, piling together the pages of notes she had been taking all day for her column. 'You promised you wouldn't.' But her deep voice held no trace of anger as she looked down at her papers. His declarations were the backdrop against which their every encounter unfolded; declarations which she chose only to half believe, lest their friendship be compromised.

'My best friend's wife –' Victor shook his head.

'Are you sure,' she interrupted him quickly, 'that I'm not over-stating the case?' She frowned as she held up a page of scribbled writing.

'Impossible to overstate the case. We're talking about a seriously incompetent government on its last legs. You'll see, quicker than you can blink, there'll be a general election and, mark my words, this new moral-majority band-wagon will do remarkably well.' He pulled a face. 'We'll find ourselves lumbered with pi politicos like that repulsive Tom Sutton.'

Nina looked up. 'Hmm. Sutton – yes, I should mention him here.'

'Michael's illustrious newspaper should start a campaign to check the progress of these new puritans.'

'If you had your way, poor Michael would be forever at the helm of some new campaign.'

'Well, what's the point of being deputy editor of a national paper if you don't defend the few principles you still believe in?'

Nina smiled at the thought of what Michael would say to that. Being deputy editor meant a great deal to her husband, but she hardly thought it was a matter of principles. She pushed the papers into a drawer, caught sight of herself in the mirror and replaced a loosened curl of the glossy dark knot of her hair. She felt the tepid sun upon her profile, saw the light fall upon the window-sill, upon the branches

1

below, on the rooftop and balconies of the houses across the street. It was a good room for dreaming. Here, during the hours of the day when she was alone at her desk, pen to paper, she could lose herself in a warm silence, among forms and shapes so familiar that they cradled her wandering thoughts and lulled her memories. It was as if in this glowing space everything seemed to promise, or had delivered, well-being.

The clock on the mantelpiece sounded three. They had finished their meal earlier than usual. Victor often dropped by for lunch during the week. Sometimes he came with a brown carrier-bag bulging with delicacies; sometimes Nina would cook while he poured her a glass of wine, and watched her at the stove.

As she sorted her papers now, she felt his eyes on her, and smiled at her memories: when he had first danced with her, at her wedding; when they had found one another in the London Library, amid a group of nonagenarian writers who scowled at their whispered conversation until they had been forced to go out for a cup of coffee; when she had sat beside him here on the sofa, poring over the proofs of his history of the Welfare State, showing him the comments she had written in the margins; and when she had thrown her arms around his neck because he had brought back from his holidays her favourite Italian amaretti – and then, with her arms around him, he had blurted it all out, the love and longing that he had suppressed for three years.

At first, Nina had taken offence, acting the betrayed rather than the beloved friend. But her vanity and her need for companionship had outweighed the self-righteous indignation she had deemed propriety dictated. Now that he was married and that five years had passed since his first declaration, they had slipped into a friendship rooted in his admiration and her wifely virtue.

He had never asked, and was never told, whether Michael had been informed of his best friend's confession. But Michael had known all along – and enjoyed teasing Nina about her admirer. 'Poor Victor.' he would say, with an exaggerated sigh whenever Nina mentioned him. 'Living proof that the best man doesn't necessarily win.' And Nina would reproach him, but only half seriously, and inwardly marvel that at Oxford it had been Victor whom everyone had earmarked for success, the brilliant First as preface to a glittering career as a writer. Michael, they had agreed, would slip into some lucrative City job.

Instead, Victor had lived up only to the First. He now wrote books about social economics that received erudite praise in obscure specialist magazines, but were only carried by booksellers near universities. He worked from home and had married a wealthy solicitor, Hannah, with whom he had had two children and enjoyed a tidy domestic life. Michael had surprised them all: he had left Oxford armed only with a Second and relentless ambition, but within a few years he had risen in the ranks of a national Sunday newspaper.

'Poor Victor.' She echoed her husband's words to herself as her eyes rested upon her loyal confidant – his black curly hair, his great nose, his thin face with its prominent cheekbones: a man who all his life had chased recognition only to be caught by failure. And once again she resolved always to be kind to him, to soothe his unhappiness and help him hide from himself his present mediocrity – all the more painful for his past ambition.

Nina approached the sofa where he lay. 'How is the work on the book?' she asked in her soft, serious voice. She stood behind the sofa, and leaned forward, her arms crossed on the striped silk.

'Ah, well enough.' But his eyes were sad and his smile false as he looked up at her, so that she quickly sought to change the subject.

'You'll never guess whom I saw coming out of St Mark's the other day. Lady Katherine, deep in conversation with that handsome vicar who has caused such a stir among the well-heeled evangelicals there. She didn't see me, she was so absorbed in whatever he was telling her.' She unfolded her piece of gossip with a great flourish, as if it were an elegant linen napkin and she were ready to enjoy an elaborate meal.

'You must be joking – an intelligent woman like that wasting her time among these born-agains?' Victor threw up his arms. 'What is the world coming to?'

'It's not quite as extraordinary as all that, you know.'

'You're right, you're right. The vicar at St Mark's has already proved himself a successful fisherman. He's caught plenty of young (and well-to-do) innocents and a handful of crafty politicians in his net already . . .'

Nina nodded, leaning closer to him over the sofa. 'The spread and spread of the Reverend Alexander Connaught's Renewal Movement.'

But he suddenly grabbed her hand, and pulled her down towards him, his lips brushing her cheek. 'Nina . . .' he whispered.

Dishevelled, blushing, almost breathless, Nina pulled away. She stood erect, smoothing her hair back in place. 'Don't, Victor, please.' Her voice trembled. 'You're my greatest friend – *his*

3

greatest friend . . .' She moved away, towards the window, her back to Victor. 'I love him, I am happy as things are.' She turned to face him and burst, impatient: 'Oh, we've gone through it a thousand times already!' Why must he strike a passionate note and ruin their finely tuned duet? 'You promised.'

On the sofa Victor said nothing. Then, raking a hand through his unruly dark curls, he said, seeking her eyes, 'I'm sorry. My untouchable Nina. Like one of those terrifying boulders overhanging a mountain road, towering, pale and beautiful, the rock seems impregnable.' His voice rose, ironic. 'Yet the signposts along the road warn of the danger that it might crumble, fall, wreak havoc and death.' He smiled at her figure, framed by the window.

'You are quite, quite mad.' She shook her head, marvelling at his constant need to analyse her.

'Not mad – just fascinated. Is Nina quite as perfect as she pretends to be?'

'Stop teasing me.' She moved from the window, regained her seat in the armchair, looked at him across the coffee table. 'Far from being perfect, I'm always having to be careful of what I say or do.' With a gesture she encompassed the room with its golden lights, books, photographs. 'I'm frightened of disrupting anything here.'

'Yes, well.' Victor narrowed his eyes. 'I don't think Nina Lewis is in any danger of wrecking her perfect, cosy little world. Here she sits, beautiful and fêted, on her way to becoming a household name with her perceptive column in one of Britain's leading weeklies, with an adoring husband and an adorable son.' She stiffened beneath his black gaze. 'Nothing to worry about, in fact.'

Nina blushed angrily, lowered her head, hands clasped before her. 'Oh, Victor,' she said in a low voice, 'you, you of all people must know that what you've just said is not true. I fight myself all the time to do the right thing.'

'"To do the right thing". What a laudable ambition.'

'Everyone has their ambitions,' she whispered.

Victor looked away from her and said nothing, but she knew he had grown as fearful of his own past ambitions as an ageing beauty of harsh lighting. She listened to the clock chime the short note with which it marked the half-hour.

'I'd best be off. I shall leave my hostess to review her spiritual progress, then.' His voice was light, teasing.

Their eyes met, and then, quickly, she looked up at the grey

4

windows. 'It's starting to grow so cold already.'

'But I'm always happy in this room.' He smiled.

Nina sat back in the silk embrace of her armchair. Yes, she thought, this room offered warmth and ease, and spoke of her careful weaving of the threads of domesticity: patience, restraint, comfort. For this existence she had tempered her passions, reined in her ambitions, softened her sharp tongue.

'I'd better go. You'll have Robbie back at any moment and I daren't be here when he comes – once again I haven't got that book I've been promising him for weeks.' He stood up, dusted off his tired blue corduroys, stretched his jumper over his slim frame, ran a hand through his hair. He followed her to the door. 'See you soon.' He smiled at her, and took her hand up to his lips. 'And don't forget,' here he winked, 'that if your evil side does take over, I'm first in the queue to help you yield to temptation . . . I shall leave you then, to return to the secret world of Nina Lewis.'

'Oh, Victor!' But she laughed, and pecked his cheek as she pushed him through the door.

She went back to her desk and sat down. Through the window the sun was trying to pierce the clouds. She took up her pen. Her secret world: it was always present, like the moon that, faint and almost unseen, lingers into daylight. She closed her eyes, slipped into a warm, window-filled place. Here, doors opened, one after the other, as she walked into a quiet sunny room where Michael awaited her. At times he would be sitting, at others standing, but his eyes were always on her. She saw his large frame cast a shadow upon the wall behind him and the floor between them. She saw his wide shoulders, sturdy and capable as a window-ledge upon which you can lean to see the world. His blond head drew closer, the better to hear her whisper, and his lips began the smile with which he teased her 'down from your moral high horse'. Her eyes rested on his forearm – the right one, always browner because he leaned it out of the window as he drove. She lifted the arm, unfolded it, wrapped it around her shoulders, so that she fitted snug against him. She felt the warmth of him, and it was the warmth of the freshly ironed dress her mother slipped over her arms as she prepared for Sunday Mass. She pressed her face into Michael's chest, and beneath the cotton it gave way like her pillow during a summer siesta, when the heat turned her sleep into a luxury as well as a need.

Beloved figures appeared in the background, remodelled by her imagination into different yet still familiar forms, so that her son

Robbie discarded his spectacles and his habitual melancholy, and gurgled with laughter, limbs grown thicker and heavier with health. Her parents appeared to her as they had when she was a teenager, younger, stronger, as they linked arms and cast a benevolent eye over her life. She never wrote of this warm, glowing space that was her fantasy: she, who could adopt the short-hand of polemic to argue her position, mock a minister or undermine an institution, never allowed inchoate sensations and emotions to seep into her writing. Her columns were for public consumption. The secret reaches of her fantasy were hers alone.

She recognised, too, that on the outskirts of this pleasant world lay clues to a Nina others should not glimpse. A Nina vulnerable to dread and fears: Michael's ambition thwarted, Michael's love dimmed, Robbie's health affected . . .

Yet today, as she sat at her desk, in this warm room, with Victor's loving presence still almost palpable, as she awaited Robbie's return and then Michael's, it seemed to her that the very air she inhabited was resonant with joyful hopes.

## Chapter Two

Her child. She stood in the corridor, just beyond the doorway, watching him play alone in his blue room. She stood hidden from him, as she often did, for hours, when he came home from school. Small, thin, his dark head bent over the three cars of a train, Robbie sat in his pyjamas on the woollen rug talking to himself, acting out she knew not what part in his games.

'They were teasing me again.' He had given a little sob when earlier she had wrapped her arms around him to welcome him home. The slightly crossed eyes had scoured her face as he issued his daily plea: 'Can't I stay at home with you?' Now he sat, pushing trains, cars and trucks as if they could help him flee the playground taunts. She stared at the small, curved figure and ached with the urge to protect him from the cruelty of schoolboys, of outsiders, of life.

She had thought that motherhood would be a replica of her own childhood: gentle warmth, soothing voices, her mother always hovering in the background, softly murmuring praise or advice, while Father's tall thin figure loomed over wife and daughter, voice booming as he outlined great plans of action. Marina del Monte had made motherhood seem effortless, at once a spontaneous act and the legacy of generations of women bent on protection, praise and support. But her own mothering confronted daily a child who seemed to inhabit a sad world, overshadowed by insecurities and infirmities, drained of energy and optimism – a world much as she imagined that of an invalid's old age.

'Robbie.' Hidden in the shadows of the doorway, she mouthed his name. He had been weak and tiny from birth; one of his eyes wandered slightly, a condition he inherited from his father, but which his doctor kept assuring them that spectacles could correct within a few years. But could she correct his frailty? Could she give him strength and inspire hope?

Every morning she saw him grow tense as they breakfasted: he ate with slow, deliberate movements, as if he could delay the dreaded moment when Mrs Rayner hooted outside, ready to drive him and her Louis to school. He would cast his mother a last desperate look as she bent over him, pushing his hands into the sleeves of his grey uniform jacket, and then he would walk off, head lowered, feet heavy. And every afternoon and evening he would sit here, acting out his escape beneath her anxious gaze.

'Robbie, time for bed.' He looked up, serious-faced, then smiled at her.

Nina approached him, bent to kiss his dark shiny hair. Together they squatted, placing the wooden and plastic toys into a large white basket. Meekly, he followed her to his bed and she watched him slip beneath the duvet.

She sat down on the bed and bent over him, laying her cheek against his. 'My darling,' she whispered. She felt his cheek burn beneath her own. Slowly she sat up.

He turned his head to face her: she could see the black irises, the left one slipping into the inner corner of the eye. Pity filled her. 'It will be fine, I promise.' She blew out her wish for him.

Robbie threw his arms around his mother's neck and again drew her face close to his. 'Mummy.'

'Good night, my treasure,' she murmured. 'Tomorrow, you'll see, will be a wonderful day.'

Robbie nodded, closing his eyes, and turned on his side. She switched off the light beside him and slipped out of the door, leaving it ajar.

She crossed the dark corridor and went into her bedroom. 'Oh, Robbie . . .' She sighed and longed for Michael: their concern for their son always bound them in whispered consultation, in shared protective anxiety.

In the drawing room downstairs the clock sounded eight. He would be back any time now. In the soft light cast by the bedside lamp, she felt her body swell, grow boneless: Michael's arrival always filled her with the same sweet physical longing. She stood up, walked into the bathroom where she ran a bath. She undressed and hung her clothes on the hook behind the door. Naked, she returned to the bathroom. While the water streamed into the tub she turned to the mirror. Nina stood completely still, holding herself tall, feet slightly turned out, like a ballerina. She stared at the white familiar curves, the round full breasts that she studied for sagging, the hips that had spread into generous curves. She turned in profile, frowning at the solid roundness of her buttocks, at the gentle mound of her stomach. What, she wondered, did Michael think when he saw her thus – stripped naked, uncovered, ready for him? She checked the water, which still only half filled the tub, then drew closer to the mirror, to peer into her anxious face. She knew these wrinkles, and the shadows beneath the eyes and cheekbones; she knew the pale matte colouring that lay across a face that had once shone fresh. She raised both hands to touch her cheeks, ran her fingers down the white throat with its three fine rings. This, then, was growing older. Did she fear middle age?

But the answer, she knew, lay not within her but with Michael. Michael's gaze, his touch, whisper, his sudden intake of breath. These were the judges whose verdict she sought.

Michael: he was her great, her terrible secret. She knew that no one – perhaps not even Victor – suspected her of the passion that had taken her captive more than a decade ago and held her still. Years ago, her mother, in whom she had confided her fear of this all-encompassing love, had tried to reassure her: 'Once the children come, the husband is never again first in your mind. So enjoy this brief interlude while it lasts, my sweet.' But it had not been so. Despite Robbie, despite the eight years of marriage, she still felt in thrall to this man, her husband.

She stared back at herself in the mirror: she had blushed at the thought of Michael. She looked away, saw the bath was now full, slowly immersed herself. She closed her eyes, lay back, her neck upon the white cold rim. Michael: he gave her such unexpected bursts of happiness that she sometimes surprised herself by murmuring prayers she had thought forgotten. For her happiness made her humble and childlike, and filled her with gratitude towards the God of whom she had learned in childhood. She had no doubt that only something divine could generate such joy.

'If he weren't my best friend, I'd hate him,' Victor sometimes teased her. 'You are, if I may say so, one of the most remarkable women I know. And Michael – well, Michael is a perfectly wonderful fellow, good enough to be my friend but – well, without treachery or any degree of malice, Nina . . . he's not a patch on you.'

'He's nice, of course,' Father had cleaned his spectacles and surveyed her with a half-amused expression, 'but you needn't make such a fuss. He doesn't have the del Monte brains and I don't see much reason to suspect great creative juices bubbling up in there.'

Nina had said nothing. She knew Michael lacked Victor's brilliance, her father's depth. But her love, perhaps leavened by these reservations, had swollen into something out of all proportion, something she herself viewed with fear, and thought she must hide, lest others mock her, lest he grow weary of it. In the beginning it had not been like this: he had been the supplicant, she the haughty muse. He had engineered their first meeting: she used to cycle to her lectures, and one day had found her bicycle chained to another. She had stared, perplexed, at the big thick chain, at the sturdy green bicycle now linked to hers. Hopelessly, she had tugged at the lock, tried to work the combination, then huffed in annoyance, looking about for help. Suddenly a large, golden-haired youth stood before her. 'I'm so sorry, what an idiot I am!' He was all concern, mumbling about how he had rushed into the lecture, late as always, hadn't seen a thing, hadn't realised that he'd chained her up – 'so to speak,' he had laughed a bit too heartily, but – but didn't he know her from somewhere? Surely – yes – she was Nina del Monte, she was reading English too, wasn't she? Nina had been too dazed by the parade of polished, determined words and far too shy to respond with more than a few muttered acknowledgements. But he, heedless, held forth, standing there in the Broad, large and smiling and self-confident, spectacles reflecting the summer sun. 'Please, the least I can do is offer you a cup of tea.' Smoothly, he took her books from her. 'No ifs or buts, I won't have this on my conscience.' And he had pulled her along, into the nearest coffee shop, where he explained the whole of his life – in a revised and heavily abridged version – while she stared at him.

From that first meeting he had telephoned, written letters, sent her books, and invited her to every play, film and concert held in Oxford. He declared his love within days, his lifelong devotion within weeks, and proposed when they had known each other barely a month. She had allowed the courtship to carry on for two years, testing his love, patience, courage. She had sipped his promises of a perfect future, avidly drunk his praise, bathed herself in the inviting waters of his adoration, and finally drowned all reservations in the pleasure of their physical encounters.

She did not know when things had begun to change, when it was that his love for her had calmed into a pleasant, manageable leitmotif to the great roaring ambition that now orchestrated his life. What she did know was that her love for Michael had become soaked in the melancholic certainty that it could never be matched by his. She had resolved that he must never know, and watched what she said to him, tempered her enthusiasm, curbed her expressions of longing, trying to hide from him the fearful emotion that had spread to every part of her. She checked herself daily, like an invalid would, for signs of deterioration, knowing that there would be no convalescence or cure. With this constant and careful scrutiny, she was certain that she could bring her passion to heel, domesticate it so that it would fit in a homely existence.

'Are you having your bath?' he called out from the bedroom.

'Yes, darling.' She felt a stab of disappointment: she had wanted to be dressed and perfect for his arrival. She hurried now with her soaping, eager to see him. 'How was your day?' She could hear the bedsprings as he sat down to take off his shoes and socks.

'Hmm . . . pretty good. Anything to eat?' She knew without seeing that he was slipping off his jacket, loosening his tie, rummaging through his cupboard for a jumper.

'Yes. There's a stew in the oven and I'll make us a salad.' She still hated the banality of married dialogue, the domestic details that she feared would dull a love she wanted to see endlessly shiny. She stepped out of the bath, donned her white robe, checked herself in the mirror: she glowed, pink-cheeked and damp-haired. She opened the door, but he had already gone downstairs. She wondered whether to get dressed but decided he would grow cross with hunger. She sighed and went downstairs, trying not to rush.

'Hello there.' He turned from the radio he'd switched on, and smiled.

'Hello.' She kissed him.

Michael pecked her cheek, but his ears were straining to hear the news. He had poured himself a glass of wine and now sipped it, leaning against the counter. He was tall, large, with thick blond hair and skin that was youthful still, pink with health. Behind gold spectacles, his cool blue eyes lit upon the world with curiosity, taking stock of everyone and everything in order to measure all in relation to himself.

She busied herself at the sink, rinsing the lettuce, the tomatoes, all the while aware of every move he made.

'I've got to commission something on the Wise Men's gloomy economic forecast – think Professor del Monte will do a leader-page piece that draws a few historical parallels?'

'Of course. He's always delighted to be asked. Papa gets bored unless he's working at a thousand and one things.' She brought the salad bowl and the pot of stew to the table. They sat across from one another.

'Apparently that's all they could talk about at the trustees' board meeting this morning.' He helped himself to the pork and vegetable stew. 'And, of course, they've come up with a million ways we're to tighten our belts at the papers. Some spanking new austerity measures being considered.' He chewed energetically, eyes moving from the meat to Nina's face.

'Jobs on the line?'

'Yes. And our budgets are being trimmed. Maurice had a fit – protested furiously at the meeting – but his profligate ways have won him few allies.' Nina nodded: Maurice, Michael's editor, was a stubby-nosed, squat man with a voracious appetite for food, women and pleasure. Any talk of austerity was calculated to upset him. 'They say his whingeing was cut short by a very dismissive Lady Katherine.'

'Ah, yes, Lady Katherine. She seems quite taken with the Renewal Movement and that evangelical vicar at St Mark's who believes only a spartan life will restore our moral fibre.' Nina took a sip of her wine.

Across the table, Michael was shaking his head. 'It does seem odd, doesn't it?' he asked. 'I mean, a woman with her past and her wealth ... What's she looking for in a church where bored bourgeois housewives go and arrange flowers?' Michael chewed pensively. He had no interest in God or the after-life, as Nina well knew: every effort, every waking moment was invested in the here and now.

'Lady Katherine may be as bored with her lot as they are with theirs.' She shrugged. 'We had Philip Stephenson at the Society lunch today. It was obvious he defers to his wife in all things, and that she in turn has come under the spell of Alexander Connaught – apparently she attends his services regularly.'

Michael flashed her a smile. 'You are quite extraordinary. You know more about the paper where I work than I do!'

She laughed, shook her head. 'Stop it – but think what this could mean for Maurice ... the final straw ...'

For three years they had plotted together at this table, over countless similar suppers, Maurice's dismissal, his resignation; for three years they had held drinks parties and dinners, attended functions and supported charities – all to ensure Michael's triumphant succession.

'Hmm. Anything's possible these days.' He broke a piece of bread. 'And he's not getting any younger. Funny how once they grab hold of the paper they just can't let go – Albert was sixty-five and still had to be dragged kicking and screaming from his editor's chair before he'd give way to Maurice.'

'The attractions of power. Something, of course, you're completely immune to,' Nina teased. Between them, his ambition was as frequently and openly discussed as their child's progress.

He stretched his hand across the table to pat hers. 'Don't you start.' He pretended to pout.

'I think I'd better befriend our Lady Katherine . . .'

He beamed, as she knew he would. 'My darling Nina, my bestest ally and most invaluable asset.' He raised his glass of wine, 'To my perfect wife, brains, beauty,' here he made a gesture to encompass the room, 'and all this too.' His blue eyes grew serious. 'I'm sorry always to drag you into this. I just couldn't do it without you.' He shook his head. 'I want it so much.'

She cleared away the plates, pushed the basket of fruit into the middle of the table. 'Robbie came home crying again.'

Michael was peeling an orange, but she saw him frown. 'They've been teasing him again, have they? Those little wretches.'

She nodded. 'The glasses . . . his eyes . . .' She watched him wince: she knew that the taunts issued by Robbie's classmates were echoes of the same ones he had suffered as a little boy.

'God, I could go to the playground and just give them a good thrashing . . .' He sighed, offering her a dripping orange segment, which she refused.

Quickly, so as not to poison their time together, Nina changed the subject. 'I saw that Victor wrote a rather wonderful piece for you on the demise of the voluntary sector.'

Michael instantly cheered up. 'I should get him to do some more, but you know how proud he is. He doesn't want me to feel pushed into commissioning him because of our friendship.'

'He's a lovely writer,' she mused.

'It never fails to astonish me that a man of his ability can't get further.' Michael shook his head and continued to eat his orange. 'I mean, why should he spend the rest of his life writing dry-as-dust tomes of little interest to anyone?'

Nina did not answer, allowing him to enjoy the not altogether displeasing contemplation of his friend's lack of success. Michael finished his orange, downed the last drop of wine, stretched his arm to pat her shoulder and smiled at her. 'I'll help you with the washing up.'

'No need. Tomorrow Mavis is coming. We can leave everything.'

They rose, she switched off the lights behind them and followed him to the drawing room.

Before he'd even sat down he turned on the television, switching from channel to channel in search of news.

'Oh, you never told me.' He was lying back in the sofa, now, relaxed by the wine and by the knowledge that the paper that was being printed as he spoke covered all the top news stories. 'Did your piece on the Christian Coalition go down well with Clive?'

'Yes.' She smiled at his effort to remember her work. It always happened about now, when, after a meal during which every aspect of his own day had been thoroughly discussed, he remembered to enquire after her own welfare. She had never minded: she liked to humour him, to forgive him these transgressions; her clemency, rooted in her love (and perhaps, secretly, in her superiority), filled her with contentment, as if here again was something through which she held him.

'He liked it, I think.' She sat beside him, sliding slightly so she could feel every part of him against her. 'Clive is convinced this whole moral revival is just hogwash, and that whether they call themselves Christian Socialists or Christian Coalition, they're just hijacking religious terminology and sprinkling a bit of holier-than-thou water about the place because it's the fashion. The minute the electorate gets bored and pines for the good old amoral days, they'll switch.'

'Hmm.' He frowned at the television set. 'Thing is, right now it does appeal to the electorate. And the newspaper buyers. They love the stuff.'

'It's hardly surprising – political scandals, crime, no sense of community left. Having seen that no politician can solve these problems, why not turn to a Higher Power?'

'Hmm.' He returned to the news.

They sat in silence, Nina feeling him stretch against her. She listened to the wind beating against the house outside, and to the newscaster's regular, sombre voice. She studied his right hand as it lay, white and large on his thigh, and felt the longing begin.

She waited for the news to finish and then linked her fingers in his. 'Shall we go to bed, then?'

'Yes.' They stood up and switched off the lights, and he led the way up the stairs to their bedroom. Quickly they undressed, Michael carelessly throwing his clothes on the armchair by the window. She slipped into bed while he was brushing his teeth in the bathroom. She lay in the pink soft light of her bedside lamp, waiting. She wondered, silent, immobile, whether he would make love to her. She never made an overture but always yearned for his strong hands and their caresses.

Michael approached his side of the bed, and lay down next to her. She switched off the light, turned on her side towards him. He reached out and patted her knee.

Nina wrapped her hand around her husband's. He lay still now, and as she waited in the dark, trying to decipher his movements beside her, predict his thoughts, understand his decision, she felt her whole body ache for him.

'Come here,' he whispered. The warm hands took hold of her waist, pulled her close up to him, till she could feel his breath on her forehead. The arms wrapped her in an embrace. 'I am so lucky,' he said, voice low and hoarse. His hands clasped behind her back as his whole body pressed against her. 'So lucky,' he whispered again and again, as slowly they made love.

# Chapter Three

Lady Katherine was dressing for the drinks party. Philip was downstairs in the drawing room and she knew he would be fretting, nervously wondering when she would appear, who was coming, who wasn't. He'd be asking Liu, the cook, about the canapés, and he'd light up a cigarette, holding the filter tightly, as if only here could he find something solid. Philip feared uncertainty. Or, rather, he viewed it with impatience for it could yield neither profits nor dividends. In his eyes, uncertainty stirred up trouble and little else – and Philip hated trouble and had always fled it, except perhaps when he, a married man, had pursued Lady Katherine in a courtship that had filled gossip columns and considerably depleted his bank account.

Lady Katherine smiled as she pulled on her sheer black tights, slowly and carefully lest her sapphire ring caught the nylon. She supposed it had been worth it. Perhaps it had not been love, but it had been exciting. She slipped off her blue kimono, without looking at herself in the long mirror: she no longer drew any pleasure from her reflection. Carefully, she took up the cream-coloured slip from the quilt of roses that stretched across the bed and entered its folds head first, arms carefully passing through the thin straps. No, those days of vanity were over. But then – though she might regret her lost looks, she had no desire to relive her past loves or exploits. She had something else now.

As she took a pink shirt from the wide wardrobe in the corner of the bedroom, she wondered what she had hoped to find in her earlier existence. The excitement of desire, the brief satisfaction of its attainment, the dangerous thrill of adultery beneath Philip's nose, the dull praise of meaningless people . . . She shook her head as it rose out of the silk folds of her shirt and ran a thin white hand through the red hair that swung down to her shoulders. She felt nothing but disbelief at the thought that this had been her life.

Downstairs she heard Philip's voice raised in annoyance, heard him slap the table beside him: Johnny must be back. They always

16

argued, father and son: it was as if each one saw his own darkest secret failings revealed in the other. She wondered if Johnny had gone to see Alexander as he'd promised he would. But from the altercation that bubbled and burst downstairs, she doubted he had done anything this evening but drink.

Lady Katherine returned to the wardrobe, chose a black skirt, stepped into it – she couldn't be bothered to pull it on as you were supposed to – and zipped it up. Now she approached the mirror, oval-shaped and flattering, and sat before it to 'apply her paints', as she called it.

She must not make a fuss with Johnny tonight – better let him be until Alexander could see him privately. At the thought of the man she liked to call her spiritual adviser, she smiled. Then, having caught the smile in the mirror, she leaned forward, up to her reflection. 'You old fool,' she said, not unkindly, to the middle-aged face.

Well, she was allowed to love him, wasn't she? He had saved her, filled her life, transformed her. If only . . . if only she could have met Alexander five years earlier. At fifty she had been a great beauty still, chased by wealthy scions and captured by famous photographers, capable of prising younger mistresses and wives from their men. She stared at the mirror as she opened a pot of 'Special Rejuvenating Radiance', and began to spread the cream on her face. Yes, something –it was difficult to put her finger quite on what – had come loose, like the distinguished and eye-catching label from a bottle of vintage wine that, once off, leaves the bottle bare and unremarkable. Yet even if she could regain her youthful splendour, what exactly could she hope to obtain from this young vicar? Her fingers pressed gently, up and outward. He was celibate: would she, forgetting His teaching, have tried to lead him into temptation, with a thousand subterfuges, wiles and ploys? Would she – snake to his Eve – have slithered to him, whispering seduction till he yielded, and tasted sin? Lady Katherine peered at the reflection that glistened, looking no more rejuvenated or radiant than before. Would she have lured him from his path of purity despite her conversion?

She'd never know now – but she could console herself with the thought that no one else would have him, either.

She took up a brush, dipped it in her powder, blew off the excess and dusted her features with quick little movements. Alexander had saved her, and he had promised to help Johnny, while she in turn had promised to help him in his mission to spread the Good News.

For that, she shook her glossy head and set her jaw in a determined manner, she would use the *Heralds*, *Daily* and *Sunday*. Philip, she knew, was uninterested: he preferred money to influence, and found newspapers inimical; but she, daughter of Anthony Brooks, the most famous press baron of all, had been brought up with talk of circulation figures, advertising revenues, splashes and leaders. She loved the big noisy newsroom in its gleaming tower, the excitement of the men, and increasingly women, rushing after stories, the sound of fingers tapping keyboards and editors shouting about the slant, the length, the importance of each story. She loved sitting in at editorial conferences where opinions gave order to facts, and welcomed the long sessions of the board of trustees, when everyone and everything was evaluated in terms of circulation figures.

Lady Katherine slowly followed the curve of her still perfect lips with a brush dipped in dark red lipstick. Philip was bored with Maurice, that much was certain: too much self-indulgence, too many editorial mistakes, the snide campaign against crusader politicians last summer . . . no, Maurice was on his way out. But who would replace him? Tonight they had invited the young deputy, Michael Lewis, and his formidable wife. Would he do? Was he capable of running the *Sunday*? And – what was to her mind, at least, as important – was he willing to promote Alexander's Renewal Movement? Lady Katherine took the miniature vase of kohl from the top of her gleaming dark dresser, applied the thin wood stick to her eyes, elongating their round blueness. She no longer enjoyed the routine – something she had once taken such pride in accomplishing so skilfully.

Johnny was stomping upstairs – she'd checked earlier that there were no bottles in his room, but God alone knew whether he wouldn't slip out while they were having drinks . . . Lady Katherine saw her face tense in the mirror, grim with anxiety.

'Don't worry,' she heard Alexander's melodious voice. 'Bring him to me. I shall heal him.'

Yes, she must save Johnny, must bring him to St Mark's. Quickly she did her hair, set down the brush. She switched off the light and went down to the drawing room.

Michael looked down at the woman's white bosom, twin mounds of vanilla ice cream.

'You've met, I presume?' Philip Stephenson raised his glass in the direction of the provocatively dressed journalist, round eyes, long earrings, dark hair heaped in a tall pile upon her head. Michael's eyes

18

moved from his host – red face, white short-cropped hair, short stature – to Ruth Anderson, feminist columnist, woman-about-town, famed in the newsroom for her answer to Maurice's fumbling pass: 'I play only with the First Eleven.'

'Of course, Ruth.'

They exchanged pecks, but he could feel her hand still pressing his. Careful, he warned himself, careful, and keep your eye on the ball. Women like Ruth needed to talk about their conquests, wear their scalps hanging visibly from their belt, and a scandal was the last thing he needed when he was chasing the editorship. He watched her push herself closer to him, address him in her breathless little girl's voice. He was glad he towered above her – he'd noticed only last week that the hair at the very top of his head was beginning to thin, looking as frayed as the Jermyn Street shirt collar worn by Philip Stephenson – a man so posh he could afford to show a few flaws. But Michael felt no desire to show anything but his attributes, and with his hand he now combed the hair over to the left, watching all the while the woman beneath him, and their host before him. He saw Philip Stephenson study Ruth with only mild amusement (Philip didn't seem too interested in the pleasures of the flesh – it was money that thrilled him). Michael didn't listen, just heard the unquenchable fountain of her speech and looked at the round whiteness of her bosom. He decided that if she were muzzled he wouldn't deploy great physical violence to get her out of his bed. But only if she were muzzled. And if he could be certain that Nina would never, ever find out.

Bored with the two men's failure to respond to her charms, Ruth Anderson moved away, into the crowded room, leaving Michael to stand by the door and his host.

He allowed Philip Stephenson to blow smoke into his face while he mused that, strategically, this was an excellent position: you could see who was coming and going between the Stephensons' large elegant drawing room and their large elegant dining room. Then again, he was already talking to the most important person there – apart, possibly, from Philip's wife. So Michael could relax, concentrate on laughing at the jokes that limped towards him, at keeping a careful check on the expressions on his face as the smoke entered his eyes and nostrils, at reassuring Philip with every gesture, word and look that he was the man for the editorship.

He wished Nina were there beside him: he would just watch her cue and allow her to conduct her diplomatic manoeuvres, cajoling Philip into an expansive mood, promoting the friendliness between them with a few flattering remarks. His eyes searched for his wife, found her by the windows that stretched from floor to ceiling and looked onto the river below. She stood next to that irritating MP Tom Sutton, looking as if every word of his would reshape her life; she was probably bored to death.

He smiled while Philip Stephenson continued to drone on about his investments in South Africa. How did Nina do it? Of course it was upbringing, in part: she must have met people like these – writers, publishers, journalists, politicians – from the time she was so high. And wonderful Marina would have taught her just how to smile, and speak, and make everyone feel at ease. That was what came from being born within the hallowed walls of the Establishment, the daughter of an influential professor. Sometimes he wondered if more than to be *with* his wife, he wanted to be like her.

'Michael, how nice to see you.' It was Lady Katherine, standing at his elbow, smiling up at him. She was, he was always surprised into thinking, a remarkably fine-looking woman. He cast her a look at once appreciative and respectful, and wondered whether poor old Philip had ever guessed how many men his wife had carried on with. Did she still?

'I've been telling Michael about the diamonds.' Philip, shorter than Lady Katherine, tipped his round white head back slightly to meet his wife's blue gaze.

'I'm sure he'd rather be talking about the *Sunday Herald*,' Lady Katherine murmured.

Michael tensed but betrayed no emotion.

'Well, not much to say. Maurice is acting up as usual. Fool – doesn't see that there are all kinds of changes going on around him that would be interesting to monitor . . .' Philip frowned at his lengthening cigarette ash, made a desperate gesture. Without a word, his wife handed him a small porcelain shell.

'Yes. Tell me, Michael,' Michael felt Lady Katherine fix him with her eyes, 'what do you know about Alexander Connaught?'

Nina knew that she was different from the way others saw her. It was as if her character were written in a foreign language that they always translated poorly, mauling her idioms and misinterpreting her meaning. Her shyness became for others 'arrogance', her earnestness 'dignity'. She watched with detachment this misunderstanding take root and drew some pleasure from the thought that her true self still proved illegible to this untutored throng.

She had never prized the social world her parents inhabited, but she had realised, since her marriage, that for Michael it afforded not only great appeal – his own background, for which he bore seemingly no sentimental attachment, had been much more modest – but also important connections.

'Nina! Come here, I haven't seen you since that brilliant column of yours on bereavement – darling, you are clever!' Nina found herself being pulled from Tom Sutton's side by the diminutive Sophie Mansel. 'So moving!' The publisher gripped her elbow while piloting her towards the middle of the crowded drinks party.

Nina cast a despairing look back at Tom Sutton. 'But, Sophie,' she murmured, dazed by the sheer energy of the woman. But Sophie was dragging her along with the same no-nonsense determination with which she had built a publishing empire on borrowed capital, had browbeaten writers, editors and agents into doing her bidding, and had imposed her will upon dissenting colleagues.

'Here, pet, let's toast. What can we toast? Well, your success and my latest bestseller,' and Sophie raised her glass, 'To Nina and *The Prophecy*.'

Nina took a glass from the waiter's tray. She looked over her shoulder, caught Michael's eye. He was talking with the Stephensons. She smiled at his unfailing ability to turn every occasion into an opportunity for self-promotion. She brought the glass to her lips. 'To *The Prophecy*.'

The publisher took a sip: 'The book's actually very good – shame we can't promote the author more – but what can I do about an unfortunate surfeit of facial hair coupled with a regrettable protrusion of teeth? No amount of air-brushing will save her, I fear.'

Sophie had pulled her into the centre of the flesh-coloured room. Above the crowded floor Zeus was seducing Leda upon a canvas, grinning all the while at the guests below. On her left, framed by wine-coloured velvet, the great windows that let out onto a balcony shone with river lights – the bridge arched bright over the dark waters where boats bobbed and twinkled, and along the Embankment the street lamps glowed, smaller copies of the great moon that sat, plump and luminous, upon the web of bare branches.

The room was hot with the crush of guests and she watched as some of the women removed their jackets to reveal sleeveless dresses. Cigarette smoke swirled with perfume and the potent scent of the giant pink roses that stretched regally from their crystal vase above the mantelpiece. Around her she saw all the familiar faces – yesterday's successes, tomorrow's failures, the wits, their glamorous hangers-on, the faded beauties, the young sirens . . . They struck the same notes she had heard in her parents' white Holland Park drawing room. She had been brought up with their liaisons, feuds, boasts, brave stands and capitulations, yet had always felt that their world would never be hers; this would never be home. She always felt she watched 'them' from without, a spectator viewing an alien world where comfortable friendships and professional alliances smudged all boundaries; her own existence instead was carried out in a clearly marked, jealously protected venue, which allowed for only respectful, ordered explorations that, as in a museum visit, stopped short of those areas that were cordoned off.

'Look at Miranda,' Sophie tugged at her elbow, so that Nina turned to catch sight of the famous actress sauntering towards Philip Stephenson, her Fortuny dress fanning out behind her like a train. 'Swanning about as if she owned the place – doesn't she realise that the only reason she's here is because Katherine still feels guilty about the weekend when she had it off with Miranda's husband *and* her lover?! Not together, I hasten to add – though with Katherine, frankly, anything's possible. Or was.' And Sophie shook her head sadly – whether in disapproval or mourning of their hostess's past, Nina could not tell.

Nina raised her glass and surveyed an old roué licking his lips as he toasted another's wife; she watched an overripe beauty whose breathless whisper drew a young man into her *décolleté*. She listened to Sophie complimenting a squat moustachioed man on his brilliant last oeuvre, and heard a young man moan about the imminent bankruptcy of his publishing house. Behind her, three women gossiped about Maurice's latest mistress. Nina sighed inwardly: these gatherings were one and the same. Like the remains of a banquet where the best dishes have been eaten or squirrelled away, they yielded only the leftovers: everyone kept their best for their writings, their deals, their jobs. Here, they chose their words carelessly and discarded them quickly.

Beside her, but invisible because of her short stature, Sophie continued, small curly head bobbing in her breathless tumbling speech: 'Look at them – oh, what a sad, navel-gazing, incestuous bunch they are!' An eyebrow rose in her small, lively face. 'No wonder that spiritual tomes like *The Prophecy* are doing so well – anything that reacts against these libertines must have enormous appeal for the man in the street!'

'What fools! Gone all soppy about their new found faith . . . Makes one shudder: I keep sentimentality strictly for Remembrance Sunday and one poppy purchase, thank you very much.' It was Clive Walton-Ellis, and Nina beamed at him: they had known one another for years, ever since she had helped him edit his father's memoirs and he had tried to seduce her on the leather sofa in his study. He had forgiven her rejection, and had hired her two years ago as a columnist for the magazine he edited, the *Society*.

'Did you hear our hostess just now? She button-holed some poor unsuspecting guest and started blathering on about her salvation through the vicar of St Mark's. She actually mentioned the words "God" and "Jesus" in polite company, can you believe it?! Anyway, theirs is a hopeless cause. What sensible soul would abandon the good life because of a few preachers shouting from their pulpits?' Clive laughed, raised his glass to Nina, winked at her.

'Clive! Clive! You must have read that column of Nina's. It was just perfect, wasn't it?' The irrepressible Sophie, dwarfed by their tall figures, clutched Clive's hand for attention.

'Read it? I commissioned it,' Clive's eyes fastened on Nina. 'You need not sell Nina Lewis to me, Sophie. I'm an ardent fan – devoted since I first knew her when she was a mere slip of a girl. I bet you didn't know her then.'

But Sophie had already sailed off.

'I must say, you look ravishing tonight. My darling,' he lowered his voice to the satyr tones she remembered of old, 'you must explain what it is Michael does to keep you looking so . . . expectant.' He chuckled at her blush, and offered her a cigarette which she declined.

'You look well, too.' She lied: at every encounter, she noticed with melancholy how soggy his once-handsome features, and the contours of his face, had grown with alcohol.

'Now, Nina, I know this is no time to talk shop but,' and immediately his tone changed from social drawl to the editor's bullet points bark, 'I want to know more about this Alexander Connaught everyone seems to be talking about. St Mark's in Chelsea – a large church that apparently packs them in every day of the week, a minister so charismatic he's managed to raise millions at every church fund-raiser, a man who it seems has our hostess wrapped round his little finger . . . They say there's more to it than hymn-singing and cosy sermons . . . and who could I trust to plumb these spiritual depths better than my most treasured columnist?'

'You realise it will be difficult.' Nina was frowning. 'If Lady Katherine supports him and I poke fun at his movement, Michael may suffer.'

'Ah, of course. Silly me not to have thought of it.' Clive was all sarcasm now, eyes narrowed and cold.

'Look, why don't I go and meet him, see what it's all about? If it's innocuous I can write it up without worry, and if it's more serious, I'll bring you my findings – obedient as ever – and you can decide how to handle the issue then.'

'I think you are wonderful.' Clive was laughing as he downed another great swallow of champagne. 'And I'm sorry if I was being snide . . . You know I worship at your altar, like everyone else.'

Lady Katherine watched Tom Sutton approach her. He made his way slowly across the guests, smiling at everyone, looking so boyish you expected his mother to be at his heels, piloting him through the throng. Every now and then he pushed back the black shock of hair that fell over one eye: he seemed pleased with the room full of important literary figures, pleased to see her, above all, pleased with himself.

'I bring you his greetings – I just popped into St Mark's.'

'I'd wanted to invite him tonight but I wasn't sure he'd come. Quite frankly, I never know how much socialising – of this kind – a man of the cloth would welcome.' Lady Katherine blushed: even to speak of him thrilled her. 'He's talked a great deal about you, your enthusiasm for the cause, your good work.' She spoke in a low voice, head slightly to one side.

'Not enough, not enough. I haven't had a chance, really, to do any proper work as of yet. But I'm determined to make a difference.' He was looking into her eyes, as all politicians were taught to do, but she felt nothing. She realised he was not interested in women, and wondered if the rumours about his past were true after all. The wife in Laurel, the baby twins: had they been hastily pulled in to reassure the constituents, the Party? Or perhaps, after meeting Alexander, Tom Sutton had undergone the same Damascene conversion that had transformed her life.

'You too must help, Lady Katherine.' Serious black eyes probed her and the young, unmarked face grew earnest. 'He needs you. Through the newspapers.'

'Yes, yes,' she interrupted him, with a meaningful look: she could see Michael Lewis standing nearby, possibly listening. A clammy warm hand on her elbow, Tom had drawn her closer to himself: 'The movement would help the *Herald* as much as the other way around. You realise how many people are tired of this moral vacuum and would welcome a newspaper that campaigned for a return to a life rooted in a value system.'

'I know that.' She caught Clive Walton-Ellis watching her: they'd been lovers so many years ago that she could hardly remember his body and had only the faintest recollection of his courtship. All she recalled was one drunken afternoon in his office . . . She stopped herself: this wouldn't do, evil thoughts led to temptation, they weighed down your spirit, and slowed your progress to the ultimate happiness. She almost smiled at her word-perfect recollection of Alexander's lessons.

'He tells me you will come to the healing session on Monday night.'

'Yes – with my son.' Or so she hoped. For a moment her heart tightened: Johnny lay in the dark upstairs, in a stupor. Then Lady Katherine beamed at the politician before her. 'You see, I think Alexander can save him.'

'Have you met your father's latest protégée?' Clive's eyes sparkled, and he drew his tall, stomach-heavy frame to its full height.

Nina wagged her finger. 'Don't you start on my father, Clive, you know I won't have any of your sarcasm.'

'He's behaving in his usual priceless manner,' Clive, unperturbed, rolled on.

'Well?' Her tone remained wary. Her father and Clive had never seen eye to eye, and their hostility erupted every so often on the printed page, erudite and ironic skirmishes that her mother thought were more tonic for Paolo than any amount of healthy eating. She had emptied her glass and a waiter swept it away before she could ask for a refill.

'A hackette. A pretty little thing with only a modicum of talent. But he's touting her about as if she were the latest genius to have burst upon our squalid little world. I think he's aiming to get her a place on your husband's august paper.'

Nina inwardly sighed: her father always fell for these pretty, unscrupulous young women. She looked around for another glass, but instead saw her parents with Philip Stephenson, her father slightly stooped, his tall thin frame almost too much for any one man to bear.

His tonsured head and his long ascetic face lent him a monkish air, quickly dispelled by his animated expression and combative manner. Beside him stood her mother, small, white-haired, plump, a dove to his hawk. Nina watched her parents perform their habitual two-step: first, Paolo attacked, frowning over his spectacles, to pose some difficult question or spout some endless list of esoteric facts. Then Marina moved forward to pacify, reassure, counteracting her husband's effect. They were, Nina mused, a perfect complement to one another. Now they approached her and Clive.

'Ah, my poor, poor Nina, stuck with the greatest bore for miles . . .' Paolo's rich dark voice boomed.

'Papa.' Nina kissed his cheek. As usual with her father a surge of conflicting emotions filled her: she felt at once protective, infuriated, loving, rooted, restless. He had loomed over her childhood and adolescence, colouring her existence, shaping her responses and aspirations. Her overriding memory of those years was of her attempts to say or do something remarkable while tugging at his sleeve to gain admission to his insulated world.

'Clive, my dear, don't pay him any attention.' Marina rose on tiptoe to peck Clive's cheek and then her daughter's. 'How's my Robbie?' she whispered. Nina squeezed her mother's hand.

Paolo's eyes were on his old foe. 'Filling my daughter with your usual nonsense, I suspect.' He straightened himself so that he was a good head taller than Clive, puffed out his chest and cocked his head to one side. 'Am I wrong?'

But Clive who, after much casting about, had found his good mood in tonight's wine, had no intention of pulling up his anchor to be marooned once again in this sea of all-too-familiar faces. 'You are wrong, Paolo. I am merely basking in your beautiful daughter's presence.'

Nina looked at the two men.

'We were just talking with Michael and Philip Stephenson . . .' Paolo began.

'Ah, yes, of course, the inevitable rise of Michael Lewis.' Clive winked at Nina. She ignored him – he was always making fun of Michael's ambition, and though she detected more than a hint of jealousy in his tone, he annoyed her with his marked inability to take her husband seriously.

'On the grapevine I hear that the Stephensons are wearying of dear old Maurice.'

Paolo removed his half-moon spectacles, held them up to the light, blew on their glass and polished them with the handkerchief he pulled from his pocket. 'Hmm . . . He hasn't exactly done much for circulation, has he?'

'Ah, well, we'll stand on the sidelines and watch the young dogs fight for the bone, won't we, my friend?' Clive smirked at Paolo's obvious irritation at being cast in a marginalised role.

'Oh, just listen to these two go on.' Marina was smiling at her daughter, ignoring the two men's traditional skirmish.

'Speak for yourself, Clive. I'm at the peak of my talents.' Paolo was looking around the room. He broke into a grin. 'Well, well, look who's here. Clive, I've found something over which we are certain to agree. Clive, Nina, meet my discovery, Allegra Worth. One of the brightest young journalists around. Don't go, don't go, Allegra, I want you to meet . . .' Paolo pulled towards them a small, dark-haired woman. She seemed very young – perhaps in her mid-twenties – dainty, with blue eyes that looked shyly upon the world from beneath lowered lids. Nina smiled: yet another pretty thing for her father to champion. She cast her mind over the female acolytes he had always drawn to himself. But Mother had never seemed to mind: 'He just needs the show, like a peacock, you have to let him strut about. And in the end he's no more capable of betrayal than a peacock of song.'

'Allegra,' Marina was gently pushing the shy young woman towards them, 'Allegra, this is our daughter Nina.'

'And the disreputable Clive Walton-Ellis,' Paolo snorted, 'upon whom you need waste no time or charm, my dear, as he can be of no assistance to you whatsoever.'

'Nonsense!' Clive had lit another cigarette and blew the smoke into Paolo's face. 'I will let you know that I have proved an incalculable asset to many a young hack – and hackette – trying to claw their way up the greasy pole of Fleet Street careers.' Here, Clive bent, smiling, towards the pretty young journalist. 'You come and chat with me, my dear. I'm not some retired academic relegated to writing dusty tomes no one ever reads . . .'

'Oh, honestly, you two!' Marina rolled her eyes.

Nina smiled, politeness mingling with curiosity, at Allegra. 'They're terrible when they get together – can't help showing off. Especially when they have an audience and she's pretty and young . . .'

Allegra nodded, and her hands toyed nervously with her glass as she cast a look about the room. 'I feel slightly out of my depth. It feels so strange still – I'm used to Sheffield where you soon know everyone.' She spoke quietly, her voice raised at the end of each sentence, as if seeking approval from her interlocutor. Nina mused that there was something in the small, hesitant figure that made her seem almost unfinished, as if she were a clay model someone had yet to complete.

'You'll soon meet everyone here, Allegra, don't worry.' Clive smiled down at her. 'There are only a few of us, in the end, and with your *cicerone* – you'll have the time of your life.'

'The trick is, of course, we must get you out and about. In fact, why don't you accompany Marina and me to *Così Fan Tutte* next Tuesday – all the arts world will be there.' Paolo was obviously enjoying his mentor's role.

'I've never heard it,' Allegra admitted, in her uncertain voice.

'What, my dear?' Paolo bent down to draw closer. 'Never heard it? Where have you been, my poor, poor little provincial Philistine!' Paolo was laughing. 'Thank goodness you've been saved from Sheffield . . . and let's hope we can inject some civilisation into you here . . .' Paolo and Clive both chortled.

Nina pierced the men with a furious look.

'Honestly, Allegra, don't pay these brutes any attention,' whispered Marina, weaving her arm into the young woman's.

'Don't worry, Paolo's been so kind. You don't know how terrified I've been for the past few weeks. I feel as if I don't know the rules of the game here, and I'm scared of saying or doing the wrong thing . . . like just now. But he's been so patient.' Allegra suddenly fell silent and Nina almost smiled at the young woman's look of panic – the vowel she had let slip lay between them: flat, drawn out, and unmistakeably Northern.

Paolo placed a hand upon Allegra's shoulder. 'Come along, Allegra, and I'll introduce you to the rest of the great and the good.'

'Goodbye, then.' Marina waved a small white hand.

''Bye.' Allegra turned and smiled at Nina and then Clive, allowing Paolo to pull her in his wake.

'A beguiling little thing. She'll soon be wrapping all of us round her little finger, I warrant.' Clive nodded approvingly. Then he laughed. 'Just look at your father, with his hand on that part of the body where others have a heart – he's smitten.'

'Enjoying yourself?' Michael joined them.

'Yes.' Nina smiled at her husband.

'Philip Stephenson was singing your praises.' He stood beside her, adopting his favourite pose – leaning against the wall, arms crossed, head slightly to one side. She felt her habitual response to his presence: a fierce, possessive yearning to be the focus of his thoughts.

'Everyone does, Michael.' Clive wrapped his arm around Nina's waist. 'I'm afraid it's the small price you have to pay when you marry the perfect woman – you threaten to pale into insignificance in her presence.'

'What rot you do talk, Clive.' Nina was only half joking: she hated the way Clive always tried to provoke Michael.

'Oh, Nina's superiority has never been questioned. Least of all by me.' Michael grinned without betraying the slightest emotion.

'Well, I'm off,' Clive, defeated in his attempt to unsettle the younger man, stubbed out his cigarette, 'before the sight of the loving couple fills me with despondency.' He looked at his watch. 'And, in fact, I think if I rush I might just about make it in time to see my new favourite.' He left, Nina and Michael laughing in his wake at the man's notorious libido.

'I saw you with Philip.' Nina lowered her voice and Michael had to draw closer to hear her. They stood beside one another, reflected with the chandelier above in the great french window beside them. Their complicity, she imagined, was mirrored by many married couples. It was like the unspoken but unquestionable understanding that springs up between foreigners away from home, betrayed in glances, smiles, nods that separate them from the natives.

'I can't do enough schmoozing at the moment . . . I can tell something's in the air. And Katherine Stephenson asked me quite pointedly about the minister at St Mark's.' He raised his eyebrow meaningfully.

'Clive wants me to look into it for the *Society* – It will afford me the perfect opportunity to confer with her ladyship.'

He ran a hand through his thick blond hair, smiled. 'Brilliant idea.'

She thrilled at his praise. She looked around the room and suddenly wished them gone, wished only to be alone with him. She placed a hand on his arm. 'Shall we go, darling?'

They walked together through the crowded room, and Nina felt conscious of being noticed, studied, envied, gossiped about.

'The golden couple,' she heard someone mutter.

## Chapter Four

It was almost Christmas. The day was cold, but glorious: sunny, fresh-aired, with every outline sharp as an intelligent argument. It had been a gloomy winter so far – rain-soaked, skies dull and grey as they had seemed to him every day of his schooling. Or so thought Michael as he stood, with a reporter's notebook in his hands, among three hundred people in the cavernous Islington Town Hall. He'd been reminded of the misery of his schooldays because Robbie had climbed into his lap this morning and lain there, sobbing into his chest till the tears had soaked Michael's shirt. They were teasing him at school again: 'Cross-eyes'. The familiar refrain echoed the playground taunts of his own child-hood. Why must his son suffer like this? The same cross eyes, the same thinness: it had taken Michael thirteen years to outgrow both – but he still bore the scars. Nightmares still woke him in which he was being held under water in the large antiseptic pool at school; or pushed against a wall, his spectacles snatched from him and thrown like a ball among a group of chanting boys.

He sometimes felt as if all those years since school had been nothing but his attempt to get away from that sense of shame. Now his son was a daily reminder. Robbie. For his parents he had felt a tepid affection in which had mingled a slight embarrassment at their humble background, guilt at having outshone them, and gratitude for their never having burdened him. Nina he loved possessively, conscious always of her as a prize he must win, and now cherish. But Robbie – Robbie made his heart crumble to a dust of loving and protective longing, so that his son's presence yielded both pleasure and pain. Robbie needed him, and the need transformed Michael: he felt himself become someone quite different from the way he was with others, a benevolent, omnipotent deity. With Nina – so perfect, so capable – he felt somehow wanting; with Robbie he felt wanted.

A hum rose from the crowd and Michael looked up: three men climbed onto the wooden platform while plain-clothes policemen moved in the background. Beneath the blue and white banner, with its bold letters proclaiming a 'Christian Coalition', stretched a long, thin table. Michael saw Tom Sutton arrive with his researcher (a delicate-looking young man with a hurried, nervous gait) and step up to one of the chairs that lined the table. Sutton was in a sober suit, his youthful face excited beneath the floppy black hair.

Now Michael spotted a tall blond man in clerical garb approaching Sutton on the platform: they hugged one another and spoke quietly while onto the stage filed the two other speakers – a bishop and a second MP – followed by an assortment of researchers, secretaries, relatives.

'Hot,' muttered a man standing next to Michael, as he wiped his forehead with the back of his forearm.

'Yes.' It was true: the audience that swelled every minute was packed into the damp Victorian hall and, with neither windows nor doors open, the air had become oppressive.

Michael was beginning to regret his decision to come himself to cover Sutton's speech for the Christian Coalition AGM. Maurice had raised a surprised eyebrow. 'Don't we have someone else who could cover this non-story? I mean, do I have to spare my bloody deputy for some born-again claptrap?' He'd scowled and banged his fist on the table in his usual controlled and polished manner, and Michael, of course, had ignored him. It had been a hunch: if he covered Sutton's speech tonight in a flattering light he might win Lady K's approval – and, who knew, even gratitude.

But he couldn't see her anywhere near the stage, and Tom Sutton seemed satisfied to talk exclusively to the tall, elegant cleric beside him. This must be his famous spiritual mentor, the Reverend Alexander Connaught.

Impatient, Michael looked around at the throng: they struck him as surprisingly ordinary – indeed, well-heeled rather than brown-sandaled. They seemed mostly young, with faces as well scrubbed as his own nails when they had had to pass his mother's nightly inspection: slightly too good to be true, conveying the distinct impression that the cleanliness was a temporary phase. They were unusually well behaved for a political gathering – but then, most of the supporters of the Christian Coalition were paid-up members of the Renewal Movement, whose followers boasted excellent pedigrees: nannies, public schools, and no heating at home had no doubt instilled in them the virtue of patience even before their conversion at the hands of Alexander Connaught. He looked at them through narrowed eyes: yes, definitely, he stood surrounded by signet rings, old school ties, and a smattering of Honourables.

Men and women wore the same expectant, gleaming-eyed look, and he could savour his own contempt for their collective hope that there was one answer to all their questions about the purpose of existence. A life beyond this one. He shook his head: only those who fail in this world need to invest so much in the next.

But now they started clapping and he stretched to see the chairman approach the podium. Behind him Sutton sat, waiting. Michael listened to the introduction – one of the youngest, brightest politicians, a devoted Christian, a man of principle as well as action . . . The platitudes flowed. He saw that the vicar with whom Sutton had been speaking had climbed down the stairs and was now back in the audience. Sutton took to the podium. Michael, who was nervous of and inept at public speaking, felt envy for those who could hold an audience's attention through successive waves of insights, jokes and melodramatic pauses. He watched Sutton as he began with words and tone to wind his way round the audience, slithering up and up till he could choke all independent life from them. As was his wont with anyone, but especially with men of about his own age, Michael measured Sutton against himself: he had done well, no doubt about it, though, of course, Sutton had had the advantage of money. In preparing for the piece about the conference today, Michael had read all the cuttings about the young MP, and had learned that the family fortune had been made by the father, in prepared food: 'I have made my fortune out of people's laziness, my son will make his name out of their sense of right – wait and see,' the old man had told an interviewer, who had profiled the successful father and son.

Michael studied the pale face beneath the black shiny hair: he had won over quite a few key ministers, young Sutton, but had earned himself also a number of enemies, with his endless talk of conservative values, women back in the mother's role, an end to legalised abortion and so forth. In addition, hovering in the background, there was always the hint of scandal: three maybe four years ago, rumours had been circulating about his pretty-boy secretaries and assistants. Still he'd married, had the children . . . Michael shook his head: why did men and women enter politics these days? All this sniffing at their heels, shaking of closet doors to see the skeletons tumbling out . . . You had to be a true idealist – or a real fool – to crave the political arena. He looked at

Sutton's gesticulating hand, at the tall brow where sweat was collecting so visibly: he had never wished that kind of glory for himself. No, from the start he had preferred the protection conferred by criticising rather than performing, of pointing out that the emperor had no clothes rather than parading naked down the high street. You could still wield power from the sideline – at least, if the sideline was being editor of the *Sunday Herald*. The thought of Maurice, infuriating, sly, smug, rose, but he quickly quashed it by concentrating on the audience around him: he needed to give more colour to the piece, he must get in a good description of the 'faithful'. Indeed, they did strike him as comic, as they stood here, wide-eyed in admiration for this politico who studded his speech with those sacred words, 'Jesus', 'Holy Spirit', 'God'. Look at them, straining to do and say the right thing, reminding him for all the world of those performances they would put on at school, where the boys played girls' parts, and every aspect of the production struck an amateur note.

'Shame. An old-fashioned word, rarely employed these days – politicians don't believe in it, the media shies away from it, the teachers in our children's schools won't teach it. Shame is a dirty word, like guilt, penance and regret. No one wants us to feel shame any more. Because to do so we would need to recognise that ideals have been betrayed.' Tom Sutton paused, looked around at the audience below. He resumed his speech, voice now swollen with anger. 'They have betrayed these ideals – and us!'

'Amen!' the reply resounded in the warm, confined space, and a few voices took up the word and repeated it. Michael couldn't help a smile of amusement as he scribbled on his pad: it would seem that many a rat was ready to follow this pious Pied Piper. He spotted a pretty blonde a few rows up from him, and allowed his eyes to feast. How strange, he mused, as he gently and slowly removed her clothes with his eyes (beginning with the pale blue shirt, then the long thick grey skirt – he might leave her standing in her lingerie for a while, just to savour her pouting prettiness) that after almost a decade of having had only a few moments of true temptation, he should now feel bombarded by lustful sensations. It happened every day, almost, everywhere he went: on the road, while he drove, in the newsroom, even at the shop, the other day, with Robbie. He couldn't account for it – he still enjoyed making love to Nina, the thought of her still excited him, but it was as if he suddenly appreciated the attractions of a thousand other women as well.

'Shame, of course, has provided one of the most powerful images in the Judaeo-Christian tradition.' Michael cast down his straying eyes, and listened to the words pour forth from Sutton. 'Adam and Eve, suddenly naked in one another's eyes, as they are cast out of the Garden of Eden for having wronged their Father. But the shame our first parents felt was rooted in their recognition of what was expected of them, in their knowledge of sin and therefore of sinning. Isn't the problem today that this recognition of the ideal and of the absolute is absent? That our understanding of wrong has become so blurred? When a baby's life is valued at less than a woman's ability to earn money, when marriage is for 'a while', when children are no longer taught right from wrong at school: what kind of moral vacuum have they replaced our ideals with?'

Allegra stood, notebook in hand, beside Ruth Anderson. She was out of breath from having run here: a wrong turn outside the tube station had taken her miles away from the enormous town hall. In the end, she'd fought her shyness and had asked a woman passer-by for directions. She must, *must* start to get to know her way around this city. But the London of her dreams had been so different from this enormous cold space peopled by expressionless men and women. She had seen, in her mind's eye, the City as lovely medieval buildings stretching by the Thames; she'd seen park upon park lie flat and lush, a green girdle giving shape to the sprawl of buildings, and white Georgian terraced homes in elegant crescents. But this, this was a drab skein of streets, where churches and houses sat encrusted with dirt like the homeless who slept in doorways.

How she longed for the regal, splendid London she'd imagined, as she walked from home through the litter-strewn roads, the sour underpass to dank, malodorous Hammersmith station. With the Christmas lights up and the sparkling miniature trees and garlands of greens, she felt as if she were in the presence of a beauty past her prime, who had miscalculated how she should dress. She hadn't dared admit her disappointment during her telephone calls home: Mum would merely chide her for her 'romantic nonsense' – 'I don't know where you get these ideas from, honestly I don't,' she would have said, the woman who'd named her only child after a beautiful actress in some forgettable Italian film.

'It's started,' Ruth hissed, as Allegra took off her coat, and folded it on her arm. Ruth had thrown hers on top of her enormous handbag on the floor but Allegra didn't dare add her own coat to the pile. In the stifling heat she breathed in the other woman's pungent scent, and watched her blacken her page in rushed shorthand: what was she writing so furiously when Tom Sutton had only begun his speech? Allegra looked up at the huge round white clock which told her that in one hour she would have to file a story for the Diary. Fear squeezed her stomach, and her hands grew clammy so that she had to change her grip on the notepad lest the perspiration made her ink run. She must find a story, write something pithy that would make her editor smile, mark her out in his mind as talent. Again she looked at Ruth's dark head bobbing over her pad that filled and filled with lines that curled and stretched across the page. Please help me, she wanted to plead with the older woman. But she said nothing for she felt wary of the columnist, notorious for her unbridled tongue and ways.

There were many like her in the newsroom, and many more around London: unconnected people searching for someone or something to keep the loneliness at bay. Allegra shivered at the prospect: these were the fears that crept over her when she lay in bed at night, like a furtive caress from a man you did not care for. These were the fears she had packed in her case when she'd come down from Sheffield, armed with pride in her 'young journalist' prize ('It's stuffed your head with airs and graces,' Bill had growled during their last quarrel, warning her that she'd soon be back, 'tail between your legs, begging me to give you a second chance, begging me to marry you after all – and I won't, Ally, I won't!'), and an introduction to a few hacks from Miles, who had overestimated the influence he, editor of the *Sheffield Gazette*, wielded over his former colleagues. These were the fears that had sent her to St Mark's, which Mum had read about on the church bulletin board.

She looked now around the crowded hall for the blond head and the black cleric's garments. Even in this throng, she felt certain he would stand out. And, in fact, she found him quickly, tall and straight as she imagined the archangels at heaven's gate. She almost shivered at his handsome, glowing face, whose features she could not distinguish at this distance but which lay imprinted in her mind: the long blue eyes, the high cheekbones that stretched fine pale skin, and the perfect curves of his lips that made his mouth seem so gentle, belying the forbidding message it issued. He filled her with more than a little fear, like the God she'd grown up with, whom Mum had described as a vengeful, ever-watchful divinity. Mum. Allegra sighed. She was so proud, she'd bored every neighbour rigid with the tales of her daughter going to London. 'The prize, you know, it's opened all kind of doors for her, she's bound for the top now, there's no stopping her!' Mum had never read anything but the odd magazine left lying around the hairdresser's where she worked; now, she could trip journalists' names off her tongue like the words in her hymn book, and knew the circulation figures of every quality, tabloid and weekly. 'Soon, you'll see, you'll have your own by-line, and picture too,' she'd told her daughter – while Allegra felt embarrassment and gratitude fill her in equal measure – as ever with her mother. It was Mum who'd made sure Allegra went to St James C of E school in Hollywell, and she who'd dreamed of the university – 'The first graduate in our family!' She'd brought her up so carefully, so strictly, all the more so after Father had died: Allegra's earliest impression of the world was of a black-and-white chessboard of evil and goodness, where every step she took would place her soul in jeopardy of sliding into the bottomless pit that Satan inhabited.

'To those who say we should do our own thing, refrain from passing judgement – to those people I would say, "We, the people, are tired of this."' The crowd murmured its approval in unison. Allegra's eyes widened: she was surprised at the transformation Tom Sutton underwent when he took to the podium. Whenever she saw him whispering with Alexander, his bowed black head close up to the other's blond one, he seemed eager to follow blindly his mentor wherever he wished to lead. Today, instead, he was all fire and certainty, a powerful Moses-like figure ready to lead his people to their salvation. 'Look who's here.' Ruth elbowed her excitedly, craning her neck to look to her right.

'Who?' Allegra asked in a whisper

'Michael Lewis, the deputy. If he's here it means they're treating Sutton's speech as a big story. Hm, attractive, isn't he?'

Allegra thought how shaming it was for a woman of a certain age to speak so brazenly. She saw Michael Lewis, and remembered meeting his formidable wife at the Stephensons' altogether terrifying party. She blushed again at the patronising way Paolo del Monte had spoken to her – though, God knew, she was grateful to him now as he'd arranged for Lewis to see her and give her a shift on the Diary. Lewis, she thought, had been warm and unassuming, as if he had had all the time in the world despite being deputy at one of the most important newspapers in the land . . .

'Come on, let's go and talk to him.' Ruth bent down, dragged up her coat and handbag, and marched towards Michael, ignoring the outraged noises from the men and women whose view she was blocking. Allegra reluctantly followed her.

'Are we tired of a society where one crime is committed every six seconds?' Again a murmur rippled through the audience.

'Yes,' said the man beside Michael.

'Are we tired of living in a world where one in three families is torn asunder by divorce?'

'Yes!' the audience replied in unison.

'Are we fed up with liars at the helm and godless intellectuals telling us to live and let live?'

'Yes!' roared the crowd.

Tom Sutton stopped for a moment, looking around the large, poorly lit hall. 'Yes, of course we are. We want to throw off this moral torpor and wake up to the call of Jesus Christ. We want to, we can, we *shall* start anew!'

'The nonsense that man speaks.' Michael turned slightly, and found Ruth Anderson at his elbow, a large red smile warm on her face. She wore a tight white woollen top that accentuated her bosom. Beside her he spotted Paolo del Monte's protégée, the little thing who'd come to see him for a shift on the Diary ... Andrea? Alison? Her name escaped him but she looked sweetly girlish in her modest navy blue dress, her face half hidden by a soft black wave of hair. He beamed at her, encouraging. 'So you don't buy it either? It's hard to believe this kind of puritanical message strikes a chord these days – though, of course, he's preaching to the converted here, isn't he?'

'Yes. Did you see his Svengali in the front row? The minister, vicar, what have you, from that posh church, St Mark's.' Ruth had sidled up to him, giving her back to the younger woman who stood shyly a few paces away. Michael saw that she, too, was scribbling away on her notepad. He remembered her name: Allegra.

'Leader of the Renewal Movement. What do we think – harmless or dangerous?' He was smiling as he asked them because his own mind was already made up.

'Oh, the Movement's harmless enough.' Ruth shrugged in her tight top, her light voice lowered conspiratorially. 'Lots of healing and chest-beating. But what I want to know is who is using whom? Sutton versus the vicar, I mean.'

'Yes, that's an interesting question.'

But he was looking beyond her at Allegra.

'Sutton, of course, has plenty of skeletons in his closet . . . but he saw the light, thanks to Alexander Connaught.'

A man in front of them turned around angrily, index finger to his lips. 'I want to hear this,' he hissed.

Allegra dropped her pen, bent to look for it on the floor, among the feet and bags there, dropped her pad, blushed, embarrassed. Michael rushed to her aid, crouching beside her, finally retrieving the blue biro from a fold in someone's leather case. 'Here,' he whispered, handing it to her. She didn't dare say anything but rewarded him with a timid smile. As they both stood up, he suddenly realised why he'd wanted to help her: in her slightly shy, slightly vulnerable manner, she reminded him of Robbie.

'Ah, look. Lady Katherine!' Ruth tried to win back Michael's attention. Michael followed her pointing finger. There was Lady Katherine, standing in the very front row beneath the podium. At her side stood the priest. They were clapping enthusiastically. Michael smiled to himself: he'd been right. He would turn in a flattering profile of Sutton and the Christian Coalition. He was certain now it would be read with great attention by all the right people.

## Chapter Five

'Now watch, Robbie,' Paolo del Monte called to his grandson, 'look at this!' He struck a match and placed the flame beneath the amaretto's white and blue wrapper. Up, up, towards the ceiling the paper flew.

'Ooooooh!' Robbie clapped his hands, dark head thrown back. 'It's beautiful, Nonno!' He jumped up to catch the paper as it wafted down slowly. 'It's magic!'

'A small miracle.' Paolo's sharp grey eyes sparkled beneath their thick brows (christened by an irreverent student 'the Professor's roof') and over the half-moon spectacles that always sat, useless, on the tip of his nose.

'"A small miracle." Honestly, Paolo!' Nina watched her mother wag her finger at such blasphemies. Marina sighed, exchanging a look of womanly complicity with her daughter across the table. 'He really is too much.' But she smiled, as ever forgiving.

Nina felt the warmth of contentment steal over her as she surveyed her kitchen table: Robbie pleading with Nonno for a repeat performance of the amaretto trick; Paolo refusing to accommodate his grandson, his large domed forehead furrowed by a succession of new thoughts; Michael, at ease and in a good mood as he poured the wine; and her mother's lovely round face, where wrinkles seemed merely the imprints of kindly emotions – frowns of maternal concern, crow's feet of indulgent smiles brought on by her husband's endless exhibitionism, wide parentheses at the corners of her mouth from laughter at her grandson's feats. Her family. Notes struck, held, and then repeated, as in the cheerful sing-songs that filled the back of Paolo's car when they had driven down to Italy for the summers: Marina's small pink mouth found again in Robbie, her father's long hands repeated in her own, Michael's perfectly round head copied, in dark brown, by her son's.

'Isn't Nonno wonderful?' Robbie rushed to his mother, burned

39

wrapper held delicately between his fingers, as if it were a butterfly's wings.

Nina smiled down at the eager face, the eyes that slightly crossed, the open mouth. 'Yes, wonderful.' She ruffled her son's curls, looked above his head at her father.

But Paolo had lost interest in the game at hand, and launched into the earlier discussion with Michael. 'My dear Editor,' Paolo had been calling Michael the editor ever since he had stepped into his post of deputy three years ago, 'they're tiring of Maurice, of that you can be certain. He's out of synch, not only with the trustees – especially our born-again Katherine – but with our troubled times. People no longer find it amusing to watch an old satyr romp about, spending money on wild parties and wining and dining young girls. In fact, to most people that kind of thing is downright offensive. Everyone's eager to start anew – they want clean-living, fresh-faced new people to be at the helm. Every member of the *ancien régime* is now discredited.'

Michael nodded. He sat back in his chair, holding a glass, wearing the courteous, attentive expression he always donned in his father-in-law's presence. Paolo had embraced Michael's ambition to become editor of the *Sunday Herald* as a new challenge for his retirement years, and Nina loved to watch husband and father scheme, study the cast of characters, plot the takeover. Her father's extraordinary connections had proved invaluable to Michael's success: Paolo had spent more than sixty university terms in the academic limelight, and a number of his former students were now influential. She always felt grateful that her husband had slipped so easily into her own family. 'From the very first I liked your father.' Michael would laugh. 'At least he's got flaws. Unlike awesomely wonderful you.'

Outside, the sky had been whitewashed by the sunlight that now filled the white and blue kitchen, polishing silver and glasses, faces and figures.

Nina rose. 'Coffee for everyone?'

'Shall we move to the drawing room?' As usual Paolo was eager to quit the mess of domesticity – whether dirty plates or emotional difficulties, he always sought to keep distressing realities at bay.

'Yessir.' Nina rolled her eyes at Michael: her husband rose to help her clear the plates.

'Patience,' he mouthed, while he filled the tray with empty glasses.

His back to them, Paolo unfolded the *Herald*. 'Oh, yes – did you see, by the by, that our old friend Luke has had pneumonia? Poor thing, it looks quite bad – and he's no spring chicken, so one fears the worst ... Merited a few lines in the *Herald*, I noticed.' Long fingers tapped against the paper.

'Come, Nonno.' Robbie pulled Paolo's arm, forcing the slightly stooping tall figure to bend lower still as they made their way into the drawing room.

Michael followed Nina to the sink. 'Your mother's canonisation must be imminent. And yours will follow suit,' he whispered into her ear, as he wrapped his arms around her waist. They kissed, quickly, laughing, and then he followed his father-in-law next door.

Nina began to fill the coffee-maker. She hummed as she tugged at the pink ribbon that criss-crossed the box from the bakery: her parents always brought a fruit tart, which Paolo was not allowed to eat, Michael never liked, and she always skipped. Suddenly she heard a strange, muffled sound behind her. She turned to see Marina, standing beside the table, white head bowed. She was weeping, one hand to her mouth, shoulders trembling.

'Mamma!' Nina rushed to her side.

Marina pressed a finger to her lips. 'Don't, don't, please,' she murmured through her tears. 'Don't let them hear us.' The pale blue eyes were terrified. Nina held her mother's tiny plump figure close. 'What is it?' And a thousand fears clouded her in that sunny kitchen – her mother was ill, her father was ill, some financial disaster ...

'Oh, Nina, I'm so miserable.' The words pushed past the small white hands. 'Nina, I loved him so.' Nina froze: her father. It was her father.

'Luke. And he's desperately ill. I had stopped seeing him – and yet every day the sadness grew heavier, the separation grew more difficult.' The blue eyes fled hers, the round white head bowed once more under its secret burden. 'And now ... he's so ill, all I want to do is go to him, nurse him. Oh, Nina.'

Nina stood completely immobile. She felt her mother's tears, warm, light, upon her own fingers. Betrayal. Her mother was confessing a betrayal. She stared at the white head that lay close to her bosom, listened to the soft sobs, felt her mother's shoulders tremble beneath her arm. Could this be true? She, who had taught her daughter about love, fidelity, marriage; she, who had humoured, coddled, praised her father for thirty-five years; she, Marina, an adulteress? Nina felt herself reject every word that had just been uttered. How could it be true – this elderly woman, with her white hair and plump figure? Marina del Monte, her father's wife, her mother – sweet, patient, forever there. This was madness. She lowered her horrified eyes to her mother's head that bobbed with grief.

Marina continued to speak in a low strangled voice. 'Luke loves me – as I've never been loved. Paolo – your father – he doesn't even know me. To this day he doesn't know that cyclamen are my favourite flowers, that I take two spoons of sugar in my morning coffee, that I never wear yellow. He bought me a silk scarf the other day. It was yellow.' Nina winced: for the first time since she had begun her confession her mother's eyes met her own, and she read the passionate longing there. Luke . . . She tried to remember what her father had read about 'Luke' in the paper.'I don't know what I will do if something happens to Luke.'

'Well, well, here they are, gossiping about who knows what – and where, may I ask, is our coffee?' Paolo came through the door, finger pushing back his half-moon spectacles.

Marina turned away from Nina. She stood, rigid and silent, while Nina stammered, 'Yes, Papa,' and rushed to the stove to turn on the gas beneath the coffee.

'I hope you didn't put the apple tart in the refrigerator, Nina,' Marina said in a strangled voice. 'It will get ruined.' She was moving about the table, collecting napkins and brushing crumbs off of the chairs. As she had always done Nina mused, after every meal: this – this domestic, helpful, active woman – was the mother she had always known. This woman would never have been capable of the secrecy, the subterfuge, the conspiracy required by an adulterous affair.

'Look at this, useless daughter!' Paolo bore down upon her, tonsured head shaking. 'She hasn't even bothered to unwrap our modest offering, Marina!'

'So ungrateful, this girl of ours,' Marina said evenly, as she continued to push the chairs into the table.

At the sink, Nina wished her parents would go, leave her to her confusion, allow her to sort through the questions her mother had thrown at her.

As her father bustled behind her, moaning about the tart, about the French bakery, about the coffee that was now gurgling, Nina felt her whole body ache, her head tense, her breathing difficult: throughout, she saw her mother, moving around the table.

She followed her parents into the drawing room with the coffee pot, only vaguely aware of Marina and Paolo discussing some school matter with Robbie, only dimly sensing Michael in a corner of the sofa, skimming every Sunday paper except his own.

Michael. For a brief, senselesss moment she worried lest her mother's liaison should become public knowledge, reach the Stephensons' ears and ruin Michael's career – if they were indeed such supporters of the new morality, a scandal could affect Michael's chances. She shook her head. Really, Nina, pull yourself together. But more mad thoughts filled her now, as she tried to imagine her mother in a passionate embrace, in a lingering kiss, sneaking away from family meals to see a faceless man named Luke.

She sat in her flowered armchair, not listening as they moved about her and chatted in the easy intimate fashion of a family without secrets. She felt as vulnerable as if she were suddenly wrapped in a drunkard's embrace – a terrifying man who might do anything. For how many years had her mother betrayed her father? For how much longer would Marina play the role of Paolo's wife? She shivered at the thought of her father abandoned – could Marina ever leave him? But she heard again her mother's voice, cold and flat, say, 'I never wear yellow.'

She looked at her mother and suddenly thought of Victor: for years now, she had told him to desist in his courtship, warned him she would never yield to him because she believed in fidelity, honour, truth . . . and all along, her mother, the woman who had taught her those ideals, a woman of seemingly unimpeachable character, had been carrying on with some man named Luke.

Can love die? Love changed, yes. It could grow lazy as a holiday-maker cradling his sunset drink, diluted like the wine with water she had allowed Robbie at lunch. But could love fade altogether? Her eyes sought Michael, half hidden by a newspaper. Could his love die?

For the rest of the afternoon, as Robbie took out a puzzle for himself and Marina, and Michael and Paolo continued to talk about the *Sunday Herald*, Nina sat silent, feeling herself loosen from her past like a page in a waterlogged book. How could she belong to something that had never existed? Her childhood and youth had been shaped by her parents' love: in every memory, the two stood side by side, almost ridiculously different in form and substance yet complementing one another as they collaborated in every enterprise from choosing their daughter's schools to choosing their holidays. She remembered her mother rearranging her father's scarf every winter morning before he strode off to the LSE; her father looking helpless and stranded in the middle of the drawing room on those rare evenings when her mother was not there to greet him. 'Yes, yes, but where is she?' he would ask, absent-mindedly patting his daughter's head while searching beyond her for the small round figure. All recollections were played out against their union: a fugue of voices, raised in happy harmony or in quibbling discord, and of expressions, as he would scowl at his wife and she would roll her eyes at him.

Nina lay back against the flowers of her armchair: she felt suddenly exhausted, out of breath, as if she were scrambling up the hill of memories, desperate to reach the top and survey all her past – to distinguish the truth from the falsehood.

She resolved not to tell Michael: she did not want her father to become a cuckold in his eyes. And, too, she was ashamed of her mother's secret, feared that it might taint her. She wanted to crumple it up, toss it in the bin whence no one could retrieve it.

She looked up now, saw her mother bend over Robbie's dark head, pick a piece of the puzzle that reproduced a Dutch flower bouquet. She studied this woman who had pretended for so long – for a lifetime, perhaps. How many lies, how deep the duplicity, how elaborate the camouflage? Anger and resentment now rose inside her: her mother had robbed her of that very happiness – uncomplicated, unwavering – that she had ensured as her legacy to her daughter; with her confession she had darkened a landscape that Nina had seen as sunny, without shadows. And yet . . . She looked at the soft familiar hands that caressed Robbie's dark head, listened to the whispered encouragements Marina issued as together they hunted for a missing petal: had it not been for her daughter that Marina had borne the immense burden of her secret love? Had she not sacrificed a life with this unknown Luke for Nina? Nina felt her heart ache. Oh, Mamma, she yearned to call out to that small figure, why tell me? And then she felt ashamed: her mother had shared her unhappiness – could she not find it in herself to be generous?

She sat up, suddenly, almost nauseous with curiosity about her mother's secret history. Her eyes searched the drawing room for the *Herald* her father had held. It lay, folded in four, on the silk arm of the sofa. Beneath the black headline, '"Godless" don hospitalised', a blurry-edged photograph smiled wanly. Professor Luke Aldridge, read the caption, and she now vaguely remembered the story of the eminent philosophy don who had caused such controversy with

44

his book about modern man's emancipation from prayer, sin and divine authority.

Nina snatched up the newspaper, scrutinised the unremarkable thin face beneath its wing of white hair, read the news brief, turned back to the photograph: black eyes, lined cheeks and forehead, a smile that startled. My mother's lover. An elderly academic who calls himself a debunker of myths; a wrinkled don with an unabashed grin. What does my mother find here? And she peered, feeling a mixture of jealousy and anger and self-righteousness, at the face beneath her.

## Chapter Six

The man of God. That was how she thought of him. When she was alone, or in silence as this morning, Lady Katherine could allow herself to slip into a world lined by images of Alexander. His face, his figure, his words: they stretched to cover her mind, pressed up against all four corners of her world. She lay in her bed, unable to sleep. It was almost five in the morning, and she could hear Philip's short sharp breaths beside her. She had read until late, but the anxiety about today had forced her awake. The house was silent around her, the wind blowing heavy against the window-panes.

Alexander. She had first seen him at the foot of the great oak tree that stretched wide above the courtyard of St Mark's. The branches of the oak spread to form a quiet place of sun and shadow. In the warm stillness beneath those branches, she had seen the black slim figure, a glowing presence that drew you near.

When she approached, she was startled by his bold beauty. He did not seem to hear her step and remained immobile, gaze fixed upon some distant spot. He stood, tall and elegant in his clerical garb, the sun gilding him. Lady Katherine saw him in profile, and he seemed inhuman: the perfect half face before her dazzled, testament to Nature's rare need to create perfection in human form. Everything around her seemed to have grown still. The blond head bowed over clasped hands. She watched his lips move and stood immobile, his figure drawing her eyes, so that all else faded into a faint world of sketchy outlines. Suddenly he knelt on the grass beneath the oak. Lady Katherine grew uneasy, as if she should not witness this moment of devotion. Softly she retraced her steps, walking slowly, lost in thought. His beauty was dazzling, yet it did not draw your touch, rather your reverence. She wondered at this extraordinary being, whose angel's face shone with a piety and perfection that struck her as less human than divine.

Lady Katherine turned on her side, away from Philip's breathing. It was so cold – she pulled up the white duvet, the rose-strewn cover,

46

so that they formed great waves up around her head. Through the open window she could hear distant cars along the Embankment, but their sound was so muted that it was no more offensive than the chorus that laced summer evenings in the countryside.

After that first sighting she had sought him out. She had heard of Alexander Connaught already, of course: with his looks, breeding, and education, he had caused a great deal of excitement since his arrival at St Mark's a year ago. He was already surrounded by a group of fanatically devoted youngsters whom he led in a weekly ritual known as the Circle – public confessions of guilt, resolutions and penance. She had approached him directly, humbly asking him for assistance; she was ready, she had told him, to forge a new life, to discard her old ways. She was ready, she had assured him, to commit herself to his cause. He had smiled at her, and wrapped her in a tight embrace that had left her breathless with happiness and longing to be with him always.

She issued a small sigh, stretched. She was feeling at once nervous and expectant, and struggled with herself to obey Alexander's orders: she must trust, trust in Him and His work. Her son would be saved, she must believe he would. Lady Katherine felt her heart beat faster at the prospect of this evening.

Beside her, Philip groaned, turned, and his foot grazed her own. Philip. Had she ever loved him, even during those years of courtship when she had proclaimed her passion to all who would listen? He had left his wife for her, she had upset her prim and proper parents for him, they had led a life studded with grand people and occasions, yet she wondered whether it hadn't been an exercise in something they both had felt more deeply than either love or lust: ownership. For two people who knew nothing of themselves, possession became the only proof of existence. Philip's ownership was about factories, industries, newspapers; hers had been men. She had been cautious, of course, in her acquisitions, ensuring that he need never confront them. It had been her secret life, and for decades she had drawn pleasure from it – or at least, amusement. The encounters had made her feel beautiful, witty, impossible, indulged; the dismissals, powerful. She had viewed her lovers' dishevelled emotions with the prim displeasure of a restaurant maître d' confronting a regular client once again in his cups.

It didn't matter any more, of course: she understood now the greater pleasure of virtue, and she would dedicate herself to Philip and Johnny, attempting to lead a virtuous life and become a perfect wife.

She smiled in the dark at the changes that had befallen her without her husband so much as looking up from his accounts. The clock struck five: she must try to sleep a bit longer otherwise tonight . . . She remembered now Nina Lewis, who had asked to accompany her to St Mark's. It would be a wonderful opportunity to promote the Movement – she wouldn't have to say anything to Michael directly, just allow his wife to see for herself the miraculous work that Alexander was carrying out. And, in any case, Michael had shown that he supported the Movement – had he not written a lovely positive portrait of Tom Sutton and the Christian Coalition? Yes, Michael would need very little to convince him of Alexander's worth. Lady Katherine smiled now at the thought of the effortless spread of the Good Word. With Michael Lewis on board – whether through conviction or opportunism it wouldn't really matter in the end – Alexander's mission would be carried out, and she would be instrumental in the process.

Next door she heard Johnny cough and her smile disappeared. 'Please, God, help him, heal him. Please let me cast off this terrible anguish,' she whispered into the cold darkness. She bore the guilt of his drinking; she blamed herself for his alcohol-soaked scenes, for his trembling hands, for his having slipped into this wretched unhappy youth. It had been her fault: she had not given him enough of her time, her love. Simon, her eldest, she had loved immediately, fiercely: from his earliest childhood he had been so good-natured, so handsome, always independent of his parents, always striding forth into a life that grew increasingly interesting, fun, lucky. Simon had led an easy existence that had reassured her that she could chase her own pleasures without worry. But Johnny – how different. Six years younger than his brother, he had been a silent, sullen, plain-faced rebuke since his earliest days. To her horror, she discovered that she did not so much love him as pity him, and that only if she applied herself could she find in her heart any real affection for this son. Simon, protective of Johnny, had warned her about his brother's loneliness and resentment. But then he had gone to Hong Kong, where he made millions and lived with a girl she didn't trust. And Katherine had lapsed into her own world, where she was constantly on the move, from partner to partner in her affairs, from house to house in weekends away, from city to city in short trips across Europe and North Africa. She had spared little thought for anyone or anything, least of all Johnny's happiness. And, unlike Philip, Johnny had known all along of her infidelities, and had faced her across the table, accusing her with eyes that saw every man, every lie, every secret assignation.

Against her pillow, Lady Katherine shook her head in remorse: she had led him to scrounge for another happiness among bottles; now she would save him.

And the same thought returned that evening, when at seven she walked through the wide open portals of St Mark's with Johnny beside her, his wide face pale, his breathing nervous, and Nina Lewis behind them. 'God help us,' she pleaded with the Being Alexander had taught her to love. As they filed into the pew, she pressed Johnny's hand.

Beside her, Nina looked around at the crowded, high-ceilinged church. It was a Victorian building, beautifully maintained but redecorated in tasteless fashion: the ceiling was a salmon pink that stretched beyond white beams; sturdy, pale wooden chairs formed even rows on this, the ground floor; a golden-coloured runner separated the church in halves. A low dais, with a lectern, musical instruments and an amplifier, stood in front of her. In one corner an ornate Christmas tree, blue and gold with baubles, shone; in another, a huge baptismal font spread white. Above them, encircling the floor like a terrace, stretched old-fashioned pews, already full with expectant faces. She saw that for these members of the flock, television screens had been mounted, lest the white beams block their view of the action on the dais. Outside, the snow they had forecast for Christmas Day was already blowing through the bare branches, filling the long driveway that led to St Mark's. But the church was well heated, brightly lit, welcoming. Nina felt as if she had entered an alien world: this place of worship had nothing in common with the small Catholic church of her childhood, where the crucifix and Ste Thérèse could hardly be distinguished in the dark dampness relieved only by spots of colour cast by stained-glass windows.

She felt ill at ease, now, in this bright place, slightly apologetic about having been less than constant in her own religious observance. Although she had accompanied Marina to Mass throughout her childhood, she had failed to continue the practice once she had married. It was as if Michael and Robbie invested her life with such an overabundance of love and meaning that she no longer needed the God she had prayed to when, as the only child of foreigners, she had knelt before the crucifix at Ste Thérèse's. Her daily life, between family and the *Society*, was so full that the rituals she remembered her mother observing – Mass, the weekly rosary, the annual pilgrimages to Lourdes – were ignored. Only occasionally would she steal into the

49

back of a darkened church, to whisper her gratitude in a flow of Hail Marys. Grateful, yes, and respectful of the moral code enshrined in His Word, of those who worshipped Him more eagerly and more regularly. It was this respect that now filled her almost with shame at the thought that she would study this faithful flock with a view to either ridicule or warning.

The faithful flock was already here, faces at once expectant and satisfied, as if they had obtained coveted tickets to a rare performance by a virtuoso. They were casually dressed – some still in the Barbours they had worn all weekend in the country, others in the leather jackets and jeans they donned outside the accountancy firm, the bank, the solicitors' chambers that employed them. The majority were young people, faces wide open, as if neither doubts nor anxiety had as yet fenced in their eagerness or hemmed in their honesty; and this unguarded expression lent them an air at once self-confident and naïve. There were older people, too, many of them couples who held hands. As Nina watched the congregation embrace in greeting, pat one another on the back, blow kisses across pews, she marvelled at the ease with which they had managed to discard the self-consciousness that for generations had corseted their class and to allay the atavistic fear of embarrassment that had hung over their ancestors. Nina, used to the silent reverence of the churches she had attended, flinched at the jollity of it all.

She stood silent beside Lady Katherine, Johnny on his mother's other side. She had tried not to stare at the youth – perhaps twenty, twenty-five, she couldn't tell because the drink had filled, bellows-like, his features, so that they stretched expressionless and ageless. He kept his eyes lowered and mumbled monosyllables in response to his mother's queries. She could see he knew how everyone, including herself, regarded him: the albatross around Katherine's neck, the one cloud on the Stephensons' horizon . . . and heads would shake and sighs issue over 'poor Johnny'.

Suddenly she heard the congregation stir: there, walking towards the lectern, she saw Alexander Connaught. Her immediate reaction was of surprise: unlike the evangelical vicars she had come across before, he wore sober clerical garb – dog collar above black jacket, shirt, trousers. This black presence struck a chord of old-fashioned piety among the loud colours and bright lights of St Mark's. His fair head shone above the black cotton, as if haloed by the lights that poured down from the high ceiling.

The audience sat silent, rapt. Alexander looked up from the lectern and she stared. He seemed to embody a host of contradictions, beautifully resolved: the manly, athletic figure, (rugby at school? rowing at university?) rose into an almost girlish face of delicate lineaments and pale colouring; the smile beckoned and promised a warm embrace that the puritanical stiffness of gestures (arms immobile at his side, hands completely still) seemed to withdraw; the longish blond hair hinted at a foppish nature that the crisp dog collar denied. As if from a great distance, she could hear the voice – public school accent untempered by the preacher's soft low tones. She stole a look at Lady Katherine's profile on her left: her face glowed, upturned, great blue eyes fixed upon the man before them. Lady Katherine was entranced. Nina lowered her head, closed her eyes and concentrated on the vicar's words as he welcomed 'the people of God'.

Lady Katherine filled with the extraordinary happiness she always drew from Alexander's presence. I am under his spell, her heart sang out, he has bewitched me. Lord, what extraordinary power You have given your servant Alexander! His spell: other eyes skimmed like flat stone over your surface but Alexander's gaze trawled round your features, your expressions, sank into you, as if determined to reach your secrets. Other mouths smiled and it was as if they offered you a little spare change, but his smile was an emptying of generous pockets, a proof that there was nothing he would not share with you. Other voices held you, but only in speech; Alexander's voice seemed to captivate in the unspoken as well as the spoken. He could feel where you hurt, when you needed praise, why you kept away from his church: she had seen him walk into a room full of people and approach immediately the one most in need. 'I am here,' he seemed to say. 'Trust in me and I shall lead you to a better life.'

He offered an intimation of spiritual excess combined with physical abstinence: he swelled with shiny, fervent prayer and denied the flesh, so that its calls rang hollow and could not awaken temptation. Between these opposites he wove his spell like a magician who used no sleight-of-hand, disappearing trick or incantation.

Lady Katherine turned to her son, joy in her eyes. She wrapped her left hand around his puffy fingers, squeezing them. Johnny gave her an uncertain half-smile, but his eyes returned to the man at the lectern.

'I ask you now to greet one another, taking a few minutes to get to know the people next to you.' Nina saw Lady Katherine wrap her son in an embrace, then turn to the row of chairs behind her and shake a young woman's hands. On her right, Nina felt a warm hand on her forearm: a plump, middle-aged woman, wearing an enormous smile was extending her hand. 'Hello, welcome!' The woman's small dark eyes looked like sultanas sunk in her dough-like face.

While Nina wondered whether she had been identified already as an outsider, she saw a beautiful, sleek-haired girl lean over, from the row of chairs behind, tap Johnny on the shoulder and, when he turned, plant a kiss on his cheek. Nina couldn't help smiling: she wondered how often in Johnny's miserable existence an attractive young woman had kissed him – there was a great deal to be said for this approach to God, she mused.

But now behind the lectern, the vicar was welcoming a band of musicians. 'Lift up your hearts, and praise Him with these songs,' he enjoined the crowd.

He stepped away, retreating through double doors. The musicians struck up a succession of hymns – rhythmic, loud music that resounded in the church. It was so warm that many of the congregation shone with perspiration; everyone had removed their coats and hats.

'Get on your feet and praise Jesus!' the lead singer urged from his microphone.

The congregation obediently rose, clapping to the beat, raising their arms to the ceiling, their bodies undulating, so that the entire assembly seemed to sway this way and that, like grass stirred by wind. Nina stared at them: many had closed their eyes as they intoned the songs, and their expressions were strained, as if they were desperate to hear some elusive word or sound amid the swelling notes.

From her pew on the balcony, Allegra watched the screen fill with the words of the hymns she was singing. 'Take me, Jesus, by the hand/And lead me down Your path . . .' She raised her voice, felt the breath fill her lungs. Beside her, Katie, the flatmate she had met through the Circle, cast a huge grin, then closed her eyes: Alexander always urged them to do so, in prayer and in song, because it was the best way to feel the breath of life, the presence of the Holy Spirit. She smiled as she sang: she couldn't help it – the warmth, the friendliness, the repetition of a ritual she had been brought up with . . . Here at St Mark's she always entered a perfect world, where somehow the cosy love of the faithful and the terrible warnings of the Almighty were reconciled. Allegra shut her eyes. 'You alone feel my pain/You alone can see in my darkness . . .' She heard her voice soar with a thousand others, and let her heart beat joyfully. Yes, here was home, a safe and welcoming place. Unlike the horrid newsroom, where faces lay white, hostile and treacherous as a lake covered by the thinnest layer of ice; unlike this sprawling, daunting city, where people did not walk but rushed, where no one exchanged greetings but looked down their nose at you, where even the buildings reduced you to insignificance by stretching so inaccessibly high. Here at St Mark's she felt wrapped in a warm embrace, as if she belonged, together with the believers around her, to Alexander's family.

Allegra opened her eyes, allowed them to sweep across the immense bright room. She looked at the white beams that met at the ceiling like long pale fingers joined in prayer. She looked at the corner where the white total immersion font sat: this was where Alexander had baptised her, his hands gentle on her head while she sank into the tepid water, eyes closed and heart thumping with joy. She looked at the long-haired male musicians and their long-skirted female lead, heads bobbing, eyes shut in a devotional trance. Her eyes rested on a familiar face here, a well-known figure there – how many people she had already met through her attendance of the services and the Circle. Now she found Lady Katherine's tall figure, crowned by her superb red head. Allegra leaned forward slightly, the better to see her. Yes, there was her son ('Johnny Baa-baa-black-sheep', as someone had laughed at last week's Circle), standing beside her, waiting for the healing to begin. 'With the Gift of the Holy Spirit all is possible,' Alexander always said, eyes alight with faith. And it was true, thought Allegra, as she belted out the last verse of 'The Good Shepherd'. He had brought her here, allowed her to dream of a life so incomparably better than anything she had been brought up with. Oh, she was immensely grateful to Jesus – and to Mum, of course, she thought with a sudden pang. She'd ring her tonight and give her a thrill with all the stories she'd found, and the praise she'd earned from her Diary editor . . .

Nina stole a look to her right. Eyes closed, right arm raised like a schoolchild who knows the answer, the plump woman sang out her exuberant devotion: 'Jesus I love you, I'll remain faithful, and You are my guide always!'

What are they doing to my God? Suddenly Nina felt almost angry: for years she had treated her faith with the casual fondness mingled with lack of deference that a hostess reserves for family members at a busy gathering. Yet now, at the spectacle before her, she felt ancient loyalties stir, and her rejection mount of this style of worship. Her eyes scoured the chanting, clapping throng: all was collective here, as if God could be reached only through the group. And this uniform troop, armed with searchlights, tireless and unquestioning in their eagerness to carry out orders, seemed bent on tracking down and exposing her God, stripping Him of mystery. They reduced Him to someone who could be chased in the same way you would stalk a human being. They were making Him, she thought, in their own image.

Nina saw that Lady Katherine had laced her arm through her son's and while Johnny stood silent and immobile, his mother was reading out the words from the hymnal.

With a last great flourish, the musicians finished their concert. The great room resonated with the clapping. Now Alexander Connaught appeared again. He stood in the middle of the dais, and without the microphone he began, 'They ask me. "What is it that you find so wrong with this world?" And I answer, there is no clarity, any longer. All boundaries are smudged and our vision blurred. The frontiers of before – lines drawn to separate evil from goodness, love from sex – these lines have disappeared, and a chaos of colours and forms have come in their wake.'

Slowly, the voice began to rise, until it rang throughout the church hall, filling the air and coating the bricks with conviction. 'Once we drop our reluctance to call sin by its proper name and are ready to fight it, we shall be able to forge a new world.' He paused. A murmur of approval ran through the congregation. 'For too many years our churchmen have taught us about God and goodness and the virtues without teaching us about Satan and his wiles. That doesn't work. How can we explain white without holding up its opposite, black? How do we know our friends if we know not what enmity is? The contrast provides the context – it gives shape and form. Otherwise we risk turning God into a vague nebulous notion, which satisfies no one.'

Nina watched the men and women nod, eyes fixed upon the black figure before them. They seemed completely oblivious to one another now, to this large hall, to anything outside the preacher's voice.

'Remember that the time for evil is nearly over. We are setting forth on a long journey and we must prepare ourselves. We shall come up against obstacles and climb arduous paths, and we must rid ourselves of anything that is unnecessary or dispensable, for we must be fleet of foot, lest the Evil one capture us.' Nina listened, but found the words unconvincing. She was intrigued by the messenger, she told herself, while contemptuous of the message. 'Remember, we must save ourselves from his clutches – but, too, we must save our brothers and sisters. We must spread the word, share the vision. Working together for the renewal of our world. And the first step is to demand that people return to a life where evil is clearly marked, as is goodness.'

Nina felt almost disappointed by the sermon: the vicar's physical perfection had led her to think that he would be inspiring, subtle, unusual. Instead, she found his world-view too simplistic in its black and white alignments.

Nina began to wonder how she would ever write about this visit to St Mark's. She knew what Clive wanted – something irreverent, cold-eyed and critical; one look at the figure standing to her left told her what Lady Katherine would want her to write. Nina felt dread fill her at the prospect of facing either one. Now the voice was swelling into a sonorous exhortation: 'Let us pray, brothers and sisters!' The words were repeated throughout the great white vaulted space. Nina saw men and women stand, arms raised, eyes shut.

'This is the house of Jesus Christ. Only those who enter it can find contentment. This is the message of Jesus. Only those who study it will find peace. You are here, at the centre of the world, rejoice! For while everyone around you is searching, searching for the threshold to this haven, we are here. When they find it, it may be too late.'

Around her the congregation lifted their voices in a hymn she did not know. Nina watched Lady Katherine grasp her son's hand and raise her arms towards the man in black before them. She was singing in a low, thin voice, and Nina looked away from that eager, almost painfully devoted face. She wished now she hadn't come, had not witnessed this woman's rapture: she could not write about this service without cringing at this exalted state, without making fun of the simplistic response these well-heeled men and women had to the preachings of the young man before them.

Now Lady Katherine was moving down the pew, the others making room for her as she pulled Johnny in her wake. They joined the long queue that was collecting in the aisle, approaching Alexander for the healing. Nina watched as young and old, men and women flocked towards the front of the church. At the lectern, the vicar stood, waiting for the faithful to reach him. He placed both hands on the believer's shoulders, then bent close to the penitent's head, as if to rest his forehead against the other's. She watched his lips move, whether in blessing or absolution she did not know. Some of the people brought before him began to weep, noiselessly, trembling; others raised their hands in the air, and sang out a single, joyful note, 'Hallelujah!'

'Hallelujah!' burst the woman beside her in full-throated echo.

The queue stretched all the way to the back of the church, and Nina watched as Lady Katherine and her son waited patiently for their turn. She could see Johnny's face finally registering an expression – curiosity mixed with reluctance – and Lady Katherine wearing a beatific smile. When they finally reached Alexander, she saw Lady Katherine's cheeks shine with tears as she stood slightly behind her son.

Nina again looked about her, at the bright faces flushed with heat and song, at the figures that swayed with their arms raised, palms turned up. As the vicar continued his healing, the congregation seemed to be struggling to keep their excitement in check. They reminded her of the fans (family, friends) clustered on the sidelines of the cricket pitch at Robbie's school, who suppressed their cheers during the game lest they distract the sportsmen. Excellent health, good pedigrees and the pursuit of their common interest lent both groups an air of uniform well-being. Any moment, now, she expected one of the women to pull out a thermos and proffer a cup of tea to those beside her.

When they returned to the pew, Johnny seemed to be in a trance. He sat, burying his face in clasped hands. Beside him, Lady Katherine was smiling, and she turned to Nina. 'Praise the Lord!' she called out, then, seeing Nina's embarrassment, smiled.

They stayed in the church for a few more minutes, Johnny bowed over while his mother looked on with a serene smile. Alexander continued to heal those of the congregation who approached him.

When they walked out, all was white: it had snowed while they had been inside the church. Nina respected the Stephensons' silence and sifted through her own confused perceptions: the beauty of the man, the sweetness of his voice, the message of doom or salvation. Alexander made it seem as if all were a simple choice by the individual between the virtuous path and the way of temptation. She could see the appeal, yet found herself impervious to it, and as she stepped onto the busy pavement she could not stifle a great sigh of relief.

She walked beside mother and son through the soft snow that had spread evenly over the Chelsea streets and beyond. Every plane, every ridge and every incline now lay beneath this protective layer, so that if your gaze remained level with the shapes and forms of the church, trees and distant houses, everything seemed part of a gentle intimacy, like a nativity scene at Robbie's school. But as she raised her gaze to take in the black skies against the snowy contours, the yellow eyes of streetlights and house windows glowing in the night, the contrast seemed to echo the alarm raised inside St Mark's by Alexander Connaught, who had seen the world so clearly divided between evil and good. She walked beneath the arches formed by bright festoons of white light-bulbs. The shops were closing and people were rushing along the white pavements. They walked past the Chelsea Town Hall and down the King's Road, where leafless trees shone with festive lights, swaying slightly in the breeze.

Nina tried to determine, from quick stolen glances in Johnny's direction, whether the healing had had any impact on him, but his face was once again expressionless as he strode beside his mother.

'He is wonderful, isn't he?' Lady Katherine placed a hand on Nina's arm. Her eyes implored Nina.

'He is extraordinary,' Nina replied truthfully. 'It is unusual, isn't it, that he should wear those clothes?'

'Yes. He explained to the congregation that it is a sign of his faith. He wants everyone, from the moment they meet him, to know him as the servant of Our Lord. He wants to be a constant witness.'

Nina nodded. 'And – is he married?' she asked.

Lady Katherine smiled and shook her sleek dark red head. 'No. He believes in celibacy. He said emotional and physical entanglements would simply get in the way of his mission. And he expects those who belong to his Circle – the younger members, the ones who meet with him on a weekly basis – he expects them to practise chastity too.'

'It might prove difficult to find many young people who would accept such abstemious living.' Nina looked at Johnny, hoping to interest him in their conversation. But the young man kept his eyes resolutely downcast.

'Oh, Nina, you should see how many youngsters attend those meetings regularly! He calls them his foot-soldiers.'

They walked on, separating at times before the onrush of passers-by.

'I'm turning off here.' Nina smiled at mother and son. 'Thank you for allowing me to come.'

'Please – it is so important that the Word be spread.' Lady Katherine cast her a long look, then, snuggling up to her son, 'We'd best be off!' she said, and waved goodbye.

# Chapter Seven

The afternoon sun pushed through the branches, through the window-pane, found its way upon the pages Nina was reading. The cold had bleached the sky of its blue, the branches of their green, the ground of its warm hues. Every line – the rooftops across the street, the trees along the pavement, the distant spire of St Stephen's that in summer was invisible because of the trees thick with leaves – had grown more distinct, as if sharpened by the cold air.

She sat at her desk, poring over her article for Clive about the Renewal Movement. She had, she thought, managed to tread a fine line between scepticism and respect, humour and understanding. Victor paced up and down. 'You are, I hope, going to dispose of them with rapier-like wit? You will expose them as the spiritual quacks they really are?'

'Well . . .' Nina skimmed the pages. 'I have to be careful for Michael's sake – and, in any case, I think it is not as sinister as you seem to think. It's high time someone held up some form of ideals, and if they have to be rooted in religious rather than social conscience, so be it.'

'Hmm . . . I don't like what I've seen of them.' Victor drew closer to her desk and stopped pacing, looking at her. 'Joshua came home from school the other day saying that a lot of his friends were going to take part in something called the Circle – youngsters sitting about reciting prayers and admitting their sins to one another – all under the careful supervision of that creepy cleric.'

Nina set down the page she'd been reading, turned to face him. 'I don't think their vicar is quite so easily dismissed, you know. He speaks very simply, reduces everything to a world where every move and thought is so clear-cut. It's immensely satisfying after the confusion we've grown used to.'

'Confusion?' he snapped, standing right beside her, angrily rapping her desk. 'You mean grey areas rather than a black-and-white world? Who but a simpleton would ever think of life as anything but?' Then he squatted beside her, a look of mischief lighting his dark eyes. 'Anyway, there's quite a lot to be said for confusion. Makes us humble, makes us long for deliverance. In short it's something akin to what I feel in your presence.'

'Oh, do stop, Victor, please.' She turned in the chair, giving him her back, while her mind filled with visions of her mother's confession. Mother. The images swirled: the soft warmth found in the plump white arms where the inside skin, translucent, revealed veins that Nina would trace with her index finger: 'The Ganges . . . the Nile . . . the Seine . . .' She would name each blue thread. The lavender scent emanating from the white linen dresses and shirts that never seemed to lose the creases Mother had carefully ironed in the kitchen, while the radio played Mozart. The thick Italianate of the consonants that issued from that small pink mouth as if heavily underlined. The pale eyes that seemed always to follow one or the other of the beloved family members. Mother . . . Nina sighed. She had not been granted another glimpse of her mother's secret: Marina had scrupulously avoided any opportunity for further *tête-à-têtes*. She wondered now if her mother had regretted her confession and wondered, too, if she expected her daughter to prod her for further revelations. In her heart of hearts she felt loath to know more about her mother's betrayal, and wished that she could cover up rather than uncover further the affair.

'You've been avoiding me.'

'No, I'd never do that.'

'You're still cross about the other day – but show some pity. I can't help it if every now and then I confess myself to you.' His voice was light-hearted but his eyes had grown serious with longing.

'I can't grant you absolution, I fear.' She smiled, but felt tense: this talk reminded her of Marina's confession, and she resented him now for raising the spectre of adulterous love. Indeed, for the first time, she feared Victor's declarations: she felt vulnerable now to his attentions, as if her own mother's betrayal had made the impossible seem feasible. And though she could protest to Victor that she would never yield before his persistence, she suddenly felt frightened at how easy it must be to be lured into this temptation. For a moment, she thought of Michael. She shivered and turned away from Victor.

Victor issued a tremendous sigh and flopped down on the sofa behind her, crossed his hands behind his head, watched her from furrowed brows. 'I suppose I should go home, get back to work. You make me feel guilty, beavering away like that. I wonder whether I shall ever finish my own *magnum opus . . .*' His voice faded.

'You will, you will,' she countered, as she always did – and wondered if her voice held conviction. In their friendship she allowed him to pass off half-truths as certainties, possibilities as achievements: in this way, she had created a kinder, endlessly hopeful world that buffered him from real-life disappointments.

'And meanwhile my poor kind Hannah continues to rake in twice my income.'

'If you were a solicitor you'd earn that kind of money but you chose glory and the pursuit of truth, remember?' She smiled reassuringly as she rearranged one of the tortoiseshell combs in her hair. 'You could never be happy leading any other kind of life.'

'Happiness is sitting here and having you prop up my flagging spirits while your cushions prop up my sagging body.'

'Oh, Victor, the things you will say.' She smiled as she shook her head. But suddenly she felt grateful to him for the presence she had only a minute before resented: his self-deprecating comments, his black gaze, even his assiduous compliments – every aspect reassured her that Victor, at least, was the same. It was as if she drew comfort in holding up his constancy against the new duplicitous image of her mother: with the discovery of the treachery that had laid hidden in her past, she required far more certainty from the present.

The key turned in the door and Michael stood before them, large and smiling, golden in the sunlight that illuminated the doorway.

'Darling?' Nina rose.

'What brings our working man home so early?' Victor called out over his shoulder, watching Nina all the while as she blushed with pleasure at her husband's unexpected arrival.

'They've appointed me. Announcement made half an hour ago. Editor of the *Sunday Herald*.' He beamed, walked slowly towards them, eyes moving from friend to wife.

'Michael!' Nina rushed at him, and was caught in his arms.

He swung her from the floor, pressed his lips against her hair. 'We've done it! We've finally done it!'

'Oh, Michael . . .' She sounded as if she would weep.

'I feel as if we've come to the end of the longest journey.'

'*Mazeltov.*' Victor rose from the sofa, pulled down his thin jumper over his stomach, approached their coupled figures. 'Congratulations, old man, well done!' Michael made as if to embrace Victor too, but Nina wouldn't allow him to loosen his hold on her.

She was half crying, half laughing, hiding her face in his chest, embarrassed by her own emotion.

'I'm taking you out.' With his free hand Michael caressed her hair. 'Tonight we celebrate!'

Nina slowly pulled away from him, rearranging her hair and dress. She cast a slightly shamefaced smile at Victor, who looked on, indulgent. 'That is, after we toast the news here with Victor,' and Michael gave his best friend a huge smile, warmed by a thousand moments shared in day-dreaming at university.

For a moment, the two friends looked into one another's eyes, then Victor shook himself as from a reverie. 'No, no.'

'Victor, you must stay!' Michael grinned at him over Nina's dark head.

'Yes, Victor, please.' Nina's voice was a half-hearted murmur.

Victor took his cue from her. 'I'm going, I'm going, I don't want to be the odd one out.' He gave Michael's arm a light punch as he passed him on his way out.

''Bye, Victor.' They stood, arms linked, waving to him as he closed the door behind him.

'Come,' Michael took her hand and led her to the sofa, 'let's sit down for a moment.' He sat and pulled Nina down beside him among the gold and cream silk stripes. He wrapped his arm around her shoulders, held her tight, tight against him. Nina leaned her head against his shoulder. He loosened his collar, removed his tie and she breathed in the faint warm smell of his skin. 'I can't believe it's finally happened. I'm so happy, Nina.' He spoke in a low voice, as if it were the release of a breath he had held for years. He took her chin now, with thumb and index finger, turned her face towards his. 'I couldn't have done it without you, I know that.' She smiled, thrilling at his words, at the gentleness of his touch.

They sat side by side on the sofa, in silence. This was happiness, as pleasantly hot as a flagstone in the sun. Nina felt him heavy-limbed and warm beside her: this contentment seemed at once solid and yielding, like the fertile earth on a country walk in summer. She laid her head against his chest and felt him breathe, listened to him inhale and exhale, lips slightly parted. Around her, their world glowed in the last afternoon sun. Framed by heavy cream curtains, the room stretched from this present into their past: the photograph of Michael carrying Robbie on his shoulders, father and son laughing, as if for that fleeting moment Michael had passed on to Robbie his belief that life could be easily confronted and successfully managed. The crystal vase Michael's parents had given her after endless anxious queries and apologies. 'We don't really know if this is suitable,' they had explained, as ever slightly uncomfortable in her presence, always aware of their own more humble origins. The tapestry pillow that Nina had had to work on under Marina's watchful eye, her painstaking stitches spurred on by her mother's warnings – 'You can't hide in your books all the time.' The volume of John Donne's poetry, a squat black-and-white book where a dry brown rose, Michael's first love token, lay pressed between pages 78 and 79.

Past folded into present here, and Nina felt a happiness that at once satisfied and promised ever more.

## Chapter Eight

The restaurant was full: it was five past one, and at every table sat well-dressed men and women, half hidden by the shiny white menus bearing elaborate descriptions of the tiny portions that would be served. The sound of voices rose, lively and indistinct, until it filled the great terracotta-coloured room and hung like garlands above the windows and the great oven from which *bruschetta, pizzette, carne alla brace* emerged.

Sitting at a table for two beneath a photograph of a Tuscan village, Allegra allowed herself the melancholic thought that even the food in London was intimidating and unfamiliar, a challenge in terms of taste and pronunciation. Indeed, everything from the clothes people wore to the expressions they used seemed calculated to fill her with insecurity. Like today's assignment: she was lunching the famed theatre director Peter Wyatt for the Diary ('A luvvie will be a cinch, don't you worry. They can't wait to dish the dirt on the rest'). He had yet to arrive, though he had set up the lunch for quarter to one. She felt the embarrassment increase with her blush: everyone round this wide high-ceilinged room must have noticed by now that her lunch date had kept her waiting for an excruciating twenty minutes. The traffic had been normal, the tubes working without a hitch: had he forgotten? Or was he slighting her on purpose, as a Puckish thing to do? She stared at the menu, unseeing, then slowly and cautiously moved her eyes to the bottle of San Pellegrino, the basket of bread, the bowl of extra-virgin olive oil before her. Please, God, don't let me wait any longer . . .

She shifted in her chair, certain that a thousand eyes were focused on her, certain that every stranger in this large noisy room was intent on placing her merits and flaws on some invisible balance that would find her wanting.

She lifted her eyes to meet a man's insistent, amused black gaze. Quickly she looked away and helped herself to more water, all the while wishing she could become invisible, slip unseen through the door . . . 'Don't you dare!' she could hear Mum bark, as she had when ten-year-old Allegra had told a friend her name was Ally. 'It's a beautiful name, and if no one else has it around here it's their bad luck.' 'Don't even think of it!' she had shouted, when a tearful Allegra had considered forgoing London after all, to stay and marry Billy. 'Don't be so daft! I didn't bring you up to end your days with a man with no dreams! Don't lose sight of your goal, girl.' And she'd suddenly wrapped her arms around Allegra and held her tight. 'My little girl in London, finding herself a big job at some great important newspaper.' And Allegra had yielded, considering that it was true, after all, that she did dream of writing for a real newspaper, not just the *Gazette*, and that she no longer loved Billy, who fell so far short of the great expectations she had of the perfect man who would enter her life to transform it. She felt someone stare and looked up to meet a woman's cool appraising gaze. Beautiful and blonde, her long neck stretching out of a fur-collared jacket, the woman turned to her companion and without much enthusiasm resumed her talk. Allegra could hear the clipped voice, the telegraphic style of conversation that involved the minimum emotional investment. She could guess how a couple such as that one would describe her: 'Small provincial girl with ambitions beyond her talent. Stop. Ineffectual diarist showing none of the stuff a true hackette is made of. Stop. Fervent Christian, friendly with a handful of like-minded youngsters. Stop. No – I repeat, no – love interest since an engagement with fellow student broken off in Sheffield.'

Allegra sighed, poured yet more sparkling water into her glass, felt herself blush beneath the waiter's pitying look as he walked past her table for the umpteenth time.

It was quite true that there was no love interest. She supposed you could count Johnny Stephenson's recent attentions as 'interest', but they were not reciprocated. He had been following her about like a puppy, ever since his first attendance at the Circle, where she had sat beside him and described to him the 'family' she had found through St Mark's. He was lonely – weren't they all? – she could sense it and instinctively knew that he would clutch on to anyone or anything that would help him through this difficult patch. She had heard about the alcoholic's tortured withdrawal, and was at once loath and eager to help him. He was like Billy, a loner who sought sweetness and someone to belong to, and this resemblance to her former fiancé terrified her – the claustrophobic attention, the all-consuming love had pushed her to London. But Johnny was, after all, Lady Katherine's son, and his devotion to her might – well, who knew what it might bring in its wake?

'Well, well, who have we here? Allegra, isn't it?' Tom Sutton stopped at her table and smiled down at her. 'Alexander tells me you've landed a job at the *Sunday Herald*. Well done, girl, well done.' He bent low to smile in her face, his chock of black hair falling across his eyes like coy lashes that protect from a too-ardent gaze. 'The more of us that get about the place,' he whispered, 'the better.'

Allegra smiled, uncertain.

'I'll put in a good word for you with your chief, then, shall I?' Again he winked, and this time pointed out a corner table where she saw her editor, Michael Lewis.

'That's who you're lunching with?'

'Yes. A bit of public relations, if you know what I mean. Well, I'd better rejoin Mr Lewis. See you at St Mark's.' He walked off, and it struck Allegra that she didn't like him.

'I see you've hired young Allegra Worth.' Tom Sutton regained his seat beside Michael, who had not stopped attacking the bread basket for new-flavoured slices: he was always starving by lunch-time, because since his promotion he was in the office by eight thirty and that meant waking up by a quarter to seven. He listened with little interest as Sutton went on about the young diarist forced upon him by Paolo. 'I have a lot of time for her – a keen Christian and a pretty, bright girl.'

'Uhum,' Michael grunted, and wondered when this insipid chit-chat would end and Sutton would get to the point of the lunch: you don't invite the editor of a national paper to an expensive restaurant to pass the time of day, after all. He dipped his slice of tomato bread into the little bowl of olive oil, looking over Tom's shoulder at the room where media types sat cheek by jowl with a smattering of literary figures.

'Look that's Michael Lewis, isn't it? The new editor of the *Sunday Herald*,' he heard a man whisper, and saw a beautiful blonde woman swivel in her chair just enough to give him a curious look and show off her perfect white throat laced by a fur collar.

Michael thrilled: people recognised him everywhere these days. He'd noticed the way the maître d' had whispered, 'One of our best tables, Mr Lewis,' even though it had been Sutton who had made the reservation. And he'd seen, as he'd waited for Sutton, how many people did that subtle double-take – eyes see you, eyes move past, eyes return to you –

that celebrities must experience daily. Even now he could hear a couple of television big-wigs at the table behind him discussing his accession and Maurice's vain attempts to get into television . . . He allowed himself a small smile: he had arrived. Not that he enjoyed these fashionable Covent Garden restaurants with their measly portions and refined dishes. His preferred eating was at Simpson's on the Strand – meat and potatoes, and a club atmosphere – but it had been Sutton who asked for the lunch, so . . .

He cast Sutton a diffident glance: he didn't enjoy having to break bread with tedious politicos like this one. Far better to be lunching with that blonde bombshell who'd turned to have a good look at him. He chewed his bread pensively. Ruth Anderson's bosoms bobbed into his line of vision, and he heard her little girl's voice invite him for drinks after work. Oh, she was interested all right: always sticking herself and her prized twins under his nose. Could he? Couldn't he? But he shook his head: a mouth as big as that oven back there and he'd get burned.

The waiter brought their plates. Michael had ordered pasta as a starter, and began wolfing it down while Sutton's fork minced about a salad plate.

'I suppose you realise what a debt of gratitude the Movement feels towards you, Michael.' There was only the slightest of tensions between the two men: they were not, after all, directly in competition, and in fact, mused Michael, an alliance might prove mutually beneficial. The politician and the editor: who could beat such a team for influence?

'We have not underestimated the impact your piece on the Christian Coalition AGM had on my career – and on the Renewal Movement.' Here he looked away, spearing the lettuce before him with a dainty fork. 'Your wife, of course, was less than kind with her profile of the Renewal Movement but, then, we could hardly expect someone to understand the religious spirit and moral rigours of our group at first glance.' He looked up into Michael's eyes, and Michael noticed with distaste the other's black hair fall almost flirtatiously over one eye. 'I think she thought the Movement used religion to advance a political party – but she missed the point. We are simply believers who want to remind politicians and the electorate that Christian values are inherent in a good, democratically run society. In fact, the electorate seems to have realised this very quickly. It has proved more difficult to convince the politicians and the media of it.'

Michael continued chewing with gusto. He noticed Sutton was so intent on talking he was forgetting to eat.

'Most political groups and newspapers, frankly, rely on people's lower instincts, on their greed or their envy, on their selfishness or their xenophobia. We rely on their best instincts – their moral sense, their understanding of right and wrong. Trust me, Michael, people out there have a very strong sense of good and evil. There is a great longing for the construction of a new and better world. We saw it, we hope to channel it. A society where all individuals have rights, but recognise that they have duties as well, a society where authority is respected, and fraternity is essential. A new world where the common good is understood to mean the end of crime, family breakdown. It might sound conservative in the present climate but the people who are coming to hear me and Alexander Connaught in droves, they seem to be in tune with this vision.'

Michael stared at him over his empty plate. Here it comes, he thought, here comes the deal he wants to make.

'Most media people are still completely in the dark about our aims – and our popularity. But I think you understand the importance of the Renewal Movement and of my Christian Coalition.'

'How, may I ask, are the two linked?' Michael sipped his wine, eyes narrowing as, over the rim of his glass, he studied Sutton's excited face. The waiter who had whisked away their plates now brought them the red mullet they had both ordered. Michael issued a small sigh of disappointment at the trio of minuscule new potatoes: did people just grin and bear it and then grab a sandwich before going back to work?

'A few of us – all committed Christians – worshipped at a small parish church called St Stephen's. The vicar there was a young man named Alexander Connaught. He was unusually bright, unusually dedicated, and a group formed around him. Many of us were MPs or politically minded, and as we saw how hungry people were for Alexander's message of Christian salvation, we realised that we could help him spread the word in our own way, through politics. We never believed the two worlds should be separate – how can proper religion be segregated from everyday life, after all? And so we set up our Christian Coalition, a kind of campaigning arm of Alexander's Renewal Movement. Of course, we would not wish to impose any religious structure upon our pluralist society.' The irony in his voice told Michael otherwise. 'We see, however, that religion – we can call it our philosophy of life if you prefer – has given our politics an extra dimension and a wider appeal. The voter has always worried about the old chestnuts, after all, the break-up of the family, rise in violence, the corrupting influence of the media, no standards and no God in education, the MP who talks good and evil, the minister who promises just punishment for sinners who indulge their vices . . .' Here Michael was pleased to catch a tiny faltering of the voice, a fleeting look of fear, but then Sutton's sermon was in full flow once more. 'These people hold greater sway than their godless counterparts. There's a new mood sweeping this country, a new instinct to purge, to undergo a catharsis – oh, they won't put it in these words, but the urge is there, strong and growing stronger every day. Don't forget, Michael, it's got me where I am – and shadow minister of education when I was a nobody last year is not bad.' He smiled again. 'Our aim is simple: we want to build a better world on those pillars He gave us. It's a takeover of society for its own good, if you want.'

'Where do I fit in?' Michael ignored the waiter who was pouring more wine.

'The government majority is down to one. Everyone predicts a general election for next summer – autumn at the latest. I think the Christian Coalition could be a big player in that election. Not as a separate party, mind you – our people are members of the opposition, and we'll get to power through its ranks. And this time around, I think we'll be numerous enough to get our priorities on the agenda. We'll clean up the mess and set up a proper working society. And you would be an invaluable ally. You are at the helm of a national paper. More important, you are at the helm of a national on whose board of trustees sits a key and eager member of our Movement. Lady Katherine.' Tom Sutton allowed the name to float down and settle upon the plates before them like a sprinkling of Parmesan. Michael didn't look up but pursued his mullet with the keen concentration of a fisherman. 'As you well know, your predecessor was most uncooperative when it came to promoting the Renewal Movement. Your counterpart on the daily seems more amenable but with little real enthusiasm. Both, between you and me, have disappointed Lady Katherine – and of course Philip Stephenson, though I don't need to tell you she's the one who cares most about the papers . . . In the blood, so to speak.'

Michael kept eating, refusing to give his host the satisfaction of seeing the anxiety spread across his face.

'Anyway, she obviously looks to you to keep her beloved newspaper as independent as it has always been, an objective chronicler of our times and so forth. But I can't stress enough how excited she was by the piece you wrote. She believes you have a real appreciation for our mission, a true understanding of what Alexander hopes to achieve. I . . . I took it upon myself to invite you today to let you know that she is so grateful – so delighted, really – with your work . . .'

'You're a goodwill ambassador, are you?' Michael asked drily, eyes cold on Sutton's smug smile.

'If you wish.' Sutton shrugged, smile wider. 'You're on the winning side, Michael. Ours is a movement for the future.'

Michael swallowed hard. Be careful, don't do anything that could upset him or your position, he told himself. Beware of the slimy bastard: he'll go back and report that you were proving recalcitrant, refused to co-operate with their grand scheme. He chased the last bite of mullet with a gulp of white wine and looked straight at Sutton, a wide smile on his lips. 'I would never have written that piece if I hadn't believed in it. I reckon you and your vicar are right: people are so fed up with the status quo they dare to say the unthinkable and the unpalatable. They want the old values dusted off, the old principles reinstated . . . Yes, yes, I agree with you, it's happening all around us.'

'So you'll help us? The *Herald* will support us?'

Michael noticed Sutton had left half his fish on the plate. Must be gay, he thought with grim satisfaction, watching his waistline.

'Count on it,' he answered, and raised his glass in an insincere toast.

Allegra felt as if her whole body and face were burning: almost an hour ago the maître d' had come to her table to inform her that Wyatt had rung the restaurant to say he would be a trifle late. She hadn't dared order a thing, and was watching her wristwatch move further and further beyond two o'clock while her stomach growled and her face grew more and more scarlet. Nothing could compare with this humiliation. All she could do was hope that the editor hadn't seen her languishing by herself, waiting against hope for her lunch date.

She stole a look in the direction of the two men. Tom Sutton was talking and talking, and she could see Lewis chewing without hazarding a response. There was something so masculine, she thought, about her editor when contrasted with Sutton. Sutton was all coy movements, as if every gesture were cramped by self-consciousness; Lewis, instead, moved in an expansive way, as if he were at ease, ready to confront everything and everyone. That wide, open face, that broad figure: he seemed incapable of shadows or concealments, a bright and warm presence that made everyone else unremarkable. He managed somehow to be at once reassuring and inspiring. Whereas Sutton, he was another thing altogether. Every image she had of him seemed to be of his confabulating with Alexander in the crypt of St Mark's, which served as headquarters to the Renewal Movement. There, among the dark alcoves and dim lights, Sutton seemed at ease, a shadow in an underworld. What was the hold he had on Alexander? Certainly anyone could sense what the vicar's hold on the politician was: you couldn't fail to miss the adoring looks and loving words that Sutton showered upon his spiritual director. Theirs was such an unlikely duo: Alexander, golden, perfect, untainted, while Sutton struck her as a dark presence that crept about in the background, among sinister echoes of stories about a scandalous past . . . Though, of course, Allegra chided herself, those were only ugly rumours no one should give any credence to.

Again Tom Sutton walked past her, this time with Michael Lewis.

'Well, well, still waiting for your lunch date?' Sutton was grinning.

'Who would be so rude as to keep a young and beautiful woman waiting for hours?' Lewis stood beside her, shaking his head, his smile warming Allegra's whole body.

'Peter Wyatt.' She named the offender, eyes demurely lowered, cheeks pink.

'Well, may I join you for an espresso?' Lewis was pulling out the chair before her. 'My host is pressed for time – you know how these MPs are, always rushing about as if the world would stop without them, and if I don't have a coffee after that lunch I'll slump over . . . It's all right, Tom, I'll join my colleague.'

Lewis nodded, Tom Sutton raised a hand to wave goodbye, and flew through the revolving doors, his mobile phone ringing somewhere within his overcoat.

Allegra said nothing as Lewis smiled at her. 'My car should be here in ten minutes – he can drive us both back to the gleaming Tower. And as the blessed trustees threaten to cut down on editorial perks you may well be one of the last people to ride in a chauffeur-driven editor's car . . .'

He chatted breezily while she felt as if she were wrapped in some extraordinary silk – a soft, sweet-smelling, flawless material that showed her to her best advantage and allowed her to feel that she belonged to some pampered, luxurious species.

Michael sighed with relief: to sit here with this fetching young woman, who was obviously speechless at the prospect of having coffee with her boss, offered him a perfect opportunity to rinse out the bad taste Sutton had left in his mouth. He sat back in his chair, crossed his legs and smiled at her: he would dedicate the next ten minutes to captivating this little wide-eyed creature, for no good reason other than his need to recoup the self-confidence Sutton had snatched from him.

'Enjoying it, then?' he asked, and watched as she turned an even more attractive hue of pink. Quickly his right hand went to his hair, moving a layer at the very top from right to left: whenever he sat, he grew self-conscious lest someone look down on him, spot the patch that seemed to expand each day.

'Yes. Yes, very much,' Allegra answered, forgetting her misery at the Diary editor's impatience, her fear of the Scottish sub's snarls, her run-ins with the man from Tunbridge Wells who rang every day with a new non-story he hoped to sell the Diary.

Michael laughed. 'You almost sound as if you mean it, though I know Bertie too well to believe working with him is anything but a torture.' He raised his hand. 'Two espressos, please,' he told a passing waiter.

'I am happy, though. It's –' she looked up from her lowered lids, '– it's my first break. And I am so grateful to you, Mr Lewis –'

'Please – Michael,' he interrupted with a regal wave.

'Michael . . . for giving me a chance.' Again the blue eyes looked at him from their lowered, black-rimmed lids.

Michael beamed, feeling all-powerful in his generosity. 'Please – where would the *Sunday* be if I didn't give young talent a start?'

The waiter arrived with their coffee. While she poured a drop of milk in hers, he noticed her exquisite slim wrists and for a moment lost himself in admiration of that small patch of skin, so white as to be almost blue, that slightly protruding bone that rounded the otherwise flat wrist. I could kiss her right now, he thought, take that thin little arm in my hands. I would trace the turquoise vein with my lips, and then place the gentlest, softest kiss upon her wrist, which I know would be warm, possibly scented. And I would feel her tremble, with surprise but also, almost immediately, with a secret eagerness . . . He shook himself: this was really beyond the pale. 'With your no-show, what are you going to produce as a story for old Bertie?' he asked, after he'd downed a gulp of steaming espresso to banish the lurking lust.

'Oh, heavens, I don't know!' In an instant, fear had bleached her of all colour: terrified blue eyes pleaded with him.

71

Again he felt omnipotent before this tiny thing. 'Well, let me see if I can come up with something.' He pretended to think while he studied her pretty mouth and the mole that sat like a dot at the end of her eyebrow, and the freshness of that young skin. Nothing compared with the freshness of youthful skin: no matter how carefully a middle-aged woman looked after herself, that feel, that look could not be recaptured. 'What about this little tale – no, I can't, confidential.' He was teasing her along, enjoying watching her face change from shiny happiness to gloomy disappointment. 'Well, all right. Lord Basingtray, the non-agenarian ultra-Catholic, super-Conservative peer, has a wayward granddaughter. Guess what she's doing?' He leaned forward, his arms crossed on the table, his voice lowered conspiratorially. 'Representing the Family Planning Association at the forthcoming women's forum hosted by the World Health Organisation in Geneva!' Allegra laughed, clapping her hands. Michael made a self-deprecating little bow but he, too, looked pleased. 'Should win you many points with your Diary chief.'

'Thank you! Thank you!' She was giggling and taking out her pad, her glossy black hair falling about her face as she scribbled.

Michael laughed as he paid the bill: his good humour had been restored.

# Chapter Nine

Nina, the phone pressed between cheek and shoulder, was unbuttoning Robbie's shirt and jeans while Clive sang her praises.

'My hair is clean – feel it, Mummy, it still squeaks.' Robbie moaned loudly, heedless of Nina bringing her index finger to her lips.

'I must say, it was a perfect put-down job. No one can tell precisely *where* your rapier cut the skin and went in for the kill, they'll just know the Renewal Movement lies lifeless at your feet.' Clive chortled at the other end of London in the Georgian townhouse that served as the offices of the *Society*.

'I'm glad you liked it,' Nina murmured, as she pulled off Robbie's jeans while her son kept his balance by pressing both hands down on her shoulders.

'I loved it! The face my former flame, m'lady Katherine, must have pulled when she read your piece – well,' he chuckled, 'I would have given anything to see it. Her beloved vicar reduced to a dog-collared Lilliputian. Ah, the thrill of it! I'm tempted to make a donation to the Movement out of sheer pity for the poor man of God!'

'I don't think it was that nasty, really. I did point out that we are very much in need of some moral guidelines.' She wagged her finger at Robbie, who was running about naked, giggling at her powerlessness to get him into the bathtub full of foamy water.

'My dear, it was priceless, irony just dripping from your every word.' Clive wouldn't be deterred. 'And what I liked best of all was that Katherine would have expected a flattering profile from Michael Lewis's wife – I mean, that whitewashing piece he did about slimy Sutton and his fundamentalist Christian Coalition. No wonder she gave him the post – he's completely bought their line. Or perhaps it's all part of his Machiavellian plot . . .'

'Robbie, don't make me cross,' Nina covered the phone as she spoke, 'or I'll tell Annie she shouldn't let you stay up past nine o'clock!'

73

'Who are you talking to? Is your husband back?' Clive immediately asked. She could hear his voice turn cold with barely concealed dislike: Michael's promotion had sharpened the antipathy that Clive had always harboured against the younger, more successful, man. Michael didn't seem to mind – it was just another tribute to his new power, influence and generally enviable position – but Nina always felt that her wifely role required her to defend him against Clive's attacks.

'No, no, it's Robbie, being disobedient and risking my wrath,' she replied, with a threatening look in her son's directeon. But he had finally yielded before the threat of an early bedtime, and, spectacles carefully placed on the counter, was now slipping into the tub, setting off small white waves. 'Michael's late as usual.' She bit her lip the moment she'd spoken the words because they sparked her own anxieties (he seemed to be coming home so late so often nowadays, and then had to be dragged into displaying any interest in things outside his own work) and because they immediately triggered another explosion from Clive.

'Well, well, well. So the self-obsession is already well and truly under way, is it? The narcissism these editors can become capable of! And those snivelling kiss-ass staff who will just lie down and form a red carpet for the boss to step on – you know how they are.' Here indignation faded as Clive remembered to whom he was talking. 'Though, of course, he's your husband, which will keep his feet firmly planted on the ground. I mean, your shining example will be there with him at all times.' He sounded unconvinced.

'He doesn't need me as an example to know what's best for him,' Nina remarked drily. She was annoyed with Clive, annoyed with Robbie, who had now taken to his bath with the greatest enthusiasm and was splashing puddles onto the floor, annoyed above all with herself for slipping into ignominious suspicions about a husband who had never given her reason to suspect his fidelity and was working harder than ever. Suddenly she caught a glimpse of her wristwatch. 'Oh, Clive! I must get ready. We're going to Victor and Hannah Strauss's and –'

'Yes, yes, off you go. Wear something pale, you look best in white and cream.' He put the phone down and she heaved a sigh of relief.

'Stop splashing about in there! I'm coming to dry you in half a minute!' she called out over her shoulder as she rushed into her bedroom to change. Quickly – and, almost despite herself, mindful of

Clive's advice – she picked out a cream-coloured dress from her cupboard and began dressing: he really was late, and Hannah was such a stickler for punctuality – and where was Annie, who'd promised to be here by eight? She picked up the brush on her dressing-table, then decided she'd fix hair and make-up once Robbie was safely out of the bath. As she stepped back into the warm bathroom, where steam rolled across the mirror, she heard Michael opening the door downstairs.

'Hello! You're late!' she cried down, in what she hoped was a cheerful voice.

'Papa!' Robbie cried joyfully.

Michael didn't answer and she could hear him fix himself a drink then switch on the television. 'Quick, quick, help me Robbie.' She rubbed her son's shivering little body with the thick white towel.

'I'm going down to see Papa!' Robbie said impatiently.

'Once you have your pyjamas on.' She handed him his spectacles and gave his bottom a little pat that sent him running into his room to find the pyjamas under his pillow.

Nina straightened up, checked herself in the mirror, combed back her hair with a hand and went downstairs.

Michael lay sprawled upon the sofa, eyes fixed on the screen, a drink in hand. She frowned down at him. 'Darling, have you forgotten we've got Victor's tonight?'

'What?' From the sofa came the uninterested query.

She checked the impulse to snap at him, and smiled. 'Victor and Hannah have invited us to dinner, remember? I reminded you this morning, Michael.' The doorbell rang. 'That will be Annie now.' She moved to open the door. While she brought Annie (a healthy, unremarkable girl who read English at King's) to the kitchen to show her the ice-cream Robbie could have and the new telephone book with Victor's number, she told herself not to lose her temper with Michael: he was probably very tired, under stress and overworked.

'I'm here, Papa!' She could hear Robbie running down the stairs.

When she returned to the drawing room, her heart leaped with happiness at the sight of father and son together: Robbie was straddling Michael's lap, hands cupped around his father's face as he recounted his day at school.

All is well, Nina thought, all is well. She smiled, sat beside Michael on the sofa, listened to Robbie's rush of enthusiastic words. Only after he had finished repeating every incident he had already described to her this afternoon did she turn to Michael. 'Darling, if you want to take a shower do it now, otherwise we'll face Hannah's dragon face and that won't be pleasant.'

'Oh, I really don't think I can be fagged to go, you know.' Michael blew out his breath in a theatrical world-weary sigh.

'What?' Nina's hand stopped caressing Robbie's head.

Annie, who had been standing in the doorway, opened her arms wide. 'Well, are you not even going to say hello to me, young man?' With a last kiss from his father, Robbie trotted off to Annie and pulled her immediately upstairs to play in his bedroom.

'We have to go,' Nina said quietly. She took his wide hot hand in hers, turned it palm up and kissed it. 'I know you're tired, my darling, but we can't let them down at the last minute.'

'Oh, for heaven's sake, Nina.' He pulled his hand away. 'They're our oldest friends, we don't need to make a fuss about them.'

'We're not the only guests. They've got two lawyers coming as well, from Hannah's chambers.' Nina tried to keep her voice devoid of anger.

'Two lawyers no one has ever heard of who'll be labouring some abstruse point of libel law. What a bore!' Michael was looking beyond her at the television screen.

'We may not have heard of them, but that hardly disqualifies them as entertaining company.'

'That's not what I meant. Honestly, I'm exhausted.' He raked a hand through his thick golden hair, yawned, and she suddenly smelled the alcohol on him. He was holding a gin and tonic – but the smell was too powerful for one drink. Had he stopped on the way home with a colleague? Or perhaps he now had a drinks cabinet in his office? She sniffed the air. 'Aha!' She pretended to be amused. 'You've been out drinking with the boys!' She wagged her finger at him in mock disapproval.

'Yes, a whole group of us.' He continued to watch the screen and avoid her eyes. 'It's still all part of the honeymoon period – they have yet to find out how nasty a boss I can be, and I have yet to suspect them of devious plots.'

'I see . . .'

'I'm afraid this after-hours socialising will continue to be part of the deal for a while, which is why dinners seem such an effort – Hold on.' He leaned forward, elbows on knees, straining to hear the newscaster. 'This is the story Ruth Anderson mentioned over drinks.'

Nina remembered with distaste the woman columnist with her

bosom-hugging top and wide red mouth, then concentrated on the screen: a little girl of four had been murdered by a ten-year-old who'd been left to watch her while her mother had gone to the shops. The toddler's dimpled face smiled from the television, her eyes wide and innocent beneath a blonde curl fixed with a bow. Her name had been Polly. The identity of her murderer could not be revealed.

'My God, what is the world coming to?' Nina murmured. Michael took her hand in his, pressed it warmly, continued to stare ahead at the screen.

'All right, you win,' he said, when music announced the end of the news. 'We'll go to Hannah's entertaining dinner.' He sighed. 'I suppose I'd better get dressed.' He switched off the television with his remote control and, without looking at her, climbed the stairs.

Nina sat on the sofa, feeling unease at Michael's mood mingle with the horror she felt for the child's murder. Slowly she climbed up the stairs to her bedroom: he was already in the shower and through the open door she could hear his humming. She sat at her dressing-table, and took up the small jar of foundation cream. With slow, cautious movements she spread the cream to cover her face, fingertips gingerly pushing along her forehead, her cheeks, her nose. She looked at the pale skin, at the light lines that cradled her eyes: he hadn't said a thing about her dress, hadn't deigned to give her a proper look. No wonder. She should have been beautifully made up before his return, instead of taking his constant attention and desire for granted after eight years of everyday exposure. Behind her he was humming out of tune. Nina held up a hand mirror to check that the foundation had left no visible mark along her jaw-line. With her index finger she pressed the smudged beige line along her throat. Did he think her still desirable, now that, as Clive had said, he was surrounded by men – and women – who were ready to do his bidding, grateful for his slightest show of interest? Did he constantly compare her with the younger more fashionable females who filled his newsroom? She set down the hand mirror, caught her reflection in the large oval one above her dressing-table. Her eyes stared back, serious, dark, filled with longing, and suddenly she ached with the memory of Michael in what must have been one of their first days in this house, lying beside her on the bed, a fingertip following a path along her features, which then his lips retraced. 'Oh, Michael . . .' The yearning suddenly blocked her throat.

'I don't know why we couldn't have rung up and said Robbie had a fever or something.' Michael stood naked in the doorway, head bent as he towel-dried his hair.

'We can't do that to them.' She smacked her lips to ensure they were evenly covered with lipstick while watching him move in the mirror, pink from the hot shower, drops of water sliding down the middle of his broad back. He had lost some of his paunch, and his hips and legs seemed thinner as he walked quickly, legs scissoring across the room. She noticed that he still withheld his gaze from her as he donned his clean clothes.

'Michael . . .' She didn't realise she had spoken out loud until he looked up at her, one leg still slipping into his trousers.

'Yes?'

'I want a kiss.' She whispered the wish, and immediately blushed, as if embarrassed by her own plea.

'I'm coming.' He pulled up the trousers, buckled his belt, came over to her. He kissed her on the top of her dark head, looking into the mirror as he did so, blue eyes first smiling at her reflection and then at his own.


The next few days, she again felt that strange mood of unease fill her: his talk of 'after hours' socialising, the drinking, the thought of the vulgar Ruth Anderson at his side . . . She felt troubled, and her new, vague anxieties hung over her like some shapeless canopy.

It was a few days after Victor's dinner – during which Michael had behaved impeccably, making Hannah laugh delightedly with his imitation of the Lord Chief Justice – that she saw the vicar of St Mark's again. She had been walking to the fruit vendor's, one hand deep in her overcoat pocket as she tried to find her scribbled shopping list, the other holding up an umbrella. It had been raining since early morning and she picked her way carefully to avoid the puddles and the slippery wet leaves. Without realising it, she had been approaching St Mark's, and saw in its courtyard an enormous sombre crowd, a television crew's shiny cameras among them. She drew closer, curious, and discerned the tall black-clad figure, face partially hidden by a large black umbrella. Alexander Connaught was walking towards the back of the church and its small cemetery, studded with white and grey tombstones and dark shrubs. He now held out his hand to a small woman who seemed bent over in grief. Nina watched from beneath her dripping umbrella as two men held aloft a tiny coffin, almost invisible beneath its profusion of wreaths. The silent crowd of mourners moved forth slowly behind it, the camera crew at their heels. Nina watched as Alexander made his slow way towards the cemetery, leading the woman and the man who followed. Dozens of wreaths lay in rondos of colour upon the shiny black hearse parked at the entrance of the courtyard. Above the cemetery thin trees stretched their bare branches, as if to hold up the sky that hung so low and threatening. The ground lay softened by rain, but bare and ugly in its winter brown.

On an impulse Nina entered the courtyard, made her way up the path towards the great grey-faced Victorian church, and the cemetery beyond. The rain was almost invisible, but constant, and the blue cloth of her umbrella dripped and dripped. The air had warmed since the early-morning frost, but it was still chilly enough for her breath to unfurl in small clouds before her.

In the cemetery that stretched away girded by a low grey stone wall, she could make out a small group of journalists standing at a discreet distance from the mourning throng. It was this that made her realise they must be burying the child Polly, whose murder had made the headlines. Alexander had led the woman, whom Nina guessed must be Polly's mother, towards the small open grave. Around them low shrubs alternated with stone crosses: everything glistened in the rain, but it was a melancholic rather than a cheerful sheen, like the gloss of the well-polished hearse outside the church courtyard.

She watched the vicar beneath the great black dome of his umbrella, one hand supporting the small woman's elbow: again, as at the healing, she felt his remarkable presence, and saw the way he effortlessly became the focus of everyone's gaze. Now he raised his umbrella slightly, the better to speak with the woman beside him, and Nina could see the perfect white oval of his face, shiny and almost translucent in the grey, rain-soaked air.

The mourners were gathered in a large silent group around the grave, and she saw now the men lowering the tiny coffin into the wet black earth. She watched the mother once again bend double, her whole body turning this time towards Alexander. The vicar did not move but held her close to him with his right arm, while with the other he held his umbrella aloft. Nina could hear the photographers behind her take countless pictures. Suddenly, Alexander shut his umbrella. It was still drizzling, but seemingly oblivious he held up his arms. 'Friends.' Nina thrilled at the melodious voice, the sweetness and gentleness she remembered from the healing ceremony. Behind her someone sobbed. She could see the journalists straining to hear every word. 'We are here to bury Polly Graham, a child of four. A child whose murderer was all of ten years old. We are here to support Polly's mother and father in this, their darkest hour, but also to bear witness to the moral agonising we all experienced when we saw the details of Polly's death on our television screens, in our daily newspapers. Seldom has a murder caused such universal revulsion. Seldom has a crime caused such a spontaneous outpouring of collective grief.' He looked around him, his arms still aloft as if to bear their communal burden; she saw that his blond head had been darkened by the drizzle, and his face moistened. 'Polly's murder has caused us to take a look at ourselves, and we do not like what we see. We had forgotten, perhaps, how strong our urge to do evil is – even from childhood, as Polly's young killer demonstrates. We had conveniently forgotten that morality is not a matter of personal interest, a hobby one can choose to take up or not. Morality is about community, about each one of us recognising that we are linked in an effort to build a perfect world. This requires a recognition of shared values. And for too long we have turned a blind eye to these values – Polly's murder reminds us that we can no longer afford to do so.'

The rain had stopped now, and a weak round sun was emerging beyond the tombs, and the vicar of St Mark's. Nina heard the sharp intake of breath from the woman beside her. 'He is an angel.'

Bathed in the extraordinary light Alexander continued, 'The time has come for us to admit that we are sinners who must cleanse their hearts and souls. The time has come for us all to examine our conscience, and to take action against its worst instincts. Only in this way may we prevent a spiralling into the kind of violence that finds root in the present moral vacuum. Brothers and sisters, let us bow our heads and pray now, for Polly, and for our nation to awaken itself from this amoral stupor, and walk forth on the true path.'

Nina watched as the crowd bowed its head in humble unison. She listened to Alexander now intoning the burial rite, and saw Polly's parents stand as if dazed on either side of the tiny grave that remained open. Slowly, carefully, she picked her way through the throng, retraced her steps down the path that led to the street. And as she walked to the fruit vendor's, then returned home to begin her column about an innovative child-care system in Scandinavia, she felt lost in a host of sensations, as if the handsome vicar's words and image remained with her even when she had left his presence. She had underestimated him in her profile, she decided. He was truly extraordinary.

# Chapter Ten

At the Stephensons' great round dining-room table, the flames of ten candles lighting his face, Alexander Connaught sat surrounded by young people. There were teenagers and twenty-somethings, all holding their breath, expectant and wide-eyed, as the vicar talked in his low, gentle voice. They sat with their chairs close to one another, Bibles in their hands: they had finished the meal Lady Katherine had laid on for them (it was Philip's bridge night, so he had not been put out) and it was now prayer time. Then, the confessions.

From the drawing room, where she leaned an elbow upon the marble mantelpiece, Lady Katherine stood watching her son through the open doors. Seated on Alexander's right, Johnny stared intently at the face of his new-found mentor, and she could see him taut and eager to please, seated at the edge of his chair, the better to capture each word. Between the muscular arms of the silver candelabra, Lady Katherine thrilled at her son's new face: less than a month, and already the changes were obvious. He hadn't been drinking, she could swear to it. Ever since the healing, Alexander had come to pay Johnny daily visits, climbing up to the darkened bedroom where hitherto no one had been allowed to venture. She could hear their voices as she sat downstairs: her son's intermittent questions, washed over by the sweet voice of the other. He would be saved, she felt certain now.

She had offered her dining room for Alexander's Circle: the youngsters met every Wednesday night at a different home to sup together, pray, confess. Lady Katherine had offered her spiritual director her home because she knew that this way, Johnny would be sure to take part in the weekly ritual. She listened to their joyful chorus as Alexander intoned the prayers. The voices rose above the cutlery and china, floated among the fragile flames of the red candles, seemed to blow like a zephyr about the richly coloured tablecloth. Her home, she mused, was being transformed into a spiritual haven, a refuge that could offer these young people solace amid the chaos of their lives.

She closed her eyes in the warmth of the fire Liu had lit in the fireplace. She wanted to be of use to him. His devoted servant. Lady Katherine felt the heat of the flames. Memory upon memory came to her, as if a hand were rubbing a misted window-pane to clear a patch here, a patch there of an animated indoor scene. She remembered the feel of her father's hand on her shoulder as he led her down the different newsrooms of his newspapers, and she would smile with confidence, buoyed by the dual certainty of her father's love and his power. The sound of the wind brushing branches against her window-pane reminded her of the voices of the women who would stop at St Mark's, on their way to work or the shops, to gossip and pledge a hand with this fête, with that flower arrangement – all the while looking out for Alexander.

Lady Katherine shook herself and opened her eyes. She looked at the vicar: she filled with love at the sight of the man who had taken her son's hand in his, and begun the long journey that would lead Johnny on the right road.

She was supposed to share this joy with everyone, yet knew in her heart of hearts that what she wanted most was to keep him to herself. She couldn't help it: the women who hung about St Mark's filled her with jealousy; the sight of Tom Sutton, his eyes lowered in devotion, his voice lowered in whispered confidence, annoyed her. Oh, she knew Tom was a good man, tireless in his mission. But she detested his wide black eyes that filled with love at the sight of Alexander, his soft smile: he was like a wet handshake that had you eager to break free and wipe your hand dry.

Still, during yesterday's lunch at the *Sunday Herald* offices, she had vociferously praised the MP, as Alexander would have wished her to, and even when she and Michael Lewis had been left to a *tête-à-tête*, she had not betrayed her dislike. Though, of course, Michael was shrewd enough to size up Sutton – and, indeed, to gauge her own true feelings about him. Yes, Michael was shrewd enough: she had done well to support him when Philip and the rest had thrashed out the candidates for the editorship at the board meeting. A bright, attractive man – he was, she mused, probably keeping his wife in a state of permanent watchfulness. She had seen him looking around the newspaper in a cocky, proprietorial way, eyes inviting as they rested on the women – no doubt about it, he was someone who would think nothing of having an affair, especially now, with his post assured. Though, of course, she wouldn't stand for a whiff of scandal, she had made that quite clear to him. But he wasn't a fool, he'd be careful all right.

With a start, Lady Katherine suddenly realised she had slipped into a forbidden way of thinking: she'd become the Katherine of old, thus betraying Alexander's teaching. She clasped her hand before her, as if to begin a prayer to restore her pure thoughts, but behind her she heard Liu: 'Mrs Lewis is here, madam.'

Of course: she'd completely forgotten that Alexander had invited Nina to come. The piece for the *Society* had been published a few weeks ago – and at first had angered Lady Katherine: the woman had understood so little, ignored so much. But Alexander had calmed her. 'It is so important, so very important, that in a magazine such as this our Movement is taken at all seriously. We'll convert Mrs Lewis later, slowly but surely. Don't worry.' They had issued an invitation for tonight, and though Nina had declined to attend the Circle, she had agreed to a meeting with Alexander later. 'Come, Nina.' She strode towards her guest. Lady Katherine pecked the younger woman's cheeks, took her hand and drew her to the sofa and armchairs before the fire.

She laced her silk-covered arm into Nina's and whispered, 'They've almost finished the prayers. Now they'll do their confession and then we can steal him away. He was expecting you and he's very grateful to you.'

'And I to you.' Nina smiled.

'He's very eager to spread the Word, to share the message He has entrusted in him.'

The two women stood, watching the ritual before them. Alexander sat back in his chair, long legs crossed to the side, Bible held in his hands. Nina studied the tall athletic figure in its chair, and nearly smiled: how appropriate the term 'muscular Christianity' seemed when applied to this youthful vicar. Around him, the young people had grown silent. Johnny Stephenson was watching the man beside him, eyes full of love.

'Who will go first?' Alexander asked. Then, softly, 'You must feel no pressure to speak out. Wait until the Spirit moves you.'

The women saw the youngsters steal covert looks at one another. No one moved.

'Remember the story of Jonah and Nineveh. Jonah was so disgusted with the city of sinners, where God's rule was ignored and

84

broken every day, that he thought the city should be razed to the ground. Instead, Our Father told him there was hope: if the inhabitants of that unhappy city repented, His forgiveness would be theirs. And they could stride forth, into the Kingdom.'

A young man, face round and freckled, now stood up. 'Brothers and sisters, I confess. I've lost my temper repeatedly . . . and I lied to my friends about my involvement with the Movement. I didn't stand up and proclaim my membership of the Circle, my apostleship of Renewal . . . I was frightened of being considered a pious born-again bore.' The young man hung his head in shame as a murmur rose among the others. Still without looking at anyone, he sat down.

'Oh, Matthew, how that pains me.' Alexander's voice was low, gentle and filled with regret. 'I would wish you to be proud, so proud of your good work, of being a member of His Movement, the Movement that seeks to reinstate His Kingdom on earth.' Again a soft murmuring swept through the group. 'I want you, Matthew, from this day forth to proclaim, to everyone you know, your transformation from sinner to Christian.'

Beside the vicar, a plump youth shifted in his chair, eyes lowered. 'Forgive me,' he uttered the words so that they sounded like a desperate bleat. Slowly he stood up, face and neck turning red as the Bibles that paved the table.

'I have had l-l-l-lewed thoughts . . . and acted u-p-p-p-pon them . . .'

The group sat silent, but every face turned to the poor puce-coloured penitent. Alexander raised his hands as if to still their excitement. 'Acted upon them?' His voice boomed.

'I slept with my g-g-g-girlfriend,' the boy's words shivered.

'Fornication.' The sin seemed to drop upon the group from a great height. 'How many times?'

'Twice. One night last week . . . I . . . am d-d-d-deeply ashamed. I swear that it will never happen again.'

'Any unnatural acts?' The vicar, Nina noticed, had the good grace to blush at this point.

'No,' the boy's voice quivered. Around the table, the young people turned to one another, silent, but with eyebrows raised like windows, the better to spy on the goings-on below; and mouths roundly open, like a telescope lens pointed at the sinner. The members of the Circle looked as guilty, in their conspiracy of curiosity, as the stuttering boy before them.

The penitent remained standing, awaiting his fate. All eyes were now on their spiritual mentor: would he punish or absolve their friend?

Alexander raised both hands: 'Listen to the words of St Paul, Justin: "Flee also youthful lusts: but follow righteousness, faith, charity, peace, with them that call on the Lord out of a pure heart." You may sit down, Justin. Think of how best to avoid temptation – no late-night heart-to hearts, watch the drinking, try to be in a group rather than alone . . . and attend, regularly, this Circle.'

Alexander opened his Bible. 'St Paul says, "Having therefore these promises, dearly beloved, let us cleanse ourselves from all filthiness of the flesh and spirit, perfecting holiness in the fear of God."'

At Lady Katherine's side, Nina shook her head at the bizarre ritual, at the prurience of the group. She wished Lady Katherine and her mentor had allowed her access to this public chest-beating while she'd been writing her piece for Clive: one glimpse of this Circle, and most people would have fled at the sound of the vicar's approach. How shrewd of Alexander Connaught to keep her at bay until now. She stared at the vicar's face that glowed in the candlelight. The long, light blue eyes, the straight nose, the full lips. She wondered whether he had any idea of his extraordinary looks. She stole a glance at Lady Katherine beside her – and was almost shocked at the naked love she saw there. She wondered if strangers could read her own expression when she looked at Michael, wondered if her own secret passion were so clearly legible. Michael. She tried to stop her thoughts from following him. She had been unable to dispel her unease about her husband. At night, when she waited for him in bed, yearning for his touch, he quickly fell asleep, leaving her to stare at his back with a thousand silent questions.

Now Alexander stood up, and Nina watched him, holding the Bible tight to his chest. 'Go, my brothers and sisters, go forth and walk with pride, knowing that you tread the path of virtue.'

The young people rose to their feet. Some began to pack up their things and remained in silence, as if pondering the vicar's words; others stood about talking, smiles open as if to betray their newly cleansed spirit.

Nina watched them, curious. Clive had told her that the scions of some of the grandest families belonged to the vicar's inner Circle. ('I fear the young evangelical has an eye on pedigree as well as piety, and on Debrett's as well as the Day of Judgement,' he'd chortled over the phone.) It was true: she recognised the young good-looking son of a Lord Lieutenant (the boy attended Robbie's school) and the daredevil daughter of a flamboyant peer (the paparazzis' darling, who smiled from every glossy magazine). She wondered how their children's spiritual endeavours were viewed at home – a young evangelical infected with religious fever and mouthing moral axioms at every opportunity would make for rather strained dinner conversation, she suspected.

'Alexander, will you join us for coffee?' Lady Katherine turned to him, eyes devoted. Then she looked past him at Johnny, who was deep in discussion with a young, plain-faced woman. 'And this is Nina Lewis.'

'Of course. I won't join you for the coffee but let me come and sit beside you.'

They sat around the low table across which two sofas faced one another. Liu had already placed a tray with small cups there, and a plate of miniature cakes. Nina was slightly ill at ease: she could sense that her hostess had been less than pleased by her piece in the *Society*, and that it was the young vicar who had invited her here. He was either more forgiving than Lady Katherine, or more anxious to change Nina's mind about the Movement he led.

Lady Katherine sat beside Alexander and looked encouragingly at Nina across the table: 'I wanted the two of you to meet properly.'

'I am very interested in the Renewal Movement . . .' Nina murmured, slightly embarrassed.

Polly's funeral had led the news for days, with enthusiastic commentators hailing the funeral oration made by 'the remarkable Alexander Connaught'. His face had filled newspapers and television news, and overnight the vicar of St Mark's had become a household name. But as she watched him now, so at ease among his adoring acolytes, Nina could not help wondering to what extent the man before her had manipulated the funeral of the murdered toddler to give himself a platform for his own campaign.

She watched him sit back in the sofa, his long hands folded in his lap, his face serene: he betrayed nothing.

'I say nothing new,' he said, smiling at Lady Katherine and Nina in turn. 'I simply listen to the men and women who come to me and say, "Mine is not a happy life. Help me change it." I listen to their cry for help. They tell me of a life where they fear violence in their streets, where children are bent on destruction – as we saw with Polly's terrible murder – where women are trying to stamp out their maternal feelings, and people at the top are engulfed in scandal after scandal.' He paused. Liu had appeared, a pot of coffee in her hands. She set it down for Lady

Katherine to serve them, then disappeared, a small smile on her face. 'Happiness eludes us while there is chaos and uncertainty. Because they realise this, an increasing number of men and women have become spiritual pilgrims, looking for the ancient and immutable truths that bring order to our existence. Truths that tell us who we are and what is expected of us.' He watched as Nina brought to her lips the cup of coffee.

'Surely,' Nina replied in a low voice, 'happiness is a lot more than this certainty you claim people seek.'

'Ah . . . what then is happiness?'

'Love,' Nina answered, without hesitation.

'Yes.' The vicar closed his eyes for a moment, as if to ponder her answer: 'But there can be too much love.'

Nina said nothing. He went on: 'Too much love of sensual pleasures, of material possessions, of oneself. Or of another.' He paused. Nina said nothing, but looked away from him, towards the young people who had surrounded him earlier. The vicar followed her gaze: 'I think the Circle is so necessary – a weekly time when these young people can sit together and pray out loud, and then, if the Spirit moves them, confess their sins –'

But Nina interrupted him: 'Medieval flagellants used to stand in a circle in front of a church or cathedral, chanting and whipping themselves in penance. Is this where you're leading them to?' She could see that Lady Katherine had grown nervous, but she ignored the older woman's pleading look.

Alexander shook his head. 'Of course not. I do believe it is important for even the youngest among us to understand penance. But I do not advocate the mortification of the flesh.'

'I'm relieved to hear that the young people will be spared,' Nina replied.

Lady Katherine again tried to intervene: 'The Circles offer a wonderful opportunity for these young people to feel boosted in their faith: they draw strength from knowing that there are others who also face trials and tribulations in their journey.' She smiled at her mentor, who ignored her to concentrate on Nina.

'I have not yet shared with them the most terrifying truth of all.'

'Which is?'

'That the end of the world is upon us.' His eyes had grown suddenly terrible in their fiery visionary's brightness. 'This is the task of the

Renewal Movement: to warn people that the Day of Judgement looms. But also to show them that there is a road to salvation and that we can show them the way.'

Nina looked again at Lady Katherine's rapturous face: 'Do you really believe the end of the world is near?'

'You mean I use this apocalyptic talk to fill fools with fear so that I may do with them as I wish?' He smiled at her. 'We live in the shadow of the millennium – this is why people are finally listening to calls for change. They may not all believe in the Second Coming, but they sense that this is a momentous era.'

'But nowadays, so few believe . . . Do you really think that outside your Movement anyone recognises this particular juncture as a moment invested with religious significance?'

'There is a new mood – look about you, and you will see that people who were once safe in their jobs have lost them, that men and women who once thought marriage was binding for life have lost that security, that the numbers of violent deaths, divorces, cases of child abuse rise with each passing day. In their despair, people long for clear-cut rules. True religions know that rules give us liberty.' He paused, as if waiting for her rebuttal, but Nina merely watched him. She couldn't really make up her mind about the vicar: was he a dangerous fundamentalist, or a harmless, saintly preacher? Was he slightly mad or sane but naive?

'We – the believers – see the new age arriving, and with it the end of the Age of Satan. A period of jubilee and renewal will ensue, for those who obey the call. But I would issue also a warning: that a dark cloud threatens this dawn of a new world, for there will be a tremendous power struggle between the forces of good and the forces of evil, and at that time, we must all declare our allegiances.' Nina remained silent. He was, she decided, slightly hysterical, a fanatic whose good looks had given him tremendous power over susceptible women (and possibly men). She sipped her coffee and marvelled at the readiness with which a sophisticated woman like Lady Katherine could accept these promises.

Allegra stood near the fireplace, felt her face burn as she watched the flames. Beside her, Johnny was whispering: 'I'm terrified at night – that's when it's worst. The temptation is incredible, it's like a mirage where you see the bottle before you . . . The number of times I wake up almost weeping because in my dreams I've got drunk . . .' He had a light feeble voice that grew more pleasing when he lowered it like tonight.

But she had begun to feel uncomfortable with his persistent attentions: he rang her countless times at home, at the paper, so much so that in the end even her flat-mate, kind-hearted Katie, had lost her patience and told him off. He would talk endlessly of his private demons that tried to lure him away from Jesus, back to the bottle and its oblivion.

Now as she listened to his catalogue of anxieties, Allegra stared at the flames that crackled like the laughter that had greeted her this morning in the newsroom. 'You can try as much as you like to throw yourself at him, Ruth,' Bertie had raised his voice, teasing, 'but I've noticed that our esteemed editor has been hanging round my Diary a great deal of late, and I think I know for whom . . .' and Bertie had winked at Allegra, who had not known what to say.

She watched the flames stretch, curl, fold into one another. Had Michael Lewis been particularly attentive? Ever since their shared coffee at the Covent Garden restaurant, he had been friendly when they had seen each other. She felt herself almost dizzy with pride: he was so handsome, bright and all-powerful . . .

With a start, Allegra tried to dispel the wayward thoughts: he was married – 'the adulterer and the adulteress shall surely be put to death' – the words of Leviticus rose before her. Michael Lewis was married – and look at his wife, the handsome, serious woman sitting beside Alexander. Allegra looked at the older woman's pale face, the great arched brows and the lips that did not move as she listened to the vicar of St Mark's. Nina Lewis, née del Monte, mother of one son, columnist for the *Society* – a formidable woman, self-confident and elegant.

Yet, despite herself, Allegra saw Michael's laughing face yesterday as he had clowned around with her when she had walked out of the lift and he had pretended to walk straight into her, so that his strong hands had clasped her arms as if to keep her from falling. And she saw the wonderful clear eyes that had filled with mischief across the table at the restaurant those weeks ago. 'Stop' she ordered herself. 'You are a wicked woman to even think like that.' And, in order to punish the little devil that was tempting her, she turned with her prettiest smile to Johnny beside her: 'If you think it would be of help, I'm happy to read Scripture with you in the evenings . . .'

As she set down her cup of coffee, Nina felt the vicar's eyes probe her. 'I want to alert every man, woman and child to this historic moment – tell them that the old way of life must – will – disintegrate. For far too long no one has asked them to choose between evil and good, between damnation and salvation. I ask them to do so now, that they may prepare themselves for the great battle.'

'How are we to prepare ourselves?' she asked.

'Repentance, penance, salvation: these are the three tenets of our faith. These are Jesus's words, after all, are they not? There is nothing unusual in what we preach. What is unusual, what has drawn so much interest in our activities, is the way people have responded so quickly and eagerly to our call. Think of the tremendous display of solidarity they showed to Polly's parents? Think of the way they greeted my call to repent? I believe they sense that we have stepped out of line with the divine plan. The millennium marks our chance to right this wrong, and to realign ourselves with His design.'

'What of those who do not heed the call? How do we instil fear of the looming apocalypse into those who have forgotten, or choose to ignore, the old lessons about good and evil?'

'We must force their hand. Push them in the same way a mother may push her child to learn his first steps, the same way a teacher may urge her pupil to finish his lesson.'

'These are adults,' Nina made an impatient gesture, 'Not schoolchildren. How do you "push" an adult? Unless of course through intimidation?'

'Well, now. Intimidation – that is a terrifying word. But if by that we mean that we are ready to shout at the top of our lungs that evil ways will bring about our fall; if we are ready to confront those who hate God and to warn them of the punishment that awaits them . . . then, yes, if this is intimidation, I support it.'

Nina said nothing, but wondered how many would march towards the New Jerusalem with Alexander Connaught and his followers. His was a stark, barren world, where life was reduced to an index of forbidden actions, words, yearnings. He levelled existence to a flat arid terrain, men and women to one-dimensional beings bent on drawing boundaries between black and white.

'I cannot believe that you expect to win many disciples,' Nina spoke quietly.

He gave her a wide smile: 'You'll be surprised at the numbers of converts we will win over, then. History has come full circle – the great battle between Truth and Untruth is imminent. This is the moment towards which man has been moving, the new millennium and the new dawn.'

Nina saw Lady Katherine nod her head, up and down, slowly. She turned away from her hostess, to Johnny and Allegra Worth sitting side by side: she could see the young girl bowing her dark head close to Johnny's while her fingers traced a sentence in the book that lay open on Johnny's lap.

Lady Katherine followed her gaze and smiled: 'She has given him a great deal of self-confidence. She has been wonderfully generous.' And she rose, and went over to her son and his friend.

'And yet he, like his mother,' Nina whispered to Alexander, 'seems to have everything. What brings him to you and your Movement?'

'It is as in the story of Nicodemus. He was well off and wanted nothing yet he knew something eluded him. The Spirit – which in the end is everything.'

Again, Nina turned to the vicar. 'Those young people who flock to you – do you really think them capable of evil?'

Alexander's eyes pierced her: 'We all are.'

That night, as she lay awake while waiting for Michael, who was once again late from work, she found his words again in the dark, and saw his face glow clearly before her.

## Chapter Eleven

For the Feast of the Epiphany, they usually went to Holland Park for lunch. Her parents still gave Robbie presents on the sixth, with Marina handing over to her grandson a large grey burlap bag 'from the Befana'. Once, a few years ago, they had even hired a clown to impersonate the stooped, toothless figure of the Good Witch, but Robbie had taken fright and the trick was never played again.

Today, with Michael expected back from Liverpool some time in the afternoon, Nina had asked her parents to come to her. They were having tea in the drawing room where she and Paolo had made a fire with endless copies of the *Sunday Herald*. She had half smiled at the thought of being able to twist those pages tightly, and set them alight: since his promotion, she felt as if the *Herald* had swallowed up Michael, leaving her nothing of her husband. When they had both planned and plotted for the editor's chair, she had loved the newspaper because it had bonded them even more tightly. But now – now that Michael was constantly preoccupied, his attention ever wandering from family matters, now that he would look at her or at Robbie absent-mindedly, asking questions she had just answered – now she hated the *Herald*.

She watched Paolo asleep in one of the armchairs, his spectacles sliding down his nose, his long thin legs stretched out towards the fire. He was hissing in his sleep and she saw Robbie tiptoe around his grandfather, studying him with great interest, then settling down beside him to play with the steamship that he had received from his grandparents today. Nina stood by the window: there had been snow early in the morning, but now a weak sun was peering over the rooftops across the street.

Marina, who had gone to the kitchen to make a cup of tea for Paolo and herself, returned, bearing the two mugs. 'Asleep, as usual. He really is the limit.' She was smiling, shaking her white head.

93

'Here, Mamma,' Nina reached out to take the mug she and Michael had bought in Bath last year.

They stood by the window, its edges blurred by steam, and watched in silence the trees sway outside, elegant, erratic pendulums that did not tell time.

Nina did not look at her mother's profile, etched against the window, did not look at the small black-clad figure that stood quite still, mug in hand: the sight still prompted a great deal of confusion, a residue of rancour. She felt tense beside her mother, as if the new Marina had superimposed herself upon the familiar image of a gentle, loyal, sweet woman – and now beside Nina stood a stranger of whom she should be wary. She sank her gaze into the milky tea before her, voice false. 'Hmm, nothing like a cuppa.'

Marina ignored her and began, voice dreamy, 'You see Luke was –'

'Mother,' Nina implored.

But Marina continued, as if she were resuming her earlier confession after a few minutes rather than a few weeks. 'It started so innocuously. And it was all your fault, you know. You remember when you went to Edinburgh for the Festival? I'd gone up with you, we'd had that lovely weekend, then I was to take the train back to London by myself.' Nina struggled to remember the weekend, tried to resurrect the fateful visit to Edinburgh, but she saw only her mother as she was now, face eager and blue eyes lit with love. 'It was the end of August, hot and muggy and I remember my compartment was impossible, like an oven. There was only one other passenger, and he was immersed in some tome, never looked up, just sipped all the time from a Thermos he'd brought. I hardly noticed him, but I remember thinking how clever he'd been to bring something of his own to drink. Suddenly he looked up, and with the kindest smile he asked me if I would join him for "a wee dram".' She laughed. 'Oh, he wasn't Scottish, but he put on this silly accent, and I laughed and accepted the drink, and then we started talking . . . and within moments we discovered that he was contributing to some book your father was editing on the history of the trade unions.'

Nina looked at her mother. She seemed to enjoy this revelation, obviously wanted to indulge herself in the forbidden reminiscences. Nina felt at once uneasy and fascinated before this unravelling of Marina's past.

'I remember liking his stillness, his low voice. I liked the way he was completely at ease, even then, when I was a complete stranger. He

94

asked me a few questions, but not, as I was used to with everyone else, about your father and his work – not even about you. He asked about me, about what I did during the day, about what I thought of London, what I'd made of Edinburgh. He asked if I missed my family in Italy, whether I missed the climate . . .' She smiled here, remembering. 'He was a gentle interrogator, you know. He didn't seem to pry – no, he seemed genuinely interested in every detail, every little word. He leaned forward, concentrating on everything I said, as if he were studying it . . . and we drank more and more of his whisky as the train sped and night fell.' Marina stopped and Nina watched the tears fill her mother's eyes. She found herself incapable of moving to comfort her. She watched, helpless and guilty, as the small figure beside her bent her head over her tea and issued a half-stifled sob. Nina studied her mother's small, plump body, a handful of generous curves now pressed together in a concertina of regret. Slowly, slowly, as if her arm bore an impossible weight, she lifted it, embraced her mother's trembling shoulders. Her hand felt her mother quiver through the black cardigan.

'Papa!' Robbie leaped up to greet his father at the door, waking Paolo from his nap and forcing Marina to dry her cheeks with a hurried gesture.

'Darling, you must be exhausted, shall I make a cup of tea?' Nina was eager, anxious, dying to wrap him in her arms and never let him go.

Michael discarded his trench-coat, his scarf, set down his briefcase and small weekend bag, all the while answering Robbie's questions about Liverpool. He pecked Nina on the cheek, waved a cheerful greeting in her parents' direction and proceeded immediately up the stairs. 'I must have a shower or I'll collapse,' he called over his shoulder.

Nina stood, silent with disappointment, staring at the briefcase and the trench-coat that had been cast over all the other coats on the wooden stand with its Hindu god arms. He'd hardly looked at her, had only given her the most rushed, meaningless embrace. She couldn't accept this new, uninterested Michael. Slowly, without a look back at her parents or Robbie, she climbed the stairs. She could hear him undress in their bedroom, whistling to himself. She walked in, a calm smile on her face. 'It must have been exhausting. How were the people at the paper company?' She kept her voice even, smooth. She watched him unbutton his shirt, pull at his belt and felt a sudden impulse to embrace him, breathe in that warm skin, feel those heavy limbs close around her.

95

'Oh, about as awful as I'd imagined, no surprises there, I fear. Still, it had to be done . . .' His eyes skimmed over her, gave nothing away, and he sat down heavily on the bed, tugging at his shoelaces.

'Shall I run you a bath?'

'No, no, I want a quick shower, that's all.' He still wasn't looking at her, and his voice seemed to sag with fatigue.

Nina suddenly broke her resolution and bent her face close to his. 'I missed you', she murmured.

'Me too.' He tweaked her nose, bounded up from the bed and, naked, walked into the bathroom. He shut the door behind him. Nina covered her face with both hands. What was happening? What was wrong? She couldn't think. Nothing came to her but waves of desire and disappointment. She wanted to bang at the door he'd closed, to scream and shout and demand an explanation. She didn't dare. Instead, she slowly, awkwardly, folded the clothes he'd cast about their bed, ranged his shoes neatly beside one another. Then she walked downstairs, where she went into the kitchen to escape her parents' looks.

She must stop this, must not always expect so much of him. He was new at the job, he felt under pressure, felt watched, examined, weighed. What had she wanted to hear? That he had missed her, had longed to come home, had been eager to hold her in his arms again? Instead there had been clipped sentences, a tired, emotionless voice.

They had supper, all together, and Michael seemed cheerful if absent-minded, Nina cheerful while anxious. That night she could not sleep, and the dawn found her awake, in tears. She wiped her skin dry, fingers cautious. Beside her, he lay asleep, breath heavy and punctuated by a slight whistle. He was on his side, his back to her. She watched the wide shoulders move almost imperceptibly with his breathing.

She could see a grey light slip through the corridor between the heavy blue curtains. As if from a great distance, she heard cars, the first calling birds.

She blinked: everything was the same. The same cream-coloured walls; the same blue chintz curtains; the same white quilted bedspread bunched at her feet. The world around her was just as she had always known it. Yet she could not silence the doubts that rose, indistinct, yet real.

Nothing had happened, nothing had been said, no one had been found wanting: she repeated the words slowly, like a prayer to be memorised. The same expression filled the face that had hung above her, reddening with effort, during the lovemaking she had initiated out of a sudden desperate need to hold him; his eyes had narrowed when he kissed the corner of her mouth, in the same way, as always; his sudden, half-stifled cry had been the one she had heard a thousand times before. Even now, as she lay in bed, amid the sounds from the street below, she could not determine what had fuelled her anxiety. Again she cast about her mind as if it were a darkened room, trying to bring up to the light of memory images of her husband. But nothing held the answer she sought, and she could only lie back helpless, in the dawn light that today seemed to hold a vague menace, feeling as if he were bobbing about in some strange new waters, out of her reach.

Michael stirred, gave a low moan. Nina waited, tense, for him to wake: she would ask him, then, ask . . . but what? She had no questions for him, only a thousand protestations of love.

'Michael,' she whispered.

She studied the smooth skin, the curls that formed golden commas and parentheses upon his neck. This love informs everything I do, she thought. I am as I am because of him. This is the centre of my whole world – I am completely at his mercy. And she shuddered, and silently pressed against him as if he could fit into the crescent of her smaller body.

## Chapter Twelve

Michael leaned back in his chair and studied Alexander Connaught across the lunch table: he was handsome, all right, a Rowing Blue type who looked remarkably youthful (a quality, Michael thought enviously, suggested and confirmed by a resplendent head of hair, unblemished by an incipient bald patch). He was urbane, at ease, and spoke with the right accent: the Old Etonian self-confidence seemed to survive the pious asceticism of his ministry, and indeed polish it like the countless spinsters who rubbed the church brass to earn their vicar's praise. But was this enough to account for the devotion he inspired in Lady Katherine, Tom Sutton and now, he could see, Johnny Stephenson, former lush now fervent Christian?

Michael's cool eyes moved slowly around the surface of the vicar's face. Look at him casting his spell upon the unsuspecting rich folk. Sweet voice, a look of concern, a few encouraging words – clever, clever man. Michael chewed the fish that he was sure Lady Katherine's cook had sweated over all morning. He wasn't crazy about the sauce (something Thai, no doubt) and for a moment wished for the old days, when the upper classes only served beef, two veg and potatoes – all over-cooked but wonderfully filling. This new-fangled 'foodism' irritated him. He looked around the round white table, with its imposing silver candelabra, impressive flowers, Imperial china: no wonder the Stephensons felt they could indulge in taking care of their souls, everything else was in perfect shape. How comfortable could this man of God feel spending his time among these wealthy people? Though he supposed the Reverend could always hide behind the parable of the camel and the eye of the needle . . .

Michael almost pulled a face: he had little patience with these pious preachers who kept cropping up everywhere these days, mouthing mumbo-jumbo about the millennium, or thumping their Bibles with talk of the Good Society and the Kingdom of Heaven here on earth. And they all seemed linked to this man's Renewal Movement and to its political wing, Tom Sutton's Christian Coalition. Yet it could not be denied that politicians like Sutton, who paraded their moral qualifications at every opportunity and who had previously been mocked for their attachment to old-fashioned values, were suddenly popular.

He took another sip of his wine – a pity that he couldn't drink properly today, he needed to unwind after these mad two months at the helm – but whenever he was with the Stephensons he felt he needed to be on guard. He scoured the table: lunch here was usually a far more glittering occasion, but today, as Lady Katherine had explained when she'd invited him a week ago, it was 'just family'. He should be grateful to be considered family, he supposed. He stole a quick glance at his hosts, exchanging a comment across the table: they gave every evidence of liking him so far. And he would do his damnedest to keep them happy. He meant to enjoy his success for many more years.

The *Sunday Herald* was his and he loved it, loved walking in and seeing the guards downstairs resist the temptation to stand to attention, loved the way his secretary Amy guarded his precious time like a miniature and pretty Cerberus, barking in her deep, scratched smoker's voice, 'The editor is in a meeting right now. Would you like to leave a message?' The editor. He stepped into the newsroom from his glass-enclosed office, amid wide windows that showed the spires, glass and lights of the city across the river and, superimposed upon it, the reflected fast-moving bodies, the bright green computer screens, the overhead fluorescent strips, the desks and revolving chairs. He breathed in the air in that large, noisy space and felt as if a hand had been removed from his nose and mouth. Now he was free, now he was liberated from the plotting, the disappointment and the nervous waiting. He was afraid he would break into a grin as former colleagues approached him with an expression that carefully cloaked jealousy while overemphasising their eagerness to collaborate. Old enemies, former competitors: he felt immensely well disposed towards them all now that he had the prize.

Philip Stephenson had finished telling one of his jokes, and Michael, though he hadn't heard it, roared with laughter, and saw Lady Katherine thank him with a wink of complicity. Oh, yes, they doted on him, he thought, and the pleasure mingled with the wine to warm him. He'd be a fool to upset them for a fleeting fling: Lady K had made no secret of her dedication to the puritanical teachings of her spiritual mentor. If he ever gave in to the temptation before him he risked discovery, scandal, a spectacular fall from grace.

99

He stole a quick look in Allegra's direction: she sat, shy and nervous, between Philip and Johnny Stephenson. As always she struck him as vulnerable, her small dark head to one side as if waiting for someone to say what she should do next. Every uncertain gesture, every faltering sentence seemed a plea for protection: 'Take care of me,' her blue eyes seemed to beg, as they rested on him when he approached her desk in the newsroom.

Oh, yes, the temptation was there all right: she was so open in her admiration for him, her need for his support, he found it difficult to resist. But, of course, resist he must.

He looked down the table at Nina, across from Allegra. She sat straight-backed and head held high, intent on listening to what Alexander Connaught was saying. She looked beautiful today, with her hair up and her face slightly flushed from the wine and the heat of this room. She was looking at the vicar with dark eyes wide, her mouth still. He felt a thrill of pride that she was his: he always knew that others admired, and slightly feared, this wife of his. His parents still treated her with the circumspection they employed with those of his colleagues they recognised from bylines or photographs. Victor was still so dazzled by her that Michael almost felt sorry for him when he saw his friend's eyes following Nina around a room.

He smiled despite himself: extraordinary Nina. Sometimes, as he marvelled at her strength and her flawless management of their smooth life, he felt as if he were once again the young boy growing up in Henley who constantly copied and ran after his best friend David. Michael had been always a step or two behind, always a point or two below, and David had always pretended not to notice. Michael could remember vividly their first visit to the sea-shore, on their bicycles: when David arrived at the bend from which the sea could be seen he turned on his bicycle and said nothing, so as not to spoil his friend's pleasure in that first sighting.

They were close until David won his scholarship to Cambridge, and Michael went to Oxford. During their vacs it was quite clear to Michael that he no longer enjoyed occupying second place – even in David's world. He had grown weary of being constantly if unwittingly reminded of his friend's superiority.

Again he looked down the table at his wife. Nina, whom no one would ever dare betray – least of all him. And he bit into a still crunchy carrot with only a tinge of regret.

*

As Lady Katherine passed the wine across to Michael, she intercepted the look of adoration that young Allegra Worth cast him. Inwardly she thrilled: she had suspected it all along. Michel Lewis was too pleased with life these days to think that any one woman could satisfy him. Then she thought of how this was just the kind of scandal that would unravel all her good work for Alexander's mission, and her expression grew serious. It wouldn't do for the editor of one of their papers to be shown to belong to the old amoral world the Renewal Movement was trying to overthrow. She would warn him, let Michael know that she suspected: if he were having an affair he would, she had no doubt, immediately leave Allegra. Ambition did not take second place in Michael Lewis's life.

'Darling, pass me the bread, will you?' she asked her son.

Johnny passed her the bread basket, then turned back to listen to Alexander's exchange with Nina Lewis. Lady Katherine issued a small sigh of happiness. Could anyone have predicted such a transformation? Johnny had stopped drinking and sought Alexander every day, attending services at St Mark's, always showing up at meetings of the Circle. He was, she could see, as besotted with Alexander as she herself was. Her mentor seemed calm, unflustered by the devotion of his newest disciple – by now, she supposed, he must be used to saving people's souls and earning their eternal gratitude. She knew he had high hopes that Johnny, grounded in his new-found faith, and with the support of the Circle (and in particular of little Allegra, whom he often visited for a gospel study session) would be able to banish the devil drink.

Though, of course, what if Allegra really was involved with Michael Lewis? What would Alexander do to one of his flock who strayed?

Lady Katherine shot him a look as he bent to hear something Nina Lewis was saying. Alexander was a strict disciplinarian as well as a loving protector – a benevolent dictator, she thought with a smile. He had made it clear to the young people who formed the Circle that sin should be confessed and also punished. Time, he stressed, was pressing: the millennium loomed and the shiny new world had to be constructed. Those who halted its progress must pay the consequences of their actions. Powerful stuff that probably inflamed these impressionable youngsters. Alexander himself had confessed to her that some among his younger members were too eager to mete out punishment. She looked past Michael Lewis at her son: Johnny would do anything for his mentor, of that she was certain.

*

'It looks as if Tom Sutton might become Shadow Home Secretary in the reshuffle,' Philip Stephenson told Nina as he lit a cigarette between courses. 'He's more and more popular outside his constituency and some of his moral high-ground speeches have been soul-stirring stuff.'

She fastened her attentive eyes on him: his heavy, wine-reddened face, the short-cropped white hair, the drooping eyes. 'There's been such a tide turning on these moral issues.' Stephenson's voice boomed across the table, demanding an audience, so that his wife had to stop serving the salad, Allegra passing the vinaigrette, and Johnny's hand trembled even more as he poured water into his glass with the maximum of care and the minimium of noise. 'I think there's quite a few readers you can pick up, Michael, if you give them more from the pulpit thumpers.'

Nina looked around the table at the familiar faces. Beyond the profusion of white lilies that formed a graceful fountain at the very centre, she looked at her hostess, in her grey-green dress, kohl-lined eyes fixed on the young vicar. She looked at Johnny Stephenson across from her, who sat, composed, calm, a thinner version of the unkempt young man she had seen receive Alexander's healing. She noted that he drank only water, and though his hand trembled as he held up his glass, his features had been almost restored. His eyes moved only from Alexander's face to look at Allegra Worth beside him.

Still nodding and replying to her host's monologue, Nina looked at Allegra who sat, listening without speaking, a polite little girl impressed by her elders and betters. The black undulating hair half covered one eye and emphasised the impression of shy modesty. The blue, almost violet eyes, dark-fringed, flitted from person to person as they spoke, without engaging with anyone in particular. A mole at the corner of the right eyebrow seemd to elongate the dark arch.

'I read with pleasure your column last week about the renaissance of self-improvement courses.' Alexander was speaking in a low voice to Nina beside him. 'I found it very interesting because, of course, self-improvement has always been regarded as dangerous to community welfare – as if by improving the individual we are somehow taking from the community. No one seems to remember that we are to love our neighbours "as ourselves".' He stressed the two words with his voice. 'I find it so surprising that until our Renewal Movement inspired the Christian Coalition no one seemed to point out that a fully realised self is not selfish, and that a good community could not be run by the wholly selfless.'

'Hmm. Yes.' Nina nodded. 'Though it must be said that in most people's minds self-improvement is allied to climbing up the career ladder rather than perfecting their understanding of gospel living.'

'Of course. In many cases, though, I would argue, the Spirit has leavened the people sufficiently for them to see their spiritual life as part of their existence, not something marginalised from their daily activities. And just as they long to change their work, their position, their attitudes, they are ready now to change their spiritual life. They heed the words we read of in Mark – "The right time has come! The Kingdom of God is here! Change yourselves completely!"' Here he dropped his voice to a low, soft tone, and Nina found herself drawing closer to him to hear.

'The right time has truly come. With the year 2000 what more significant threshold could we cross?'

'Ah. Of course. So you mix the millenarian fears and the spirit of change and what you get is a Renewal Movement that can attract the superstitious, the New Ager, the born-again Christian . . . a perfect catch-all, in fact.' Her sarcasm was palpable, and she almost regretted it as she saw him blush slightly.

'My Movement may not offer the answer that you seek, but I imagine that you pose the same questions about how to reform our world. How do we get men and women to remember that rights come with responsibilities, that another's life is not in our hands but in Jesus Christ's, that neither father nor mother can make a child and then walk away from them? I imagine that you place a value on the very same things I do.'

Nina nodded, distracted, her eyes on Michael. Dear God, what is wrong, what is wrong? Why can I not shake off this feeling of unease, this sensation of loss?

Nina remembered when Robbie, too young to talk, would cry in his cradle. She would lift him in her arms and gently probe, with her fingers, every part of his body, searching for the hurt. And now again she probed, looking for the source of this nameless unhappiness, seeking out the pain that would yield the reason for her anxiety about Michael. A few nights late at the office, an absent-minded air, the long periods between love-making – she knew the warnings, and for these months since his promotion, she had watched the tell-tale signs collect, a threatening stockpiling of weapons.

Was he, could he be, having an affair? And her mother's face superimposed itself upon Alexander's, so that for a moment Nina wanted to shout accusations at the kind round face: her confession had transformed Nina's world into a dark undergrowth where treachery and lust tangled their branches to obscure all light.

'Mrs Lewis . . . Nina . . .?'

Nina checked herself. She swallowed hard, took a sip of water, turned her face to the young man.

'You saw, when you came last month to witness the Circle, how eager the young people were. They are thirsty for the words of God. They long for the beauty and the horrors, the passion and – yes – even the hatred shared by the true believers. They have no time for the anodyne religion of yore, a church with cotton-wool walls that insulated it from the people.'

'The beauty and the horrors . . .' Nina murmured, and winced at the memory of the loud music and inane expressions of the congregation collected beneath the salmon-pink ceiling of St Mark's.

It was as if Alexander guessed her thought. 'You see, I need to attract them with warmth and to engage them in . . . some form of collective rite, even if it means employing, well, what you might regard as banal means. When they raise their voices in song together, bow their heads in prayer together, it makes them feel they belong to a new world with a great new vision.' He wasn't touching his food, but looking at her so intently Nina had to turn away. 'And the word has spread. The young are so enthusiastic . . . They are determined to fight against lies and empty words. They want no part in our society. They want to build a new world.' His hands made a broad gesture as if to contain that new world.

Nina nodded, then saw their hostess watching them: her blue eyes were clouded, and it suddenly occurred to Nina that Lady Katherine was jealous of the attention Alexander was bestowing upon her. She did not wish to incur Lady Katherine's wrath and, with a smile at Allegra, forced the younger woman to join in the conversation. 'Have you ever set foot in St Mark's, Allegra?'

'Yes' the voice was low, unsure, 'I . . . attend service regularly,' but the eyes remained resolutely downcast, as if fearful of meeting Nina's gaze.

Alexander nodded in confirmation. 'Yes, Allegra takes part regularly in the Circle . . . or at least did, before the *Sunday Herald* replaced St Mark's in her affections . . .' He smiled benevolently at the young woman, who had lowered her head to hide the blush that now covered her face and throat. 'Allegra has become a diarist on your husband's paper. She said it was a humble start, but she seems to be going off to all corners of the island – Bath one day, Liverpool the next.'

'Really,' Nina murmured, as she slowly considered his words and their meaning.

'Your husband is a hard taskmaster, I fear,' continued the sweet, soft voice.

Nina repeated his words in her head while a sequence of images filled her: Michael's late nights at the office; Michael's new indifference; Michael's aloofness after the Liverpool trip. She felt fear slip its hand around her own, drag her from this table into an empty room where she began howling her suspicion. Michael was betraying her, Michael was cheating her with this false little woman before her. Nina swayed in her chair, took hold of the table with both hands to steady herself. Slowly she stood up; quietly she excused herself to Philip Stephenson. She crossed the room, climbed the stairs and locked herself in the bathroom. She turned on the light and immediately the great mirror above the basin shone with her face and figure. With a cry, she switched off the offending image, and pressed her back against the wall, embracing herself as if she were freezing. 'You can't be sure,' she repeated to herself. 'Be sensible. For eight years you have been happy together, for eight years he has been faithful, honest.'

She was shaking, her head bowed as if she were facing punishment. She could not go on like this. Why was she allowing herself this fit of jealousy? Why did a business trip have to involve a betrayal? And why had she found him guilty of an affair just because he'd failed to mention that Allegra had gone up with his team? Surely, in a group of colleagues, she would be the one he would have most easily overlooked and then forgotten? She was trying him at a kangaroo court where sitting in judgement were her basest instincts, her darkest fears, her most secret suspicions.

If she were sensible and level-headed, she would recognise that his erratic, suspicious behaviour was nothing but commitment to the new job. A job he had aimed for all their life together. Wasn't it true that her anxiety had grown since his editorship? Of course it was. She must put a stop to these strange, irrational fears . . . Michael loved her, loved Robbie: nothing would go amiss in the perfect world circumscribed by their three linked, loving figures. All would be well.

Nina approached the white porcelain basin. She turned on the cold water, let it splash onto her right wrist, watched the water flow.

'All will be well,' she told herself, aloud in the dark.

*

'Lunch almost doesn't feel like a proper meal when it's not followed by a pudding, does it?' Lady Katherine gave a little sigh: she wanted to remind Alexander of her Lenten sacrifice. But the vicar took no notice, a look of concern on his face as his eyes remained fixed on Nina Lewis, who had regained her seat. 'Let's move into the drawing room for the coffee, shall we?' Lady Katherine threw down her folded napkin and stood up. She led her guests through to the pink room.

Michael and Philip immediately sat on the sofa, discussing the *Herald*'s position on Sutton and his ilk. Johnny took a seat on the sofa facing them, and struck her as thin and pale against the profusion of coloured silk flowers. She watched Allegra sit beside Johnny, and Nina wander towards the windows where Alexander soon joined her. Lady Katherine checked her impulse to interrupt their *tête-à-tête*: she must play the good hostess.

She saw Johnny smile at something Allegra was saying, and for a moment Alexander was eclipsed by the two young people before her: it would do Johnny so much good to become involved with a nice young girl, and unless Allegra really was seeing Michael Lewis, who better for her son than a fellow member of the Circle who had a bit of a life outside the group and St Mark's?

Liu now appeared with the tray of coffee cups and saucers. She brought them to the low wooden table between the sofa where Johnny and Allegra sat and the one opposite, where Michael and Philip continued their conversation, already shrouded in Philip's cigarette smoke.

Lady Katherine approached the tray, began to pour the coffee. 'Thank you, Liu,' she whispered to the disappearing tiny figure in black. 'Allegra.' She smiled as she handed over the cup and saucer.

'The thing is, you seem to be doing very well as it is so we must not rock the boat,' Philip, body crumpled against the sofa, was saying to Michael.

'Well . . . I don't know about that.' Michael ran a hand through his blond hair, pretending humility.

'Oh, Michael, it's true.' Allegra was blushing as she spoke, her fervent admiration for her editor ringing in her tone. Lady Katherine served the men.

'And tell us, Allegra,' Philip teased, 'what is the atmosphere like in the newsroom – do they like him?' His drooping dark eyes studied the young woman with amusement.

'Oh, yes, everyone likes Michael,' Allegra enthused, then suddenly embarrassed, she looked down. 'He's very . . . very professional.'

'Well, at least we know you have one fan!' laughed Philip.

'Don't be so silly, Philip,' Lady Katherine admonished him as she sat down next to her son – neither Nina nor Alexander had wanted coffee. 'Allegra is just saying what Michael is too modest to tell us.'

She smiled at Michael, then at Allegra. She studied the young figure in her simple navy blue dress, suede feet neatly placed next to one another, like the gloves in her own top drawer. Oh, she was in love all right – and dangerous. She knew how to buff and polish the man's ego, how to take a step back at all times as if the better to admire; and she didn't mind looking slightly foolish and naive if this was necessary for his greater glory.

Lady Katherine drew a sigh, sank her gaze into the sugary black liquid in her cup. Perhaps she should be warning poor, unsuspecting Nina: a woman's woman probably would, sitting her down with a cup of strong tea in the kitchen, all motherly wisdom, sisterly concern. But Lady Katherine preferred to give a wide berth to that emotional marketplace where women exchanged secrets, bartering with one another to gain greater intimacy. She disliked the confessional atmosphere that lingered over women's friendship, feared the baring of souls that made for claims and betrayals. And she suspected Nina Lewis felt the same way.

'You are all right?' Alexander touched Nina's elbow.

'Yes . . . of course.' But as she stared at the wet grey garden framed by heavy curtains, beyond the french window, she wanted only to be at home, away from here, burying her face in Robbie's curls, listening to her son and her parents describe their day together.

'You know, if ever you should need me, I'm always at St Mark's. I won't try to convert you, don't worry.' He smiled. 'I just want you to know that, should you need to talk, my doors are always open.'

Nina stared at the vicar: he was uncanny, with his sixth sense, knowing exactly when to strike with his profession of compassion. It was as if he had stood beside her in silent witness as she had voiced her fears and reassurances in the dark bathroom upstairs. Nina nodded, more out of politeness than conviction. 'Yes,' she whispered. And then, smiling into the clear eyes, 'Yes.'

# Chapter Thirteen

The morning her father was taken to hospital, Nina was trying to write her weekly column for Clive while preparing the vegetable soup for supper. She sat at her desk in her apron, half listening to the bubbling from the great pot.

'Darling?' Marina's voice had come over the telephone in a little sob.

'Yes?' But she knew immediately.

'It's Papa. He's had a heart attack. I'm at the Chelsea and Westminster Hospital,' and Marina's voice broke.

'How is he?' Nina slipped unnoticed into the hospital room, to stand beside her mother at the foot of the bed. Marina lay crumpled in the chair, like a small tear-soaked handkerchief. Nina felt her heart thump beneath her raincoat, beneath the wool of her dress. Her father lay immobile, grey-faced, eyes shut, with clear tubes springing from his chest and arms leading from his seemingly lifeless form to the machine that, like a monstrous guardian angel of steel, stood beside his bed. Nina felt the tears rise to her eyes and blinked them away. Marina did not turn her face from her husband's thin grey form, merely raised a hand to be clasped. Nina took her mother's cold hand into her own. She could not speak and felt fear – weighty, dark, clammy – fill every corner of her insides. Nina stared at the extraordinary stillness that wrapped her father's figure, at his furrowed brow, at the shadowed lids. Silently, she whispered her plea, Dear God, spare him, please, please spare my father . . . Beside her, her mother bowed head and body.

Nina raised her head, with her eyes slowly swept the hospital room. It was square, whitewashed by a strip of ceiling lights; a grey curtain separated her father's bed from the one where a middle-aged man sat up, free of the tubes that seemed to chain Paolo's body. The man, pensively chewing some grapes, nodded at Nina, then gave her a quizzical smile. Nina looked down and saw that her apron strings were trailing on the floor. Slowly, silently, she took off her raincoat, her apron, placed everything on the window-sill where her mother's black jacket had been cast. She pulled a chair towards the bed, sat down and placed her hand upon her mother's knee. 'What . . . when . . .?'

'He was complaining of a tingling sensation in his left arm all day yesterday. I didn't worry until today, when he said he felt as if there were some oppressive weight against his heart. I begged him to ring Dr Sands, but you know how stubborn he can get. And then, just two hours ago, he had terrible pains, and just – just turned white. Oh, Nina . . .' Marina wept.

Nina wrapped her arm around the frail, hunched shoulders. 'He'll pull through, Mamma, don't worry.'

She stole another look at her father as he lay back against the white pillows.

A male nurse padded in to take Paolo's temperature: both women stared at him, apprehensive, anxious, watching his every move and expression as if it were a thermometer that could register their beloved Paolo's progress. 'He's doing well. The temperature is down to normal, and the blood pressure's fine.' The nurse buried both hands in his pockets, as he had seen the doctors do on their rounds of the ward, and cast a long look at the monitor that hung over the bed. 'Heart's all right – none of those big peaks and troughs we had before.' He spoke in a low, soothing voice that had calmed a thousand relatives, a thousand friends, before them. He had a wide, pleasant face, handsomely taut between Slavic cheekbones. His slightly slanted eyes filled with soft concern as they now rested upon Marina. 'Can I bring you anything – a cup of coffee, water?'

Marina merely shook her head. Nina looked over her mother at the young nurse. 'I'm here, don't worry. I'll take care of her.' And she clasped her mother's hands in her own, so that they disappeared.

'Oh, Nina,' Marina sobbed, and laid her head upon her daughter's shoulder, and Nina wrapped her arms round her mother's seated figure, rocking gently back and forth, all the while wondering at this extraordinary reversal of their roles: Nina offering her mother a maternal protective embrace into which Marina slipped, childlike in her greedy need for comfort. Nina rocked gently, remembering Robbie as he had lain thus in her arms when, a few years ago, he had been afraid of the dark; when, a few weeks ago, his classmates had taunted and teased him into heartbroken weeping. 'God, please help us, please help us,' she murmured. 'Spare him, dear God, spare him.'

But suddenly as she stroked her mother's figure, she felt a stab of resentment: did her mother now realise what she had risked losing? Couldn't her mother see how much she cared for her husband? She must, she must give up Luke.

Nina now looked away from her mother's head, away from her father's grey face. She focused on the man sitting up in his bed to her right, his thick-set figure, serene and beatifically smiling as it lay back against the pillows. She saw him peel a grape he chose from the bowl at his side, then pop it skinless into his mouth. The card hanging from his bed-post proclaimed him to be a Mr S. Tyler.

Paolo stirred, left leg bending slightly. He whispered, 'Mamma,' and stretched out his hand over the coverlet, where it trembled. Marina reached out her hand to his. At her touch, Paolo opened his eyes and Nina almost gasped: the desire, curiosity, ambition and arrogance, usually struggling within Paolo for supremacy, had been spent. The eyes rested upon her mother, then turned slowly to her: dull, faint, unresponsive. He drew them shut again, as if life were a book whose pages no longer held any interest for this man, once its most avid scholar.

'Marina . . .' he whispered now, eyes closed. 'Marina.'

Nina watched her mother draw close to the inert figure, so that her forehead almost touched his, and her hands propped her up by pressing down on the white sheet. 'Yes, my darling, I'm here.'

Paolo's eyes opened once more and Nina began to weep because she read there his fear. But Marina smiled her familiar warm smile, and laid a gentle hand upon her husband's furrowed brow. 'Shall I wipe your forehead with a nice cool cloth?'

And before Paolo could answer, she was standing up, folding the washcloth into a small square and holding it under the jug of water from which she now poured a few careful drops. Gently she placed the cloth upon her husband's forehead, eliciting his murmur of approval.

Nina looked on, but said nothing. Now Paolo stared at his daughter from beneath the wet white cloth, looking like one of the war wounded he had described seeing during his visits to his own father in an Italian hospital. 'Nina . . . you too . . . here . . .' He motioned her to draw closer. 'Thank you.' His eyes, still weak, sought hers.

'Papa, you must get better. We want you to get strong again.'

Marina took the cloth from Paolo's forehead. She held up the empty jug. 'I'll fill it in the corridor.'

'Nina . . . if I should die, promise me you'll take care of her.' His hand clutched her own, and the brown eyes shone, suddenly feverish. 'She has no defence against the world . . . She wouldn't survive.'

'Papa, don't talk like that.' Nina heard herself sob. 'I can't bear to hear you speak as if . . . as if . . .'

But Paolo looked beyond her. 'I've been careless with her. I loved her in the best way I could – but I know it wasn't enough for her . . . I couldn't blame her for trying to find happiness elsewhere . . .'

He closed his eyes, and before she could reply, she sensed her mother's return. She watched Marina replace the jug at the foot of the bed, then stretch the coverlet, tuck the sheet beneath the mattress, smooth out wrinkles on the pillowcase, fussing and murmuring as if the hospital ward were a guest room at home.

Marina squeezed her daughter's hand and motioned that they should move back to the chairs at the foot of the bed. They sat side by side, watching in silence as the suddenly frail figure drew sharp short breaths, eyes firmly shut. Nina studied the small hand in her own, then again the grey head against the pillow, the tall body that seemed embalmed in the hospital coverlet. Everything seemed to tremble around her: with her father lying helpless here, his words and her knowledge of Marina's betrayal, her world, once so well ordered and rooted in certainties, was being shaken, a rattle in a cruel child's hand. She filled with a sudden terror of an existence whose course she could no longer determine.

Beside her, Marina dropped her head. 'Where will I be without him?' She hunched forward, and her head seemed to bob up and down with the strangled sobs.

'Mamma, please . . .' Nina stretched her arm to embrace her mother once more.

But Marina pushed her away. 'You don't understand. You have a life of your own, separate from Michael's. You are someone. Who am I? I'm his wife, I'm your mother . . . but nothing else.' The words tumbled forth, rolling into one another. 'Every other life I could have led, every other role – I gave up for him, for you. You've left me and now he may leave me too.' And her mother buried her face in her hands.

Nina crouched at her feet, embracing her and murmuring, 'Mamma . . . Mamma . . .' like the mantra it had always been.

Paolo remained in a critical condition for five days. Nina visited daily. Always, at his bedside, sat her mother, immovable, indefatigable, eyes red with grief. She would hold onto the large hand, and silently stroke its long fingers, age spots, palm. Paolo lay inert, silent, as if wrapped in a strange film of fear and helplessness that insulated him from the women.

Propped up against his white pillow, the silent Mr Tyler peeled his grapes and looked on benevolently, smiling every now and then at the two women.

Nina would drive from home to hospital, shuttling from her warm domestic haven to this cold room that with its fluorescent lights seemed to bleach the life from her father and Mr Tyler.

Michael, throughout, was attentive, supportive: he left her the car to drive back and forth from the hospital, cooked supper for Robbie, rang the hospital each day for progress reports. With her inarticulate anxiety about her husband supplanted by the very real fear for her father's life, Nina basked in Michael's kindness and her heart filled with sympathy for her mother, who risked losing a similar love.

Then, one night, she drove home earlier than usual from the hospital and had to park the car in the next street. She walked in the January darkness towards her home, head heavy with fatigue and worry. She noticed a car parked at the end of their road, two figures seated side by side. Suddenly a car door opened and in that instant light she recognised Michael and Allegra, facing one another. Michael stepped out of the car, began to walk towards the house. The car remained immobile. Then Michael turned and ran back. Nina watched her husband open the car door, sit beside Allegra again, then wrap his arms around her. The two figures remained perfectly still, lit up inside the car. Nina stood transfixed. He loved this woman. She saw it in the tender embrace, saw it in the expression of his face caught in the light shed by the open door. She did not stir. She did not move when Michael made his way again back home; did not move when Allegra, after a few minutes, drove off. She remained standing on the pavement, while despair rocked her world as if it were a dried-up nest of fragile happiness.

With her gaze she followed Michael as he approached their home. She watched him switch on the lights – first in the hallway, then in the drawing room, finally in their bedroom. She knew, without seeing, that Robbie was now rushing up to him, boasting about his father to the temporary au pair she had hired to cover for her hospital visits. Now Michael would loosen his tie, run a large hand through his hair. He would be calling out, even if she hadn't appeared yet, 'What about a

112

nice stiff drink, then?' and pouring himself a whisky. She knew he would check his watch for the television news, then switch on the radio, moving about in his lazy, self-confident way. She knew his every step, his every gesture. 'Michael,' she whispered, 'Michael.'

It began to rain. Along the road, cars drove past her, their searchlights fixed upon her coated figure. She could hear the windshield wipers move back and forth, hear the wind that was swelling the trees. The night air hung heavy, filled with the promise of a storm. The wind stole into her coat, began to loosen her hair, whispering all the while. She drew herself up, wrapping her arms around herself protectively, as if to avoid a lecherous man's unwanted attentions. Slowly she walked home, the rain slipping down her coat collar, into her shoes, dampening the wool of her coat. Michael greeted her with a drink. She listened to Robbie's school tales, smiled at Michael's outrage over the gas bill, and paid the au pair. She heard herself chatter pleasantly, saw herself pour a glass of wine as she joined Michael at the table once Robbie was in bed. She felt herself climb the stairs, slip off her clothes, lie on her side in the bed while she waited for him.

When she opened her eyes the next morning, for a moment she remembered nothing and began to plan her day as usual. Then, dread engulfed her. She found herself unable to get up and lay on her side in the bed from which he had rushed – at six, hours before he usually woke up. She brought up her knees to her breasts, and allowed the fear to seep into every part of her. She saw Allegra's face, Michael's face, Michael's golden head bend close to Allegra. Had this kiss been the overture to, or the seal of, their love? Her head filled with snatches of their conversation, their whispers, visions of two figures entwined. She felt as if she were in danger of losing her balance and slipping for ever into a harsh new world.

Outside, she could hear a neighbour start his car, children call out to one another and, right against the window, a bird burst into song. She marvelled at life going on, unchanged, oblivious to her misery. Through the wall behind her, she now heard Robbie cough, turn in his bed: she must not allow him to see her like this. She tried to concentrate on Robbie, tried to pull him into the centre of her thoughts. Slowly, she sat up, pushing down her hand against the mattress, feeling weak, almost ill. Pain filled her head, her bones, her skin. With an effort she focused on her son next door: she pulled herself up, took her bathrobe from the back of the door where it hung. Downstairs, she began to prepare breakfast: she arranged the cereal and milk neatly upon the table. Automatically she began to make the coffee, her movements slow.

'Mummy . . .' Robbie stood before her, barefoot and without spectacles, right fist rubbing his eye.

Nina bent to wrap her arms around his thin little frame. 'Good morning.' She tried to smile, overcoming the heaviness within.

'Bad dream . . .' Robbie moaned.

Nina buried her face in his blue and white striped pyjamas, in the warm, sweet smell of him. Behind her the coffee gurgled.

'But now you've woken up, and it will be a lovely day, you'll see.' She kissed his cheek. 'Go and sit down, and have your cereal. I'll make the toast.'

Without thinking she picked up the espresso maker from the stove. The handle slid from her fingers, and she sent the machine crashing to the floor. Coffee splashed everywhere, collected in a puddle at her feet, steaming. 'Damn!' she shouted. 'Damn!' Suddenly she burst into tears, her body rocking with pain. From his chair, Robbie watched her, worried face half hidden by his bowl of cereal.

Nina crouched by the coffee that covered the white and black tiles. She placed one hand on the floor, and stared blindly at the brown liquid. 'Mummy!' Robbie flew from his chair, rushed at her crouching figure, wrapped his arms around her neck. But Nina did not move, and the sobs spilled forth, dry and harsh.

'It hurts, it hurts, it hurts,' she moaned, shaking her head while her son's warm arms clasped her throat. Robbie began to cry, scared by her anguish. With a wrench, Nina pulled herself up, her maternal instinct stirred: she could not let go like this, she must look after him. She dried her face with her bathrobe, cast him a weak smile. 'I'm sorry, my darling, it was just that the coffee maker burned my fingers.'

Robbie stared up at her, tears still glistening upon his pale cheeks. Nina took him up in her arms and pressed her lips against his forehead. 'I'm sorry, darling, I'm sorry to have frightened you like that.' Robbie smiled, still uncertain.

She watched him eat breakfast in silence, while her head pounded with fearful images as she mopped up the floor. When he had left for school, she tried to dress herself for the hospital, but with every move she began to weep and was forced to sit, her eyes blinded, her breathing frantic through the sobs. She did not dare stand up, in this room where

114

everything seemed to shift around her, changeable, mutable – treacherous. She buried her face in her hands, feeling almost dizzy with her own disorientation. Michael's love, the fixed point in her life, had disappeared.

## Chapter Fourteen

Allegra wished she hadn't opened the door but she had been so certain that it was Michael that she had not even checked through the entryphone. When she'd seen Johnny's large head coming up the stairs she had stifled a gasp of disappointment and now, as he sat awkwardly before her, she was terrified lest Michael arrive with Johnny still here. It usually took him forty minutes from Canary Wharf, but perhaps the traffic was bad or he'd been delayed at the paper. Michael, Michael . . . She repeated the name secretly, and felt like a little girl who steals sips from a grown-up's glass and grows deliciously tipsy. The longing had been with her since this morning, when Katie had told her she was on duty at the hospital until midnight. Immediately, she had done her calculations: it was Saturday, he'd be working late, he could be here for an hour without raising suspicions at home . . .

Johnny sat stiffly on the very edge of the yellow flowered armchair beneath the poster of Van Gogh's sunflowers, fingers leafing through some magazine he wasn't reading, legs stretching out then bunching up again beneath him.

'You've missed the last three sessions and I didn't even see you last Sunday. What's happening?' He was staring down at the pages before him, reddening as he spoke.

'It's work.' Allegra sat on the shabby two-seat sofa, back erect, wearing a prim, expressionless face. On the coffee table sat St Mark's parish newsletter – Katie had brought it back last Sunday, placing it under her nose with a look of reproof.

She tried not to stare with hatred at Johnny's brown head bowed over the magazine, his slightly trembling hands, his newly thin body. Out, she wanted him out, so that she could enjoy these rare precious moments when Katie was away and Michael could free himself.

She felt herself so tense she thought she would burst before him, pull him from his armchair, push him out of the door. He sat there, a lump of accusations, a stern-faced judge ready to pass sentence on her, without even knowing, as yet, what sin she was guilty of.

For a moment, the excitement of Michael's imminent arrival gave way to the empty darkness of guilt. Oh, she didn't need Johnny Stephenson's recriminations to remind her of what she was doing: she had turned her back on Jesus Christ, on Alexander, on the Circle. She was sleeping with a married man, a man whose vows bound him to another, a man who had a child . . . From that first night, when he'd stopped his car as he gave her a ride home and took her face in his hands, kissing her without pause; from that first night, when he'd shamefacedly led her into a hotel room on the Gloucester Road and made love to her while she clung to him weeping, she had watched the large dark shadows gather over her. Yet she could keep the anguish at bay by concentrating on him, anticipating their moments together or reliving their passion. Her existence had become a Morse code of dots of contentment, dashes of unhappy dread, spelling out a wordless message that only he must hear.

Over the past month, she had dreaded her mother's phone calls (every Sunday, and sometimes in the middle of the week as well), with her innocent questions about the newsroom, the young people at the Circle, the discreet probing about any particular young men. She hated lying to her mother. And she hated lying to Alexander. She now avoided St Mark's, and kept away from the Circle. Alexander had rung her and written her a note, but she had pleaded work, ill-health, fatigue, a whole list of lies that had filled her with shame and left him unconvinced. Sometimes, she would wake up in the middle of the night, overwhelmed by the need to confess to her spiritual adviser: he had been, after all, the first person to show her kindness and extend a welcome to her when she'd arrived in this city. But as she lay, anxious and lonely, across her bed, the visions of the vicar's fearful wrath, his accusing eyes, his thundering warnings of divine retribution, melted her resolve. She would never have the strength to confront his righteous anger, nor would she ever find the courage to leave Michael, as she knew Alexander would demand of her. And so she had kept away, avoiding Johnny's phone messages and Katie's silent disapproval (although she didn't know about Michael, her flat-mate had sensed that a new relationship was keeping Allegra from her usual friends and worship).

'You're seeing someone, is that it?' Johnny's eyes probed hers, his expression sullen, his voice dead.

'No.' Allegra wondered at the ease with which she could now lie: like a woman recently initiated into motherhood, she had discovered unexpected strengths while gaining a new and terrible vulnerability. 'I am simply so under stress. I need a little bit of time to adjust to this new job on the Diary.'

'But you know that it is only through the Holy Spirit that you grow in strength and energy. It is with Jesus beside you that you reach your destination. But if you stay away you'll get lost, Allegra.'

Allegra stood up to avoid those watery blue eyes. She pulled down the blinds, kept her back to him as she spoke. 'You know that I love coming to St Mark's. I'm coming tomorrow. It's just that the Circle right now is a bit difficult for me to get to.'

She didn't realise he had stood up to join her at the window until, with a start, she felt his breath on her hair. 'And what about me, Allegra? I need you there. I need you to help me stay on the right track – remember how you used to read the Gospel to me? You said that I could come to you whenever I was in need.' His breath was hot, his voice low and pleading.

Allegra wanted to recoil from him, but she turned slowly and shook her head gently. 'I am always here for you, as you see.' She made a gesture as if to show him the room, where she stood at his disposal. 'I have not forgotten my friends,' she said, in a sombre voice that rang with conviction. Again she wondered at her own new-found duplicity, at her extraordinary capacity for deception. She thrilled at it, then sank again into shame when he spoke of Alexander.

'He is so worried about you – it was his idea that I should come and find you. Allegra, you must beware, there are many out there who would wish to lead us – any one of us – astray. When Satan comes for us, he knows to don handsome features and show pretty manners. That's how he leads us into temptation . . . I fear that you may be too innocent to recognise him for what he is.'

'And you are not?' she whispered, eyes cold.

'Unlike you I have not led a sheltered life.' Here his face twisted in a grimace so sour she looked away, lest it poison her happiness. 'Think of what I told you about my earliest memories . . . my mother, those men she saw . . . I've experienced Satan's wiles well enough to recognise when someone is being lured into his trap.'

Allegra turned around: his face was so close to hers that the breath she took smelt of him. She took a step back, so that her body pressed against the window's blind. 'I . . . I think you're getting carried away, Johnny. I haven't attracted Satan's interest, don't worry.' Quickly she regained her seat on the sofa, stealing a look at her watch.

'Do you remember what Alexander said at the very first Circle I attended? That we should look after one another, make sure that our brethren in Christ are not in danger of falling? I could never forgive myself if I didn't fulfil my duty and obligation towards you – or any other member of the Circle.'

'Darling Johnny.' She wanted him gone, away from her, and decided to adopt a lighter tone, to jolly him out of his suspicions. 'I'm so grateful, really I am. But you mustn't read so much into my absences. Anyway I'll be there tomorrow, you'll see, in the very first row.'

But the young man stood unmoving. 'Why don't we go tonight to St Mark's? A prayer, a few hymns, you know how you always said that you felt safe there –'

'No!' she burst out, impatient, and nervous now that Michael would buzz at any moment. She was on her feet again, hands clasped. 'Please, Johnny.' She drew close to him, eyes wide and beseeching, fighting her instinct to push him away. She adjusted his collar over his jumper, saw him flush at her touch. 'I'm going out and I've got to change now.'

'Who are you going out with?'

'Oh, you don't need to worry, a girlfriend.' She smiled coquettishly, spoke lightly. 'But honestly, I'm late as it is, and if I arrive after the curtain's gone up . . .' She patted his arm, then rushed to the coat hanger and pulled down his coat. 'Off you go, there's a good boy, and save me a place beside you tomorrow.'

He shot her a look sharp with suspicion, but Allegra was now in a frenzy of excitement. Michael would be here, they'd make love, she'd lie in his arms and whisper endearments. 'Bye-bye.' She pushed Johnny towards the corridor, her eyes shiny and her cheeks pink. The moment the door closed behind him she rushed to her room, where before the small round mirror on her chest of drawers she began adjusting her hair and applying a new coat of lipstick. 'Michael, Michael, Michael,' she repeated to her image in the mirror.

Michael pulled up a few hundred yards from Allegra's shabby block of flats: it wouldn't do to park right in front. It was freezing tonight, and as he rushed along the pavement he pulled up his coat collar to his ears and hoped she'd have some wine or a gin and tonic for him. Though in that flat he was more likely to get a thimbleful of sherry – the holy roller she lived with led a terrifyingly Spartan lifestyle. Allegra did, too, he supposed – until now, of course. He felt a pang of guilt – she was such an innocent, really – at the surprisingly easy seduction he had initiated in a car and sealed on a brown coverlet in a hotel room above a casino. Poor Allegra. It was because she had been so needy, so unsure of herself, that he'd taken her up to the disinfectant-smelling, weakly lit room. Afterwards she had wept about her evil sin – she, too, he had noted to his exasperation, belonged to the group Alexander Connaught had gathered round himself – and confessed her love for him while he had cursed under his breath at the scratch she had left on his shoulder: a thin tiny redness that shouldn't give Nina a second thought, but still . . . Allegra had been properly grateful, of course, that her editor had found her worth entangling with; she had been sweetly clinging since, her adoring eyes following him around the newsroom. He didn't think anyone had guessed at work – and at home he was careful not to arouse Nina's suspicions by staying away too late or too often at the paper. But you could never be too sure, and Nina was clever enough to smell trouble from miles away. He set his jaw with renewed determination: he must pay his wife more attention, must try to arrange some family outing. It was when they didn't think they were getting enough of your attention that wives began suspecting infidelity.

He walked quickly, growing excited at the prospect of Allegra splayed beneath him on the bed. He was, he thought with some degree of satisfaction, her hero, and in this admiration he found the courage to continue their secret meetings. Indeed, her obvious infatuation fuelled his desire far more than her young slim body or her dark blue eyes. He loved the way she saw him rather than the way she looked, was more interested in the way she interpreted him than in anything she said. He recognised that he had no wish to get to know her better. Though he wanted to ensure that she was happy, and to protect her from others' harm, he didn't want to share her thoughts or understand her motives. This was very different from how he had felt during his courtship of Nina, when he had wished to be in sole possession of Nina del Monte's every thought and sensation.

Memories of Nina at Oxford were jolted from his mind: was that Johnny Stephenson walking slowly on the other side of the road, staring at him? With one hand, Michael held his collar tight around his face, and ducked his head, pace quickening: all he needed was for Lady K to find out, and that would be it. When he reached Allegra's front door he turned: the figure he suspected of being Johnny Stephenson was crossing the road, looking right and left, and Michael felt suddenly vulnerable – he was still within sight. He hurried past Allegra's door, walked aimlessly for a few minutes and then retraced his steps. Better safe than sorry.

'Did Johnny Stephenson come to see you just now?' he asked her, as she pressed her whole body against him when he walked through the door.

'Yes, yes,' she murmured, as she kissed his eyes, his lips, holding him tight in an embrace that bent him down to her eye-level.

'I hope he didn't recognise me.' Michael unclasped her hands behind his neck and walked to the window. He moved the blinds from the pane, and tried to peer through the crack into the darkness below; he couldn't see a thing. He turned back to her and smiled despite himself: how young she looked, and how overcome with emotion. 'Come here.' He opened his arms, voice low with desire. She rushed into his arms, and he lifted her clear off the floor, relishing this sensation of power that Nina – so tall, so statuesque – had never afforded him. He took her into the bedroom, where she kept moaning his name while he rushed to pull off her clothes. Suddenly the telephone rang beside them.

'Damn!' Michael snapped crossly: he was midway through removing his trousers and felt foolish at the sight of his naked thighs and the blue corduroy bunching at the knees.

'Shouldn't I . . .?' Allegra asked timorously, while her lover sat on the bed and awkwardly pulled up his trousers. She lay naked and quivering on the rumpled duvet.

'Yes, pick it up.' He wouldn't look at her.

Allegra stretched out her thin white arm, picked up the telephone. 'Hello.' She tried to regulate her breathing. No one answered, but in the silence at the other end of the line she could feel a presence. She gave a small shudder and hung up. She sat up beside Michael, and gently unbuttoned his shirt, fingers caressing the white chest that, little by little, emerged through the pinstripes. 'It was a wrong number,' she whispered as he began again to remove his trousers.

But after their lovemaking, when Michael had showered, dressed, and left her with a quick kiss on the lips, the telephone rang again.

'Hello?' Even as she spoke, she knew who would answer.

'I saw Michael Lewis going into your flat. And then leave again an hour later. You're lying, Allegra. You're a hypocrite and you're leading someone into adultery. You'll be punished, Allegra.'

She said nothing, her hand turning clammy around the receiver. She waited for him to continue, but he'd hung up. She sat, stunned and terrified, in the dark bedroom where only a few minutes before she had cried with pleasure.

## Chapter Fifteen

Nina watched, passive, while life, like an evil Penelope, secretly unravelled her every patient stitch. Soon nothing would be left of her familiar world, only markings upon the cloth she had so lovingly embroidered.

There is nothing I can do. She repeated the words and filled with panic. She could not confront him. The thought of watching him blanch or look away, shifty-eyed, of hearing his lies or evasions, of his losing his temper – this horrified her. Keep still, she ordered herself every day, keep your own counsel. Within this self-imposed restraint, her wretchedness swelled till it lay so heavy upon her she thought she could no longer breathe or move.

Throughout, she watched him like a wary sentinel, alert to every sign of danger. She would listen for his waking yawn, feel his stretching limbs beside her and draw her lips into a smile, preparing words of false cheer. She heard herself greet him, felt her body rise from their bed, move to the kitchen to prepare him and Robbie breakfast. She moved about the cool white and blue kitchen with heavy, slow steps, her gestures constrained as if by an invisible rope.

When Robbie had left for school and Michael for the paper, she allowed herself to slump into an armchair and view once more Michael and Allegra, their profiles lit up by the yellow light of the car. Once more she saw him walk away, then return to embrace Allegra. She would sit, bent over, arms crossed on her knees and see the scene again and again. She would follow his day's schedule with her mind. Would he engineer a meeting with Allegra? Did his secretary Amy know? Did the whole newsroom gossip about their boss's liaison? Her head throbbed with questions and she tormented herself with fearful answers. When she was alone in the house, she would spend hours going through his desk, his cupboard, his chest of drawers. She unlocked every drawer of the battered Victorian desk that sat in a corner of the drawing room, green leather top fading in the window's sunlight. She would take out sheaves of papers, piles of envelopes, sift through each, again and again: one perusal could not suffice. She would pull open his cupboard drawer and push through the suits that hung there, leafing through them. Her frantic hands would burrow into those cotton, linen or wool pockets, reach into the inner lining, the trousers, the sleeves, seeking she knew not what proof. Sometimes one particular suit or jacket would suddenly yield Michael's odour and she would bury her head in that empty fabric shaped like Michael and weep. She would hold her breath while she carried out her search and feel her heart beat hard as she brought to light a garage ticket, or a receipt from the deli near the *Herald* offices. She never found any clue to Allegra.

Fatigue filled her: when she tried to tidy up the house, she felt as if she had to sculpt every action and every step from some enormous heavy rock.

The telephone would ring during the day, but she merely listened to the messages – Victor, her mother, Sophie, Clive – on the answering machine, motionless. She fled others: no one must ever know, no one must ever see her prey to this helpless fear. She must not allow the revelation that she – the much-envied, the much-admired Nina Lewis – had been rejected. She fled her own reflection in the gilt-framed mirror that hung over the fireplace: she had come to hate the body that Michael had turned from, the face that no longer inspired his caress. She hated her hands when she caught sight of their pale, translucent skin, hated the dark strands of hair that sometimes loosened from the hair-clip with which she pulled them back, hated her feet in their neat shoes, her body that filled clothes she had bought to please him. She wanted nothing to do with these reminders of her failure. But she forced herself to dress for him still, to brush her hair and keep it neatly up, to bathe each evening and wear her scent: she feared that otherwise he would guess her discovery.

Only with difficulty could she remember her father's illness; when she did, she filled with panic: whom could she turn to now? She realised, to her shame, that she'd begun to regard her father's heart attack as yet another act of betrayal.

She began to divide the day into different parcels of time. Mornings were difficult. Always, awakening brought habitual pleasure in the light that seeped through the pale bedroom curtains: as yet unformed, filmy sensations filled her with well-being – 'I am alive to another day' – and then she was stunned by the violent blow of the realisation that always followed: Michael no longer loves me.

The breakfast hour was easier: it brought the three of them together and forced her into familiar activity, allowing no time for doubt or sorrow as she re-enacted their morning ritual.

The hours in the day lay heavy, suspect, hardly ever yielding anything but torment. Sometimes she could spend the entire day slumped in her armchair, weeping till the afternoon shadows swallowed her drawing room and she would rise, painfully, to tidy the house for Robbie's return.

Only her column for the *Society*, which took up her Mondays and Tuesdays, could free her from the unhappiness that held her. She would push herself onto the chair at her desk, pile the newspaper cuttings she had culled over the weekend on her right, and take up her pen. Here, among newsprint and ink and paper, she could order the world again, organise her responses and discern a logic that her own life had lost.

The worst hour came in the evening, delivered by the grandfather clock that swung its heavy brass pendulum. What if, tonight, he stayed away? What if, tonight, he did not come home? She would watch the pendulum swing and feel herself grow faint, almost nauseous with the fear that tonight he would stay with Allegra. 'Please, God,' she would murmur, straining to hear his footsteps, his key in the lock, 'dear God, please bring him home to me.'

She felt as if, physically, she had shrunk. She looked down at her limbs and knew she had lost weight. Even her stature seemed diminished. Every object, in this her beloved home, seemed to loom, threatening, over her, towering above her till she was reduced to a ground-crawling creature of insignificance. The curtains, the cupboards, even the mirror took on a new terrifying dimension. Vulnerable in her new stature, she moved about with circumspect step, every gesture as deliberate as if she inhabited a foreign landscape. At night, though, at night he was hers. She would let him fall asleep – 'Fatigue and nerves are no aphrodisiac, darling,' he would murmur, when he planted his half-ashamed kiss upon her cheek before turning over – and then she would begin her watch.

'Michael,' she would whisper into the darkness, turning towards the slumbering figure that stretched, at arm's length. She felt the tears cover her face as she reached for him, fingers light and tentative. She would caress the broad pyjama back, caress the curve of the shoulder, the collar where her fingers found soft curls. 'Michael, come back . . . come back.' She would listen to the heavy breathing that was so regular and felt love liquefying, overflowing.

A thousand memories floated in that dark space between them: Michael as he stood, defiant, by the bicycles he had chained together; Michael weeping at Robbie's birth; Michael humouring Paolo; Michael praising her to Clive . . .

'I'll wait. I'll wait,' she assured him.

At Easter, Robbie's school holidays meant he stayed at home with her. His presence – his dark innocent eyes, his happy hugs because he didn't have to go to school for weeks – forced her out of the passivity into which she had slipped. Instead, anger now came. It was sudden, like an unexpected guest who arrives late but takes over your whole house. It swamped her and left her powerless as she watched it crash into her prized self-possession, destroy her precious instinct for forgiveness, overturn her patience.

She would not accept her loss or his betrayal; would not silently, passively stand by as Allegra took possession of him. As she sat in their bedroom at night, waiting for him, she repeated these resolutions to herself, polished them with her silent resentment, sharpened them with concentrated fury, and found comfort in this secret gearing for battle. The unhappiness she had felt before had hollowed out her life, pulled away certainties and stripped her of hope; but this new anger filled her, like a strong, full-bodied wine that made her slightly dizzy and gave her the illusion that she could still prevail. She began to consider everyone in her life in relation to Michael's betrayal: she viewed her mother once again with resentment – had she not betrayed, as Michael had?; her friends with suspicion – had they known all along, the Victors, Clives, Sophies, had they colluded with her husband?; even Paolo drew her anger, because it had been through his enthusiastic support that Allegra had entered their world.

During the rest of the Easter holidays, spent at home because of Michael's job rather than on one of those short happy trips to Italy or France that they had enjoyed in the past, the anger kept her awake, late into the night, like a sinister intermittent sound. How much further can I go on before I erupt? How much longer before he comes into my bed bearing marks of their love-making? How much longer before he calls me by her name, or I stumble into a lie that exposes everything, and am forced to confront him?

Michael, her enemy, took his place beside Michael, her husband. She began to marshal her weapons against him: Clive, Piers (the editor of the *Daily Herald*), even Victor became arms in her campaign to damage him. She would invent criticisms they levied against his ability or his intellect; she made up rumours about conspiracies to take over his stewardship of the *Sunday Herald*. In a thousand different ways, she tried to undermine him, and studied him for his reaction – a frown, a rebuttal, an offended look. It was as if the man whom before she could touch with a smile or a look could now only be reached by inflicting pain. Her father, whom illness and prolonged convalescence were keeping from his habitual social rounds, became a perfect weapon in her private war. He became her stooped and slightly limping Mercury, conveying warnings to Michael which she carefully planted in him. 'I'm worried about Michael,' she would confide in her father during one of her visits. 'Apparently Philip Stephenson thinks the paper is failing to pick up in circulation. He's getting edgy, and there are a number of talented young contenders for the editorship . . .' She could be certain that her father, so eager to show off his inside knowledge would soon repeat the message, unconsciously exaggerating it in the process; she could be certain that pride would keep Michael from checking its veracity, and stoke his fear of failure. 'I understand that the trust wants Michael to adopt a more supportive tone when it comes to the Renewal Movement – Lady Katherine's been complaining that he's half-baked in his enthusiasm for her cause . . .'

Sometimes, in the middle of the day, she would stop in her tracks and realise that she could hardly recognise herself. Who was this liar, this vengeful, calculating woman? Was this the same woman who had loved and protected and supported Michael for ten years? She could not believe how easy it was to wish him ill, or to plot for retaliation. Evil sat comfortably inside her, a relaxed and eager passenger who looked forward to a journey to a place at once foreign and familiar. Her great fear was now coming true: her will to rein in her instincts had been replaced by her desire to mete out her own justice.

She would study Michael when he came home, into their bedroom: large, slightly fatigued eyes skating over her as he talked and undressed. She would watch him sit at the edge of their bed and with a clumsy pull and tug remove his shirt and tie; she would watch his throat, strong and wide and pink framed by blond curls; his spectacles that, in reflecting the overhead light, seemed to deflect her own gaze. She studied his forearm, the right one, that he leaned out of the car window: lightly tanned, showing a white wristwatch mark whenever he undressed. She watched the way his stomach filled his striped shirt and then the blue wool of the jumper he always wore. She noticed the new patch, at the back of his head, where the hair had thinned to betray a pink scalp. She listened to his effortless way with lies.

'Sorry I'm late – we were sitting about the newsroom howling with laughter at a piece Victor's just filed for us. Unbelievably funny – mocking the Renewal Movement. His caricature of the hairshirted vicar had me practically in tears.' He stretched, head slightly turned back, arms reaching high up as if to grab at everything. 'Though, of course, I had to turn it down, as I had to turn down his excellent portrait of Luke Aldridge last month. Who can afford to anger Lady Katherine?'

'Oh, I don't know.' She chose her words carefully, studied him for their effect. 'Even sacred cows can afford to have their tails pulled a bit, can't they?' She shot him a look. 'I think what your trustees really care about is actions – what people do, especially, of course, their employees. You can imagine the rumpus if anyone should be caught in a scandal when the Stephensons and their gang have been mouthing pieties on behalf of Alexander Connaught!' She was accompanying him down the stairs. They had not touched since his arrival.

'Well,' he grinned at her as he uncorked a wine bottle, 'you may have a point. Though it does seem a bit harsh, when Lady Katherine at least has done it all . . .'

'Yes, like St Augustine she is all the more fervent in her virtue for having sinned so greatly.'

Mechanically she searched for two glasses, set them before him. They stood in the white and blue kitchen, facing one another. 'You must be careful, darling.' She stripped the word of emotion. 'They say she means to screen every appointment at the *Herald* to ensure that the place is purged of the less than virtuous.' Her serious dark gaze fastened onto him, and she watched him flinch. 'I think the kindest thing you can do at this point is to warn those among the hacks who . . . enjoy questionable lifestyles.' She sipped the wine slowly, watching her husband, flushed and flustered, lapse into silence.

Nina thrilled at the success of her calculation: she had helped make Michael who he was, now she could threaten to bring him down. For he would fear a scandal above all else – not the exposure as an adulterer, but the stripping of his powers, his demotion.

# Chapter Sixteen

'It's getting worse. It's three months now that my post is full of green-ink letters of accusations, threats and – to my mind at least – anti-semitic slurs . . .' Victor stood at the stove, stirring the white sauce, while beside him, Nina poured out two glasses of wine. Rows of dark aubergines sprinkled with salt lined the white ceramic dish on her kitchen counter. 'All this because of that comment piece I wrote for the *Recorder* last month.' He continued to stir while she handed him a glass. He cast her a wry smile. 'A piece your husband commissioned but didn't dare publish, let me stress.'

She heard the shadow of bitterness in his voice and issued a half-hearted defence of Michael's decision. 'Well, it was a bit strident, wasn't it? "Religion of apprehension" and the "rise of the Christian ayatollahs".'

'So, because I dissent from their views these wild-eyed fanatics are allowed to wage a campaign of intimidation against me? They are allowed to keep me awake at night, worried for my children's welfare? They are allowed to send me vile threats like "Death to the unbeliever"? Honestly, Nina, you're not going to defend their guerrilla warfare as faith, are you?'

'Well . . .' She was surprised by her own lack of interest in his difficulties – it was as if she were too engrossed in her own woes to accommodate his. She had avoided him for weeks and watched him warily, with his elbow-patched arms, the tousled greying hair, brows furrowed in concentration, as he re-enacted their routine. He had pleaded with her for this lunch, and in the end she had agreed – though almost ungraciously, for it went against her better instinct: she didn't want him prying, didn't want to register a pitying look on his familiar face. And she didn't trust herself to keep him at bay – he knew her so well.

'Anyway, I don't believe you support them. You're just provoking me. Otherwise, you wouldn't have written such a lukewarm column about that vicar Alexander Connaught. And your column last week – it was practically mocking their sacrosanct MP Tom Sutton.'

'I don't like Sutton, he's a one-issue politician and I think a lot of the arguments he makes are simplistic. It's all very well to say we should always choose life over death, but the choices are usually more complicated. Still,' she sipped her wine and watched him over the glass, 'the Renewal appeals, Victor, you can't deny it. It even appeals to me. I'm fed up, like so many others, with this indifference to moral obligations, this wilful ignorance of duty and responsibilities. They've struck at the right time – they're harnessing our disappointment with slipshod morality.' She was surprised at her own conviction. It was true. When she thought of Michael's betrayal, the ease with which it had been perpetrated, her certainty that many would condone it as 'an adventure', her suspicion that some might even have connived at keeping her in the dark about this secret adulterous tryst, she felt as if her allegiance had shifted. Where before, those who, like Alexander Connaught and his Renewal Movement, had thundered against lax morals, had struck her as simplistic, now that very simplicity seemed to her infinitely appealing.

'Listen,' Victor turned to her, wooden spoon raised in one hand, 'they aren't just a pocket of pious parishioners in Tunbridge Wells. I've been trawling through the regionals and what I've discovered will make your hair stand on end.' He took a sip from his glass, set it down beside hers. 'Item: at a young people's rally in Portsmouth last Wednesday, seventeen young men were pushed onto the stage and publicly confessed to the "sin of fornication". Whereupon their vicar presented them with a rod with which each, in turn, flogged himself, and then publicly repented.'

'What?' Nina set down her wine.

'There's worse. Item: in a churchyard in Leeds a bonfire was made last week in which a hundred books were burned by locals who were chanting prayers as they piled them upon the logs. Item: a congregation in Manchester stood for three hours as one after the other they queued to pledge to their vicar that they would sin no more and – get this! – would inform the community of anyone who broke this pledge.' He shot her a triumphant look. 'Is this what you wish for us?'

He turned back to the stove. Slowly he poured the sauce over the aubergines, then grated Parmesan upon the white concotion, carefully distributing the cheese up and down the white mounds that rose from the dish.

There was no sun, and afternoon shadows wrapped the blue and white kitchen, colouring Victor in sombre tones.

'Yes, it all sounds excessive. But that's not what Alexander and his Renewal Movement are about – not, at least, what I saw and heard. He spoke of our need to return to old-fashioned moral values. Back to virtue, order, discipline, respect for others, for the sacred. They offer rules where we have had none. And most of us find comfort in being told what to do.'

'Hand me the oregano.'

Nina smiled, scoured the neat rows of spices, herbs and condiments that lined her kitchen cabinet. Her fingers ran lightly upon the glass jars, touched now this tin now that: here, all was as it should be. She gave him the jar of oregano.

'You can't possibly believe this is proper, Nina.'

'Perhaps I do. Don't we all seek something, or Someone, that can ensure some modicum of fairness, some degree of justice?'

'But surely this God of theirs offers neither?' he huffed impatiently at her, all the while putting the finishing touches – a flick of butter, a dash of pepper – on his concoction. 'If my reading of those articles is correct, those who fall outside the fold, or stray from it, risk punishment by their vengeful, forbidding God – who, may I point out, looks very much like the cruel Yahweh your Jesus was supposed to have delivered us from.'

Nina watched him push the casserole dish into the oven, then retrieve his glass and frown at her over its rim.

'Oh, you are exasperating! I give up!' He raised his arms high up, spilling a few drops of wine from the glass he held. They both laughed, but she felt that a new self-consciousness had crept between them and taken up its vigilant position beneath their gaze, eagerly awaiting the chance to bound up and drag either one away from this suddenly fragile friendship. Victor slipped the dish into the oven. 'About fifteen minutes.'

They moved to the kitchen table where they sat across from one another, in the grey light shed by a sunless sky. She had not set the table yet, and she rested her arms on the bare dull wood that stretched between them. Victor sipped his wine then leaned across the table, face animated. 'I want you to meet Luke Aldridge. I've been in touch with him since that profile. We've been planning a series of conferences, writing articles – pulling the wool off people's eyes about this Movement. We've even got plans for a protest march.'

130

Nina was surprised into silence: surprised that he had kept from her something so obviously important to him, that her mother's great love should now be allied to her own great friend, that he exhibited a vigorous conviction, an enthusiasm of which she thought him no longer capable. She studied him now. It was true: this new campaign had transformed him. His eyes shone, the melancholy that had so often stolen upon his features had given way to a new energy, a determination to move, to do, to speak. He looked years younger.

She watched him and suddenly she wanted to throw her arms around him, bury her head in his chest. She wasn't sure whether she sought the caresses and kisses that her husband was cheating her of, or revenge, by giving herself to his best friend. She needed him now, she thought bitterly. Why couldn't he see that, in her misery, she needed the pledges of devotion, the offers of comfort – yes, even the admissions of desire – he had shown her before? Yet, after all these years, he seemed uninterested in Nina, preoccupied with something wholly separate from her, and she felt the regret seep into her.

'You seem galvanised into a whole new life.' She tried to smile as she touched his sleeve that lay upon the tabletop.

Victor seemed unaware of her touch. 'Nina, he's a fabulous speaker, a fantastic old man. Promise me you'll come and meet him.'

'Hm.' She checked her watch. 'Your fifteen minutes are up.'

He rose and she followed him to the oven, then suddenly as he bent to retrieve his dish, she laid her hand on his back. 'Victor,' she spoke the name firmly, the overture to an important request, 'I've been such a fool . . .'

He stood up and cast her an amused glance. 'It's all right, Nina, plenty of others have fallen for the Reverend's litany.' He had misunderstood her, but she didn't correct him. He bent again to withdraw the aubergines from the oven – burning his thumb in the process – and continued to unfurl his fears of Renewal plots. 'If Michael doesn't watch her, I'm sure Lady Katherine will start censoring his articles. I think my own humble offering was a case in point.' Nina began to set the table, moving slowly, her eyes fixed on her china and cutlery. She didn't want to draw too close to any subject that might lead him to discuss Michael. She brought the dish of aubergines to the table, and spooned him a helping, smiling brightly. 'Let's see if you've retained your culinary skills through this conversion.'

131

'Well,' he laughed, as he unfolded his napkin with a flourish, 'it seems to me you're the one undergoing the great conversion.'

Unusually, she walked him home that afternoon: it was as if she sought his presence to the last. As she walked from his house through the cool grey April day, her thoughts now slipping from the anxiety she felt about Michael into the regret about Victor, she felt herself pulled down to the very depths of her unhappiness: it was as if she had fallen into icy black waters and was thrashing about, desperately trying to regain her footing.

In the damp greyness she walked by the river, past the row of houseboats that bobbed on the water and the sequence of bridges that, with their pastel-coloured arches, seemed magical rather than real. She walked past the Stephensons' house and its canopied entrance, and past dozens of similar houses that stretched, tall and red-bricked, along the Embankment. The air hung limp about her, offering no comfort. The gulls called out in the darkening afternoon, and their cries swung in great arches overhead. She walked slowly, almost welcoming the chill that entered her bones, as if only through this sharp, unpleasant sensation could she remember that she was alive. Otherwise, all seemed a grey numbness, like the strangely passive mourning with which an unexpected death is first greeted.

Death . . . Sometimes she allowed herself to picture Michael's ashen face, listen to the sobs his guilt would certainly tear from him. Would her death break him, shatter his world, or simply free him of obligations he had sought to forget? But before she could follow these thoughts, Robbie's face came before her and her whole heart and body contracted with the longing to protect him from any hardship. Her son. She saw him stand at the window in his room, blowing a rondo of steam upon the window-pane. She saw him stretch on tiptoe, small finger drawing upon the glass. What was he drawing? Was he trying to create a special view of his own, as if to see another world? How much did he know of his parents' strange, secret enmity? Did he understand the words no one spoke, guess at the recriminations, defences and pleas? Robbie wandered around the house softly and muted, a footstep on a rain-sodden field. He held his head down, fearful, it seemed, of drawing his parents' attention. At times, Nina would find him sitting at his desk, hand propping up his tilted head, pen immobile but still clutched in his hand. At other times, he would steal covert glances at her as she sat beside him at the kitchen table where increasingly the two were alone, Michael having rushed off in the morning or being delayed in the evening. Sometimes, every part of him seemed to strain to understand or comfort, and she could see him tense, his face taut in expectation or fear. Even when she wrapped her arms around him, buried her face in his dark, sweet-smelling hair, she knew he was not reassured.

'Tell me a story,' he pleaded at night, as she put him to bed. He rolled onto his side, face towards her, eyes shut.

'Once upon a time . . .' she began, unfolding the fairy tales of her own childhood. Robbie breathed evenly, forehead now smooth. She spoke softly, studying the dark head shining in the glow of the bedside lamp, the curved arm that disappeared beneath the pillow propping his face. She studied the crescent shape of his body, half covered by the blue duvet's folds. He had never been fearful of sleep. Yet now, night after night, he sought her story-telling, urging her to continue at every pause, opening his dark eyes when she drew breath, as if frightened that she would stop. When she finished the tales, she could see he was still awake, troubled by unspoken worries, as obvious a testament to unhappiness as an unconscious sigh.

Nina walked on slowly, head bent, and registered neither passers-by nor buildings until a hand touched her shoulder. She spun round, almost frightened, to meet Alexander Connaught's smile. 'Nina Lewis. I thought I recognised you.'

'Hello.' She was so taken aback that the word faltered, uncertain, as if it were a question rather than a greeting.

'May I accompany you?' He adjusted his longer gait to hers.

'Of course.' They walked in silence through the damp air. Nina stole a look at the flawless profile beside her and wondered what she should say to this strange being in his clerical clothes. But he seemed content merely to stroll with her through the Chelsea streets, walking on the side of the road, like a well-brought-up young man.

When they arrived in front of the pillars between which stretched the long winding driveway that led to St Mark's, Alexander stopped and took one of her hands in his. He smiled down at Nina. 'I've been reading your pieces in the *Society*. I admire them very much. You write with great passion when it comes to issues of right and wrong – few columnists do. I just wanted to tell you how very impressed I've been.' He bowed slightly over her hand, then looked up and met her surprised gaze. 'If ever I can be of use to you, let me know.' He retreated down the driveway.

Nina stood still, unsure of what to do. She wanted to follow him into the church and beg admission to his world: he seemed so genuine, so serene, so far removed from the sordid world that she had been dragged into – first by her mother's revelation, now by Michael's betrayal.

She shook her head, quickly moved away, as if frightened that he might return to claim her.

How ridiculous, she chided herself as she walked on without looking up. A handsome man of God gives you a few words of praise and you are ready to forget the chilling stories Victor told you this afternoon, forget the fanatical gleam you saw in the eyes of his congregation, forget your own reservations about his evangelical millenarian vision.

Yet from that chance encounter, she began to seek out Alexander. She, who in her distress had not thought to enter her own parish church to light a candle, began slipping into that wide, ever-bright, salmon-coloured house of worship where she had first seen him. She would come in the afternoon, almost shamefaced, and sit in the row of capable chairs that lined the back wall. Eyes lowered, she would listen to the elderly women who in their long tweed skirts proceeded in quick little steps from one corner of the church to the next, whispering his name all the while, 'Alexander . . . Alexander . . .' The first days, she did not see him and sat, impatient, wishing him to appear. Then on the fourth day of her secret pilgrimage, she found him conversing with one of the frail women. He saw her, came towards her, smiling. 'I knew you'd come,' he said softly. 'Do you . . . do you want to come downstairs? There's no one in the office, we could talk without . . . without being overheard.'

She followed him meekly down the stone stairs, into a dimly lit crypt that was more cellar than office, with its low arched ceiling. 'You seem – so worried, so unhappy . . .' He held out a chair for her while he himself sat humbly at her feet, on the bottom step. Nina didn't respond. He sat so close to her, eyes raised to hers, that she could see his body tense as it leaned forward. She had to remind herself that she didn't really believe in what he sought, did not wish to follow him in his path of virtue. She only wanted to be in his presence to soak in that extraordinary, shiny certainty. She wanted to hear his ringing tones denounce the fickle world outside that was Michael's world. She wanted to see him raise his fist against the corrupt non-believers. She wanted him to wage her war for her.

'You are troubled,' he whispered, coaxing the confession from her.

Nina hung her head. 'Yes. My husband . . . He is seeing – someone else . . .' she spoke the words slowly, lingering over consonants and vowels, indulging in their sound as if they would in this way be impressed upon the air between them and never disappear, witnesses to Michael's guilt. 'It's . . . it's all so disgusting and banal. You must come across it a thousand times from a thousand housewives.' Her voice was so low the vicar had to lean closer to hear her, 'But it's my life, my world, and it's come crashing down around me.' She felt the tears, but did not move to wipe them away. She wanted him to see her at her weakest, so that he would know what she expected of him.

Alexander made a move as if to touch her, then rose and walked away towards the bookcase. He stood with his back to her. 'How dare he? How dare he?'

Nina looked up, 'Help me . . .'

He turned. 'You are an extraordinary woman and I shall help you in every way I can.' He drew to her once more, clasped her hands, raised one almost to his lips, then lowered it again.

'You will find it comforting to come here, I think. At times like these we need to be in a quiet place, far from those voices that shout their evil nonsense. I shall tell my assistants to leave you in peace when they see you. And I'm always here for you. I want you to pray, Nina, in whatever words you have been taught. Remember that, as you make your way, if you can fix your eyes on one point, you won't get lost.'

She looked at him, slightly disappointed by his rhetoric. She wanted to urge him not to speak, not to ruin the effect he had had on her. She looked down at her hands, his captives. 'I am so grateful to you,' she whispered. 'I'll come back.' She slipped from his grasp, and moved away, up the stairs.

As she walked home her heart pounded and her breath was sharp, uneven. For the first time since her discovery of Michael's betrayal, she felt a warmth steal over her that felt like the prelude to contentment.

## Chapter Seventeen

Did she suspect? She had given no sign if she did. But why should she suspect? She was too certain of his love, too confident that no one could possibly leave her, Nina Lewis, née del Monte, the beautiful, the talented, the perfect wife. And, of course, she was right: how could he ever leave her? It was almost midday, bright-skied and cold, and Michael had decided they would walk to Holland Park. Paolo and Marina had invited them to lunch.

'It's so beautiful out,' he'd said at breakfast, in the new jolly voice that guilt forced him to adopt with them, 'and we can walk through the park. It will be a treat for Robbie.'

The three of them had set off, Michael trying to walk between wife and son. But Robbie wilfully hung back, clutching his mother's hand, gaze fleeing his father's. It was as if he knew, Michael thought, with a sudden stab of guilt. He walked on the pavement that stretched almost deserted in the sun, and listened to their soft footfall behind him. Please, God, no, he thought, even his unbeliever's heart moved to prayer, don't let me have ruined everything. He had been so foolish – coming home too late, trying to pull a counterfeit absent-mindedness over his very real juggling of a thousand commitments. He must stop this nonsense, or all would be lost.

Michael looked up as he walked, at the black ridges of the rooftops, the grey squat columns of chimney stacks, the fragile limbs of tall trees: all sharply outlined, distinct edges, solid certainty. Hope stirred inside him: in this light, his guilt – towards his family, towards Allegra – grew dim, faded, called into question by the contrast provided by this startling bright day.

Still, it was difficult not to feel guilty about poor Allegra. She was being persecuted by the foul Johnny Stephenson – she'd shown him the pile of threatening letters. They struck him as so sick, with their scriptural warnings and foamings at the mouth, he'd almost wanted to call in the police himself. But, of course, that would really cause

136

scandal: with the present cast of characters – married Michael, a pretty girl, not to mention a Stephenson – it would end up splattered on the front page of every other newspaper. In the end he had advised her not to do anything, but he'd felt a coward as he'd watched her large blue eyes shed their terrified tears. He sighed: it was strange how this little thing who'd once made him feel omnipotent, so great and good, should now make him feel terrible about himself. He was forever denying her pleasure, turning his back on her needs, disappointing her. And he felt at once ashamed of his failure to make her happy and of the relationship between them. It was as if the space that he occupied with Allegra were an unmade bed, no longer fresh and inviting. He already almost preferred the Michael he was to Nina – a none-too-perfect, somewhat wanting specimen – to the cruel, frustrating one he had become with Allegra.

It was, quite simply, time to put a stop to it. Everyone in the newsroom now knew, and even though Michael had merely shrugged his shoulders and made a few jokes about his irresistible magnetism, it wouldn't do for the gossip to reach the Stephensons. He would wrap it up as soon as he decently could without doing untold damage to the poor girl's heart. He almost shook his head at the thought: of course she would be upset and wretched, but he could not, would not risk destroying his precious, smooth-running existence for a young, pretty, slightly uninteresting girl.

He wasn't really looking forward to lunch: usually he found Paolo entertaining as he bored on about some ridiculous abstruse topic while Nina and Marina exchanged glances, eyes rolling, and ignored him. But today he felt ill at ease at the prospect of his wife's parents, devoted and blissful after forty years of matrimony, welcoming a man whose betrayal they were unaware of. He doubted there would be anyone else, as Paolo was still frail and being carefully monitored on a diet of heart-sinking strictness. They might, of course, invite Victor and Hannah, who were practically family. That might prove difficult: he was pretty sure Victor thought something was up. He had shot Michael a couple of probing looks and the other day he had actually turned to him over drinks, when Nina had been in the kitchen with Hannah: 'Why is Nina so restless these days? Something's the matter – I hope it's nothing to do with you, my friend, or I'd feel duty-bound to give you a real talking to. You cannot have a treasure such as this one in your keeping – and no, I don't mean your blessed paper – without being accountable to her admirers.'

Michael, who had wanted to confide in Victor at the outset of this ridiculous fling, thanked God he hadn't and merely shook his head. 'Yes, she's been slightly odd with me as well . . . I just don't understand. You don't think she wants to have a second child before it's too late, do you?' And then, pleased with this smokescreen, he had brought up the Renewal Movement, calculated to distract Victor's attention from the Lewises' domestic arrangements.

They crossed Kensington High Street, came to the entrance of Holland Park. Michael turned to smile at them both. 'Come on, you two, hurry up or we'll be late!'

'We're coming!' Nina huffed crossly. Robbie didn't answer him.

'I know what – why don't I put you on my shoulders, like when you were little? That way, I'll rush for the two of us.' He looked down at the dark head that hung slightly.

'I'm too old for that,' Robbie muttered, without looking up.

'Oh, yeah? We'll see about that.' Michael bent, swooped his son into his arms, hoisted the frail little body onto his shoulders. He was so light, so terribly light . . . He waved with one hand at Nina, who frowned, and began to canter up the pavement.

'Papa!' Robbie was giggling despite himself, and Michael felt his habitual rush of powerless love.

'Will you tell me your new friend's name, then?'

'Max. He's taller than me. He lives in Hammersmith.' Robbie unwound the words that had been coiled tight inside him. Michael smiled between those cotton-clad legs, felt the trainers kick against his chest. Allegra could not hope to wrest him away from this.

Nina walked behind the leaning tower formed by father and son. Her heart ached for her son. She knew he had sensed her own unhappiness, had guessed that it related somehow to his father. He would steal quick glances at her in their moments together, but if she looked at him, his brown eyes behind their spectacles fled her own, as if fearful of what she might tell him. Sometimes, unprompted, he would bury his dark head in her lap, and with his arms wrap her waist in a wordless embrace. She had found him sucking his thumb – something he had not done for years. Today she could see Michael trying to win back his son, and she felt certain that if she alone could not succeed in keeping Michael, Robbie would.

The familiar anxiety pressed down on her: she hadn't been to St Mark's to see Alexander this weekend, and she found herself missing that interlude of calm and peace. Since her strange confession in that crypt of his, Nina had returned almost daily to the great wide church hall with its capable chairs and its red Bibles in neat rows. Alexander's beautiful face was now superimposed upon the awfulness of that salmon-coloured ceiling, of the memory of the singing, swaying throng with their eyes firmly shut and their arms humbly extended. Although she could not bring herself to attend the Renewal's two-hour-long Sunday service, during the weekday afternoons Nina liked to step into that place where she felt no holiness but a great deal of warmth and comfort. She sat, unable to pray, bowed beneath her wounded pride and hurt, while tensely expecting his arrival. She would hear the whispers of the pious parish women as they arranged the flowers, distributed song sheets; often she would spot Johnny Stephenson skulking in the back, stealing curious glances at her without ever daring to approach. Alexander had obviously done as he'd promised, warning his acolytes to keep their distance and allow Nina room for quiet reflection.

Always, towards the end of her quarter of an hour of silent wait, she could be certain of his arrival, sober-faced, eyes fluent in their message of hope. He would sit beside her, and they would converse in low tones. He never tried to convert her but asked her about her family, and volunteered information about the Stephensons, the members of his Circle, the continuing success of Tom Sutton. Throughout, she felt conscious more of his physical presence than of his words, more of the feel of his cool hand upon her arm or his blue gaze upon her face than of his hopes for the Renewal Movement. She did not hide from herself that it was Alexander rather than his vision that drew her to the portals of St Mark's. Yet it was not merely his beauty that attracted her. She found tremendous appeal in his spiritual certainty, that burning indignation with which he had exploded when she had told him of Michael's betrayal. In the strange new world in which she found herself, where even her mother and her husband led secret lives and openly lied, Alexander's stark, unforgiving sincerity provided a reassuring contrast.

'Can you pray?' he had asked her.

'No. I long to. I used to, in my youth.'

'You do have faith – faith is longing.' He had placed his hands on either side of her joined ones. The touch of him had been so potent that she had felt her whole body enveloped by him. She remembered now the shiver that ran through her: what she had felt then had been akin to the desire she felt for Michael, and had little in common with the spiritual longing she had seen reproduced in the paintings of saints in ecstasy. Yet she had been struck by his words: was he then, despite his serenity and certainty, a soul still seeking a happiness that eluded him?

All around her the day gleamed in the cold sunlight. The sun shone, through trees that stood immobile, and beamed golden upon the wall that separated the park from a row of tall houses. Spring had arrived, slightly reserved still, like a friend who, after a long parting, needs a bit of time to grow accustomed to you once again, and she felt impatient with its tiny leaves, its tepid warmth, its buds, for she wanted it to herald a new life immediately. She yearned for the future to change the present into something softer and kinder.

She stared at Michael's wide back in its leather jacket, and longed to taunt him with her knowledge of his secret, to show him her disbelief and watch him tremble before her righteous anger. But that way lay destruction: she could only reclaim him if the world she offered him was easy, flawless, unmarked by doubts, accusations and ugly scenes. Of that she was certain, and every day she swallowed her anger and buttoned up her jealousy.

'I wonder who'll be there – or do you think it'll just be us?' Michael half turned, smiling between their son's legs.

'I don't know.' She grew taut, eyes narrowed in scrutiny. 'Perhaps,' she said slowly, 'Mother will have invited Papa's favourite, Allegra, to cheer him up. She hasn't been round for ages.'

'Not for ages, you're right. And I hardly ever notice her at the *Herald*, she keeps such a low profile.' He didn't flinch but grinned, didn't look away but held her probing eyes, and Nina wanted to scream at him that he fooled no one.

'In fact,' he turned his back on her and continued to march with his little burden on his shoulders, 'I'm surprised you haven't heard about her from Clive. The rumour is that she hangs about the *Society* offices after hours, visiting your editor.'

Nina almost laughed: his duplicity took her breath away. 'Really? That's news to me.' She spoke in a flat, emotionless voice. 'It's one of the few flaws in working from home – you never hear the juicy gossip about who is doing what with whom.'

Yet his blindness to her discovery continued to amaze her. How little he knew her that he could not see that beneath the calm exterior everything had changed. She studied Michael's back, his arms raised to hold her son's hands, his head hidden from view by Robbie's body. How could he be so smug?

The house in Holland Park was, as it had always been, full of light and the smell of cooking. Marina had roasted lamb, and she greeted them with a twig of rosemary in one hand. 'Come in, come in. Your father's doing better, though I fear Luke's presence is calculated to irritate him. They're arguing furiously already about the pious MP – what's his name?' Marina embraced each in turn.

Over her shoulder Nina saw her father's tall gaunt figure in a corner of the sofa, a plaid wrapped around his legs. Standing to his left was another man. Nina turned back to her mother, speechless: Luke Aldridge here!

'Come, come, let's have a glass of wine!' Paolo's voice was still feeble, and he waved at them with a weary hand. On the table beside him stood a bottle of water and a bottle of wine, uncorked. He was drinking water and gave them a sad smile. 'Doctor's orders – only half a glass at this stage. I'd better have it with the meal.' The Lewises trooped in, were introduced to 'the famous Luke Aldridge', and Michael immediately sat beside his father-in-law. Nina tried not to stare at her mother's former – who knew, perhaps present? – lover. He was not tall, with a long and ascetic face that contrasted with his robust body. His white hair curled about his lined, suntanned skin, and beneath thick white brows small sharp black eyes shone. He grinned now to reveal untidy grey teeth. My mother loves this man, Nina kept thinking, as she asked her father how he felt, asked her mother if she needed a hand in the kitchen, asked Robbie to sit beside her.

'Their petty-minded puritanism divides the world into us against them – "them", of course, being the Chosen People who alone possess the truth.' Luke grimaced. 'To think how our forefathers fought to rid society of this kind of self-righteous tyranny. Why are we now so ready to yield before it?' He paced the length of the red Persian carpet, speech throbbing with conviction, then returned to stand before Paolo's seated figure.

'Oh, it's all so predictable!' Paolo, eyes suddenly lively behind their spectacles, couldn't wait on the sidelines any longer. 'We approach a time of momentous symbolic significance – the dawn of a new millennium – and someone with some degree of magnetism pops up like a sinister jack-in-the-box to instil fear of the end of the world, speaking of our need to overthrow the decadent order.'

'Did you hear,' Luke turned his bulky body to face Paolo, 'about their dirty tricks campaign?'

'No.' Paolo frowned. He hated to admit ignorance of anything at all.

'Higgins – that loud Midlands MP who's been Sutton's greatest opponent (even attacked the Renewal Movement as "pernicious" on the floor of the House). Well, someone paid an escort girl to pose as a parliamentary secretary. She gave him a bit of encouragement and – wham! bam! – he was photographed canoodling with her in a seedy hotel lobby. Higgins discredited, the movement untarnished – and unstoppable.'

'Renewal one, Liberals nil,' Paolo said.

'Could you take a breather, please, the two of you? Lunch is ready, and I won't have my lamb grow cold while you settle world problems.' Marina led them to the large white kitchen where this Sunday lunch ritual had been re-enacted for so many years.

Around the long refectory-style table they sat, and Nina watched Michael carve while her mother spooned out a vegetable stew which was all Paolo could eat. This was how she had always thought of her mother. In this warm kitchen, hands busy serving others, rings still as she had placed them, in order to cook, in a shiny row on the window sill. This was the figure of her childhood: Mother at the sink, her sleeves rolled up as she rinsed supper plates after each course; Mother, needle and thread in hand, bending over Nina's shirt or dress or slip, replacing a button, basting a hem, while her daughter urged her to hurry, hurry, lest she miss her ride or arrive late at her party; Mother straining to listen to competing claims on her attention as Paolo read out bits of his lectures or books or newspaper articles while Nina moaned a complaint, whispered a fear, voiced a dream. Nina felt a twinge of shame, now: why had she never asked herself if her mother had been satisfied with this life?

'These Renewal people see the liberal establishment as their great enemy.' Luke was once again setting forth into his campaign, forgetting to eat the food before him, turning his black eyes upon each one of them in turn. 'Liberals like us are guilty of everything from the increase in crime to the multiplying of political scandals. They accuse us of placing too much emphasis on the individual. Which, of course, these fanatics wish to see quashed, trodden underfoot.'

'Dear Luke, please, will you eat?' huffed Marina exasperated. Nina watched these two who had shared a bed, a love story, a chain of memories, as they traded quips beneath her father's nose. What did her father think? Did he know, as she had suspected during her visit to his hospital bedside? Had he forgiven, or did he pretend ignorance?

The thoughts filled her like heavy food, and she almost felt nauseous. And as she looked from father to mother, she thought how extraordinary it was that she, devoted daughter, felt she could not seek her parents' counsel about Michael's affair. Throughout her childhood and adolescence she had wanted their advice and asked for their insights. But now the image she remembered was of Marina drawing the curtains around Paolo's hospital bed before she would wash him with the white facecloth soaked in warm soapy water; Nina, too, wanted to draw a curtain of silence around herself, protecting her betrayal from those around her.

She looked across the table at Michael: how happy he was, deep in conversation with Luke and Paolo, discussing the world of spirituality as if he knew anything about it, describing Alexander Connaught as if he had ever drawn close to him, making out that he, Michael, knew the extent of the membership, power and influence of the Renewal Movement. She swelled with anger. Here he sat, meeting a man leading the campaign against the Renewal and therefore key to the world of the *Herald* – and as ever Michael Lewis was making his connections through his wife and her parents. And Nina had to look away from his complacent smile, lest she burst into a violent attack.

Michael was considering, for the umpteenth time in his life, what a formidable alliance a good marriage was: here were his parents-in-law, performing their successful duet, contrasting voices raised in an elegant harmony that embraced the widest possible range of notes. Here sat Paolo, eager thoughts spilling forth in a tumble of words, while beside him, smiling, Marina raised her gentle voice, restoring a sense of balance to the whole. Perfectly suited, delightfully complementary, their union was, he mused, what he aspired to, for his old age with Nina.

Across the table from him Luke Aldridge – Lady K's nemesis, as he was dubbed in the newsroom – sat mopping his plate with a bit of bread. Hair wild and jacket frayed, he couldn't look more the academic if he tried. Michael smiled benevolently: these were the kind of older men he enjoyed meeting, against whose worn demeanour he could contrast his youthful vigour and adventurous life. Though he had to admit Luke Aldridge gave little evidence of being worn: despite the long bout of pneumonia, he shone with energy and enthusiasm for what he obviously saw as his crusade against the puritanical excesses of the Renewal Movement. But in all that impassioned condemnation, was he not, in the end, just like those he professed to hate, a fanatic? He sipped his wine. Paolo was going on about the half-starved millenarians who had waged war against Church and State in Münster, and ended up slain during a siege. Michael kept himself busy with his wine. Sometimes, really, being in Paolo's presence was like being force-fed vegetables by his mother when he was little – the mouthfuls just kept coming and coming.

'Of course,' Luke interrupted, 'there would be one sure-fire way to stop them in their tracks or at least to discredit them. Tom Sutton. The Renewal people and their Christian Coalition see their chance with the next election – and even a fool can tell that's imminent. They've got a lot of people marching to their tune, and they can hope for quite a few of their numbers to be well placed. But the rumours about their beloved Sutton are true – I know there are plenty of young men who'd give evidence.' Luke paused to utter a no-thank-you as Marina tried to press a second helping of meat on him. 'No matter how much the Renewal people would claim that now he has seen the light – and you know they would – it would strike most people as pretty sinister that he's banging on about the moral life, about abortion, when only a few years back . . .' Paolo nodded approval, Marina smiled, but Luke pointed an accusing finger at Michael. 'Though you, of course, would not be allowed to print the story, would you?'

'We would print any evidence that might compromise a national politician,' Michael snapped, smarting at the insult to his paper's independence, 'I cannot say that I agree, though, that his past sins will severely cripple Sutton's campaign. There are many who would prefer him if he had undergone a Damascene conversion.'

'Hm . . . And what do we make of his devotion to a man as devilishly handsome as that young preacher chap? An OE to boot, you heard.' Luke grinned.

'I didn't know about Eton but I'd heard about his good looks,' murmured Paolo, obviously cross that he did not know the young vicar any better.

'Yes, it's all a bit odd. We'll have to see what else our investigations into Sutton's life unearth.'

'He's not homosexual – I mean, Alexander isn't.' Nina spoke up, voice loud. 'And he's comforting, intelligent, not at all the zealot you've been describing.'

'Oh my, our daughter seems to have changed her mind about him since that none-too-positive profile she wrote in the *Society*.' Paolo, who'd pushed away half his vegetable stew in disgust, was cleaning his spectacles with his napkin. He smiled at her blindly. 'Nothing to be ashamed of, my dear. Changes of heart are good for the soul because they teach that we are fallible.'

'And how does my beloved wife know about this evangelical vicar?' Michael grinned at her over his glass. Robbie, always silent and well-behaved at grown-ups' meals, looked from father to mother.

'I followed Lady Katherine there a couple of times . . .' Nina murmured, unwilling to reveal her secret to him.

'Did he fill you with end-of-the-world doom and gloom?' her husband went on, voice raised in mild teasing.

'Not about the end of the world, but about how we should put a stop to those who lead their corrupt lives, disregarding the rules, indulging in betrayals . . .' Her voice lay flat and bitter between them. Michael looked up, suddenly frightened, but his wife met his probing gaze with cool brown eyes that said nothing.

After lunch, Nina insisted on clearing up. While Marina, with Robbie's hand in hers, led everyone through into the drawing room, Michael sat and watched his wife silently take his plate, her own, and walk to the sink.

Michael remained completely immobile for a few moments. What should he do? He felt suddenly terrified. He stood up, took the bowl containing Paolo's stew and followed his wife to the sink. She didn't turn round.

'You're so edgy today.' He stole up behind her, set down the bowl on the stainless-steel counter. Nina did not move but he could see her breathe in deeply, as if to calm herself. He didn't dare touch her.

'I'm not edgy.'

'Just listen to you!' His voice sounded false and petulant to his own ears.

'Michael.' The name hit him like a slap. 'These have been difficult times. You are hardly ever at home, and Robbie and I can't even remember how to be with you.' She spoke in a low, staccato voice, and panic filled him.

'The job, Nina, the job.' He rushed through the excuses, wondering if he should wrap his arms around her, then deciding against it. 'It's taken up so much of my time. There seems to be an endless scramble, things to do, people to see . . .'

'And in the endless scramble Robbie and I are forgotten.' Nina kept her back to him.

'Never. But what did you think?' His voice rose in an exasperation with which he sought to cloak his fear. 'That I would be around as much as before, when I have an entire news operation to run? Nina.' He lowered his voice again to a whisper, and then wrapped his arms around her waist. He felt her tremble, but she wouldn't turn to face him. 'Why are you forcing me to defend myself when I've always thought of you as my ally?' He tightened his hold so that he could press himself against her, and with his lips brush the soft, scented skin of her neck. 'Nina . . .' he murmured. 'We both knew when we were preparing for this that there would be a price to pay.'

Her head bowed. 'I never thought the price would be so high,' she whispered, and still he could feel her quiver against him. He felt her sadness replace the anger of before and he now grew incredibly strong, confident that this woman whom his embrace reduced to a trembling silence must love him still – and this love would continue to blind her to his betrayal. A tremendous joy seized him as his fear receded: she was his wonderful, his perfect Nina, and he must never be party to her unhappiness. No, never again. He kissed her bowed white neck while she wept silently.

## Chapter Eighteen

She was feeling quite sorry for herself, Lady Katherine thought, as she helped the silent, ever-smiling Liu set the table for tonight's meeting of the Circle. Of course, as a good Christian these were just the sort of thoughts she should banish. She had everything she could possibly wish for, and had made great strides towards improving herself, stilling those dreadful little voices that urged her to forsake Alexander, Jesus and the Spirit and return to her wicked pleasures . . . Yet the serenity she had experienced with her conversion under Alexander's loving eye, and which she had enjoyed until a few months ago, seemed to have evaporated.

There was Johnny, for one: she had thought that with his finding God and attending the services at St Mark's and the Circle, he would undergo a wonderful transformation that would bond him to his mother and somehow remove the shadow of animosity that still overcast their relationship. Instead, he had grown enamoured of Alexander – seeing him daily, either at home or at St Mark's, following him from Circle to Circle, volunteering to help him and those dreadful twee spinsters in that grim office of his – but had maintained his distance from her. He could not, would not forgive her – for what? Her lovers? The love she had showered upon his older brother? She had tried to build a bridge between them with stolen caresses and gentle questions that did not seek to probe but rather to acknowledge her new interest in his welfare. Yet nothing seemed to work, and her son's gaze fell upon her as if it were ripping off her coat and forcing her out into a cold night.

Lady Katherine shivered. She picked up a silver knife that seemed tarnished, breathed on it, rubbed it with the linen towel she had draped over her arm for this very purpose: she believed in never stinting when she had guests. And this was, after all, for her beloved Alexander. She sighed, glance skimming the sparkling table. It was a warm night, and Liu had opened both windows in the dining room: the sweet scents of

147

the garden wafted in. Lady Katherine adjusted the white thick-petalled roses in their crystal vase. Alexander . . .

She looked down at her image in the knife – thinned and silver-plated and unhappy. Unhappy because of his new obsession with Nina Lewis. For weeks now Alexander had seemed more interested in 'saving' Michael Lewis's wife than in keeping the rest of his flock safely penned in. 'It's very important,' he had explained to her – and had she not seen him blush as he did so? – 'that we get her on our side . . . She could influence not only her husband's paper but the *Society*. She desperately needs us. She is in turmoil, doubting everything. She must find faith, or be lost.'

'What about her own faith – I thought she was a Catholic? Surely there are Roman priests she could go to?' Lady Katherine had asked crossly.

Alexander had merely smiled, shaking his head. 'I think she is gravitating towards us, Lady Katherine, and we must do everything in our power to draw her in.'

Lady Katherine had tried to overcome her resentment, but every time she saw Nina Lewis she could feel the jealousy stir. She couldn't help herself: she wanted to claim his every look and every word. And she honestly could not understand his fascination with an earnest young woman whose unsmiling presence and prim manner struck her as ridiculous. Didn't Mrs Lewis realise she was in her prime?! Lady Katherine shook her head at the ingratitude of youth.

Liu moved into the kitchen. Left alone, Lady Katherine surveyed the table: everything shone, awaiting the arrival of the members of the Circle. Alexander had asked her to invite Nina tonight, which she, ever obedient, had done. Nina was not to take part in the Circle, which was reserved for the young people, but she was coming in time to witness the concluding rites, from which Alexander was certain 'she would draw great strength.'

'Well, I'm off, and I trust the pious brigade will be gone when I come back?' Philip was adjusting his tie as he came through the double doors. It was his bridge night, and he was in a good mood.

'Now don't be nasty.' Lady Katherine smiled, bent slightly towards her husband's throat, finished the knot for him, kissed him.

Philip beamed back. 'I think we see even less of our son than when he sought company in the bottle.' But he was pleased, she knew. 'See you!' he called out over his shoulder, as he retrieved a cigar from the box on the mantelpiece.

For a moment his wife filled with well-being. Yes, she and Philip now occupied a comfortable space – it was as if, on a hot, sunny lawn, they had found a perfect retreat in the shadow of a large tree and sat there, looking out from its cool dome at those who were forced to sweat in the exhausting heat and brightness.

But when she heard the front door close behind him she slipped once again into a confusion of images embracing Alexander and Nina Lewis. The way she had seen him cover both her hands with his, in the back of the church, one afternoon; the smile of welcome that lit his face when she had stepped into his office the other day; the sight of their handsome figures walking down the Embankment yesterday after lunch, heads close together – his light, hers dark – in a communion that had knotted Lady Katherine's heart.

Stop this nonsense, she bade the woman now reflected in the window. Then the doorbell rang, and she smiled: he was here.

She was granted only a few minutes alone with her spiritual guide, for in quick succession first Johnny then the other members of the Circle appeared. Tonight's lot represented the core group around the vicar of St Mark's. There were many Circles taking place tonight around the city – indeed, around the country – but the ones collected here were those Alexander called 'the old faithfuls': youngsters he had converted when they were still in their teens, who were now embarking upon their first jobs. They were ten in all: well-bred, decent-looking, enthusiastic. Their shared belief, their common dream of being good Christians, lent them an air of security – almost brazen, in some – that belied their age. What indecision she had experienced when she had been as young as them! Lady Katherine thought with a pang of envy. How much heartache, how many doubts they would be able to avoid, with their armour of faith. Still, it was an armour they had taken on only recently: she had suspected, and Johnny had confirmed, that among the youngsters who crowded round her mentor were a number who had had their share of past disappointments, and felt flattered, their self-esteem caressed, by their membership of this select group. At every opportunity, after all, Alexander repeated his admiration for their commitment, their abilities, their spirituality. And this group, losers in other competitions, found here much more than conviviality: a new sense of coming first.

After much praising of their hostess's table, the young people sat down for their meal. Lady Katherine, as was her wont, retired to the drawing room: she pretended she had already eaten, though in truth she usually fasted on the Wednesday nights they met here. A fast dictated, she admitted rather shamefacedly, by her fear of putting on weight with age rather than any notion of participating in a holy ritual. She sat in the pink drawing room, where the french windows stood ajar and the picture lights shone upon Zeus's face, one of Philip's ancestors and her own youthful beauty captured in a portrait painted so many years ago. She sat in a corner of the sofa, awaiting Nina Lewis with a *Herald* she was not reading in her hands. She had left the doors to the dining room open, and now she stole quick glances at the assembled gathering: how earnest they looked, those eager disciples who seemed to drink and eat the words he uttered! She smiled despite herself at this tableau of youth in need of guidance.

They ate noisily, cheerful and loquacious, often seeking Alexander's voiced approval, and she felt as if she could see her own desire to please him reflected in their faces. After the meal, Liu cleared the table, Johnny helping her with the bottles. Everyone's eyes turned to Alexander, and Lady Katherine strained to hear his voice.

'I am warning you of the end of the world. I have heard the hooves of the Four Horsemen draw near, and I have seen a white cloud upon which sat the Son of Man, a crown on his head, a sickle in his hand.' He paused, and then resumed, voice low: 'And an angel said unto the Son of Man: "Thrust in your sickle and reap, for the time has come for You to reap, for the harvest of the earth is ripe."'

A murmur rose from the group.

'The time is ripe: with the new millennium comes the New Dawn. You must prepare for it, and I am to help you see the light and tread the right path, so that He will choose you as His own, and place upon you His seal, the Seal of the Lamb.' The vicar raised his eyes to the ceiling: 'All others will be visited by the beast, by the Antichrist, whose arrival will be foretold by meteors and earthquakes and volcanoes.'

Again a murmur rose among the Circle. Alexander smiled: 'Fear not, for the year 2000 is a glorious moment, for those who have surrendered their lives to Him, as you have done. The year 2000 is that moment in the history of Creation for which I have been waiting for all my life.'

Liu was suddenly before her: 'Mrs Lewis,' she whispered.

Lady Katherine sighed, put away the unread paper, stood up to greet her guest as she strode in, holding herself tall and proud, a small bouquet of flowers in one hand.

'Thank you, you needn't have . . .' murmured Lady Katherine as she handed the flowers to Liu and drew Nina to sit beside her on the sofa. She raised an index finger to her lips and motioned to her to join her in contemplating the pious spectacle beyond the open doors, where the handsome figure sat, addressing the upturned faces that glowed in the candlelight.

'You've asked: Why confession? Why a public admission of guilt? I tell you: because we must repent of our sins lest the end of time find us with an uncleansed conscience. Shortly we shall all be judged. He will mete out terrible and eternal punishment to those who do not wear the Seal of the Lamb. But do not think that because the harshest of fates awaits them, we should refrain now from judging our fellowmen: it is better to be harsh with those who sin than weak – for weakness they will misinterpret as connivance. We cannot allow our world to be infiltrated by evil, my friends. We must protect ourselves from the onslaught of the sinners' battalions, lest they overturn our world.'

'Amen,' Nina heard someone pipe up, only to be quickly silenced.

Nina glanced at her hostess, who nodded her approval. Once again, she felt slightly ashamed of being able to read so clearly Lady Katherine's love of the young vicar.

And what of you? Nina asked herself. What do you feel for this extraordinary being? She saw him almost every day. In her presence, he hardly ever spoke of the Movement, of the end of the world, or of the Circle. Instead he spoke of his rejection of a world that had turned its back on truth and virtue and respect. 'All I want to do is to help people to see that there is evil and there is good – and to find the strength to be virtuous,' he told her, eyes tenderly seeking hers.

Slowly, Nina had felt her reservations about the strange young vicar melt: it seemed to her as if the silence of the church lent their moments together a kind of enchantment. In the great soundless space their voices shivered in the air, their seated figures cast one shadow across the empty chairs before them, upon the carpet that covered the floor. All was a quivering of sounds and shadows, a magical mingling of words and sensations within the calm house of God. These meetings sometimes struck Nina as stages of a pilgrimage that led to she knew not what shrine; she followed him meekly, certain that he knew the path, and would lead her to their destination. At other times, she felt as if they were engaged in a strange courtship, a mutual wooing that did not seek intimacy as much as a shield against the inimical outside world. If she ever thought of it as love, it was as a

151

peculiar form of love – as if it could only offer, like a figure glimpsed through a gauze curtain, a vague, teasing impression of the real thing.

Only in his presence, she realised, could she forget Michael.

'Forgive us, sweet Jesus, for our sins.' Alexander had resumed a low, low voice, and he bent his head, eyes closed. 'Let me make my confession to You now, so that I may with my repentance earn your ready forgiveness when I stand at the doors to Your Kingdom.' He paused. 'I have not, dear Jesus, been all-embracing in my love. I have picked and chosen among my disciples and my friends, showering affection upon some while rejecting others. For this failure, please forgive me.' He waited a moment, then raised his head, opened his eyes. 'I beg you too my brothers and sisters, for forgiveness.'

Again there was a pause. Then Johnny, pale-faced and large eyes fixed upon Alexander, clasped his hands on the table before him as if he were praying, and addressed the table: 'I . . . I sin in my urge to wreak revenge . . . I find myself considering possible ways to extract penance from those I know to be sinners . . .'

Nina sensed her hostess grow tense beside her: Lady Katherine's hands trembled in her lap. But now a young woman had taken up from Johnny and was confessing her sin. With a self-conscious little cough she stood up, eyes fixed before her. 'I have sinned, because I have indulged in fornication . . . with a man who is also a member of the Circle.'

Around the table, eyes moved left to right, but no one dared speak.

'Is he – here?' Alexander asked of the young woman who remained standing, as if ready to continue her 'J'accuse'.

'Yes,' she whispered.

'I am guilty.' Before she could continue, a handsome young man shot up. 'Isobel is right. I too yielded . . .'

Alexander bowed his head as if considering their sin – or their punishment. 'Let me remind you both of St Paul's words in Ephesians: "But fornication, and all uncleanness, or covetousness, let it not be once named among you, as becometh saints." He looked up at the couple who, at opposite ends of the table, remained standing. 'You've been brave, Isobel, to acknowledge your sin before us. Your sin – and Geoffrey's. The same courage will help you regain your virtue. But keep a watchful eye on one another. Virtue is three-quarters vigilance, as I have taught the Circle. Transparency is what we seek. A world without secrets or subterfuge. Thank you, Isobel, for your honesty – and your humility. Geoffrey,' the vicar turned to the handsome youth, 'learn from your friend to account for your actions.' Alexander raised both arms. 'Be seated, you two, and let us now pray that the Spirit may fill us.'

'Forgive us blessed Jesus and fill us with Your Spirit.' Around the candle-lit table they held hands, heads bowed, eyes shut.

'It's finished now, they'll come through,' whispered Lady Katherine to Nina.

Through the open door they came, two by two, so docile and subdued, they reminded Nina of a group of old age pensioners coming off a tour bus, slightly wary of their new surroundings, completely dependent on the guide at their heels. As she watched the young vicar now, she wondered why she felt no outrage at the spectacle – *mea culpas* mixed with finger-pointing – that she had witnessed: had she no indignation left for anything but Michael's betrayal? Or did the Circle mirror her wish for Michael's repentance and a chance to accuse him?

'Nina, you came . . .' Alexander strode directly towards her, eyes alight, smile widening. 'You realise who that was?' he had reached her, and spoke in a *sotto voce* that could not mute his pleasure: 'The Duke of Farley's daughter . . . a new recruit.'

Nina nodded her congratulations on his aristocratic prize. But Lady Katherine stepped in before he could take a seat beside Nina. 'Alexander, I've been so troubled by reports of this backlash that Luke Aldridge plans.' Lady Katherine was whispering, drawing him with her into a corner of the room, just beneath a Stephenson holding his monocle.

Nina overheard her. Should she mention the plot she'd heard at lunch the other day – Luke's plan to reveal Tom Sutton's skeleton in the closet? But she could sense Lady Katherine's desire to be alone with her mentor, and dared not disturb her.

'What did you make of it?' Johnny sat beside her. Nina was taken aback: he had never approached her during those afternoons she had seen him hanging about the church. Now he was watching her with careful eyes, ignoring his role as host as around them the youngsters from the Circle talked in small groups, taking the cups of coffee that Liu handed round on her silver tray.

'I think . . . oh, I think I envy you all for your certainty. I envy you for sharing an ideal of how life ought to be. It's a vision so many outside this group fail to uphold.' She spoke with feeling, and he seemed pleased.

He drew closer, now, though with his eyes upon Alexander

standing beside Lady Katherine at the great french windows. 'He speaks brilliantly of his vision – infects us with it. But I feel he's a bit slow in carrying out the cleansing he knows we must undergo if we are to save ourselves and our brethren.'

Nina looked at the pale face and strange half smile: he was quite, quite mad, she thought, with this talk of cleansing. She pulled away from him, into the silk softness of the cushions at her back.

'We need a scorched-earth policy. Sinners should repent, accept punishment – or be somehow disposed of. We just can't risk contamination of the innocent and the naive . . .'

'The sinners – removed? Johnny what do you mean?' She was whispering as if to keep his insane ideas from the others.

'I mean that we should think of a way to contain the wicked – curb the power they wield. Otherwise, their evil will infect us . . . and we have so little time, so little time before we are called to account.'

'Johnny . . . surely you accept that we cannot eradicate evil . . . that our world will always accommodate both the instinct for the good and the bad – it is up to the individual, in the end, to make his choice.'

'Not if that choice affects others,' again he drew close to her, so that she could feel his breath upon her face, hear his soft voice: 'think of Allegra Worth for instance.'

Nina stiffened. She stared back at him, at the blue eyes that seemed innocuous because so watery – as if he were permanently moved to compassion or grief. But there was contempt, not compassion as he continued now: 'Women like that – they are the most evil of all, those who betray our love, our trust, those who will tempt others to follow in their footsteps towards the gratification of the self . . . they deserve nothing but pain,' he hissed, and Nina again withdrew into the pillows, her eyes wide and filled with fear.

'How do you know?' she whispered.

'I know.' He moved closer to her, following her into the silken embrace of the cushions. 'She is terrifed it will destroy her, you'll see. She cannot bear the strain of all the secrecy, the guilt, the realisation that . . . that we don't approve of her turning her back on His teaching.'

'You don't approve,' Nina repeated mechanically, still so shocked to be speaking about her secret with this strange young man.

'I am letting her know, don't worry. I've bombarded her with letters, she must receive one with every post now, and I've rung her too. She must not be allowed to delude herself that what she has done

154

will be allowed to slip by.' He shot Nina an appraising look, scoured her face for expression, but found none. Johnny carried on, pressing his fingertips together. 'I cared, you know, I cared about Allegra. Not in any – special – way,' he flushed and she wondered if he had not been infatuated with the young woman himself. 'I thought she was pure, innocent . . . I thought she was . . . different . . . from the women I had known . . .'

Nina watched him, silent and unblinking, trying to suppress her desire to shoot up and run away from him.

'But she isn't, is she? Seducing your husband, torturing you, probably laughing at your expense.'

Nina flinched. She cast a cool look at his feverish face: it was extraordinary to think how he had immediately concluded that it was Allegra who had lured Michael into adultery – and then, as she followed his gaze which fastened upon his mother, she realised that that was how it had always been in his life.

'Anyway, I think if we gave her a good scare she would leave you – and him – alone.'

Nina lowered her voice: 'And do you think that Alexander would go along with your idea of – retribution?'

'Oh, of course he will,' Johnny again cast her a half-smile, 'Not directly, of course – the vicar of St Mark's must keep his spotless reputation. But then – he need not get his hands dirty with people like me around.'

'What do you mean?' she asked.

'I am his faithful vassal. His messenger and agent. I carry out his orders – it's efficient, and it covers his tracks. As for Allegra, his condemnation would make her life unbearable . . . a living hell. He still has a great hold on her. He has a great hold on us all.'

## Chapter Nineteen

'We cannot afford this kind of scandal!' Tom Sutton was almost shouting. 'The general election could be called at any moment, and I can tell you at Party Headquarters they love the Movement – they've been dusting off words like duties and values and trotting off to church in droves – but everything we've worked for could be jeopardised by this!'

The voice seemed to rush up from the crypt, two steps at a time, eager in its anger to collar someone and explode. Standing in the doorway to the crypt, invisible and silent, Lady Katherine listened in surprise to the politician's fury: she had never known him like this. The voice continued below her, and she decided not to descend into the dark space where he was addressing Alexander.

'You realise the scandal! She belongs to the Movement, he is the editor of a paper which has always championed us – it would be a God almighty fuss. Oh, I'm so angry, angry, angry!' He sounded so petulant that she could not refrain from smiling as she looked down. Where was the famous jolly manner, the characteristic sweetness of tone and ever-smiling presence? She cast a quick look about the church: it was empty, with rows and rows of sturdy chairs, a Bible sitting like a russet-coloured brick upon every second one. She bent, the better to peer into the shadows below, and made out Alexander's figure, Tom Sutton beside him.

'Calm down, calm down, Tom.' Alexander's sweet voice wrapped itself around the loud exclamations like the cool wet towel she would place upon Johnny's fevered brow when he'd been unwell. 'I told you,' even if soft, Alexander's voice filled the low-ceilinged room, 'I know how we can contain it.'

'I just can't believe Lewis,' Sutton spluttered on. 'He had seemed such an important asset, and now he's become a liability.'

'Tom,' Alexander's voice was cool, calm, unruffled by the other's explosion, 'I know what Michael Lewis wants and I know how we can get him to behave. As for Allegra,' the voice had grown hard, 'Johnny is trying to woo her back to us. With little success so far, but . . .'

In the faint light shed by the lamp on the desk, Lady Katherine could see Tom Sutton pace, hands clasped behind his back like some elderly Victorian statesman in a costume drama. She kept hidden behind the door to the crypt, watching, unseen.

'Alex . . . I just know that if we don't slip up, I could be Home Secretary. All our dreams – all our dreams are coming to fruition, and you're letting those two ruin it for us!'

'Rest assured, my friend: I shall not allow anyone to destroy our dreams. But,' Alexander's voice seemed to taunt, 'you may do well to remember that other illicit affairs could threaten our campaign far more. It would be impossible to bring the Renewal Movement to the fore of public life if one of its leading lights were discovered besmirched by some secret scandal . . .'

Lady Katherine froze: she'd caught sight of Alexander's pale angry face, illuminated by the desk lamp. What was he alluding to?

'Alexander . . .' From Tom's corner came the low-voiced plea. He remained hidden in the shadows.

'Tom,' from her position she could see the vicar's fearsome face, 'you and I believe in redemption. True penance brings with it Jesus Christ's forgiveness. But there are many out there who don't share our view and would hold a man responsible for past sins, no matter what his present resolutions. This is all the more so,' he lowered his voice, but it vibrated with conviction, 'if the scandal involves male prostitutes and a young man who claims you raped him.'

'Alexander I didn't!' Tom almost screamed, bouncing out of the shadows to confront his mentor. 'I told you, he was leading me on, flirting, teasing! It was sex between consenting adults!'

Lady Katherine couldn't breathe as she listened. Revulsion seized her, and she was forced to look away from the young politician below.

Alexander held up a hand to stem the man's cries. 'I believe you, I believe you, my dear Tom, but you and I both know it wouldn't look good if this ever came to light.'

Tom Sutton's hands reached out for the vicar's, but Alexander pushed him away. 'Meanwhile, try not to panic – you might make a wrong move.' The vicar had walked to his desk, and bent over now, leafing through papers. Suddenly he looked up and, as if the sight of the immobile Sutton had moved him to pity, he smiled. 'Look, with regard to Lewis and Allegra, I'll simply bring it to the attention of Lady Katherine. She'll be more than willing to help us out.'

Lady Katherine felt a shiver at the sound of her name issued by his lips. What was he asking of her? The secret he had unveiled – it had made her recoil, determined never to deal with Tom Sutton again. Did her beloved mentor demand compassion of her, forgiveness for this foul hypocrite? How could Alexander ask her to collaborate with someone who had lied about his past – and, who knew, might be found guilty of a terrible crime? 'Oh, Alexander, you cannot ask this of me!' she told him in her heart.

The creaking of the portals behind her made her jump. One of the two spinsters who, in thrall to Alexander, kept the church and crypt tidy for him, was pushing open the heavy wooden doors. Fear seized her: they must not realise she had overheard them. She rose from her bent, spying position, tiptoed a few steps back into the church. Then she approached the door of the crypt again, this time with heavy, resounding footsteps, feeling childish at this ploy.

'Alexander?' she called out, giving them time to prepare themselves. Slowly she descended the stairs, at once shamefaced at, and alarmed by, the secrets she had stolen. She stood among them in the soft light cast by a corner lamp. Bookshelves lined the walls, a few desks sat beneath piles of papers: this was the headquarters of the Renewal Movement, where files, accounts and correspondence were kept by the two devoted women. She walked slowly past the Elizabethan stones, and wondered why she had never thought of discovering whose remains lay buried here, whose sepulchre this had been, centuries ago. Yet somehow, she thought as she smiled up at her mentor, it seemed impossible in Alexander's presence to think of the dead. Every part of him seemed to beckon to her to explore every aspect of *this* life.

'You asked me to come?'

Alexander drew close to her. 'Thank you, Lady Katherine.' He was smiling, voice light.

Lady Katherine gave Tom Sutton a quick nod, loath to look at him now that she knew his past. The politician looked exhausted, pale, miserable, and Lady Katherine turned her back on him as she hung her handbag and linen jacket upon a chair. 'Well, Philip keeps telling me how well the Movement is doing – gaining momentum throughout the country, it seems.'

'There are many reasons to celebrate, Lady Katherine, though I fear there is also cause for serious concern.'

Lady Katherine turned wide eyes upon him. 'What has happened?' She tried to sound both surprised and worried.

Tom Sutton sat on the chair, crossed his hands upon the blotting pad: following the confrontation with the vicar he seemed spent. Behind him Lady Katherine saw the pastel colours and block lettering of the calendar of parish events. Next to it hung a parchment-like scroll with some passage of the scriptures she could not read.

'It would seem that Michael Lewis has been carrying on with Allegra Worth – you may remember, one of our young recruits, friend of your son . . .'

'Michael and Allegra,' Lady Katherine repeated.

At the desk, Tom Sutton suddenly stood up, hand pounding the grey paper before him. 'What do you say now about your carefully chosen editor, eh?' Silent, Lady Katherine watched this outburst. Tom went on, 'Not very clever, is it, for the great media supporter of our Movement and its moral renewal to be found toeing a very different line in his private life?' Tom stared at her, his gaze hostile. Lady Katherine realised that he, the millionaire, approached her with none of that fear mixed with envy that her wealth usually inspired. Indeed he approached her as if, in his eyes, she were to blame for the affair between Lewis and the young girl Paolo del Monte had championed so tirelessly, and she felt her indignation mount at the thought of being judged and found wanting by a man like this one. She looked away from Sutton's pale face.

'How do you know?' she asked Alexander. 'She confessed to you?'

He shook his head. 'No, she's keeping away from the Circle. It was Johnny – he saw Lewis going into her flat. He stayed. Long enough.'

Lady Katherine tried not to think about her son standing about Allegra's house, waiting for her married lover to leave her. Was he devastated by this betrayal? Poor, poor Johnny, she thought, her heart compressed with pity: women had not been kind to him.

The vicar linked his fingers, as if he were beginning to pray. He bowed his head, and Lady Katherine felt a terrible impulse to stroke his thick, glistening hair.

Alexander raised his head, cast her a smile. 'Will you help us, Lady Katherine?'

'Yes,' she answered, and realised as she did that he could make her forget – or at least forgive – even the politician before her.

'Good.' Alexander's eyes were bright, loving. 'There is nothing that would frighten Michael more than the realisation that he might be jeopardising his job. If you were to hint delicately at your displeasure . . .'

'Of course.' She nodded: she knew now why he had telephoned this morning.

'As for the girl . . .'

'I'm keeping an eye on her,' a disembodied voice boomed down the crypt.

Johnny's feet came slowly down the stairs, and his shrunken body slowly emerged as if lowered by an unseen hand into the crypt. He came to stand beside his mother and the vicar, but his gaze was fixed on Alexander's face. 'Women like her should not be allowed near your flock. Surely you should either punish or banish her.'

Lady Katherine was taken aback by her son's outburst. It was to her mentor she turned. 'But are we not asked to forgive . . . ?' Her voice was faint.

'I would never have thought her capable of it,' Alexander was saying, as if to himself. Then he looked up at Lady Katherine. 'She was extremely devoted to our Church, to the Circle, to your son. She had helped him.' Here Johnny shuddered, his head shaking violently as if to deny the vicar's words.

'Let Johnny see what he can do with her. She may come crawling back.' Tom Sutton had sat down behind the desk again, and was tapping impatient fingers upon a blotting pad.

'Meanwhile, we must not overlook our work of conversion.' Alexander was looking at Johnny.

'But as we work to convert, we should also be purging the bad elements in our community,' Johnny continued from his dark corner, eyes fixed on the vicar. 'Lest they infect the rest . . .'

Alexander approached him, placed a hand on his shoulder. 'Yes, Johnny, but be careful with your campaign of intimidation.' His voice was kind, soft, patient. 'There have been complaints from some of the other members of the Circle. Your talk of the punishment they deserve – it is appropriate, Johnny. But it lacks subtlety. Conceal the hand, rather than wag your finger, and you will achieve far more.'

Lady Katherine hardly dared watch her son as he stared, silent, at Alexander.

Alexander once again turned to Lady Katherine. 'Have you moved any further in those discussions with the trustees about the *Society*?' His tone was unemotional, but she could detect an eagerness as he awaited her reply.

160

'The trustees have shown some interest, but it is still too early to tell.'

'Hm.' Alexander did not hide his disappointment. He moved back to Lady Katherine, took her hands in his. 'It would prove such a powerful weapon. The media, it spreads evil now but it could spread the Word too. Counter the attacks of those who mock us.'

'Like Luke Aldridge in the *Recorder* last week.' At the desk Tom Sutton kept his fingers playing upon the imaginary keyboard of the blotter. His gaze was fixed on Alexander. 'The man has been vehement in his opposition to us – hates the Christian Coalition, hates the Movement. He has made more than one veiled attack on me personally. We have to watch him.'

'You saw how easy it was to dispose of Higgins . . .' The vicar spoke softly.

'What clout does Aldridge have?' Lady Katherine took a few paces about the room. She was looking at Alexander, and as she spoke she realised that they had all been addressing themselves exclusively to him. 'Aldridge has the reputation of a mad old professor – and it's a bit late in the day to shed that image, don't you agree?'

'He is influential among liberals, though,' Alexander leaned back against the bookshelves, smiling slightly at each one in turn, as if conscious of his power over them. 'Aldridge is part of that nucleus of so-called forward-thinking intelligentsia. His attacks cannot be so easily dismissed.'

'Well, what do you think we should do?' Lady Katherine asked, raising an eyebrow.

Tom Sutton stood up, walked around the desk, came to stand beside Alexander, his eyes on Lady Katherine. 'If we could rely on both the *Herald*s and the *Society*, we would become unbeatable.'

'Of course. I'll bring it up again at next week's meeting of the board.' Lady Katherine stiffened slightly at the proximity of Tom Sutton.

'Thank you.'

She made as if to speak to him again, but was forced to draw back as Tom Sutton placed a hand upon his arm. 'Alexander, will you come up to Laurel for the fête?' She watched the politician: his face had softened into a pleading expression as his eyes caressed the vicar's pale profile.

Alexander did not remove his arm, but shook his head. 'I fear not, Tom. Work is pressing here.'

'I was so looking forward to it.' The disappointment was clear in Sutton's face, and he could hardly bear to look up. 'I mean, we all were – Annie and the children . . .' He sank both hands into his pockets.

Again Lady Katherine felt distaste for the petulant manner. Tom Sutton behind the scenes was even worse than the public persona. But as she saw him now embrace the young vicar, gripping him with both arms as if the better to study him, she felt a shiver of recognition. What she truly disliked in the politician was that his love of Alexander placed him in competition with her. Shame, shame, she thought to herself, you are no better. Her eyes turned to find Johnny's implacable stare. Lady Katherine picked up her jacket, her handbag. 'Alexander, if I may, I shall be going back. I know what my task is – rather, what *they* are.' She gave him a quick nod, cast a swift, frightened look in her son's direction, then slowly climbed the stairs.

'God bless!' she heard Alexander's voice call up to her.

'God bless,' she answered sadly.

When she reached the bright, warm church upstairs, she stood for a moment completely still, staring at the salmon-pink space, at the rows of chairs and the benches above, in the terraces. 'You ask so much of me,' she wanted to tell the vicar downstairs, 'more than anyone ever has . . .' And yet, as she stood in the church where he had received her, and remembered the endless services where, pressed between the congregation, she had watched him with love, Lady Katherine knew she would not seek to rebel but to obey.

# Chapter Twenty

The summer had grown hot and heavy as a well-fed diner. Nina leaned against the open window and felt the sun beat bright upon her face. The leaves outside had grown thick, lush, hiding the view of St Stephen's in the distance. The sunshine glossed the wide-faced white houses across the street, making them shine with new-found benevolence. It was as if the day beckoned to her to step away from Victor and his questions and this house with its reminders of unhappiness, to leave behind all this for the life without.

She wanted to escape Victor's searching gaze: for the past half-hour he had tried to engage her in a discussion of the Renewal Movement, of Luke Aldridge's campaign against it, of Alexander's hold on Lady Katherine. She wished she could let Victor talk for both of them, that he would stop seeking her answers. She wanted to be left alone with her thoughts, her visions of Allegra and Johnny and Alexander, above all of Michael. She wanted to mull over the next few moves: if Johnny did not relent in his campaign of intimidation, if he kept his hold on Allegra's guilty conscience and tightened it so that she would gasp for air . . . if . . . if . . .

She had not seen Victor for weeks and this morning he'd suddenly come over, 'Like old times,' he'd said in a falsely cheerful voice, though from the moment he had stood before her they had known this was not so. The old easy friendship they had treasured had given way to something far more circumspect, as if they were tailors eyeing up the way an expensive fragile fabric ought to be cut. Nina mused that even if Victor did not know how Michael's betrayal pulled her in Alexander's direction, he could sense that they had embarked upon new, diverging paths.

Now she kept him under careful scrutiny, conscious of his every move, listening out for every inflection in his familiar voice. She didn't want him to pry, nor did she want to snap at him that she saw Alexander as holding out a promise for a better future. Above all, she didn't want to admit that she had woven her life into the Movement, and saw her aim to regain her husband as linked to theirs – or, at least, to the purge Alexander hinted at but of which Johnny Stephenson spoke openly.

He had sensed her wariness – oh, there was no fooling Victor, he knew her too well – but he would not desist and kept up his enthusiastic talk of "our counter-Renewal campaign" and its thousand meetings and splinter lobby groups and posters and fliers-through-the-letterbox.

'You seem totally different,' she told him from the window, eyes closed and a smile on her face.

'I think you should come to the park on Saturday for the rally – Luke's an extraordinary speaker, Nina, you'd be impressed.' She could hear him behind her as he paced up and down the drawing room. Without looking at him she pictured the worn collarless cotton shirt, half pulled out of the shapeless trousers, the frown of concentration furrowing his lean brown face, the nervous gesticulating hand.

'Hm.' She wouldn't rise to the bait.

'Well, I can't bear,' he approached her, and leaned out of the window, elbows on the sill, blocking half the sun from her face, 'just can't *bear* the thought of your seeing that hellfire and brimstone vicar at St Mark's.'

'He has always sounded very mild-mannered to me,' Nina demurred, keeping her eyes shut.

'He is not mild, he is mad. Have you listened to his prophecies? End of the world upon us, sinners punished or cast out . . . anything to whip our fear into a frenzy that will blind us to his fundamentalism.'

'What fundamentalism, Victor?' She would not allow him to stir her into an argument.

'It will become very obvious very soon – Sutton is tipped to be Home Secretary if the opposition gets in with the next election, and you know that's only a matter of weeks now. Then we'll see them rushing through new measures to further tighten access to abortion, tough new plans for single mothers – and God alone knows what the hypocrite will do to homosexuals. Oh, they'll make a puritanical new state all right – this is how the roundheads *de nos jours* hope to instil a new sense of values in our society! It's all about scapegoats not about real ideals. And with the Stephensons trying to extend their control over the *Society* as well, we'll have a media monopoly and a moral majority all rolled into one.'

'Yes, I know.' For weeks now, Clive had been reporting to Nina rumours that the trustees who owned the *Herald* and the *Sunday Herald* had been 'circling my poor magazine like vultures a carcass. I fear the insatiable Stephensons may want to buy it – and I warrant it has not a little to do with the fact that Lady Katherine wants to push her cause. Nina, what is the world coming to? When I knew that red-headed vixen she was a praying mantis. Now they've turned her into a praying bore.' Clive had laughed, but she had sensed an edge in his voice: he had been receiving some strange letters at the *Society*, accusing him of lax morals and a libertine lifestyle and concluding that a man of his disposition should not be editing an influential magazine. She, who knew of Alexander's plans to take over the *Society* and oust its present editor, said nothing but listened to Clive's flood of recriminations and suspicions, his words of hatred against his former lover. Poor, poor Clive, 'a pawn in the greater scheme of things', as Alexander had murmured.

'And do you know,' Victor's face drew near hers, his voice low, 'that there is evidence that their Tom Sutton is not the knight in shining armour he pretends to be? Luke and I have been assembling quite a portfolio on the future minister, including rent boys, a male brothel and one young man who went around claiming he was raped.' Victor's scowling face pushed close to hers.

'Victor!' Her alarm obviously satisfied him, for he half smiled.

'It's true, my dear. We're working on the story, trying to trace the youth. With him as a witness, well, we certainly would discredit that man.'

Nina said nothing. She looked into his shining black eyes. 'You couldn't begin to suspect Alexander of allying himself with such a man?'

'Why not?' Victor shrugged. He began to roll up his sleeves. 'Sutton's a perfect ally – money, a political career that's made him some powerful connections, and tremendous ambition. I'm sure Alexander Connaught can think of a few psalms or proverbs with which to whitewash his friend's past.'

'I'm not convinced.' She leaned back against the wooden window casement.

'You see? You, too, you've fallen for his charm.' Victor threw up his hands in exasperation.

'If one of his disciples turns out to have been wicked, do you hold him responsible?'

'Of course.' He shrugged. 'Anyway, Luke and I will soldier on with our campaign to thwart the Renewal Movement's expansionist ambitions.' He gave her a lopsided grin. 'Who knows, if the story's good enough, the *Sunday Herald* itself may decide to buy it!'

'I doubt Michael would think it wise.' His name pained her, though, and she pulled away from the window, retreated into the drawing room and onto the sofa.

Victor followed her in, stood before her. 'Well,' he stared down at her, 'who knows what Michael might do any more?' As he said the words, he suddenly flushed, his eyes fleeing hers. Quickly, he began his pacing once again.

'Who knows what Michael might do any more?' She repeated his words and felt panic overwhelm her. Did Victor know? Was this the reason for the wary concern she had read in his eyes? Was this why he had come to see her? Her head was spinning.

'Nina, are you all right?' He had stopped his pacing and stood before her, peering down at her, eyes large and dark and full of sympathy. Or pity. She swallowed hard, brought a hand to her mouth. No, not Victor, don't let Victor know of my humiliation.

She placed both hands on her knees, as if to steady herself. She stared up at him, trying to divine his thoughts. But he gave no hint of harbouring any suspicions.

'Nina,' his voice was soft.

'I'm all right, I'm all right . . . It's a migraine, I've been getting them lately.' She tried to keep her voice calm. She looked away from him. 'You'd better go,' she whispered.

'You don't need anything?' He now crouched beside her.

She shook her head and in a loud, hard voice said, 'Please. Go. Now.'

When he'd gone, she burst into tears. The thought of his having known about the betrayal all this time – it was too much for her, too horrible to contemplate. Victor, whose love and admiration she had taken so much for granted, Victor must not see her fall from her pedestal.

She sat back in the sofa, watching the sun glitter, harsh as a hostile gaze. How could she go on? How?

Slowly she stood up, walked to the mirror, dried her face with a tissue from her skirt pocket. 'You must get out, walk outside, move,' she ordered the pale face. Quickly she turned away from its misery, grabbed her handbag from the coat-rack, stepped out into the white light. She rushed, eyes on the pavement, and made her way towards the King's Road.

She fought the vision of Michael and Allegra, entwined, smiling, whispering. They deserved nothing but pain. That was what the horrible Johnny Stephenson had said: they are the most evil of all, those who betray our love and trust. They deserve nothing but pain.

How had he found out about her husband and Allegra? What kind of threats had he been capable of, this strange young man so alive to the satisfaction of punishing evil-doers? He had struck her as mad, in his convert's zeal, his eagerness to rush into battle for society's soul.

As she thought of him she arranged and rearranged images and plans, knowing that she was trying to plumb, somehow, his wild-eyed fervour for an opportunity to further her own aim. His link to Allegra, and the young woman's to the Circle: did they not offer her the lever she sought against her husband's mistress? No matter how sheltered Allegra might feel by Michael's love, the shy young woman from the provinces who had sought the Renewal Movement for companionship could not have cast off its influence so easily. Guilt would darken her joy and fear her ardour every day of her adulterous affair. In Allegra's guilt, Nina mused, lay her own deliverance.

The King's Road was already busy, though it was only ten o'clock. People walked past her without a glance, consulting maps and staring at the landmarks they announced and explained to one another in a flurry of foreign languages. Nina walked among them, and felt as alien as they were, her body and spirit completely detached from this surrounding she had called home: in the wide avenue of glossy shop windows, handsome houses, thickly leaved trees she felt insignificant and out of tune. She found no pleasure in the confident, shiny road, in the blue shallow waves of the inviting sky, in the greenness of the trees that swayed discreetly round St Luke's Church and the Farmer's Market. She walked quickly, head down, and saw only a few puddles left over from last night's burst of rain and the dust that rolled, as if it were seized with laughter, from side to side of the wide pavement.

Michael. What had he forced her to become? She, who had been above envy, jealousy and petty suspicions, she, who had felt so strong and so unimpeachable in her righteousness, she had become a lesser woman. She had been forced into a narrow, coffin-shaped despair that had belittled her spirit and reduced her vision so that all she could see or sense were the consequences of his betrayal. Allegra, too, she had no doubt, had been distorted by her illicit affair, no longer the innocent hopeful disciple of the Renewal Movement who had so protectively sat by Johnny Stephenson.

Alexander's face imposed itself on her thoughts: she hadn't gone to see him for a week now. Partly because of a series of interviews she'd been doing for the *Society* . . . partly because, she admitted to herself, she felt he was beginning to wield a great power over her. She had begun to find his physical appeal troubling: she'd grown uncomfortably conscious of the muscular body that seemed increasingly impatient with the restraining vicar's suit; of eyes that lingered over her figure; of his own confusion when she drew close.

The town hall stood ahead, unassuming in height, its grey faded elegance like an elderly society hostess's. 'No to pornography!' She heard the words raised in a chant, taken up and repeated by a chorus. She looked up and saw a group of people standing on the pavement, in front of the cinema across the King's Road. They were a shapeless group, noticeable for the placards they bore. She looked up at the cinema: it was showing *Mimi's First Love*, the new 'arty' French film that had caused a stir for its sexual explicitness. She caught sight of one placard: the poster of the film (a naked photograph of the starlet, her long blonde hair flowing in a strategic cover-up) had been cut in half, to make room for black bold letters proclaiming, 'Do not lead me into temptation.'

Standing beneath one of these posters, his head a fig leaf of modesty against Mimi's most treasured asset, she saw Tom Sutton. He was red-faced and in shirtsleeves, his black hair dancing across his face as his head bobbed up and down. 'We'll put a stop to pornography, we'll barricade our cities against the onslaught of this foreign filth . . .'

The words were diluted by the onrush of cars, the words of passers-by. She crossed the road and approached the group that huddled beneath the swaying placards. They were mostly women, uniform in their ferocious expression and nondescript looks – as if virtue had blunted their features, and prayer bleached their colouring. She noticed a man handing out leaflets. As she drew nearer, she saw that he was a youngster, puffed up with self-importance.

Nina looked at the middle-aged housewives, the children they had brought along. 'Stop the corruption of the innocents! Protect us from evil!' A group held hands, swinging their arms as if to gather momentum for a more strident declaration of war. She could see them encourage one another with glances and whispered comments.

'Where is he? Where is Alexander?' one of the women asked. Nina felt disappointed that he should have anything to do with these people.

They were, she mused, as unworthy of representing Alexander as her ancient recording of *I Pagliacci* was incapable of capturing (with its intermittent dragging of notes, its tinny sound and many scratches) Beniamino Gigli's incomparable voice.

'What will they do to our society? Don't they understand how they will affect us with their lewd visions and their display of gross and bestial acts?' Tom Sutton was raising his arms like a conductor trying to lead his orchestra's response.

Beneath the truncated body of the naked starlet, the group nodded vigorously and issued a great chorus of 'Yes!'

'What kind of a society allows for this filth? What kind of people watch these foul spectacles?'

Nina watched the youthful politician work himself into indignation, with large, febrile arm gestures and exclamations of ire. Above him, the blonde starlet smiled on beatifically.

'Get out of here! You're interfering with my business. I'm going to call the police!' An elderly man had come out of the cinema, shirtsleeves rolled back as if for a fight. Squat, neckless, he glared at the protesters through thick, black-rimmed glasses.

A few women rushed at him, like angry hens. 'Stop showing this filth!' they hissed.

'Filth? How dare you! It's a masterpiece!' He held his ground, his black-bordered gaze fierce.

'Put a stop to this obscenity or we will!' a woman shouted from the back of the group.

Nina suddenly saw a trickle of men and women making its silent way behind the cinema, towards a side street: the cinema customers were slipping out of the back door. She realised now that the manager was bent on diversion tactics. No one else, in fact, had noticed *Mimi's* audience sneaking out.

'Have you even seen *Mimi's First Love*?' The cinema manager snatched a leaflet from the young man, and waved it in the air before the women. 'I bet you don't even know what's shown and what isn't.' He threw his arms up in the air, relinquishing the little leaflet, which flew up and then, as if its wings had turned leaden, sank to the pavement. 'God preserve us from self-appointed censors! From all censors in fact!' The cinema manager shook his fist at them once more, then went back inside, through the glass doors, mission accomplished.

Nina saw Alexander approach, his tall, black-clad body striking a mournful note among the bright colours of the King's Road. She watched as the women and children immediately surrounded him, and he placed his hands upon the children's heads. Nina did not move while the vicar bent low to share a secret word with the youngsters, then with the women who touched his sleeves, his hands. 'We shall win this battle if we continue,' a woman's voice rose triumphantly.

'Yes, yes,' she heard Alexander reply. He raised his eyes as he caressed a young boy's sleek head, and spotted Nina. He blushed and she saw him look slightly taken aback, as if he were not certain of how to proceed.

Then he came forward. 'Nina.' He loomed over her. She took a step back, embarrassed, happy.

'I . . . you haven't come for so long.' He was smiling at her. 'I was beginning to worry . . .'

'Alexander,' she whispered.

'Have you been ill?' he asked, and such concern trembled in his voice that Nina felt excitement run through her.

'No, no, just working terribly hard on a column – it needed a great many interviews.' She hoped he could not see her confusion.

'What brings you here?' He surveyed the group of chanting protesters.

'I found them by accident. And you – are you organising them?'

He sensed her tone of disapproval and frowned. 'Pornography is one of the main issues on Tom Sutton's agenda so I am here to lend a hand.'

'I see,' she said, thinking that if Alexander were allowing Sutton to get on this bandwagon he must be convinced that the rumours about the politician's skeletons in the closet were false.

'The corruption of the innocent . . .' he began.

'I'm sure you'll find that *Mimi*'s fans are none too innocent – and no one has coerced them into buying admission tickets.'

A young woman, blonde and plumply pretty, drew near to the vicar. She seemed oblivious of Nina as she addressed the vicar. 'They want to move on to the Oxford Street cinema.' She looked to him for a lead.

Nina said nothing but watched the young woman before her listen, rapt, to the vicar's every word. Nina stole a glance at the delicate lineaments, the half-smile that lit his face as he listened to the young woman's praise. And immediately the image of Allegra appeared: it was as Johnny had prophesied, a word from him and her spirit would be broken.

'Aren't you scared,' Nina whispered as the young woman left their side, 'of your power over them? The influence you wield is tremendous.'

'I approach it with the greatest of caution. I realise how impression-able most of these men and women are. They have but started the long pilgrimage along the right path and are like children, seeking advice and humbly accepting it.' Suddenly he smiled. 'Do you fear me irresponsible?'

'No. No, I don't. I think you are very conscious of your great influence on – on us all.' She blushed as she spoke the words, and looked away from him.

She felt his eyes on her. 'Nina, I told you that faith is longing – but it is also a burning need to share with others what you see as the truth.' He drew closer, so that she could feel his warm breath on her face. This proximity shook her, and she could decipher his words only with the greatest of difficulty. 'I feel as if it is through your . . . ordeal . . . that you will find the true path. And that I have been placed in your way for the explicit purpose of leading you into the fold of our Movement. I see you draw close, closer . . . and I fervently hope one day you will become one of us.' He took hold of her hand.

She said nothing: she did not want to reveal to him that in allying herself to him she was motivated by concerns that were much more base. No, she would not disabuse him: she was prepared to be whatever he wished her to be.

Suddenly he laughed, 'Let me live in hope,' and he made as if to wrap her in an embrace. But he dropped her hand, and the arm that he had extended towards her, and looked down. 'Yes, I live in hope,' he murmured.

'Alexander!' Tom Sutton hurried towards them, brandishing his mobile phone with great excitement. 'They rang to say there is a camera crew making its way here – they're on the King's Road. I think I should stay – you too, Alexander, we could make an impromptu speech.'

He was exhilarated as he smiled at his mentor.

'Yes, you stay. But I was on my way back to St Mark's.' He turned from Tom's disappointed face to Nina. 'Shall I walk you home?'

She nodded. Tom Sutton hunched over to murmur into his telephone. Slowly he walked away from them, speaking all the time into the small black box pressed to his ear.

As she strode away with Alexander, Nina turned her head and saw the placards bob up and down, the women linking arms as they continued their chorus, the young man handing out leaflets to passers-by.

Nina and Alexander walked for a while in silence. Then the vicar, without turning to her, asked, 'How has it been? Michael? Has anything changed?'

'No changes.' Her voice was dark with bitterness. 'Johnny told me that he knows about Allegra Worth, that he's been following her.' She took a deep breath and resumed, as if each word were an immense high step that would require great effort and must be approached with care. 'I think she is still trying to see my husband.' It was strange, she thought, how easy it was to make Allegra sound like the aggressor, when in fact she was certain that it would have been Michael who seduced the admiring young woman. But if Allegra were cast in the role of temptress, she, Nina, would become the victim of evil rather than the spurned wife.

'Yet only a few months ago she was completely devoted to Jesus Christ, to our Movement and the Circle.' Alexander walked on, as if there were no more that he could say.

Nina studied his profile for reaction as she spoke the next words. 'My friend Victor Strauss tells me that he and Luke Aldridge have unearthed some very damaging information about Tom Sutton.'

The vicar stopped walking. He remained rigid, unmoving, for a moment, then turned slowly to face her. 'What did he say?'

'They have heard about a young man who claims that Tom Sutton raped him. They're trying to find him – get him to tell his story.'

Alexander placed both hands on her shoulders. He stared into her eyes and she could feel his hands tight on her cotton shirt, as if they sought to squeeze every fact out of her. 'Nina, this is important. What do they plan to do with this information?'

'Publish it.' Nina felt the excitement rush through her blood like a heady mixture of alcohol. 'Victor is Michael's best friend and he's told Michael – though he doesn't think the *Sunday Herald* will run the story. But the worst of it is that if I know Michael, he won't be able to resist telling Allegra. He may have done so already. My fear is that she'll use it against you.'

## Chapter Twenty One

Michael was sweating in his car as he crawled home along the Embankment, and for the umpteenth time he cursed the trustees for having decided to curb expenses by dispensing with – among other things – the editors' chauffeurs. He had enjoyed it so much for the brief months it had been granted to him. It was the one thing Maurice had had over him: he remembered his erstwhile editor lolling about in the back of his Jaguar like a well-upholstered sultan amid the leather.

Oh, well, he wouldn't wish to trade places with Maurice: he must be writhing in his penthouse flat above the river. Yes, writhing with jealousy as he watched the *Sunday Herald* improve its circulation – and get those two scoops (the whip and his misdemeanours, and the Swiss bank scandal . . . not bad, after only a few months in the editor's chair). No, he was certain Maurice must be livid – and the trustees pleased.

The sun beamed down, stifling. It was midday, and he'd decided to surprise Nina by coming home early: he'd take her out to lunch or something, cheer her up. A bit of attention, a little flattery would do her no end of good.

Damn. His arm, leaning out of the car window, was getting burned and his shirt was sticking to his back, his wet neck to his collar, and meanwhile no one was moving along this stretch because of the road works. He cursed Westminster Council with its urge to resurface the roads; cursed the trustees with their austerity measures. Couldn't a hard-working man be left in peace? But no, it had been problem, problem, problem blocking his path over the past few weeks, what with Nina keeping him at a distance and Allegra breaking down in tears every few minutes. 'You don't understand, they're hounding me! Johnny Stephenson keeps frightening me with threats about the fate scarlet women deserve. Oh, Michael, please help me,' and Allegra had clung to him as he had tried to make his escape from the horrid little flat in Hammersmith. It was uncanny, he thought now, in the sweltering

173

heat compressed by the car, her sixth sense about his decision. It was as if she had guessed that he meant to stop their affair, and had shrewdly understood that her best weapon would be to stoke his pity.

Michael honked at a cyclist who brushed past him and wove dangerously between his car and the one in front. But it was no use. He'd already made up his mind to put a stop to this madness. Well, if truth be told, Lady Katherine had made up his mind for him. She had called on him unexpectedly, late last Friday night, when he'd been so under pressure that the sight of her had filled him with panic. She had sat herself down on one of the two small Italian armchairs in his office, taken off her great hat, shaken her head and pierced him with narrowed eyes. Without spelling out a thing, she had let him understand she knew about Allegra, would brook no scandal, and that he must 'gently but firmly set the poor thing down'.

Michael, red-faced and speechless, had merely nodded agreement, and Lady Katherine had embarked on a completely different subject.

At the memory, his left hand at the bottom of the steering wheel grew clammy and he felt the fear squeeze his stomach. Yes, Allegra had been a false step along the climb to the dizzying heights to which he'd always aspired. Thank goodness he hadn't fallen. Now he must obey his trustee, take a deep breath and continue his climb. He could smell the sweet scent of success all around him, see its attractive blooms, feel enclosed in its embrace. Nothing must distract him now. He must never stray from Nina's side again.

For it was Nina who stood in the very heart of his successful world, and he must cling to her. She had led him out of the Henley existence where everything was small, grey and compact, where everyone was an accountant like his father or a bank clerk like his uncles. She had shown him onto a brightly lit stage, beneath an immense, high, vaulted ceiling. Here he was suddenly important, illuminated, and his voice carried within the great domed space while a huge audience watched his every move. He had loved it from the first, and he was ready to make what was, after all, a small sacrifice in order to stay there, lit up, important, the focus of so many eyes.

The implacable sun blazed, turning the car in front of him into a blinding steel object. He felt almost unable to breathe: the heat lay tight around him.

He had been careful, damn careful, but he should have known, the moment Allegra had told him about Johnny's threats and of her written confession to Alexander Connaught: 'I wrote to him that, yes, it was

174

true, but that no matter what he or Johnny did I could never give you up.' She had sobbed in his arms. 'I felt I owed him the truth –'

'I wish you'd felt you owed me your discretion,' he'd cut in, appalled by the possibility that she had jeopardised his security.

'Michael, pleeeease.' In her distress, she stretched the word into a long Northern vowel, and he grimaced involuntarily, 'I feel like I'm living through hell. I've lost the only friends I had here, I've betrayed someone who'd been so kind to me.'

Michael had said nothing but had thought about Paolo, that other man who'd showed Allegra such kindness and with whose daughter's husband she was carrying on. Allegra seemed to pick and choose her guilt.

'I felt I ought to tell them they would never win me back with their vile tactics.'

He had looked at her eyes, smudged with tears, at her trembling mouth, and had felt nothing but fury. 'Did you need to cross the t's and dot the i's in order to feel better? Couldn't you have left it in the "general adultery" category rather than name your partner in crime?'

'They made me feel so dirty, terrible –' She had broken into sobs, and her weeping had dragged him back onto the bed, where he sat with his arms around her bowed body.

'Don't cry – don't. I can assure you that he has encountered worse sinners. You should see what dirt we have on that MP he has allied himself with. You are virgin snow in comparison.' And though she had not seemed relieved he found some comfort in his own words: if that cleric ever started making sinister noises about revealing his affair, he could counter with his own threat to publish the evidence against Tom Sutton that Luke Aldridge and Victor had assembled. But that plan had been aborted with Lady Katherine's visit: obviously she had swallowed the party line, and would never allow her newspaper to make any embarrassing disclosures about a Renewal member. Yes, he decided once again, as the traffic ahead began to move. He would stop seeing Allegra, and stop mulling over what was, after all, a small mistake. His life had no room for regret: regret was for those who have not found enough in their present to fulfil them and must always look back. Regret was for the accountants and the bank clerks he'd left behind in Henley.

Nina could not make out whether the vicar had known about Tom Sutton's past: he had walked on, silent, ashen-faced, and she had hurried to keep pace. In the end, it didn't matter: all she needed was the look of anger mixed with fear that had transformed his face to know that he would act.

They were coming to her street and Nina placed a light hand on his arm. 'Please, Alexander, will you come in? I could make you a cup of tea?'

He seemed happy as he answered, 'Yes. Yes, I would like that.' They walked on quickly towards the house, again lapsing into silence. When they reached the door, she ushered him in, suddenly aware that this was the first time he had ever set foot inside her home – and that they were alone. It was as if the realisation had struck the vicar as well, and she felt him nervous beside her as she led him to the armchair. 'I . . . I don't think I will stay for tea, after all,' he almost stammered. Then he relaxed as he surveyed the golden room and watched her stand beside her desk, one hand on its green leather surface. 'Do you know, I have often imagined you at your desk in a room very much like this one . . . Yes, it is almost exactly as I pictured it.' He was nodding and smiling as he spoke.

Nina moved to the sofa, sat in front of him. She marvelled at the strange intimacy between them, a sudden and complete understanding, as if they had been siblings or a couple well versed in one another's ways. This new ease, which she felt all the more keenly because it had so recently disappeared from her friendship with Victor, filled her with self-confidence. They were now, she almost smiled, accomplices.

'How it must pain you to see women like Allegra make a mockery of your teachings,' she murmured.

His cool hand touched hers and she saw him blush. 'I must face the hardships that come with my ministry, as well as its great joys.' He was studying her, as if searching for some clue to her own feelings. 'It has been such a revelation – and a relief – to find someone who can share my vision.'

'I don't think I'm capable of your vision,' Nina said truthfully, not daring to look into those eyes where she had read such yearning.

'How can you say that, Nina? You would not be here with me now.'

She wondered if she should tell him that she only wished to believe in his God because he came with a Devil. She wished to believe in his idea of salvation because it meant there was damnation, too. But she saw him tired now, almost hollow-eyed, as he lay back against her sofa. 'What is it, Alexander?'

He shook his head slowly. 'Sometimes I feel as if I'm so very inexperienced as a reader of souls. I understand what He wants me to do and where He wants me to go. But as for others . . . I fear that I fail them.'

'How can you say that?'

'I look about me, and I feel that they all seek something different, something that I either cannot or should not give them. Tom, Lady Katherine, Johnny, even the youngsters in the Circle. So many of them seem more excited by the prospect of personal success than communal welfare, of revenge than joy of salvation.' He sighed. 'They ask, where is the purge of evil I have promised them? And I have to answer that the cleansing of our society cannot be accomplished in a few days. They ask, why have laws not been enacted that would safeguard the family and protect the lives of the unborn? And I have to reply that so far, every politician speaks of their belief in a return to morality but only a handful are prepared to work for the cause. The truth is they want me to deliver my vision now, immediately. They don't understand that they must help me construct it.'

'Alexander,' her tone was loving, 'you must not think that. You have helped so many – surely you must see that.' He shut his eyes, leaned back against the silk. 'Where would Tom Sutton be without you, or Lady Katherine or Johnny? And what about me? You have given me courage when I had spiralled into such despair.' She was whispering, and took one of his hands in hers. 'I am so grateful to you.' She pushed her fingers in his, then brought up her right hand and kissed his fingers locked in hers.

'Oh, Nina . . .' The words were barely audible.

Her heart pounded as they sat, immobile, in the bright sunlight.

When Michael walked in through his front door and found Alexander Connaught with his wife, he felt a rush of fear. What was this vicar – more important, this vicar who'd read Allegra's confession – doing in his drawing room? What was he telling his wife? Why did the two look so guilt-stricken when he walked in? Why did Nina avoid his gaze?

'Hello.' He forced jollity into his voice as he threw down the jacket and tie he held far from his overheated sweaty body.

'Alexander just dropped by.'

Michael frowned as Nina stated the obvious: he scented danger, something was not quite right. He fumbled through his memory as if it were the chest of drawers which, in the sunless winter mornings, he ransacked unseeing for his socks and underwear. What was the teaching about confession? Was a vicar bound by secrecy? He knew about Catholic priests – encountered plenty of maddening, black-cassocked creatures who wouldn't give up criminals to the police or talk to the press, hiding coyly behind the secrecy of the confessional. But what of their Church of England counterparts?

He scowled at Alexander, then, remembering that he was Lady Katherine's mentor, he relaxed his face into a smiling countenance. 'It's terrible out there . . . beastly hot.'

'Yes.' Alexander stood up, looking flustered, embarrassed.

Nina said nothing, but kept her gaze from her husband, even as he pecked her forehead.

'I must . . . must be going.' The vicar gave a little cough. 'Thank you, Nina, and I hope I may see you soon again at St Mark's.' He blushed as he said, 'We miss you there.'

Nina nodded. 'Yes.' She walked him to the door.

'I didn't realise you were so chummy with Lady K's spiritual director.' Michael spoke in a light voice, but again his eyebrows bunched in a frown.

'Oh, I see him from time to time.' She shrugged, keeping her eyes averted as she took his jacket and tie from the armchair where he'd sloppily discarded them, shook them out, draped them over her arm like a weary waiter with a napkin.

'You don't think . . . I mean, he looked as if he were a bit in love with you.' Michael studied her as he threw out the words.

'Hm.' Again she shrugged. 'Perhaps he is. I hadn't thought of it. He's very kind to me – very . . . protective.'

She made as if to move past him, to go to the coat cupboard beneath the stairs, but Michael's arm shot out and he grabbed her wrist. 'Are you all right?'

'Yes.' She didn't pull away her wrist, and now looked into his eyes with a dark and inscrutable gaze. 'Why?'

'You,' he couldn't resist adopting the counter-attack mode he always employed when he felt defensive, 'you are so cold and distant these days . . . makes me feel edgy, miserable.' Then, seeing she was impervious to his words, he wrapped his arms around her. 'Nina,' he tried to press his lips to hers.

'Get off!' She pushed him away from her, threw tie and jacket in his face. 'Don't touch me!'

She was screaming, her face contorted. Michael took a step back, afraid of her outburst. 'Nina . . .' he whispered.

'How dare you ignore me for months on end, treat me as if I were some object in this room and then, when the whim takes you, push yourself on me? You fill me with disgust!' She was shaking, and sobs kept breaking through.

'Please, Nina.'

'Who do you think you are?'

'Nina . . .' Terror filled him as he watched his wife's body bend over and spill forth the sobs. She knew – she couldn't know, she suspected . . . and he was dizzy with the images of the strange, eerily beautiful face, the look of fear on Allegra's face raised to his, Lady Katherine's cool bright eyes as she told him to put his house in order.

'I won't be taken for granted like this!' She was screaming, as he'd never heard her scream before.

Suddenly he heard the knocking on the door, and opened it mechanically while behind him Nina screamed, 'Don't!'

Robbie stood before him, eyes large behind their spectacles. For a second, he confronted his father, and Michael felt the accusing eyes look from himself to Nina beyond him. Then Robbie rushed wordlessly past his father to throw his arms around his mother. 'Mummy!' he whimpered.

Michael watched, helpless, as Nina lifted their son in her embrace, and made her way up the stairs with him.

But downstairs, as he hung up his jacket, folded the tie to pocket size, and poured himself a finger of neat vodka, Michael felt his guilt mingle with relief. Surely if she'd known about Allegra it would have come out now. She couldn't have suppressed it during that scene. And he downed the vodka in one go. She'd accused him of ignoring her – of nothing else. The odds were that she didn't know about the affair. From now on, though, he must be above suspicion.

# Chapter Twenty Two

Allegra came out of the tube, walked up the stairs slowly. She felt tired – it had been a long day at the Diary, and she had still not recovered from the horror of the move. Katie had said nothing but had stared at her with patent disbelief as Allegra mumbled that her decision to live in Bow was a matter of finances. She had volunteered to drive Allegra and her belongings to the new flat – in the same car, Allegra had thought with sadness, that she had borrowed for those secret happy assignations with Michael. Allegra had quickly turned down the offer: she didn't want anyone from the Circle to know her whereabouts. 'Goodbye, then.' Katie had stood at the door. 'God bless.'

The flat itself was in a converted council block, a bare and tight little place that she feared would never be home. Mum had been the only person to telephone her so far – but that had been more painful than reassuring for Allegra had had to answer almost every question with a lie. Mum had asked if she'd quarrelled with Katie, whether she could urge Alexander to visit his followers in Sheffield, whether the new editor at the *Sunday Herald* had made any difference.

But even worse than betraying her mother had been Michael's reaction to her move, of which she had expected him to approve with enthusiasm. That moment had transformed her world into a loneliness that seemed to pull her down, further and further, into its black drain. He had watched her silently, with cool blue eyes, as she had tried to explain how much easier it would be to see one another without worrying about Katie's movements or suspicions.

Slowly, he had unclasped her hands, gently pushed her body away from his own. 'I'm not sure this was a wise step. You're miles from anyone you know and you can't expect me to drop everything and run over when you feel lonely.'

She shuddered at the thought of him, and her stomach felt the void that seemed to grow with every passing day. He was trying to absolve himself of all responsibility for her happiness, to distance himself from her, adopting a brusque new tone, all expression retreating from his eyes. Michael . . . She trembled at the sight of his angry face as he exploded with rage when she told him she had written to Alexander.

Oh, Michael! She almost sobbed his name aloud as she walked the dirty Bow Road, with its cheap shops sporting saris on blonde-hair white-skinned mannequins, used electrical appliances, tired fruit and vegetables. The fluorescent light of the fast-food shops alternated with the red lanterns hanging in the windows of Indian restaurants, and the dying sun rays hit the glass panes obliquely so that they reflected in an unpleasant glare.

She walked quickly, as ever slightly frightened by the turbaned men who stared, the appreciative whistles of the white boys who hung about outside the pubs. Sometimes she felt certain that they re-cognised her for what she'd been branded by Johnny – a scarlet woman, a temptress who had led a husband from his wife's bed. And she would lower her head, lest the tremendous stigma of guilt she bore would somehow become manifest, shining like a blood red marking on her forehead.

Dear Jesus, why, why? Why had it been so easy to turn her back on her God, to withdraw from the safe, cosy world of St Mark's and the Circle? Why had it been so simple to run from Alexander's arms and fall into Michael's? Why had no one warned her of the guilt and the dread and the loneliness that would await her if she attached herself to a married man?

She walked on amid the newsprint pages that skated along the dusty pavement. She hated London now. When she had been so certain of Michael's love, she had come to see London as a huge tree whose capable branches welcomed her into their fold, forming a bower in which she could feel at once safe and raised above the ordinary. But now she saw only the filthy pavements, the narrow dark alleyways, the low weakly lit skies that seemed to creep along the rooftops and the minaret of the mosque rather than soar above them.

She was frightened by Michael's hold on her, by the terrible lies she repeated to her poor mother, by the memory of those threatening telephone calls and anonymous letters that had stopped only with her move. Johnny's disembodied voice, light and slightly breathless, had lowered into a hiss and spluttered warnings and menaces; his letters had been cheap paper upon which he had glued newsprint words and single letters to spell out Biblical warnings and calls for redemption.

A slight breeze swept round her as if to rid her of the day-long heat, muttering like the street cleaner whom she saw every morning on the pavement before the council block.

She walked quickly now, beneath the bridge, turning right into a narrow street of grey houses. A car swerved to avoid her. For an instant she thought it was Michael's: she must stop seeing him, hearing him everywhere she went. Her obsession filled her with fear: could everybody read his name, hear her longing, see his face, detect her love when they met her? Certainly, the entire newsroom knew. They probably pitied her, realising how precarious her situation was. Nina del Monte would not sit passively by while her husband cavorted with some young nobody and the Stephensons would quash any scandal that brewed in their hallowed newsrooms. But the hacks probably also envied her the pillow power that would ensure her own job safety and possibly, who knew, some degree of influence on the editor's actions. As long as their affair lasted. Allegra suddenly stopped, took a deep breath: it was as if, every time she recognised her own position, she felt bludgeoned. She couldn't bear to think about it, couldn't bear to uncover the secret instinctive knowledge that he wouldn't leave his wife and son for her. Allegra looked up at the feeble sun: she felt herself tremble and sway.

'Stop this.' She spoke aloud, trying to steady herself. Slowly and with heavy steps she moved on, trying to keep herself from stumbling.

She had no one to blame but herself: she had yielded to his advances without reservation. She had thought herself invincible when he, the all-powerful, much-envied editor had chosen her among all others. She had somehow thought this meant that she and he . . . that they would remain together for ever, bonded to the end, a couple. It had been so easy then to dismiss Nina, to overlook Robbie: Michael could not have been satisfied, after all, if he'd come seeking her. The ease with which, as he first kissed her, remorse had given way to joy, fear to hope and guilt to triumph still dazzled her, like a sudden burst of sun in a cloudy sky. But that hope-soaked trance, which had enveloped her for those first weeks, had now dissipated. In its stead she felt a terrible dark fear, like a prowler she sensed but could not see in the dark. 'Dear Jesus, help me, help me,' she repeated to herself.

'Stop! Allegra!' She thought she had imagined the call but turned to find Johnny Stephenson running towards her. Allegra immediately walked away, broke into a run, raised her hands to her ears to block out his cries. 'Allegra! Stop!'

She ran, her heart almost hurting as she pounded the pavement, turned into her street, the tears of fear and anger streaming down her face.

'Watch it, luv.' A man with drink on his breath staggered towards her, bearlike as he tried to embrace her.

Allegra tried to make way for his tottering figure, and in that instant Johnny grasped her elbow. 'You can't keep running away like this,' he shouted.

Allegra tried to pull away her arm, but he held fast. She wouldn't look up to face him but kept her head low, the tears burning in her eyes, her nose dripping, as he grabbed hold of her shoulders. 'Don't you realise there's nowhere to hide?' When he raised his voice it was different from the one that had whispered her sins over the telephone, entered her sleep at night, and seeped into her hours of loneliness during the day.

The memory of his persistent threats angered her now so that she raised her face to his and, lips trembling, screamed at him, 'How dare you send me those threats? How dare you ring me with your foul accusations! Leave me alone!' Again she tried to wrest herself free of his hold, but his hands held on to the sleeve of her cotton shirt. His expression remained set, impervious to her outburst. In his ashen face the wide watery eyes shone grimly. 'Stop hounding me! Why must you torture me so?' She trembled violently, feeling herself powerless in his grip.

Johnny did not blink, did not even attempt to deny her accusations. He merely shook his head in sad reproof. 'Have you really shut out the Spirit, Allegra?'

Allegra shuddered at the proximity of those large eyes, that pale dull skin. She closed her own eyes, head dropping. 'Oh, Johnny, please . . .' Her voice broke and the sobs burst out so that her torso rocked back and forth. 'Please,' she sobbed, engulfed in the dark guilt and the cold fear of being abandoned by Michael and by the world she had been so quick to reject.

'Come along.' He took her arm in his and was almost pulling her along down the pavement.

She felt her feet drag, her head fill with a confusion of thoughts and sensations. He pulled her and she couldn't resist. She followed him, unseeing, tears moistening her face, as he hurried towards her block of flats. They came to the stairs and, as she looked up to begin their climb, she saw him: Alexander, standing in front of her door.

'Noooooo!' Allegra howled her dismay. She felt terror fill her.

'Come now, Allegra, don't be like this.' Johnny's voice was low.

'Can't you leave me alone?' She was weeping. 'Go, please, go!' Her words were indistinguishable, as if worn down to some indistinct matter by her sobs.

'Come . . .' His arm beneath her own, he was hoisting her up the stairs.

Allegra felt her knees give way, and thought she would fall in a faint on the first step. Above her, standing immobile at the top of the stairs, Alexander looked down upon the two figures. He remained completely silent. Allegra could not look at his face.

'How did you find me?' she wailed. Her legs buckled beneath her, but Johnny would not desist and practically dragged her to the top of the staircase.

'Allegra.' Alexander's gentle voice shimmered in the air between them.

She kept her head bowed, refusing to meet those judging eyes. Alexander reached out a hand, lightly touched her shoulder. Long, white, cool, it sent shivers through her body. She was as if paralysed between the two figures.

'Allegra, may we come in? I would like to discuss a few things with you.'

'No!' She screamed the word so that Alexander flinched before her.

But then, with a thin smile he addressed her. 'My dear, you can keep away from our church, you can keep from the Circle, but you cannot continue to hide from Him. He will find you wherever you flee. But not,' here the sweet low voice dropped lower still, 'to seek revenge, Allegra. He loves you, and will not let you lose your way or turn from Him.'

'Allegra, open the door.' Johnny's voice sounded brittle, distant.

She did not move.

'Open the door,' Alexander's voice was strong, and would brook no disobedience.

Allegra sank her hand into her bag and removed the keys. Helpless, she turned the key in the lock, and opened the door. Both men waited for her to step into the dark dingy corridor. She heard them follow her in. She did not offer a seat or a drink, but stood immobile in the middle of the white square room.

'Allegra, I have been praying for you for many weeks now.' Alexander sat down on the green sofa and she saw a split on the cushion smile with yellow foam next to his black jacket.

Johnny sat beside his spiritual mentor. She did not look at them.

184

Alexander's words filled the room, bearing down on her. She felt as if, in a cruel rewriting of her baptism, he were holding her underwater, his hands pressing her down into the tepid stillness, determined that she should never resurface.

'You must understand that it pains me to know you are unhappy. For it is clear to those who love you that you are a decent girl, and will soon become terribly unhappy in this ungodly situation. You are guilty of tempting a man from his duty, Allegra, of trying to wrest him away from his family, his beloved wife and child. Allegra, you have turned a weak man into a contemptible sinner – an adulterer.' He enunciated the word very carefully, frowning as he looked at her. 'But I care nothing for Michael Lewis – I will pray for his soul but will waste no time trying to persuade him. It is you, *you* I want to recall to the path of virtue. You, who I know in her heart of hearts cannot abide what she has become. You must give him up, Allegra, free him to return to his wife.'

Without looking at him she could feel his eyes upon her. 'I am guilty,' she whispered. 'I know what I have done, I know how I have offended Him, you, the Movement . . .' She refused to look at either man. 'I have disappointed you, those who care for me. I know what I have done!' Her words came in small bursts, like sobs.

'You'll ruin yourself and you'll ruin him. A whiff of scandal, and his life will be destroyed. Think of what the trustees would do, were they to discover your secret. They would oust him without a moment's hesitation.' Alexander clasped his hands before him. 'And you see, Allegra, I cannot allow that to happen. I cannot lose our best ally because of some indiscretion. Michael Lewis at the helm of the *Sunday Herald* has been important to the Movement. I won't let you destroy that for us.'

'It's too late, it's too late,' Allegra said, and saw the vicar frown. She could not still her trembling: even her voice shook. 'I'm not worthy of being a member of your Circle – don't you think I know that? I've betrayed you. I've betrayed you all!'

Alexander flinched. She saw him and Johnny exchange a look. 'You have betrayed us?' he repeated softly.

'Yes, yes, with Michael.' Again, as she uttered the words, she saw the vicar tense. 'I have let you down.'

Johnny made a move as if to stand up but Alexander held him back. The vicar kept his eyes on Allegra. He rose from the couch and took her by the hand. 'Allegra, what have you done? What have you said?'

Allegra did not raise her head but remained stooped before him. The

185

cool long fingers held tight her quivering hand. 'You have betrayed us, you say.' She looked up to find the vicar staring at her with a terrible expression.

'What do you mean, Allegra?' Johnny's question shot out.

She could not speak, her eyes on Alexander's face before her, fearsome, unforgiving.

'Tom Sutton, Allegra, is one of us. His campaign is our campaign.' The vicar spoke in a staccato voice.

Allegra looked at him, uncomprehending. 'If our dream to create a new world is ever to be fulfilled, we need men like Tom.' The voice now grew louder. 'We cannot allow you to ruin this for us, my dear.' She wept now, her hand trapped in his.

'Allegra.' He intoned her name like a lamentation and drew up close to her, lifted her chin with his index finger.

'I'm sorry, I'm sorry.' She sobbed. 'Please . . . leave me . . . I can't come back, I can't come back!' and she brought up her hands to cover her face. Immobile, she stood with her hands like a shield.

She heard Johnny stand up, approach Alexander.

'Allegra, Allegra,' Alexander murmured sadly. She would not lower her hands.

'We shall have to pursue this later, I can see, when you are calm.' Alexander's soothing voice seemed coated in forgiveness.

Allegra could hear Johnny whisper that they ought to go before 'anyone' arrived. She lowered her hands and, as if through a distant window, she saw Alexander nod, cast her one last look of concern and move away towards the door.

Johnny placed an arm around her and brought her to the armchair, where he lightly pushed her so that she fell within its green cotton embrace.

The two men saw themselves out, and she heard the door close gently behind them.

'Jesus, help me, help me . . .'

## Chapter Twenty Three

'Johnny! Johnny!' Lady Katherine called her son. She could have sworn she'd heard him come in earlier on, and shut himself in his bedroom as, increasingly, he was wont to do. She was at her dining-room table, stuffing envelopes for Alexander: every member of the Renewal Movement was being asked to pledge as much as they could afford to help build the headquarters for the new Circle in Manchester. She had worked her way through at least fifty names by now, but the white damask was covered still with piles of manila envelopes and sheets of headed paper bearing a photocopy of Alexander's elegant sloping handwriting.

Lady Katherine sighed as she sponged the glued flap, pressed the envelope closed, began writing yet another London address: it was hot, even with the windows open, and her hand was growing tired. She bit back the blasphemy that floated to her full, subtly reddened lips: she must not, she must not. Though, in her time, she had crunched those words like popcorn, spat them out, shocking her nearest and dearest – and earning a delighted laugh from Clive. 'I love it when you talk dirty,' he had murmured, oozing desire whether they were lovers at the time or not.

Poor, dear Clive: she could picture him pacing up and down in his Soho flat, glass in hand, cursing the 'puritan brigade', as he no doubt called them, and their destruction of his *dolce vita*. She had felt dismayed at having been instrumental in his overthrow: within days of the trustees' purchase of the *Society* – a purchase she had been so eager to promote, for Alexander's sake – they had decided to dispense with Clive's services. Too notorious, they had said, too far removed from the new mood of morality sweeping the nation. Lady Katherine had praised his editing skills and brilliant writing – but she had been half-hearted in her defence: between Alexander's gratitude and Clive's, she now sought only her mentor's.

She smiled as she remembered the vicar's warm praise when she had told him about her meeting with Michael Lewis and the ambitious young editor's obvious discomfiture. Lewis would, she had assured her mentor, quickly comply.

Alexander seemed happy these days: he was confident, he told her, that the Movement was unstoppable. And it was true, she could see it in the newspapers, hear it on the radio and on the television: people were dusting off all those old-fashioned words like values and duties, and championing politicians like – well, like Tom Sutton . . .

She frowned at the memory of the exchange she had overheard: she did not like to think of her beloved spiritual guide being tainted by association. Sutton had been adamant that the youth of eighteen had been 'asking for it' and the vicar had been so ready – indeed too ready, she had thought – to speak of redemption. But if Tom's homosexual past were to surface, now that he had publicly launched his campaign of Christian family values, what would happen to the Renewal Movement? What would happen to its leader?

She tried to close her mind to the thoughts that beckoned. Apart from Liu, whom she could hear moving about in the kitchen, the house was silent. Even the garden beyond the open french windows seemed to have slipped into a soporific stillness. Lady Katherine went into the drawing room and took Philip's small transistor radio from the bookshelf, switched it on as she carried it back to the dining-room table.

'Two people were killed when a bomb exploded at an abortion clinic in Oxford Street earlier today.' Lady Katherine raised the volume and stood quite still. 'No one has claimed responsibility for the explosion, which took place at two o'clock this afternoon.'

She walked to the table, set down the small black radio on an envelope. Inexplicably the image of Alexander amid his Circle of young fanatical faces rose before her. She strained to hear more, but the woman's voice had already moved on to cover the deselection of an MP. Lady Katherine switched off the radio. 'Johnny!' she called.

Quickly she climbed the stairs to her son's bedroom. His door was shut. Lady Katherine took a deep breath and knocked. Silence answered her. For a moment she hesitated, not daring to enter his room without his permission. Then she tried the door handle, and it turned easily in her hand. She stepped inside: Liu had drawn the blinds, to keep the sun from the mahogany furniture. The room was tidy, impersonal: all the old posters and magazines, the empty exotic bottles he had collected in his youth had been discarded. She saw a St

Mark's parish newsletter on his desk, the Bible on his bedside table – as in a hotel room, she thought.

She approached the desk by the window: a stack of papers stood to one side and her eye was caught by their newsprint cutouts. 'Death to the unbeliever,' she read, in letters and words culled from different newspapers. She raised her eyes to the recipient's name: Allegra Worth. Astonishment seized her, and then made way for shame, and fear. 'Johnny,' she whispered, 'Oh, Johnny.'

'Two people were killed in the explosion. Police said no one has claimed responsibility for the bomb, which went off at two o'clock this afternoon . . .' Michael watched the grim-faced newscaster and shook his head.

'What's happened?' Nina was coming in through the back door. She had gone into the garden to daub sun-block on Robbie's nose: he'd been out all morning, pushing a giant car along red plastic tracks Michael had laid out on the dry grass.

'A bomb. Two people killed.' Michael pressed the remote control. 'Do you know what they were predicting last night in the newsroom? That fanatics from the Renewal Movement would turn to terrorist tactics to speed along our conversion. That bomb could have been their first attempt at intimidation.'

'I don't believe it.' Nina frowned. She stood at the window now, watching her son in the garden without shade. The Sunday church bells of St Stephen's began to peal. 'Alexander keeps talking about building a new world, not about destruction.'

'Ah,' Michael raised his arm and wagged his finger in the air, in mock-prophetic mode, 'but the Renewal people would argue that it is from the rubble and ashes of the old sinful world that the new society can rise, phoenix-like.'

Nina kept her back to her husband: she was preparing her speech for him about Robbie.

'I haven't seen them around here,' he continued behind her, 'but do you know that they've put up posters in the Docklands? The threats would make your hair stand on end.' He was unfolding the newspaper on the coffee table, probably to find the television schedule. 'I tell you, the trustees have bitten off more than they can chew. But what's so strange is that no matter how strident the Movement becomes, people are buying it.'

'Why not?' She spoke over her shoulder, her eyes still on her son.

'People have grown tired of all the lies, deceit, selfishness . . .'

Michael, made uncomfortable by her tone, stood up, stretched self-consciously. 'I think I'll have a beer – do you want anything?'

'No.' Nina's voice trembled.

He was fearful as he asked, 'What is it, darling?'

'It's Robbie, Michael. The teachers are concerned. The school rang to say his marks have slumped and he seems so distracted at all times. They say he's become difficult, his behaviour obstructive. He continues to be bullied.'

She heard him draw up to her, felt him taut behind her as he joined her at the window. He gave an immense weary sigh. Nina continued, 'They say he suffers because he misses you, he needs a more constant presence at home.'

'Jesus . . .' He ran a hand through his hair. 'I don't know, I just don't know what I'm supposed to do any more.' He was talking as if to himself, his eyes on their child outside. 'This job brings such pressure, and the trustees are always hanging over you like some bloody great sword of Damocles. If you knew how everyone one rung below me has been plotting to replace me since the day of my appointment . . .' Again he sighed. 'What do you expect me to do?' He didn't look at her, but still at Robbie in the sun.

'I don't know, Michael. We'll both just have to try harder to be with him. Make as much effort as we possibly can.' She was careful to keep her tone measured, to say 'we', to keep the accusations from her voice.

He put his arm around her suddenly. 'Why do things have to get more and more difficult? It seems as if we were happier before . . . before the editorship.'

Nina said nothing: was he admitting that he wanted to change, wanted to turn the clock back?

'Papa! Mummy! Come!' Robbie stood up amid the rubber tracks and the grass, legs wide, arms beckoning to the window.

'Look at him! He's so happy when you're at home.' She smiled up at Michael.

'Yes.' He squeezed her shoulder. 'You go, I'll join you in a second. I just want to check what they're doing at the paper about the bomb.' He walked to the telephone and began dialling. He watched her go through the open back door, saw her outside in the bright sunlight as she bent over Robbie. His heart constricted with love as he asked his deputy (sulky, as always, on Sundays) who was covering the bomb.

He had sat down on the sofa to make the call, and after he hung up, satisfied that everything was running smoothly, he lay back against the striped cushions and stared at the sun that had gilded the afternoon sky. For a moment he felt the impulse to ring Allegra at her new flat, to make sure she was all right. It was only three days ago that he had left her weeping on her bed in her new home – a tiny converted council flat in a neighbourhood he thought desolate and dangerous.

'I can't go on with this – it's no good, Allegra, we'll end up suffering far, far more if we don't put a stop to it now.' He had repeated the words as he caressed her head, lying against the sheet amid a glossy, tangled black mane. Naked and trembling upon her unmade bed, Allegra had reminded him of the dog he and Nina had had put to sleep when Robbie had been a toddler: a vulnerable being, quivering upon a white sheet, eyes terrified in the full knowledge of the fate awaiting him. Michael had had to look away then and he did so now. Allegra had wept, accused him of callousness, but he had stood firm, knowing that far worse would be discovery by Nina. 'If you're worried,' he'd told her, 'you should go and stay somewhere else, at a friend's,' but he'd known the answer already. She had no friends, only him, now that she had severed all ties with the Renewal Movement.

He stood up and went to the open door through which he could hear Nina's low, sweet voice and Robbie's murmured rejoinders. It was all getting too much for him: hell, he hardly had any time left to worry about his newspaper, what with the trustees calling him to endless 'policy' meetings, his trying to avoid Allegra in the newsroom, his worrying about Nina, and now Robbie. Even Clive Walton-Ellis – to whom he'd succeeded in giving a wide berth for years, despite his being Nina's editor – had come, cap in hand, asking him for a job. But, of course, Michael knew that would be impossible: it wasn't Clive's editorial skill that was unacceptable to the trustees, it was his hedonist (or libertine, depending on whether you were one of the countless women he'd bedded) lifestyle. So that the same reservations they'd shared about him at the helm of the magazine would hold true were he to work for Michael. A point that Michael had tried to make as delicately as he could, only to earn himself a furious tirade from the older man. 'You're in league with them, aren't you, printing pious platitudes that should make you ashamed of yourself. I know why you were chosen as editor. Katherine knew you wouldn't have the balls to fight her on anything. She wanted a puppet whose strings she could pull, and she got one.' And he'd turned on his heels and walked out of Michael's glass office.

Michael's mouth twisted at the insult that still smarted. Outside, the crouching figures of wife and son seemed to glow. His eyes filled with tears. What had he risked losing?

Puppet . . . If anything, it was Lady Katherine who had become the puppet – and the puppet master, with his dog-collar, untouchable good looks and millenarian vision, struck Michael as downright sinister. It wouldn't surprise him if the bomb today really was the work of those spiritual terrorists: he'd worked long enough in a newsroom to know how many innocent lives religious fervour could claim. He didn't like the new moral majority that was flexing its muscles in Parliament, Tom Sutton smiling and smug among them; he didn't like what the trustees were up to, with their 'suggestions' of feature pieces and leaders in support of the 'great new social and moral renewal'; he didn't like having to turn away a man as obviously talented as Clive on what he regarded as fundamentalist principles.

He looked down at his drink, checked his watch: news in five minutes. He sat down again. Yes, he felt uneasy with the way things were going. Secretly, he even endorsed Victor and Luke. He knew all he'd have to do was say the word, and Victor would show him the dossier he was compiling about Sutton. A dossier that sooner or later, maddeningly, he would place on the desk of some other Fleet Street editor.

'Lady Katherine's puppet.' Again Clive's words rang in his ears. Well, maybe so. But he would see them all out, the Renewal puritans, the crotchety old trustees, Piers at the *Daily Herald* . . . He would survive them all. He took the remote control from the coffee table and switched on the news.

## Chapter Twenty Four

July had been hot and without rain and the heavy air hung over London like a low-ceilinged canopy that seemed to block out the light while increasing the temperature. Nina had agreed with Marina's suggestion that she and Robbie come to spend the morning in the tiny garden at Holland Park: it was Sunday, and Michael would join them for lunch when he came back from the newspaper, where he "had to settle a few things".

Nina stretched in the *chaise-longue*. She shut her eyes. Her head was throbbing: she was finding it impossible to sleep and felt fatigued, listless during the interminable days. It had been Johnny she had called, for a report of the vicar's meeting with Allegra – as if between Alexander and herself, this incident must never be discussed. 'Alexander was splendid,' the young man had assured her, 'and she as good as confessed her betrayal of Tom. Alexander has given me the all-clear with my campaign – she will buckle under, you may be sure. She was in despair the other day.'

What of now, though? Impatient, she had wanted to press Johnny, over the telephone, to make him sense her own despair, to share with him her urgency. Had Allegra repented, or was she still seeing Nina's husband? She could not be certain. Michael had been coming home late, and she would lie in her bed alone, tensely waiting for the sound of his key in the door. She could feel her heart beat hard, nervous, as she lay between the sheets. Even her bedroom no longer seemed familiar to her: it was not the haven where she would lie in Michael's arms, or where in the dark after love-making they would discuss his career, her writing, Robbie's progress. These nights, in the hot dark air, the room had taken on new shapes and distorted shadows so that she felt alien, almost in danger as she awaited his return. She opened her eyes in the brightness. Robbie was trying to set up a hammock between the plum tree she had never seen bear fruit and a post of the green trellis Marina had dug against the wall years ago. Paolo sat beside her, in the shade that the Levinsons' great oak tree cast over three neighbouring gardens. He was studying the *Daily Herald* obituaries with the attention no news story about the bombing of the abortion clinic could elicit.

Her mother was putting the finishing touches to the table she had laid for the *al fresco* lunch. Her small white hands fluttered about the china and glasses, as she bustled busily from one end to the other.

Nina's childhood seemed always only a step away in this garden: it was as if just beyond this rosebush or once around that corner, she might suddenly come upon her own schoolgirl self, with her long dark plaits and navy blue sandals, checked pinafores and always a book in hand or pocket. Here, enclosed between white brick walls, studded with rose bushes and miniature flower-beds, was a green space where everything had seemed so certain, so well planned. Nothing in the existence she had led here had prepared her for the despair over Michael, for the unsettling revelation of her own mother's betrayal: life viewed from this sunny garden had held promises, not hinted at disappointments. Michael and Allegra . . . She felt the bitter taste rise in her throat, reach her mouth: in her new anxiety, everything seemed strained to breaking point, and the pleasant languor of summer that habitually enveloped this sunny garden seemed as alien as some extraordinary folk costume from a distant land.

'You've seen the posters that have started springing up everywhere? Now they're buying ads.' Paolo was pointing to the full-page advertisement in the *Daily Herald* before him: a face of Jesus on the Cross, His crown of thorns digging into His skull. '"For your salvation I have died. Soon I will come again, to judge the living and the dead."'

'Now Paolo, don't start,' Marina reproached her husband before disappearing inside.

'There was a poster on the way here – some quote from the Book of Revelation.' Nina shrugged against the white and green canvas of her *chaise-longue*. She wished she had come out in a sleeveless dress rather than this short-sleeved white shirt.

'Well, it's appalling what they're up to – smash the whole liberal intelligentsia, that's their mission. Forget all this nonsense about preparing for the new millennium. This is a cultural war not a spiritual battle!' Paolo lowered the newspaper slightly so that his eyes peered at her through half-moon spectacles. 'And I don't want to hear any nonsense about you hanging about with these people, you understand? Our family is proud of its long liberal legacy and no vicar is allowed to tarnish our reputation.'

Nina gave him a long look. 'Alexander Connaught is a good man, not a wild-eyed schemer. And anyway we're up to our necks with this Renewal Movement because of Michael's trustees.'

'Hm.' He snorted, unconvinced. 'You have that column in the *Society* – you could have struck out there, or at least examined the group.'

'You may have seen what happened to Clive. Had I struck out against the Movement that Lady Katherine is so enthusiastic about I'd be out of a job right now.' She heard her voice, grown cold and aggressive. She was not used to quarrelling with her father and she stopped, swallowed, looked at him beseechingly: she could not bear to feel him so disappointed in her, and slowly began to construct a more acceptable reality. 'It's not very easy. Both Michael and I feel we have been muzzled by his trustees. Of course I'm worried about the new morality, the talk of punishing sinners, but I daren't write a word lest it get Michael into trouble.' She looked down at her hands, hoping this would suffice.

'Doesn't Lady Katherine have any understanding of a paper's independence? Your husband would do well to show he's got some spirit. We can't allow more soft-focus portraits of that creepy Tom Sutton to fill every page of the *Sunday Herald*.' Now another item caught his brown eyes. 'Well, well, I could have guessed it. They say this year will be the worst drought since 1879 – I do wish I'd had the courage to tell your mother not to bother planting tomatoes. Did you see? Already dried up on their stalks,' Paolo grumbled from his chair. Inside, the doorbell went.

Nina looked up to find her mother leading Victor and Luke into the garden. She felt her heart sink: she did not want to confront Victor, to see her fall reflected in his pitying eyes.

'Hello.' He came towards her, slightly uncertain of his welcome. She rose, dusted off her white skirt. She smiled at Victor, marvelling once again at his youthful, vibrant new self, and then shook Luke's hand. Luke's eyes shone with mischief as they rested on her. 'Is it true you're one of them, then, young lady? That you attend those meetings at St Mark's and are a dedicated disciple of the dreaded vicar?'

Nina shook her head. 'I never attend the services, I simply know Alexander.' She pretended that her attention had been captured by Robbie and moved over to her son, crouching beside him. She resented having to defend herself to a man who had cuckolded her father.

'We're pretty close to having all the evidence we need. Exposing Sutton will be one of the great pleasures of my life.' Luke had taken a chair from the table and pulled it next to Paolo. Nina cast a hostile look at the lean, mobile face, its suntan emphasised by the white floppy hair that framed it. Luke was leaning forward, hands on his knees, his voice excited. 'All their talk of reintroducing morality into our society and yet one of their key members stands accused of male rape.'

'I'll feel like a *tricoteuse* at the guillotine when the blow is delivered,' Paolo smirked, folding his newspaper and dropping it on the grass.

As she crouched next to her son, pushing his toy train, Nina strained to hear what Victor was telling Marina in a low voice. 'He wouldn't publish our piece, despite all the evidence supporting the boy's account. Can you believe it? It killed me. My best friend didn't have the guts to do what he thought right. We're going to have to go to the *Recorder* – they're independent enough to want to thumb their nose at Sutton and the new moralists.'

Nina rose from her son's side, regained her *chaise-longue*. She looked at Luke, beside her father: expression chased expression across his face, as his speech rushed past them. 'You heard about Clive Walton-Ellis and that feminist columnist Ruth Anderson receiving threats through the post? Their writings are deemed to support a – get this – "slipshod morality". No prize for guessing who's behind the letters.'

'Censorship,' Paolo spat out in disgust.

Victor had overheard them. 'I've had those threats myself. There seem to be many scapegoats of the Renewal Movement.'

'Will you stay for lunch?' Marina dug her hands in her apron, looking from one to the other, a smile warm on her face: 'I've made *vitello tonnato*, Luke, I know that's your favourite.'

'No, my favourite was last week's spinach thing – what did you call it? Anyway, no, we shouldn't stay.' Luke slapped his knees, rose and approached Marina. 'The most generous hostess in London . . .' and he took her hand and drew it to his lips. Nina stared in horror, not daring to look at her father in his chair beside her. Had they returned to their ancient love story? Had Paolo been forced to accept their carrying-on right beneath his nose? She shuddered. Luke had talked about last week: how often did he come now to her parents' home? She turned, confused.

Victor was squatting beside Robbie, whispering to him, making her son laugh. 'Uncle Victor!' Robbie exclaimed, gurgling.

'It also might be awkward, you know, with Michael having turned down our stuff, and although there are no hard feelings on our part, he may well . . .' Luke was whispering to Marina.

From his chair Paolo raised his arm, still holding the folded copy of the *Daily Herald*. He waved at them as if he were hailing a taxi. 'Come along, Luke. Michael knows on what side of this new cultural divide his parents-in-law stand.'

'We see each other all the time, we needn't inflict our presence during your Sunday lunch.' Victor looked over Robbie's dark head at Nina. 'Michael may feel he's walked into the lion's den with all of us here. Nina would have to defend him from our barbed remarks and veiled accusations . . .'

Nina said nothing. She felt weary, hot, above all uncomfortable in the presence of her friend. Victor had said they saw each other all the time: had her parents begun to collaborate with Luke and Victor in their mission to fight against the Renewal Movement? When had this begun? Why had she not known about it? She stared at her father's great domed forehead, his sharply outlined profile, the spectacles that glinted in the sun. Was he really involved with those other two in organising a counter-attack against Alexander's Renewal? Why was he collaborating with his wife's former, perhaps current, lover? The questions shot before her like cross-fire between enemy camps. Nothing seemed to make sense any more: not their collusion, not the secrecy which they had obviously maintained with regard to herself. Again she closed her eyes. She felt as if she stood alone in the silence that follows the roaring departure of a car bearing your loved ones. Michael's affair, Victor's allegiance to Luke, and now her parents' engagement in a campaign they had kept from her: she, who had once felt at the centre of a skein of loving relationships, now felt plunged into a dark loneliness where she could not get her bearings, but must rely on someone who, taking pity on her, threw down a rope. Alexander struck her as the only person who might. Only in his presence did she feel herself to be the Nina of before, the much admired and slightly feared Nina Lewis.

In this sunny garden, where only the birds' calls disturbed the silence, Nina mourned the past. She opened her eyes, blinked in the light. Everyone but her father had gone inside. She saw him in profile as he skimmed the paper once more in the receding shadow of the

Levinsons' oak. He sensed her gaze, looked up at her and smiled. 'The guests wouldn't stay, despite our protestations.'

'Good.' The word was out before she could consider the wisdom of uttering it.

Over the paper, her father raised an eyebrow. 'Don't we like our pal Victor any more?'

'It's not that . . .' She rose, approached her father, looked down at him, a hand shielding her eyes. 'It's Luke I don't much like.' The sentence hung between them like a tightrope that he might or might not brave. She watched him through careful, shielded eyes: would he broach the subject, as he had that day at the hospital?

'You don't care for Luke.' He sighed, dropped the newspaper on the grass beside him. He crossed his hands and looked at her. 'Because of the past?' he asked, in a low voice.

Nina nodded but remained silent.

'He loved your mother, she loved him. But . . . it's over.' Paolo's pale brown eyes filled with tears.

'How can you forgive them? How can you bear to have him around you?' she heard herself almost hiss at him, and drew a step back, as if frightened by her own anger.

'Nina.' Her father sighed. 'Can you not forgive?' She looked on, uncomprehending. 'Can you not find it in your heart to forgive your mother? Michael?' Beneath her hand, Nina's eyes widened in fear. 'Can you not forgive your husband?' he asked again, eyes probing her.

Nina felt dizzy there, in the sun, before her father. He knew. Perhaps he had known all along, as had her mother. Perhaps the two of them had discussed Michael's betrayal, had raised their voices in a duet of sorrow and pity every time they left her side. Nina blinked. Dear God, let it not be so. She tried to deflect him, to bring up something else, but the words would not come. 'Nina,' he reached for her hand, took her cold, clammy fingers in his own, 'sometimes we have to learn we are less than perfect, and must accept the consequences. It hurts our pride, our self-esteem, but,' he shrugged, 'how could we not forgive those we love?' Nina stared back at him, unseeing. 'How could I forget what a wonderful wife your mother has always been to me? How could I overlook the easy, happy life she made for the three of us for all those years?'

Nina felt the garden spin round her, her foothold so uncertain she feared she would fall.

'Forgive,' she whispered to herself.

'Michael's come! Let's start lunch, shall we?' Marina came through the door, bearing a platter of *vitello tonnato*, adorned with tiny ruby-red tomatoes.

Paolo stood up, brushed down his linen trousers over his thin legs, and cast a look of concern at his daughter's pale face. 'Nina, are you . . .'

'Of course, of course,' she answered mechanically. She turned her back to him, to ask her mother if she needed a hand, to greet her husband. But when they all sat round the table that Michael and Paolo had had to move to one side to find more shade, she could hardly speak and had to force herself to eat the food before her. All she wanted was for this meal to end so that she could ring Johnny and make sure that they had not let up on their intimidation of Allegra Worth.

'Ah, my mother-in-law has outdone herself – spectacular sauce.' Michael smiled his most ingratiating smile. Not much success today, though: here he was, in high spirits and ready to enjoy a homey Sunday, and the glum and taciturn ensemble seemed linked in a conspiracy to cheat him of his hard-earned pleasure. Marina and Paolo kept exchanging worried glances over the plates and bottles, while in front of him Nina was out of sorts, eyes resolutely downcast. Only Robbie was cheerful, yapping about Uncle Victor.

It was Uncle Victor's car parked outside the house that had delayed Michael for half an hour: he'd recognised the aged, untidy Citroën (honestly, not even one of his junior reporters would be caught dead in such a scrap heap) as he'd turned into the street, and had done an about-turn of such speed he had almost dispatched a neighbour's dog to his Maker. The last thing he wanted on a Sunday was to have to defend his position to his best friend. Surely Victor understood why Michael couldn't publish a damning piece about a leading member of Lady K's favourite cause? Had he been in Michael's shoes, with those trustees on his back, surely he would have acted in exactly the same way.

Through the green oak leaves the sun peppered the white table-cloth, the plates filled with thin slices of veal.

'Some wine, Michael?' Paolo poured him a glass, taking only a thimbleful himself: doctor's orders. Michael raised his glass. 'Cheers.' He addressed himself to Nina but she did not meet his eyes. She looked white and troubled.

'Is it true, then, about the ghastly Renewal fanatics being behind the bomb at the abortion clinic?' Paolo, who had been allowed only white chicken meat and a salad, sat miserably cutting a bite-sized chunk out of the chicken.

'That's the rumour doing the rounds of the newsroom.'

'Then they are madmen who've hijacked religious talk for their own sinister gain.'

'Nina, you're looking so pale, are you sure you're all right?' Marina poured some water into Robbie's glass while her kind blue eyes searched her daughter's face.

'I haven't been able to sleep for ages . . .' Nina blew out in a whisper.

'Camomile after lunch for you, then,' Marina said decidedly, then turned her attention to serving her grandson more veal.

'God only knows what will happen next. Tom Sutton as minister of something or other, no doubt.' Paolo took off his glasses, breathed onto them, began polishing them with the handkerchief he'd produced from his pocket. 'Who is using whom in the holy rollers' game, I'd like to know?'

'They're inextricably linked. Tom is their political arm and, as you pointed out, he'll be a cabinet member in no time at all, and Alexander's church mice will become very powerful indeed. It's incredible, really, how quickly they've managed to become a force in the political arena. People think that if you talk with sacred words your agenda must be sacred too.' Michael shook his head.

Paolo growled in disgust. 'Just you wait till the backlash starts once they discover about Tom Sutton's dirty habits . . .'

Michael laboriously avoided this bait, stuffing a huge forkful into his mouth. So far, thank goodness, he had not had to confront the issue of Sutton's past – the skeletons had remained firmly shut in the man's closet; he had not had to probe too deep regarding the bomb at the clinic either, as no one had claimed responsibility for the killings. Thank God. He broke off a piece of bread and soaked up the thick tuna sauce. If the bomb were linked to Alexander's little band, would Lady K fall out of love with this nonsense? Michael frowned for a moment, then turned to Robbie. 'After lunch we'll play with the train, shall we?' He winked at his son.

'Please.' Robbie smiled.

From here, Michael couldn't see the slightly slipping iris, and Robbie looked as if he'd put on a bit of weight. His little cheek, tanned by the summer sun, curved more roundly under the dark rim of his spectacles. My Robbie, Michael filled with paternal love, I'll make it up to you, you'll see. No more bullying, no more teachers talking about absent father figures. He downed a great sip of wine. No one and nothing would disturb his son's peace of mind.

Allegra's face rose before him. It had been much more difficult to wean her from himself than he'd bargained for, and he still feared her ringing him at home as she'd done the other day, right under Nina's nose. Poor little thing – you had to feel sorry for her, with those great big blue eyes and skinny limbs. But even a sniff of scandal, now, was enough to ensure you pariah status – and even, in the world of the *Herald*, your dismissal. Piers had called him in just last week, white with fury at the trustees. 'I can't put up with it any longer, Michael. They asked me to get rid of one of my best columnists – they were all upset because of some so-called "libertine" column he'd done.' Piers's small thin frame strode about his office, while Michael told himself that these scruples were the luxury of the man who at the pinnacle of his career can decide if he can accept the terms set before him. 'I can't sit there and mouth pious pap I don't believe in and give the push to someone whose writings I enjoy simply because he doesn't toe our trustees' moral line! What the hell do they think we're running? A Sunday school? I warn you, I'm ready to throw in the towel. Can't do it any more.' He looked over his desk at Michael. 'And don't think they'll let you be. I warrant you'll be getting a summons soon enough. You'll be asked to fire someone or other, wait and see.'

Michael had made some inarticulate noises, trying to be at once incensed and consoling – but secretly he had exulted. The *Daily* was his logical next step, and here was Piers practically renouncing it. As for his columnists, he knew the trustees would probably soon ask him to get rid of Ruth Anderson, but it was a small sacrifice at the altar of promotion.

He downed the last sip of wine and smiled beatifically at those familiar faces around the table. Yes, things were going smoothly. The only problem that remained was his certainty that Victor and Luke would bring their file on Tom Sutton to some other newspaper that would publish it. It would kill him to lose out on that story – sex scandals were perfect for circulation boosts, no matter how great the moral revival. In fact, the greater the moral revival, the better it would sell. Still, he shouldn't forget Piers's distraught countenance, and his determined air as he spoke of leaving.

He sighed with contentment, then caught Nina's sad gaze, and for a moment froze. But remembering that he'd reformed, and that he was leading a blameless existence, he gave her a confident smile. He had nothing to worry about any more.

## Chapter Twenty Five

Allegra lay in bed. It must be almost midday but the fatigue still held her down, her bones aching and heavy. She could feel the sweat coat her forehead and wondered if she had a fever. The light seeped through the curtains, sending a faded square onto the floor.

She turned on her side to look at the blue cotton that barred the entrance of the sun and tried to gather her strength. She must get up. Alexander had called a press conference for three o'clock at St Mark's, and she was to cover it for the Diary. The prospect of stepping back into the church hall and seeing the members of the Circle, seeing Alexander glow with self-righteousness, filled her with dread, but she knew her refusal would send her editor, Bertie, into a furious rage. Already, she had not gone into the office this morning, and she trembled at the thought of what Bertie would be thinking – or rather, saying, as he was not one for observing a dignified silence. Not about staff problems, certainly, and she realised she was very much a staff problem now. Her endless days off, her floods of tears in the women's room, her sudden flights from the newsroom when the sight of Michael beyond the glass wall proved too much . . . Oh, Bertie had noticed it, all right. Allegra was certain he was holding off firing her on the spot because no one could be quite sure whether Michael had left her altogether or whether her unhappiness was just a lovers' tiff. But it wouldn't take them much longer to determine how the ground lay, and then . . . then she'd be cast out without so much as a thank-you.

Cast out. She winced at the memory of one of Johnny's horrific letters. They hadn't stopped, always in different envelopes, ink and handwriting, so that inevitably she unwittingly opened one. The Renewal Movement had been determined to force her to repent, and she had conceded defeat: she had written to Alexander yesterday to let him know it was over with Michael. She could no longer bear the pressure of their censure, the burning sensation of those letters slipping through her fingers. Yet her admission of failure had not alleviated her guilt. It was as if she had given joy to Alexander and his followers without being able to experience the sense of catharsis she had sought. In her misery she had been robbed even of the relief of confession.

She could hear the vicar's gentle voice describe the deliverance offered by penance before a group of wide-eyed faces . . . No, she mustn't think about him, or she would never dare step into St Mark's today . . . But she would sneak in at the back: she could be certain that all of Alexander's followers would be at the front, near their spiritual mentor. Again, she filled with images of the Circle sitting around Lady Katherine's elegant table, of Johnny smiling at her with a rapturous face, of the loud singing sessions in the bright warm church . . .

She tried to push them away. She could never return, after Michael: in their eyes, as in her own, she would be the adulteress ever after. Tears stung her as she thought that there was nothing, nothing left in her life. Mum had been so angry because she'd heard, through some members of the Circle in Sheffield, that Allegra had stopped attending the sessions. She had scolded her, then raised her voice at the other end of the line at Allegra's weak denials. 'My God, girl, what are you doing to yourself? Whom have you fallen in with, that you don't remember to keep the Lord's own day?' But Allegra had burst into sobs and hung up: she couldn't bear any more recriminations, she had no strength left.

The neighbours upstairs raised their music so that the ceiling seemed to move above her. They were noisy, but for days on end theirs were the only voices she heard and she almost welcomed their unseen presence. They reassured her that she was not completely alone.

She heard a car screech to a halt outside. Michael? She managed to raise herself onto her elbow, to push aside the cotton fold and peer out of the window.

But it wasn't him, and she sank back against the pillows. Her forehead and eyes burned. She placed both hands upon her belly: she sometimes thought that the grief had hollowed her out, and she pressed her hands onto her stomach as if to feel the painful void.

Oh, Michael . . . and the tears ran down her cheeks. Oh, Michael, how could you leave me? She sobbed now, and allowed herself to be convulsed by the anguish that swept over her daily.

She saw him walk past her in the newsroom, casting the briefest of nods in her direction. Through the glass wall, she saw him on the telephone in his office. He stood, facing the river view, his back to her, one hand holding the receiver, the other sunk into his trouser pocket. Sometimes she even stayed late enough to see him leave for home, jacket slung casually over his shoulder, crossing the great room with proprietorial strides. It was as if she had meant nothing to him: he had returned to his existence without the slightest pause for breath.

The realisation made her moan aloud, in her sweaty pink nightgown, in the unkempt bed where he'd never return.

Oh, Michael . . . Suddenly, Allegra saw her. It had begun of late, Nina Lewis's intrusion into her thoughts. She stared at Allegra, eyes burning in a pale face, one hand raised, accusing. Allegra turned, brought up her knees and her hands to her eyes to keep the vision at bay. Nina, whom she had relegated to a corner of her mind during her affair with Michael, had gained prominence in her new-found loneliness, haunting her.

Allegra felt the perspiration course down her back. Upstairs the music continued relentlessly. She should get up. Should get something to eat – she couldn't remember when she'd last eaten – and then get dressed and go.

Slowly she set her feet down on the floor, sat up. She tried to feel the carpet under her soles, but could not: everything seemed to move around her. She raised a hand to her head, pushed back the hair from her face and throat. Mum, forgive me . . . God, forgive me . . . God: the loving face of the Jesus Christ painted on the corner of the prayerbook used by the Circle filled her eyes. Dear Jesus, help me . . . She shivered, and began to weep loudly. Suddenly the gentle features of her youthful Jesus grew faint, to be replaced by the glowering visage of a cruel and vengeful deity who resembled Alexander as he had sat in her living room. She cowered before the image, and pushed both hands down on the mattress to hoist herself up. She must go, must go to St Mark's.

Lady Katherine stood alone in the dark crypt. Upstairs she could hear the church filling, voices and footsteps reaching her in a resounding echo. She had had to push past the television crew and the photographers: Alexander Connaught had invited them to hear some important announcement, they claimed, when she berated them for entering the house of God.

Yet yesterday, when he had asked her to come along, he'd said nothing. In the humid heat of this vaulted space, Lady Katherine felt slightly faint: she had walked from home and the afternoon sun had been unbearable. The drought they had been predicting had struck the city and beyond, and in the squares along her route the grass stretched dead and brown. The air seemed to hang thick from the trees with their slightly burned leaves. As she waited for Alexander to come, she studied the room for his traces: his black jacket slung over a chair, one button dangling over the floor by a thread she could not see; his diary opened blankly on his desk; his sloping handwriting on the calendar of parish events. And in a corner of the room, upon a little milking stool, a pile of red Bibles. A life that required only a few belongings. A life dedicated to others. She shook her head: she should, of course, regard it with reverence, and envy him the spiritual discipline that allowed him to contain his world in a handful of humble objects, but instead her heart tightened at the sadness of it. How lonely. She reached out a hand and caressed the cotton jacket with pity.

She had wanted to see him earlier this morning, but he had been unable to meet her: Tom Sutton was down, and the two men were as ever in some confabulation she dared not interrupt. In truth, since the day she had overheard Tom's secret, she had done her best to avoid the politician: she could obey Alexander in letter, but not in spirit.

She looked about the crypt for her mentor: she had wanted to share with him her unease about the bomb – what of the rumours that the Renewal Movement had been behind it? She needed to speak to him, alone, find out the truth, ask him why increasingly she felt shut out from his inner circle. She paced up and down in the crypt that lay at the heart of his work. She must see him. Must have him calm her fears about her son. Ever since finding the threatening letters on Johnny's desk, she had been terrified lest her son had become involved with some splinter group of fanatics who, in the name of the Renewal Movement, were venting their anger against the Establishment. The news of the Oxford Street bomb had further worried her: was Johnny in any way linked to it?

The sound of voices above her had grown into a loud hum, and still she could hear footsteps marching in from outside.

'Alexander?' Someone was rushing down the stairs and before she could answer Johnny stood before her, his face red and sweaty, his expression one of excitement.

'Johnny,' she whispered, and made as if to move towards him.

'Where is he?' Johnny asked, looking suddenly as he had when she had watched him playing hide and seek in their garden in the country.

'I don't know, but he told me he wished to see me.' She spoke in a low expressionless voice. She raised her face to the humming ceiling. 'Why are those journalists there?'

'Hasn't he told you?' He smiled suddenly, and she didn't know if it were at the secret in his keeping or at his delight that Alexander was withholding something from her.

'No,' she answered, straining for calm.

'He'll let you see, soon enough.' He cocked his head to one side, placed an index finger on his lips.

Down the staircase came another figure: Nina Lewis. Lady Katherine felt defeated – with Nina around, she would never manage even a few minutes alone with Alexander. She watched the younger woman approach her son with an interrogating look. 'Have you . . .?'

'Yes.' Johnny nodded, a look of gleeful triumph spread across his face. 'As promised.'

'Has Sutton arrived?' Nina looked from Lady Katherine to Johnny. 'They're getting restless up there.'

'Is he meant to speak, then?' Lady Katherine asked.

'Of course!' Nina looked surprised, and then, seeing Johnny's face, 'Oh, perhaps he didn't tell you. Yes, Tom Sutton is supposed to speak – that's what all the fuss up there is about.' The noise above them had suddenly stopped. 'They're starting. I'm going up.' Without waiting for either of them Nina rushed up the stairs.

Johnny made as if to follow her, but his mother placed a restraining hand on his arm. 'Johnny,' she whispered, searching his face with a loving gaze, 'my darling, please, please don't let us have this terrible strain between us.'

Johnny placed a foot on the bottom step. He shook off his mother's hand. 'I'm moving out tonight. I'm going up north for a while – to start a new Circle for him.'

'Johnny . . .' She issued the name like a sigh, and now clutched the banister and his elbow, pulling him back. 'Please don't leave us, don't leave me – I want so much to make it up to you –'

'You can't. It's too late. Let me go now!' He pulled himself free and ran up the steps, two at a time.

Nina leaned against a white pillar at the very front of the church. She could hardly breathe: fears and hopes swirled in confusion before her eyes. Johnny had confirmed that the pressure on Allegra had not let up – but did he have any evidence that she had repented and that the affair was truly over? She had suspected that a few turns of the screw from the Renewal disciples would deliver her from Allegra, but she couldn't be certain what Michael's role would be. Would he sigh secretly with relief at the thought of being let off the hook by his lover's stirrings of conscience, or would he balk at being pushed about by a group of evangelical Christians whose influence he already resented?

She could see Alexander, face inscrutable, moving in the shadow amid the white pillars to the right. She drew sharp small breaths in the heavy air: the church was stifling despite the open windows and doors. The great Victorian edifice was packed, with rows and rows of people standing, craning their necks the better to see, whispering their expectations, faces gleaming with sweat as the regular congregation stood cheek by jowl with journalists, cameras, television crews. An air of anticipation hung over the throng, and she saw the eagerness fill the eyes of the faithful, the curiosity shine in the journalists' gaze. Each member of this crowd awaited something different – an announcement, a miracle, a sermon. She, too, had her expectations – that through Alexander and his Renewal Movement justice had been carried out, and her perfect world restored.

The lectern stood just to her right and beyond it, amid the slim pillars, she could see Alexander and Tom Sutton in deep consultation; a step or two behind them stood a small blonde woman, whom she recognised as Mrs Sutton. Her head hung in a penitential pose and she seemed lost in secret contemplation. Nina's gaze crossed the crowded aisles, and suddenly she spotted Michael. She wanted to push her way to him, but the church was too packed. She stared at him, studying his demeanour for clues. What of Allegra?

Allegra arrived at St Mark's and tried to make her way to the back of the church. She could hardly breathe, and her legs were unsteady as she whispered, 'Sorry, sorry, sorry,' from the vestibule to the church hall. She kept her eyes lowered, fearful lest she recognise anyone from the Movement or from the *Sunday Herald*. In fact, she could see only television people, holding cameras and microphones, jostling into position. It must be an important announcement. Suddenly she saw Michael, standing towards the front of the room: she felt as if someone had pushed her off balance. Then she saw Nina. She looked at the pale, handsome face, the serious, almost unhappy expression, and her heart filled with guilt rather than envy. Nina Lewis, whom she had wronged, whose serenity she had destroyed. Nina Lewis, whose husband she had tried to steal . . . Oh, Jesus, how I have sinned!

Before she could continue her prayer, Alexander came to the lectern. He stood completely still, tall and imposing. Silence immediately fell upon the congregation, and Allegra found even her misery suppressed by his sheer physical presence.

Alexander clasped his hands before him. 'I stand here before you with pride and shame struggling with one another for possession of my heart. Pride, because my friend Tom Sutton has shown himself to have that strength and fortitude of spirit that we of the Renewal Movement would wish instilled in every man, woman and child in this blessed land of ours.' His voice was low, immeasurably sweet, carried by the warm air. 'Pride because he has the humility to confess his sin – here – before us. Pride because this man, a member of my Renewal Movement, has begged me to hold this public confession so that the whole world can hear his remorse and see his regret, and so that the Renewal Movement need not be tainted with his sin.'

Allegra trembled before the vicar's face alight with faith, stared at the mouth that spoke the words of the righteous. She saw him as an avenging angel, a holy presence meant to remind her that she had wronged her God, wronged her fellow men. Again she felt the sinner's misery engulf her. 'Jesus, help me, help me . . .' No one stirred, and she could see the faces around her taking on an air of absolute concentration.

'He pleaded with me last night, tears in his eyes, that I would allow him this public act of contrition so that no one in condemning him would condemn the Renewal Movement.' He hung his head suddenly, so that the lights shone bright to gild his head. He dropped his voice to the merest whisper. 'But I feel shame, too, for I find that I feel repugnance and disgust for this sinner before me – and I am desperately fighting my own instincts to find the forgiveness and the compassion with which I know we must embrace our brethren, no matter what their faults. Tom, come, speak.' He raised his arm towards Tom Sutton.

As he stood beside Dick Snell, the large, grey-haired reporter he'd sent to cover the story, Michael stared in awed admiration at the two men before him. What an audacious gamble they'd taken. This morning, when the telephone call had come from Sutton's office, inviting him to St Mark's for a special announcement, Michael had handed over the task to Snell and thought little of it. But as the morning wore on and Piers, too, had been invited to attend the meeting at St Mark's, and he heard that television crews were besieging the church, he knew he'd best accompany Snell. He'd rushed over, pushing and shoving everyone round him to get to the very front of the packed church, and from the people he saw, he knew Alexander had planned a big revelation. Somehow, he must have got wind of Victor's and Luke's file on Sutton – and guessed rightly that in their fight against the Renewal Movement the two were ready to hand over their evidence to the first Fleet Street editor who dared fly in the face of public opinion and print the stuff. How perfectly cunning of Sutton's spiritual director to beat them to it with this extraordinary public display of humility.

Michael studied the vicar who stood a few paces behind the lectern. A brilliant coup, he thought, worthy of the dirtiest and most canny politico. With this confession, Alexander was throwing Tom Sutton to the wolves – while giving him a lifeline. He was successfully distancing himself from Sutton and at the same time maintaining his hold on him. If, as they hoped, the people, when faced with a broken man on bended knee begging their forgiveness, would indeed embrace the penitent, then Sutton would be allowed back into the Renewal fold. If the people turned their back on the young shadow-cabinet minister, Alexander would simply walk away from him. Michael almost grinned at the sheer daring of it.

Sutton approached his mentor with a slow, heavy step. His youthful jovial manner had disappeared: his expression was grim, determined. His face had turned a strange grey hue, and the easy confidence of the wealthy man on his way up had been replaced by a leaden clumsiness. Would he survive this? Would the audience here and at home, watching him on their television sets, clasp this prodigal son to their bosom or would they cast stones? Michael wondered, as his eyes remained fixed on the spectacle before him.

Sutton gave Alexander a brief nod, then took the microphone at the lectern in both hands. His voice trembled as he began his confession, eyes downcast as if he dared not meet his judges' gaze. 'Brothers and sisters in Christ, I come to you today with a heavy heart. I come to you pleading for forgiveness. I have sinned.' Sutton now raised his head, face ghastly in its pallor. 'I have committed a grave sin that cries to the heavens for vengeance. I am guilty of an abomination for which in Leviticus we read that I should be condemned to death.' Michael gasped as he saw tears streak Sutton's cheeks. The penitent's voice vibrated with conviction, with sincerity, filling the entire church. To his left, Michael saw the television crew fixing their cameras upon the figure: he could almost feel the excitement of the cameramen as their unblinking machines caught these extraordinary images.

Michael stole a look at Snell beside him: the journalist stood completely immobile, staring, as if transfixed by the weeping man at the lectern.

'I have committed, repeatedly, acts of sodomy.' Sutton cast the word like a stone. A murmur ran through the crowd. He raised his wide tear-filled eyes to the ceiling that soared above the throng. 'I do not know why, but –' here his voice broke, turning raucous with grief '– but since I was a young lad, these urges have been with me. Is this a disease we are born with or a terrible challenge Jesus places before some of His children? I do not know, but I know that, though I tried to combat it from the very first, my flesh proved weaker than my resolve. For years, I fought my desires, for years I tried to still the voice that urged me to yield to the temptation.' The round grey face shone now with tears.

Allegra felt faint: it was as if her own confessions had been woven into the politician's, her own guilt linked to his. Sutton was pleading for forgiveness as she should do, he was prostrate with guilty grief as she should be . . . She shuddered and felt the tears run down her cheeks as she saw Annie Sutton bow her blonde head in grief and shame and Alexander approach the poor wife, place an arm around her shoulders. The pain, the hurt that people like Sutton and herself had caused . . . and Allegra stifled the sobs that wanted to break forth.

'I failed. I gave in to my secret despicable desires. I slept with older men, with men of my own age, even with young boys of eighteen, twenty . . . with any consenting homosexual, in fact. I knew I was betraying my vows to my wife and to my electorate. I knew I was being a hypocrite, pretending to practise as I preached. I fought and fought my evil impulses, and sometimes months would go by without my succumbing to any overtures . . . and then I would fall again and my spirit would sink to the lowest depths known to man.' Again the voice broke, and Sutton paused for a moment, while the crowd held its breath to see if he could continue. Allegra trembled as she watched him bow his black head. 'I have gone through a dark night of the soul and repented. I have wept my shame at the foot of the Cross. I begged Him to tell me what to do in order to gain His forgiveness and to be welcomed once again into the fold. I believe I know what He wanted me to do. He wanted me to beg forgiveness from those who had trusted me and whose trust I had betrayed. He wanted me publicly to prostrate myself before my beloved wife, and before you, my beloved brethren.' Sutton looked out over the silent crowd: he pointed to the woman beside Alexander. 'My wife – my wonderful wife – has forgiven me. Annie has decided to stand by me. I now turn to you, my brothers and sisters. Can you find it in your hearts to forgive this repulsive sinner before you? Can you feel any compassion for this disgusting man?' The head dropped once more, and the tear-stained face was hidden. 'I implore you – I implore you to be merciful.' Sutton had finished. He took a step back from the lectern, then stood quite still, head bowed in penitence.

Allegra pushed past the men and women around her, past the cameramen who stifled an imprecation, past the journalists with notepads at the doors. She ran from the church, eyes blind with tears, the sobs she had stifled during the speech surfacing, spilling forth. She stumbled, a sandal slipping off her foot, and then picked herself up to run she knew not where.

Michael watched the Rev Alexander Connaught study the audience, as if to gauge their reaction to Sutton's plea. The throng remained silent, and it seemed to Michael that Sutton's last words hung in the warm air. Sutton had not mentioned the rape allegations: had they silenced the boy? Paid him off?

Michael did not move. He tried to outguess the crowd's response, but everything had remained frozen in a silent immobility. Suddenly amid the silence, he heard someone begin to clap – slowly, slowly. A second person took up the clapping, and now, scattered throughout the church, others joined in, at first uncertain and then with conviction, their beat louder and louder. Soon the entire church was rocked by rhythmic clapping.

Tom Sutton slowly raised his face, where the tears now ran anew. This time, Michael thought, they were genuine: he had been truly saved.

An exhilarating performance, a spellbinding act: their gamble had paid off. Nina watched the look of elation take hold of Alexander's glowing features. There, in the half shadow, with poor Annie Sutton beside him, he seemed to shine like the tall thin church windows through which as a child, kneeling in her pew beside her mother, she had watched the sun's rays flow. He had succeeded in retaining both public support and Tom Sutton's allegiance. Around her, amid murmured comments, praises and even embraces, the crowd was beginning to disperse.

Nina looked up to find Alexander beckoning to her. She made her way to him, trying not to get pushed by the men and women who streamed towards the doors or towards Tom Sutton. Sutton had been able to move only a few feet from the lectern: he was surrounded by

212

well-wishers and journalists. Some patted him on the back, others embraced him. Nina saw a film of sweat and tears covering his face, and every now and then he took out his handkerchief to mop his brow.

'Annie!' he called, and pulled his small thin wife to his side. Cameras flashed, and Nina saw two journalists scribbling the couple's words.

'Nina . . .' Alexander was pale, tired, as if he himself had just undergone Tom's ordeal. 'Come.' He pulled her through the columns, into a dimly lit alcove. He was whispering, and had taken her hand in his.

'You must be so proud . . . relieved . . .' She did not know what to say about the performance.

'Yes, the people want us to continue, no matter what. I'm delighted for Tom: the boy withdrew his allegations yesterday, and the *Recorder* was forced to back down. They won't be printing their dirty scoop now.' He smiled suddenly. 'But you, Nina, you too must rejoice. Johnny and I saw her and you can rest assured that from now on she will leave you alone.'

'Ah . . . oh, thank you.' She felt as if the relief would burst forth, swamp him. She shook her head in disbelief and placed a hand against the white pillar beside them to steady herself. It was all over and she could resume her life. Michael . . . She turned to try to find him amid the group that still hung about the vestibule. She could not see him.

'Allegra has written that it is over between her and your husband. She understands that forgiveness can only be hers if she repents properly. And she knows now that you – you have become one of us.'

'Yes.' Nina looked away. She was not one of his people, she thought with impatience.

'Promise me you'll continue to come to St Mark's,' he pressed her hand as if to extract the promise from her, 'even now that the justice you sought has been carried out. I – we – don't want to lose you.'

But Nina had seen Michael standing towards the back of the church, by himself.

'Please, I must go.' She pulled her hand from Alexander's. 'I must find Michael.'

'Of course.' The vicar looked disappointed, his hands clasped now before him.

Nina read his face and rewarded him with a smile. 'Alexander, I am grateful to you . . . very grateful. Had you not persisted Allegra would

213

never have repented of her ways.' She pressed his hand in hers. 'She would never have freed my husband.' She saw him draw closer to her: 'I am truly grateful.'

His eyes held her, probing, seeking . . . Seeking she knew not what. Had he hoped for her conversion to the Renewal Movement, or had he thought that she would succumb in some other way to his spell? They stood, their hands linked, beneath the pillar. Nina studied the face before her as if to imprint its every lineament onto her memory: she knew she would no longer seek him, this fellow-conspirator. She would consign him to the painful past; his presence would now serve as a reminder rather than an aid – she needed neither now. Already, she felt something akin to distaste colour her responses to him, as if he alone were responsible for the lie she had delivered him and for the plotting she had demanded of him.

Suddenly, she thought she heard Michael's voice, and turned her face from the vicar's. 'I must go.'

'God bless,' Alexander whispered.

'God bless,' she replied, as she began to push past the men and women swarming around the Suttons.

'Michael!' She rushed up to him and almost threw her arms around his neck. He smiled down, surprised at her unusual outburst. Then, one arm stealing around her waist, he motioned to the cameras pointed at Tom Sutton. 'What a spectacle,' he whispered.

She stood next to her husband, pressed against his side by his strong warm arm, and she felt a rush of happiness fuelled in equal measure by love, possession and victory. She felt as if her impatience to bring him home, to be alone with him, simply stoked her pleasure, and she was content to stand there, watching him watch Sutton, while through her cotton dress she felt the solid warmth of him.

He turned, pressed his lips on her forehead. 'I am so lucky,' he murmured into her hair, 'to have you.'

She trembled with joy: he was hers, once again he was hers.

'Oh, Nina . . .' Again he laid his lips on her forehead.

'Shshshshsh. I'm here, darling, I'm here. Always here.'

In the white square bathroom the light fell, meek, through the blue cotton curtain, gentle as it touched the porcelain tub and Allegra's dark head against it.

The music upstairs continued its regular pounding, and in the street below a car's brakes screeched and let loose a shower of abuse from a passer-by.

Fully dressed, her body lay inert in the stillness of the now tepid water. Only her black hair moved in the red liquid, the strands tangling then freeing themselves as if they had come alive.

# Chapter Twenty Six

Twilight glowed in the drawing room, softened the white and gold stripes of the sofa, muted the sparkle of the chandelier. Michael sat forward on the sofa, head in hands.

At her desk, Nina studied her husband, who had not moved since the newsroom had called: it had been the Diary editor, Bertie, to inform them of Allegra's suicide – she had recognised his clipped voice as he'd asked for Michael. Nina listened to the unseen bells of St Stephen's overhead, to the laughter of the children next door. Her eyes roamed the perfectly ordered, quiet elegance of this room, where nothing seemed changed. She caught her reflection in the window: a glass woman, whose proud head emerged from capable shoulders. Almost transparent, the figure framed by the window seemed unshaken by recent betrayals – and untainted by them.

Alexander's image suddenly appeared to her: he was not the uncertain man who today had pleaded with her amid the pillars of his church, but that other man of God, alight with righteous anger and vengeful words. Nina trembled: those words and that unyielding fervour had led to Allegra's destruction – as she always had known they would. She shook herself, as if to banish Alexander and with him her guilt. The cleric, his allies, her own collaboration – they threatened to extinguish the sense of triumph that, even amid this guilt, coursed through her. Michael was hers again. Nina studied his immobile figure. She felt as if she had cast a stone into a dark pool, and awaited now the echoing response. Silent, tense, she stood listening out for him, though she knew not what she expected of her husband. He had known nothing that could lead him to accuse her; had admitted nothing that could absolve her. With everything withheld between them, they would inhabit a new limbo where they would discuss Allegra's suicide as a dreadful item of news and make as if to scour her blameless life for motive. Nina would pretend to grieve, and Michael that his grief was that befitting a kind-hearted editor. He would mourn in secret, of course, and blame himself for the young woman's sufferings, but soon the bright lights of his newsroom would dim the memory and the excitement of the present blur the unpleasant past. She would watch over him, undemanding, loving, discreet.

'Oh, God . . .' Michael moaned into his hands, still slumped forward on the sofa.

Nina slowly approached her husband. She sat beside him, but so that their bodies did not touch. He would not bring down his hands to look at her, but she waited, patient, silent beside him, to reclaim him.